THE MALDIVES
ADVENTURE

by

ROYSTON ELLIS

KICKS BOOKS
NEW YORK, NEW YORK

Books by Royston Ellis
published by Kicks Books

GONE MAN SQUARED
Collected beat poems, 1959-1967

BIG TIME
The autobiography of an pseudonymous pop
star in Britain's Swinging Sixties

THE FLESH GAME
Beach boys in Las Palmas in the 1960s
live by the rules of the flesh game.

RUSH AT THE END
A respectable city clerk falls for a young
student in this tale of forbidden gay love
in London suburbs in the 1960s.

SWEET EBONY
Four women in search of romance discover
more than they expect in Kenya in the 1970s

THE MALDIVES ADVENTURE
A swashbuckling historical yarn
by a master storyteller about the
Maldivian hero who saved the islands
from Portuguese colonization
in the 16th century

THE MALDIVES ADVENTURE
by Royston Ellis

This is the story about the Indian Ocean tourist destination, the Maldives, that tourists don't know.

In the 16th century, the Portuguese invaded the islands and imposed colonial tyranny.

The inhabitants, devout and simple fisherfolk, traders and rustic islanders, were powerless to resist... until a young man, Mohamed Thakuru, who became a favourite of the Portuguese governor of the Northern Atolls, returned from martial and religious training in India.

Appalled by the ruthlessness of the invaders, he led a seaborne guerrilla campaign to oust them.

This is a swashbuckling yarn of adventure, intrigue, lust, passion and faith in the face of adversity.

(This Kicks book is the unexpurgated version of the novel by Royston Ellis, A Hero In Time, previously published in the Maldives in 2000.)

CONTENTS

PROLOGUE
Male', Capital of the Maldives
Tuesday 20 June 1573 1

PART ONE
Utheem, Northern Atoll, Maldives
1552-1558 10

PART TWO
Utheem, Northern Atoll, Maldives
1562-1568 106

PART THREE
Exile & Vengeance
1568-1573 233

AFTERWORD 280

GLOSSARY 281

PROLOGUE
Male', Capital of the Maldives
Tuesday, 30 June 1573

From the dusk descending on the avenue of palm trees, where gathering gloom engulfed a cluster of thatched huts, came the sudden dint of a gong being banged.

A voice called out: "Hear ye! Hear ye!"

Aboobakur was about to light the cloth wick in a coconut shell of palm oil. He stopped and sighed, looking up. From the depths of his hut through the open doorway he could see down the sandy avenue. A man was tramping along it and the clanging of the gong grew louder as he approached the beachside hamlet.

Although the man had the rolling gait of a fisherman going home after a day at sea, Aboobakur sensed it was the wine of the Portuguese occupiers of the islands, not the retained sway of the ocean, the propelled him.

Aboobakur placed the unlit shell lamp on the wooden dais that filled half the space of his simple home. Bending his head, he stepped out through the low doorway onto the apron of brushed sand in front of it. He was accustomed to proclamations, but something in the man's boastful, if unsteady, swagger suggested that this was more than the usual call to take notice of the latest dictum of the Portuguese invaders.

He stood outside his hut and waited. The voice of the town crier as he shouted "Hear ye! Hear ye!" had a menacing edge to it. From other huts among the palm trees, people were emerging cautiously to see what the fuss was about. Young boys, ambling up from the beach where they had been playing, hastened to a run, puzzled by this disturbance in the placid routine of sunset.

The town crier lurched to a halt in a nave formed by the coconut palms. He appeared pleased at the commotion he was causing. Boys ran around him until one, tugging at the flapping waistcloths of his friends to restrain them, pointed at Aboobakur standing motionless in the shadows.

Aboobakur was a man the children feared and their parents respected. He was a man steadfast in his religious beliefs, a man who tried to maintain the traditions of Islam, despite the presence of the infidel foreigners. For the children, the sight of him glaring at the stumbling town crier as he clashed his gong promised confrontation. They fell back, some of them running to join their fathers who, like Aboobakur, had been drawn out in the dusk to determine the reason for the ruckus.

The town crier leered at the boys and they shrank further from his evil gaze, puzzled by his manner. They had heard him before on the roads and paths of Male', shouting proclamations issued by the occupiers. But he had never seemed threatening like he did now.

The children of the hamlet had grown used to the Portuguese as ill-mannered, red-skinned people who sweated a lot. When they drank a liquid that looked like blood, they quickly became agitated and roared like the devils of the sea. Then the boys had to hide lest they be seized by them and carried off to their beds for the night, returning in the morning wracked with pain and scarcely able to walk.

While the children had known no other life but the hazards of being under Portuguese occupation, for their parents and Aboobakur it was different. Before the infidels came Aboobakur prayed in the mosque five times a day; now he had to pray alone in the privacy of his hut. To go to one of the island's mosques, long locked up on the orders of the Portuguese half-caste governor, would have brought the wrath of the soldiers down on him. That's why there was no *Mudin* any more to lead the people in prayer.

Aboobakur had tried with friends to remember the prayers he had learned from his own father, who had been a judge, but it was difficult without guidance. The only discipline the islanders had now was the whip and sword of the foreign occupiers.

"Hear ye! Hear ye!" the town crier shouted hoarsely as he reached the climax of his refrain. His final shout was directed deliberately at Aboobakur. The children wilted, cowered by the vehemence in the man's voice.

"All *Malins, Mudins, Katheebs* and people, small and great, of this island and outside islands, hereby take notice."

The town crier pulled from his tunic a parchment and unrolled it with a great show of importance, and a hearty scowl at Aboobakur. In the dying light he read its contents aloud, his voice thick with alcohol as well as menace. Reaching the end, he rolled up the parchment with an attempt at a flourish and stabbed it in the air to emphasise his words.

"Should anyone hear this notice or get word of it and not attend as directed, woe betide him!" He smote the gong clumsily and uttered a grunt that bellowed into a loud belch.

His uncouth manner filled the children with terror, even though they did not understand the meaning of the proclamation. Aboobakur did. He looked at the men standing outside their huts, their wives and children grouped around them, most of them confused by the words. But to Aboobakur it was a moment of dreadful clarity: the hour of destiny was upon them.

During the years that the Portuguese had occupied Male' and the islands that formed the Sultanate of the Maldives, the proud Maldivian people had gradually been reduced to vassals. The islands had been independent and prosperous before the Portuguese invaded. Fishing, exporting coir rope and cowry shells generated a good income for everyone. When the Portuguese invaded fifteen years before, they had taken over the trade and its rewards for themselves. Now they wanted the souls of the people too. As the gloom of dusk descended, Aboobakur knew the final surrender was to dawn at sunrise.

◆ ◆ ◆ ◆ ◆

The town crier's announcement was an ultimatum. It contained the official orders of the Portuguese governor, Captain Andre Andrade, the man the islanders knew by his Maldivian name of Andhiri Andhirin. He had governed the

Maldives on behalf of the Portuguese Viceroy in India since the Portuguese invaded in 1558.

At dawn the next day, according to the proclamation, all adult inhabitants of Male' were to assemble outside Captain Andhirin's palace. There they must swear a pledge of loyalty to the Portuguese crown in front of Andhiri Andhirin himself. All must then quaff wine as a symbol of their acceptance of the Portuguese fief. Soldiers would hunt down the islanders who did not present themselves; they would be bound and beheaded before sunset.

Aboobakur turned slowly, his shoulders bowed as though pressed by some heavy weight, as he entered his hut. Two of his wives were sitting on the hut's raised wooden floor with his sons clinging to their skirts. He waved them to silence as he picked up the coconut shell lamp to light it. Instead, with a deep sigh, he placed it back on the dais, still unlit.

This was the ultimatum he had long feared. It meant death for any islander who disobeyed the Portuguese order. The islanders had been powerless to stop the red-skinned invaders usurping their supremacy in the trade of the seas, but they had been left alone to fish and eke out a living as long as they remained passive to their presence. They dared not openly refute the arrogance of the Portuguese that their religion was the correct one. Men like Aboobakur who retained their faith as well as belief in the independence of the Maldives, dared speak of it only in whispers.

Now it seemed the end had come. Aboobakur had vowed a decade before that he would never submit his soul and spirit to these infidels. He would never drink their blood wine, forbidden as it was by Islam. If the Captain carried out his threat of death to those who refused his commands, then Aboobakur was truly doomed.

He sat down heavily on the dais as reality struck him. Death waited with the dawn. He sighed and as he did so, a strange feeling swelled through him, making him tingle with a frisson of fulfilment. His heavy sorrow lifted and he suddenly no longer felt frightened of the future. He *knew* what had to be done. By accepting what would be his fate, with the strength of his belief in Allah, he felt inspired and emboldened by his resolve.

Minutes after the town crier had staggered down the sandy path as he headed towards the next settlement, the shadows of the palm trees outside Aboobakur's hut grew bolder. Men were threading their way through the bushes, pausing silently by the palms to see if any soldiers were watching. One by one, they tiptoed over the threshold into Aboobakur's darkened home, as his wives slipped out of the hut, dragging his sons with them.

There were ten of them; sheltered by the hut's gloom, they glanced at each other cautiously. Aboobakur was surprised they had come. These were his neighbours, simple fishermen, boat builders, a merchant, a toddy-tapper, and a goldsmith. He was gratified that his words of encouragement to them in the past, urging them to maintain their beliefs in secret despite the Portuguese harassment, had been heeded.

"You heard the proclamation," said the toddy-tapper gruffly, still with his wooden mallet stuck in the waistband of his loincloth. "What shall we do?"

"As the Captain commands," said another, a dealer in cowry shells. "Let's just drink the wine and pledge loyalty to these invaders and then forget all about it. It's what we've done before."

"No!" Aboobakur's determined voice startled even himself. He signalled the men to join him sitting on the palm-weave mats on the floor. When they were settled, he began to speak slowly, gradually unravelling his thoughts.

He gently told his neighbours that if they did not resist the Portuguese this time, they would forever condemn themselves to a life of servitude. By refusing to drink the wine and abandon their belief, they had been offered a chance to die in defence of their faith and freedom. Death would rescue them from falsehood and they would die honourably as martyrs.

He pleaded with each of the men gathered around him to go out and seek others to join them. They should bring weapons, knives, mallets, clubs and rocks, anything with which to fight the soldiers. He told them all to meet him at midnight outside the tomb of the missionary who had brought Islam to the islands four hundred years before.

How the Maldives had become exclusively a Muslim realm was part of the lore of the islands, passed from teacher to pupil, from father to son. It was during the reign of Tribuvana Aaditya, the king four centuries before, that the High Priest began speaking about a demon of the sea, called Rannamaari. The High Priest said that Rannamaari would destroy the island with a tidal wave and only the offering of a virgin girl once a month would placate the demon.

So great was the islanders' fear of the angry ocean, they believed what the High Priest preached and brought a young virgin to the temple on the night of every full moon. In the morning the people would find the girl dead, ravished by the demon, her naked body lapped by crimson surf at the lagoon's edge. The High Priest smiled on them benevolently, and no tidal wave disturbed the island.

The girl to be brought to the High Priest when the moon was full was chosen by drawing lots. A Muslim missionary and trader from Morocco who was visiting the island happened to be staying with the family whose daughter was selected for sacrifice to the sea-demon. His name was Abul Barakaath; he was not a brave man but he was confident in his faith. He volunteered to take the place of the girl that night.

The legend that all Maldivians believe tells how Abul Barakaath had entered the temple by the shore disguised as a girl. He sat on the floor where the High Priest instructed the islanders to leave the girl for the sea demon. When the islanders left him he began to recite the Holy Quran continuing throughout the night. The shadow of the demon monster rising up from the lagoon in the moonlight drew closer and closer. Abul Barakaath chanted louder, his gruff voice reverberating through the night air. The monster paused, drew his robe around him and disappeared back into the shadows.

In the morning, the people were astonished to find that Abul Barakaath was alive, and still reciting the Holy Quran. They took him to the king and explained his deed. The king listened in amazement as Abul Barakaath recounted how the Holy Quran's verses had protected him. He was so impressed that he banished the High Priest and decreed that henceforth the religion of the Maldives would forever be Islam.

To Aboobakur, the legend he knew from childhood had become alarmingly real. There was a new demon that had come from the sea intent on destroying the Maldives. As he hurried to the tomb of Abul Barakaath, he drew strength from the story of the brave man who had challenged the demon and brought the protection of Islam to the islands.

Aboobakur, however, was not a brave man. He had hidden a dagger in his robe; it was the only weapon he could find and he knew it would be useless against the firearms of the Portuguese soldiers. He proposed instead to do what the missionary had done. He would stand in defiance and recite what he could remember of the words of the Holy Quran.

He remembered that his father had warned him about the Portuguese. Led by Vasco da Gama they had arrived in the Indian Ocean seventy-five years before, in 1498. They were foul-smelling, brutal people who patrolled the ocean in ships the size of a fortress, arresting every trading vessel they encountered and seizing its cargo.

Their atrocities puzzled the gentle folk of the Maldives who depended on maritime trading for their livelihood. As the Portuguese conquered more of the coast of India, their reign of terror spread. Ships from China and Asia and Africa had to divert to Male' to discharge their cargoes instead of taking them direct to ports in India where they would be confiscated by the Portuguese. The tiny island of Male' began to flourish as an entrepot for the transhipment of goods. Inevitably, the more Male' and the islands prospered, the greater the danger the Maldives was in from the Portuguese.

The Portuguese tried several times to invade, attacking like pirates in the night, ransacking islands and killing innocent islanders who dared to resist them. Finally, sixty year after they first sailed into the Indian Ocean in their tall ships of war, the Portuguese were successful in conquering the islands. The Maldives was doomed. Sadly,

Aboobakur's father had been right in prophesying the end of freedom at the sword of the Portuguese for the islanders who trustingly called themselves children of the sea.

♦ ♦ ♦ ♦ ♦

Aboobakur paused for a moment as he approached the tomb of Abul Barakaath. A single coconut oil lamp burned by it, as if defying the Portuguese to carry out their threat. In the shadows around the tomb were the men who had gathered to join in this final struggle.

Aboobakur sighed as he counted them. There were only thirty-nine, out of the one thousand men who lived on the island. It was not enough. The Portuguese numbered at least three hundred, every one of them a devil. Then Aboobakur realised that, by including himself, the band of the faithful numbered forty. That was a fateful number. It gave him courage. He asked them all to draw close to the mouth of the tomb. They kneeled down, facing northwest, the direction of Mecca.

"If only there were someone to save us," whispered the cowry dealer as he sank trembling to his knees.

"There is no one except us to resist," Aboobakur chided him gently. "Only Mohamed Thakurufaan could save us now but he and his fast boat have gone. He cannot help us any more. We are alone. But alone we shall show the infidels they can no longer force us to do their bidding.

"Take comfort, my brothers, for tomorrow we shall be martyrs. Our name will live forever."

With their heads down, touching the ground, none of them saw a youth in the livery of the Portuguese emerge from behind a tree. Listening from his hiding place he had heard every word Aboobakur said. He slipped silently away from the group praying at the tomb and made off in the direction of the Captain's fort, disappearing swiftly deep into the dark of that terrible night.

—◆—

PART ONE
Utheem, Northern Atoll, Maldives
1552-1558

—◆—

CHAPTER 1

"Mohamed! Mohamed Thakurufaan!" The girl's voice sang out his name, its sweet tone soaring above the lazy splash of surf on the white sand of the beach.

Mohamed turned from staring out to sea and looked back to where coconut palms fringed the beach. His sister was beckoning him at the end of the path. Mohamed had been gazing at the horizon, to where the sea and the sky seemed to touch, dark blue changing to light blue, light blue becoming dark. What mysteries, he wondered, lay beyond that distant merging of sea and sky?

"Do stop daydreaming, Mohamed."

He smiled at his sister's words. He knew she wasn't angry but he didn't want to upset her so he ran obediently to her side. He put his hand in hers and looked up at her, waiting for her to speak. She was like a mother to him and he loved her dearly.

"What are you doing here, Mohamed? The children are all at the other side of the island, playing on the beach and swimming. I looked for you there."

Mohamed withdrew his hand and glanced back at the sea. A flutter of dragonflies danced suddenly from the bushes at the beach's edge. He jumped as they pirouetted around him. He tried to hold one in his hand but he wasn't tall enough. He laughed.

"I suppose you want to fly like them?"

"No, sister," he said politely, falling into step behind her as she began to walk along the sandy trail through the forest. "They dart around without any brain."

"Just like you, Mohamed."

"Is that what I do?"

"I don't know what you do, Mohamed. One day here, another day there, always looking, always thinking. I wonder just what goes on in that young head of yours. Does it really have a brain?"

Her question made him laugh. "All sorts of things are in my head. There is so much to know. I want to know as much as our father."

"And how much is that?"

"Surely it must be more than most people?"

"You are right, but why do you say that?"

Mohamed sensed that his sister was trying to humour him. He was eight years old and she was ten years older, so he regarded her as an adult. She was actually the only woman in their father's house. His mother had died when he was two, just after his younger brother, Hassan, was born. He couldn't remember her at all.

Ali, his elder brother by fourteen years, and his sister, Fathimafaan, were his father's children by his first wife. Their mother had died too but his father had waited until Ali was almost a man before he took another wife.

Mohamed decided to humour his sister in return, since she was trying to tease him. "Our father has made you and Ali wise so you will make me wise too."

"Hear the boy!" Fathimafaan exclaimed. "You think wisdom is like those dancing dragonflies to be plucked out of the air? You must study, learn and live by the Holy Quran and – " She broke off as she tried to change the subject, but Mohamed spotted her sadness.

"And leave this island?" His young voice squeaked with excitement as he finished the sentence for her.

"Your father, your brothers and I, your home, are here in this island of Utheem, Mohamed. What more can a boy want?"

"One day," he said, without looking up to see his sister's eyes were moist, "I shall sail away from here, beyond that line of blue on the horizon."

"Then you'll fall off the edge of the world!" His sister sounded annoyed.

"Does Ali fall off when he sails to Male'?" Mohamed paused, pursing his lips as a new thought struck him. "Our father says the world is round, but I've heard some fishermen say it is flat. That's why they don't sail far from here and come back every day before nightfall. Why does father say it is round?"

"Round or flat, you talk such nonsense!"

He fell silent immediately, knowing he had somehow upset Fathimafaan. He couldn't fathom how. Then he began to wonder why she had come for him. Usually he returned home by himself as the sun went down. Darkness fell so quickly and, although he could easily find his way home in the dark on their small island, he knew his sister worried when he was late.

His routine at the end of each day was to bathe before sharing his evening meal with his younger brother, Hassan. Then he would curl up with Hassan on a mat and sleep in his father's room on the *ashi*, a kind of wooden dais. His father, who was the *Katheeb*, the island chief and a religious leader, always rose before dawn so he could go to prayers.

Other boys on the island, even those as young as he was, had to go fishing with their fathers or uncles. Because of their father's wealth through trading, Mohamed and Hassan were spared having to work and spent their days at home in study.

Being a trader, not a fisherman, his father owned boats that were big enough to sail to Male' and he was often away from Utheem on fishing trips. In his absence, Mohamed could wander off to play by himself, instead of studying. Sometimes he would sit on the beach and wonder wistfully about the world that lay beyond the horizon.

"You're a funny one." His sister patted his shoulder, signifying she was no longer in a bad mood with him. "You weren't even on the beach when Ali returned."

Mohamed was shocked at his own bad manners. "Has he come back from Male' already?"

"Of course he has. He was away for more than a month. Far too long."

"Is he at home with father?"

"Wait!" He felt his sister catch hold of his shoulder as he was about to run off to the house. "You must go to the well and bathe before you meet him."

"What did he bring for you, sister?"

"His safe return is enough, Mohamed." Again her voice revealed an inner sadness.

Mohamed thought about that when he was at the well, ladling out water with the coconut shell cup attached to a long pole. He poured the water into a brass jug, one his father had brought back from India on a trading voyage. Emptying the water from the jug over his head seemed to clear his mind. His sister, he understood, had devoted herself to caring for their father, his brothers and himself. Other girls of her age were already married and had children of their own. That must be why she sometimes sounded thoughtful and sad.

He wiped the water from his bare chest, noticing how the droplets sparkled in the dying sunlight, giving his golden-hued skin a soft, burnished sheen. He took up the clean tunic his sister had laid out for him on a bush and pulled it over his head. He smoothed down the loose-fitting garment so it reached his knees, and peeled down his wet loincloth from underneath. His head was shaved, as was the custom for children. It exposed his strong-boned face, emphasising the intelligence of his husk-brown eyes.

He was eager to see his elder brother again. Due to the age gap between them, Mohamed thought of Ali as being of his father's generation. Ali had sailed many times with their father on voyages to Male', carrying coir rope and cowry shells and returning to Utheem with sacks of rice from India. His father depended a lot on Ali. The two men were alike in personality: strict, serious and steadfast.

Satisfied he was properly dressed, Mohamed hurried through the compound to the front of the house. He paused under the thatched eaves overhanging the outer wall of the wooden house, where they created shade for the sand-floored veranda. Carefully, he knocked his bare feet together to shake off loose sand. His excitement grew as he heard the soft drone of conversation inside and recognised Ali's deep voice as he talked with his father.

He was eager to rush in and embrace his brother, but sensed he should wait. When there was a lull in the talking he stepped up to the side of the open doorway and coughed quietly. There was silence from within yet Mohamed knew he had been heard. The voices began again and it seemed his father was finalising some business. Then all was quiet again and Mohamed shifted his weight impatiently from one foot to another. At last, his father called his name.

"Mohamed, you may enter."

He stepped through the doorway, greeting first his father

with the traditional salutation in the name of Allah and then turning to address Ali. "God is my Lord, Mohamed is my prophet, I am a poor ignorant being..."

Ali replied formally and nodded at Mohamed. He and their father were seated cross-legged on the raised platform in the room, the *beyru-ge*, the hall for the men of the family and for visitors. His father waved him to a mat in the corner, indicating that Mohamed should sit and hear what Ali was saying.

It was an enormous privilege for him to be invited to listen to the talk of men. At first, he barely heard the words as he watched his brother and his father together. While it was still hot outside from the dying sun, the interior of the thatched house was cool. The sliding panels of the long louvered windows were open, as were the shutters of the house's wooden walls, so gentle puffs of evening breeze fanned the room.

Mohamed thought how great his brother must be to sail their father's boat to Male' and back. He wished one day he would be able to do the same.

His ears pricked up as he heard the worried tone in Ali's voice. He was saying something about the Sultan who ruled the Maldives. His name was Hassan, which caught Mohamed's attention since that was the name of his young brother.

Sultan Hassan, he understood, was only twenty years old, which made him younger than Ali. He had come to power two years before when his brother, who was the reigning sultan, died. It was rumoured that Hassan had murdered his brother so he could take over the throne. Although events in Male' seemed remote, Mohamed remembered how shocked he had been when he heard the news. Hassan seemed such a ruthless man, unlike any he knew.

"Sultan Hassan has fled?" It was his father's question.

Ali shrugged his shoulders. "Some people say he has, others say he has gone to raise support and will return to consolidate his hold on power."

His father threw up his hands in dismissal of Ali's words. "It is too late. The House of Hilali, the Sultan's birthright, is doomed. What Hassan did will be done to him. He is scared, that is why he has fled."

The Sultan of the Maldives scared? It seemed incredible to Mohamed, but wasn't his father always right? He listened carefully, trying to understand the unusual events in the capital. Ali was describing how, secretly at night, the Sultan had taken his young bride and members of his court and embarked on a foreign ship anchored off Male'.

"Where did he sail?" asked his father. "The southern atolls?"

Ali would not be hurried; he was savouring the details of this extraordinary news, as though tantalising his father's thirst for information. "For days, no one knew," said Ali. "The people left in the palace were in a state of confusion. I spoke to some myself. There were some foreigners there too, one of them the captain of a ship from the land called *Port-u-gal*. I sold him our coir rope."

"What has that got to do with it?"

"They said that Sultan Hassan was accompanied by a nobleman from that land when he left Male', a man known as *Dom Gaspar*. He tries to speak our language, but Dhivehi is not a tongue for foreigners."

Mohamed saw his father nod knowingly, without a smile. "Ah, yes, I know of Dom Gaspar. He is the officer in charge of revenue and trade for the Portuguese Viceroy in India. This is indeed serious." He paused in thought. "The Portuguese must be planning to use Sultan Hassan for their own designs. They want to control our seas and take over our trading."

"There was talk in the palace that Sultan Hassan sailed to Cochin. He was received with a salute of cannons and afforded the respect due to his status as Sultan."

Again his father nodded, his face stern. Mohamed squeezed his thighs tightly together to prevent him blurting out the questions he wanted to ask. If he drew attention to himself, his father would send him away. There was a pause before Ali concluded with the choicest piece of news that he had been saving for the end.

"They say Sultan Hassan drank the blood wine and has become a *Christian*."

The silence in the room was complete as both men, and

Mohamed, digested this information. His father was not an impulsive person so he would take time before commenting. Mohamed didn't know what a *Christian* was but since all Maldivians were Muslims and Sultan Hassan was their ruler, what did this mean?

"This news does not surprise me," his father was saying. "Sultan Hassan is ambitious, although he is a coward. He sees in the Portuguese a way to consolidate his position here. He has doubtless become a Christian to please them, now he hopes they will please him." He fell silent.

"What will happen to us, the children of the sea? We are Muslim." It was Ali who spoke but it could have been Mohamed since he longed to ask the same question.

"The Portuguese are not to be trusted. They have long wanted to control our seas and take over our trade. They want to profit from our coir rope and our cowry shells. Now they want to enslave us too through influencing our Sultan.

"If we lose our independence and our religion and let the Portuguese gain control of the Maldives we shall suffer. We are a peaceful people, we are fishermen and traders and craftsmen and farmers. We have neither the will nor the ability to resist."

"Perhaps it will not come to that." Ali tried to sound hopeful. "If the Sultan wants to be a Christian that is no concern of ours. We shall choose another Sultan."

"From what House? The Hilali dynasty began nearly two centuries ago with Sultan Hassan the First. He was the grandson of Muslim Abbas of Hilali, and the son of Hilali Kalo of Hulule. Hassan has no successor so the dynasty is doomed and it will end with that Hassan, the last. These are grave times, my son."

Before he had time to reflect on what his father meant, Mohamed saw the two men rising to their feet, so he scrambled to his feet too.

"Come," said his father. "It is time for prayer."

As his father strode out of the house, with Ali following him, Mohamed glanced around the room. He was in time to catch sight of a shadow moving away from the curtained entrance to the inner room, the *ethere-ge*, and knew that his sister, Fathimafaan, had been listening. Good. He would ask her about Sultan Hassan and why couldn't the people find another Sultan now he had gone to India? And why were the Portuguese feared so much, even by his own father? And anyway, what was a Port-u-guesey? He had never seen one in Utheem.

◆ ◆ ◆ ◆ ◆

News of the events in the capital of the Maldives during the next two years came to Mohamed's ears sooner than to most, because of his father's status and his coterie of keen informers. Katheeb Hussain Thakurufaan was respected, not just for his position as island chief, which he had inherited from his father with the then Sultan's blessing, but also for his prosperity as a trader. He was known through his voyages in all the atolls, from the northernmost one of Tiladu Mati where they lived to the southernmost one of Addu. That was a distance of over two hundred leagues, with the capital of Male' roughly halfway between the two.

The people of all the islands in all the atolls brought him news, sought his advice, and respected his learning. During the months that followed Sultan Hussan's unexpected departure, many chiefs from other islands came to visit his father. There was uncertainty among the people about the future. Katheeb Hussain advised them to remain calm, to go about their prayers and duties as usual, and trust in Allah.

"What happens now our Sultan has gone?" Mohamed asked his sister a few weeks after the news brought by Ali of the Sultan's departure. He was watching her as she crouched in the sand grating coconut for the day's meal. His father and Ali were away from the island and Mohamed was growing anxious for news of the outside world.

"Do you never stop asking questions?"

Mohamed bit his lip and remained silent. His younger brother was romping on the sand of the compound, shouting for him to come and play. He turned away from Hassan and looked up at his sister. She had stopped rolling the hard flesh of the coconut across the ratchet that shredded it, and was watching him seriously.

"Soon there will be a new sultan, Mohamed. We children of the sea are Muslim. We cannot have a Christian king."

"Are Christians bad?"

"I don't know, Mohamed. The Portuguese are bad, and they are Christian."

"Why are those foreigners bad?"

His sister looked exasperated. "I don't know. They just are. They have killed Maldivians they encounter at sea, without any cause."

Mohamed had to wait until his father and Ali returned before he could find out more. By eavesdropping on their conversations with the island's elders, he discovered that the presence of the Portuguese in the region was actually advantageous to the Maldives.

Because of the stranglehold the Portuguese had on the ports of India, arriving vessels from other countries were instead unloading their cargoes in Male'. This increased the opportunities for trading and brought prosperity to the islands. The Maldives was famous as the Money Islands because of the abundance of the small cowry shells that were used throughout the world as currency. The islanders also supplied visiting ships with coir rope made from the fibre harvested from coconut husks, as well as dried fish and ambergris.

As time passed a new Sultan, Abu Bakur, was installed on the throne in Male'. The islands and the people had grown prosperous and a measure of stability returned. Even Mohamed could sense the excitement of the times. While he never expected his father to express satisfaction openly, he sensed his father was content with the success that he and Ali were achieving in their trading.

◆ ◆ ◆ ◆ ◆

The seasons, the time of humid heat and relentless sun from October to March, and the days of rain and storms from April to September, passed peacefully at Utheem. Mohamed studied the Holy Quran, went swimming and fishing with his friends, and led the idyllic, carefree life of a child of the sea. Yet there was a deeper side to him. For days, he would sit gazing out at the horizon wondering about his destiny. He wanted to sail away from the island as Ali did, to see Male' for himself, to gaze on those strange foreigners who were considered evil but whose presence in the Indian Ocean and demonic deeds actually brought prosperity to the islands. He wanted to sail with his father and help with the trading; he wanted to be a man.

One evening after prayers, as his father sat on the dais in the house apparently deep in thought, as was his custom, Mohamed coughed politely, hoping to attract his father's attention.

"What is that burning in your brain with such a bright fire, my son?"

His father's words surprised him. He believed his presence, and his yearning, were carefully concealed.

"Most respected father," he said quickly. The words he had planned for days to say as politely as he could tumbled from his lips without even the traditional courtesy of salutation. "Let me go voyaging with Ali!"

Before he could apologise for his rudeness, his father held up his hand, gesturing him to silence. He dared not speak any more.

"So that is the reason for this restlessness that has seized you with the power of a monsoon?" His father pursed his lips, looking at him with interest.

"Mohamed, you shall see the world when you are ready, if Allah so wills. As yet you are too young. I need you to stay here and care for your brother and be helpful to your sister when Ali and I are away. Learn, enhance the spirit surging within you, study the Holy Quran, be a credit to Allah and to me, and perhaps when you are fifteen and a man, you may be able to sail on one of my boats."

His father's words filled Mohamed with joy and he bowed deeply, withdrawing swiftly from his presence.

That night, as he fell asleep on his mat beside Hassan, he felt his loins stirring. It was a strange feeling. It made him resolve to learn all he could, so that one day he would be ready to sail on his father's boat to see Male', the Portuguese, and the Sultan's palace for himself.

He hugged Hassan, pulling him closer and wrapping

himself around him, silently praying to Allah that the day he would be recognised as a man would soon come.

CHAPTER 2

Mohamed was on the beach. He was playing in solitude as usual, yet for him it was not play but a serious part of his self-instruction. He had studied for a long time the behaviour of birds on the beach. He had learned that it was impossible to rush up to them with a wild shout and catch them, but if he blended into the landscape and approached a bird patiently and stealthily, he could scoop it up in his hand before it had a chance to fly away.

His father despaired of Mohamed's pursuits. He followed him to the beach, unknown to Mohamed, and observed him at the task he had set himself. He watched Mohamed wait for the whole morning, just to seize one special bird he had grown fond of. It was not an easy task; he had to win the bird's confidence before he could pounce.

Mohamed laughed with delight when the bird was in his hands. The words he uttered then carried across the empty beach to where his father was watching from the bushes.

"So, my young bird, you forgot how you got caught last time? Do you not understand my strategy even now? I am cleverer than you are, even though you can fly. See, I will catch you yet again." Then he raised his hands in the air and released the bird. "Go with God."

That evening, his father admonished Mohamed for spending his whole day catching and talking to birds. He told him it was a waste of time and a sign of a feeble mind that he addressed birds as he would people. He urged him to enjoy the company of other boys his age and not to spend his time playing alone.

Mohamed was completely tongue-tied when his father asked him to explain his actions. How could he? He bowed his head and kept silent. When his father finished, Mohamed saluted him, bearing his rebuke like a man, and stepped backwards out of the *beyru-ge* to escape his father's censure.

He sat down on the sand outside the house, wondering why his father was so displeased. Yet even as he brooded he heard his father addressing Ali. Mohamed knew he should not eavesdrop but the words came to him so clearly. It was only much later that he realised his father had deliberately spoke louder than usual so he could hear.

"Mohamed is a peculiar boy. There are people in Utheem who see his solitary ways as a kind of madness. Oh yes, Ali, I know all fourteen-year-old boys try to catch birds, but Mohamed has taught himself how to succeed." There was a pause during which Ali obviously felt obliged to keep quiet.

"I believe Mohamed is touched by destiny. Now he trains himself to catch birds. Is he not also training himself for other things? The technique is the same whatever you hunt."

Ali couldn't contain himself any more. "But he lets the birds go free!"

"Exactly. Other boys would tease the creatures or put them in cages and let them die. He gives the birds their freedom. The birds sense when he catches them that they will be safe. He can inspire such trust, even in wild birds." His father made a clucking noise with his tongue, his thoughts remaining unspoken.

Then he said words that puzzled Mohamed. "Ali, we must aid the boy. When he does something odd, we must not appear displeased. Always we must feed and care for him. That way he can prepare his body and his soul for a great cause."

For days after he had been rebuked to his face, and yet apparently praised when his father thought he was not there to hear, Mohamed wandered on the beach and through the palm groves of Utheem by himself. He returned home for meals, ate silently and then wandered off again. He began to sleep on the beach at night, burying himself snugly into the sand not because he was upset but because he felt he should become familiar with the embrace of the night, the caress of the stars, and how to survive alone as one with nature.

He was watching a flock of birds on the beach, how they darted down to the surf to seize crabs scuttling back to the water for safety, when there was a commotion behind him. He glanced up and saw Hassan burst from the undergrowth.

"Mohamed, I have been looking everywhere for you!" The birds rose up in panic at the boy's voice and flew off with cries of alarm.

"Now you have found me, Hassan, and told others where I am."

Hassan looked around him and was puzzled. "I see no others. Who are you playing with? Are they hiding?"

"They have flown away, Hassan. Do not concern yourself."

Hassan looked along the beach. This was the loneliest part of their island. The fishermen lived in thatched huts on the other side where it was easier to push their boats into the water. The houses of more prosperous people, like their father, were closer to the mosque, built in shady glades. Although there were about three hundred people living on the island, few came to this side unless it was to pluck coconuts.

"It is so quiet here. Only the splash of the sea." Hassan didn't seem to like it.

"Are you frightened?"

"No."

"Then you should be!" Mohamed lunged at Hassan with a shout, tugging at his loincloth and toppling him to the ground. The two rolled over and over together in the sand, Mohamed pulling at the cloth until Hassan was naked.

Hassan tried to pull away from the strong grip but relaxed as Mohamed held him firmly. Climbing on his back and pressing him down into the sand. Mohamed gave a shout of triumph and then suddenly released him and fell back on the beach, his legs spread open. Hassan rolled over and sprawled beside him, gazing at him with adoration.

"I nearly forgot," he said breathlessly, breaking the intimacy between them.

"Forgot what?" Mohamed looked fondly at his younger brother.

"Why I came to find you. Our father calls you."

Mohamed moved to grab him again. "So he does every day."

"He says you are ready. He has told Ali to take you to Male' in the big boat. Ali is preparing to sail after dawn prayers tomorrow."

Mohamed felt his heart skip a beat. He looked at Hassan carefully and then smiled at his caution because he knew his brother would not lie to him, even as a joke. "This is a great occasion, Hassan. I am pleased our father asked you to carry this news to me. Soon it will be your turn to see the world. You are twelve years old now, so you must prepare."

Hassan said nothing.

Mohamed nodded his head, feeling himself growing taller even as he leapt to his feet. "Don't be envious. I shall go to sea first and return to tell you everything. Everything! My knowledge will help you understand things I can only tell you about.

"You promise?"

"I do." Mohamed ignored the sulkiness in Hassan's voice and leaned down to pull his brother to his feet, handing him his loincloth and wrapping his own around himself. Linking his arms in Hassan's, he led him up the beach into the shade of the coconut grove to take the path home.

♦ ♦ ♦ ♦ ♦

Ramazan was to fall in twenty-four days, when the solemn month of fasting and prayer would begin with the new moon. That was the time when the Maldives people fasted all day until nightfall. As Muslims they were scrupulous in denying themselves anything to eat or even to taste, and they would partake of no liquid either. After sunset and prayer, they would break their fast and entertain their friends in lively feasts. It was a time when no one did any work, or even travelled from one island to another.

"You must go to Male' and return before the new moon," Katheeb Hussain cautioned Ali as he prepared to leave. He explained to Ali that it was necessary to dispose of their coir rope and dried fish at the market in Male'. Traders from the Malabar Coast would be there then since during the month of Ramazan no commerce could take place.

His father was stern with Mohamed, warning him by his gruffness of manner instead of words of advice that he should behave well. Mohamed appreciated his father's trust and realised that beneath his dour expression he was full of concern at sending him away. There was no wish of goodwill for the voyage, nor even a wave of farewell as they left, since that was not in his father's nature.

Mohamed turned quickly from where his father stood on the beach and busied himself curling up the coir rope that had moored the loaded vessel to the shore. He did not want to look at the face of his sister who seemed to have a grain of sand in her eye, or at Hassan who was pointedly ignoring him by trying to stand on his head in the sand.

From his short voyages to neighbouring islands in the same atoll, Mohamed was familiar with the basic routine of shipboard life, and set about to make himself useful to Ali. When all was stowed neatly and the palm-woven sails were plump with the wind billowing in them, he sat close to his brother.

Ali stood at the stern, guiding the tiller of the boat with one foot. Mohamed watched him keenly, his awe at his brother's competence giving way to impatience to try to steer for himself. There was no deck and only a palm-thatched canopy for shade. Like all the boats in the Maldives, this was built entirely of coconut timber, without iron or any material that was not from the palm tree. The vessel's anchor was made of coconut palm with a stone attached to give it weight. Even the ship's planks were lashed and secured with cordage made from the fibrous husk of coconuts.

The cargo of the vessel was merchandise from the same kind of tree; there was cordage, mats, sails of plaited leaves and fibre, comfits, oil, palm wine and vinegar, and the deliciously sweet palm honey. These commodities would be in demand in Male' as the people prepared for Ramazan.

To Mohamed it was a disappointment that he would not

be there then to see how the Sultan and his court observed the period. He had heard the nights were passed in much feasting with many lords attending the Sultan in his court.

From Ali he had learned that there was a new Sultan, also called Ali, who had been in power for only a few weeks. Before becoming Sultan, he had won the respect of people for leading resistance to the Portuguese galleons of war that tried to attack Male'. It was said that the former sultan, Hassan, now living in Goa where he was close to the Portuguese Viceroy, was behind the invasion attempt, which was to re-occupy the Maldives in his name.

There had already been two such attempts, the news of both causing much concern to Mohamed's father. Although Kathheeb Hussain did not discuss such matters with him, Mohamed had listened closely, unseen, to what the elders discussed. Thus he knew that a Portuguese ship had come from Cochin in India bringing an envoy who had told important people in Male' that Sultan Hassan wanted them to meet him in Cochin. They had refused and, led by a nobleman called Abu Bakur, had attacked the ship, killing all the Portuguese on board and seizing their goods.

The second attempt was after Abu Bakur had himself become Sultan. A small armada was sent from Cochin with the intent of taking the Maldives. Again, the wiles of Sultan Abu Bakur were too much even for the three Portuguese vessels. They were all captured, their crews slain and their goods conveyed to the Sultan's treasury.

Sultan Abu Bakur, however, did not reign for many months before he was succeeded by Sultan Ali.

◆ ◆ ◆ ◆ ◆

"You intend to pass the voyage in dreams?" His brother's voice shattered Mohamed's thoughts.

"Oh, no, elder brother." He jumped to his feet wondering what he should be doing. Already the sun was high and he could feel its powerful warmth under the cloth he had wrapped around his head like a turban.

"Take this line." Ali handed him a skein of twine and a crudely fashioned hook. He showed him how to fasten the hook to the line so it would not be pulled off by the race of the sea's current, then told him how to throw it overboard.

Of course, Mohamed knew how to fish. He crouched down quietly again beside Ali and wrapped the end of the line around his hand so he would immediately feel when a fish snapped on the hook where it trailed behind the boat. It didn't take long, for the waters around the islands abounded in fish. He continued to play out the line, pulling it in a dozen times until Ali stopped him with a laugh.

"We shall not starve with you on board. Now mark that island well."

Ali pointed ahead and Mohamed rose from where he was hunkered down on the stern board, quickly rolling up the twine into a ball. He almost lost his balance as a swell rocked the boat and Ali looked at him disdainfully.

"Come, boy, you must see the marker."

He looked at the island in the distance. They were in the deep water of a channel between two atolls. All he could see on the island were coconut trees, the bright flash of sand at their base glistening in the sun. It looked just like any of the islands in the atoll they had just left.

"Now watch carefully," said Ali, touching the tiller. "You see?"

Mohamed strained his eyes, wondering what he was looking for. To his amazement, the island appeared to split into two. A channel large enough to sail through opened up.

"Now look to the west."

He did so and saw where the waves were pounding a reef that he had not noticed before. Had Ali kept the boat on course to the islands they would have run into it.

"Every island is like a verse in the Holy Quran," Ali said. "Study it properly and you will be guided by it."

Ali explained the atolls were in a line running end to end from north to south, each separated by a channel of deep ocean. Many atolls had openings, or entrances, opposite each other, two on one side and two on the other. It was only by those openings that vessels could pass from one atoll to another.

"Thus," said Ali gravely, "we observe an effect of God's providence, which leaves nothing imperfect. For if there were only two openings to each atoll, that is only one at each end, would it not be impossible to pass from atoll to atoll?"

Mohamed frowned as he tried to understand what seemed like a riddle.

"Remember the strength of the current that is bearing us onward even now. The current runs sometimes east and sometimes west and suffers you not to cross but carries you down. With one opening towards the east and the other to the west, you could not return until the current changes. With two openings you can choose the one that suits the current and sail back and forth as you wish."

For the whole morning, Mohamed listened to his brother telling of the ways of the sea. He tried to memorise the characteristics of each island as they sailed past it, and to remember the marks that Ali used for navigation. They sailed without a compass although the channels between the atolls were broad and they were often out of sight of land.

At noon, Ali handed the tiller to Mohamed and showed him in which direction to steer. For a moment Mohamed was puzzled about why they were heading west when Male' lay to the south. Then he realised why, as Ali and the two men who were the crew washed their feet and hands and went to the bow to kneel in prayer.

A few hours later, as the sun was losing its strength and sinking towards the sea, Ali steered the boat from the rolling waves of the channel into the calmer waters where the islands of an atoll afforded shelter. Mohamed marvelled at Ali's skill in manoeuvring the vessel through jagged heads of coral protruding darkly from the waves dashing against a reef. Then suddenly they were over it and in the languid waters of a lagoon.

Without being told, Mohamed knew what to do. At a glance from Ali he was over the side of the boat in an instant, diving down to the bottom, his eyes open for a suitable rock that could be used for mooring the boat. Like all boys born in the islands, he was a natural swimmer and accustomed to diving and staying under water for a long time. He soon found a rock and swam back to the boat, signalling to Ali to throw him the bow rope. He plunged down again, taking the rope with him and securing it to the rock. Then he surfaced again for the stern rope.

With the boat secured fore and aft, he and Ali waded through the surf to the shore as the sun set.

CHAPTER 3

"What island is this?" Mohamed asked his brother eagerly as he splashed after him on the white sand of the narrow beach that fronted a curtain of jungle. "Do people live here?"

Ali seemed not to have heard him. He was staring along the beach into the sunset, raising his hands to shield his eyes so he could see better. He stood as straight as a ship's mast, tall and confident, his long mane of dark hair billowing around him in the breeze that played at the sea's edge. He was darker than Mohamed, the colour of teak, and the soft light from the sun's afterglow highlighted his craggy, weather-beaten features. To Mohamed, he looked like a hero, and the boy was relieved when he lowered his hand and the frown on his brow vanished.

Whatever Ali had seen in the distance he seemed satisfied although Mohamed could make out nothing ahead of them except the beach stretching between the tangle of bushes and trees and the splash of surf from the lagoon. Ali glanced back at the boat where it bobbed close to the shore, retained by its mooring on the seabed. He shouted a command to the men on board and one jumped out carrying a long rope, which the one remaining on board fastened to a wooden cleat in the boat's bow. The man played out the rope as he waded ashore and Ali indicated a tree to which it should be tied. When he was satisfied the boat was secured properly, he nodded to Mohamed to follow him.

"Where are we going?" Mohamed was too excited to stop asking questions. Again his brother remained silent. It was a habit Mohamed realised he should adopt too. Ali was always taciturn, never speaking out of turn, concentrating hard on what he was doing. He observed everything and said little. Tramping along in the sand, anxious to keep up with him, Mohamed hoped that he would some day be like Ali. But how could he learn anything if he didn't ask questions?

Gradually, as they walked and the sun's red glow softened beyond the trees on the western shore, Mohamed made out the silhouettes of three men sitting in the shade of a large banyan tree at the edge of the island's canopy of greenery. Beyond them, around the curve of the island, some *dhonis*, small fishing boats, were anchored in the bay. Mohamed looked back the way he had come and saw they had already walked too far around the island for him to see their own boat at anchor.

"Don't worry," said Ali, as though reading his thoughts. "She is safe but I prefer to anchor away from people. Why give strangers an easy opportunity of knowing our business? It is our concern, not other people's, how many skeins of coir rope we are carrying and how many cowry shells fill our hold." His stern features relaxed for a moment.

Mohamed felt elated by Ali confiding in him, sharing his wisdom. He understood he was being cautioned about how to behave in the company of the people he was about to meet. He wanted to tell Ali that he knew what he meant, but already his brother was leading the way up to the men under the banyan tree.

"Peace be with you."

"With you be peace."

The men greeted Ali formally, taking no notice of Mohamed beyond responding to his echo of the salutation. They did not seem surprised at seeing Ali and soon returned to the conversation they had been having. Ali hunkered down beside them, listening patiently, while Mohamed gazed around him. He could see dwellings in the clearing beyond the banyan tree. The huts' brown, dried palm-thatch walls and roofs made them seem part of the undergrowth that smothered the island.

From the distinctive, cloying odour that wafted around him on the evening breeze, he guessed the island was devoted to the boiling, drying and smoking of fish. Those hard, blackened batons of dried fish were a staple his father traded in, buying from islanders and selling to visiting vessels to ship to India, Ceylon and Sumatra where it was much in demand.

Ali rose to his feet and started to walk towards the houses, accompanied by a small, wiry man whose waistcloth was folded up above his knees, his bare back burnt black by the sun. He was obviously a fisherman but his bustle of importance made Mohamed think he might also be the island's chief. He followed at a respectful distance, looking around him to see if there were any boys of his own age. If there were any on the island, they were elsewhere.

The fisherman invited Ali into one of the huts. It was small, its sole room serving as living and sleeping quarters. Ali seemed to know his way around for he pointed out the well to Mohamed and told him to go and bathe. He did as he was bid.

When he returned, feeling greatly refreshed after washing the salt from the sea off his skin and cooling his body where the sun had changed his golden complexion to russet, he saw Ali swinging on a board suspended by a rope at each end from the branch of a mango tree. A coconut shell of oil burned in front of the house, piercing the gathering gloom of night.

"Come, sit." Ali beckoned him to his side.

He clambered onto the swing seat and relaxed to its gentle motion, not unlike the rhythm of the sea they had just left. He wanted to ask so many questions but surrendered instead to the serenity of the evening. He knew Ali would talk when he was ready.

From behind the hut came the sound of women murmuring softly; he hoped they were preparing dinner, for the ripe smell of drying fish that hung over the island stirred his appetite. He snatched at a mosquito buzzing around his ears, his sudden motion jolting Ali into speech.

"What do you know of the Maldives?"

The questions surprised Mohamed. He wanted to ask Ali about the island they were on, about how long they would stay, about where the children were. He realised Ali was waiting for him to reply.

"Very little, elder brother," he said cautiously, wondering what Ali expected of him. "I would like to know more."

Ali grunted, just like their father did when he wasn't impressed with something he or Hassan had done which they thought so clever. "Where do we live?"

"Why! On our island of Utheem, of course." It seemed a silly question.

"Take nothing for granted, Mohamed." Ali's voice was sharp. "Where is Utheem?"

Mohamed paused. The swing seat had stopped swaying. He glanced around quickly and then pointed. "In that direction."

"How do you know?"

"I observed where the sun set, so I know where is north."

"And the stars, do they tell you anything?"

"I have heard so, although I am not sure. Will you show me?"

Ali cuffed him gently around his ear in a rare show of affection. "You have a charming way with you, Mohamed. It will stand you in good stead, as long as your heart is in the right place."

"I try to follow what is written in the Holy Quran."

"I am your brother, Mohamed, not your father. You cannot deceive me."

"I would never seek to do that, elder brother."

"Fathimafaan says you waste your time on Utheem when father and myself are away. You go off alone, leaving Hassan with the other boys. She says you prefer your own company to that of others and you sit outside houses when the elders are talking, listening to them discuss matters of which you should know nothing."

Mohamed was shocked. "It is through my desire to learn," he said quickly. "Please do not misunderstand my intentions."

"Very well, Mohamed. Let us see what you have learned. Tell me about our realm. Who is our Sultan?"

"His name is Ali, like yours. He is the son of a courtier. He became Sultan but recently. He is a brave man who killed many Port-u-guesey when they tried to invade Male' so they could collect taxes for our former Sultan, that's Hassan, named like our younger brother, who is now a Christian living in India."

Mohamed paused to take a breath and realised that Ali was staring at him. "Have I made a mistake?"

"Where is Male'?"

Mohamed pointed to the south.

"And India?"

Mohamed pointed to the northeast.

"Look at the sky." Darkness was complete and the stars were bright as they gathered around the quarter moon. Ali stood up, sending the seat swinging, but Mohamed was alert enough not to lose his balance and topple off. He jumped down and followed Ali to the beach.

Ali pointed to the stars, naming them one by one, making him repeat their names after him. Mohamed desperately tried to remember what he was told and managed to name them all correctly when Ali tested him.

"Know the sky as your guide," Ali said. "When you sail to India on our father's ship to trade, there are no islands like this where you can shelter from storms or sleep when night falls. The ocean is open, no reefs, no lagoons, no landmarks; you must learn nature's starry signs so you can navigate."

Mohamed was thoughtful, wondering how he could ever learn enough to be like Ali or their father. "Tell me about the Maldives, elder brother," he asked still eager for knowledge. "How many islands are there?"

"You may as well ask how many stars in the sky," Ali said softly. "We cannot count them."

"Then you haven't been to them all?" This was odd. He was discovering for the first time that Ali did not know everything.

"No man has. Some say there are twelve thousand islands but that is just a phrase to say there are many. I know we have twelve plus one atolls and in each atoll there are dozens of islands, some no more than sandbanks that come and go at the whim of the tides.

"Others have only trees and no people. Some have villages and mosques. Others are like this with a small community of fishermen who dry and smoke fish away from their home islands."

"That explains why this is such a lonely, lifeless island without children?" Mohamed wanted to impress Ali with his observation.

"It explains why we are here," Ali looked stern. "To collect a cargo of dried fish tomorrow to sell in Male'." He put his hand on Mohamed's shoulder and steered him off the beach. "Come, boy, let's eat and sleep. Tomorrow you shall help us load the fish. We must leave at daybreak."

"Is Male' a great distance?" Mohamed asked, taking advantage of Ali's mood. He had never heard his brother speak so much before.

"Male' lies some seventy leagues south of Utheem, so we have a few more days' sailing depending on the wind and tide." They had reached the house where the lamp still burned. Ali crouched down by it and ran his finger in the sand, drawing circles in a line, each one below the other. The completed drawing looked like a necklace, with three circles on one side and five on the other, and a pendant of three circles at the bottom. With two circles at the top, there were thirteen when he had finished.

"This is the northern atoll," he said, pointing to the circle at the head of the line. Utheem is at its centre. See those circles on the west, those are the western atolls and those on the east, the eastern ones. See this."

He scored a deep line in the gap between the last circle and the others. "This line is where the sun is at its highest. Cross that line, and you are in the southern part of the world, two hundred leagues distant from the northernmost atoll." He sat back on his haunches and said no more, leaving the night air heavy with silence that had a strange hint of menace.

◆ ◆ ◆ ◆ ◆

Mohamed had trouble falling asleep that night. Images of distant islands filled his mind, of sailing on seas to unknown destinations, of people he would meet. He was nearly fifteen and he felt he was beginning his life. He was far too excited to sleep. This was the voyage he had been preparing for over the years.

He rolled onto his side. He was aware how his body was developing, his young muscles strengthening from the solitary exercises he practised on the beach. His legs were firm from swimming and running and shinning up and down coconut trees. His chest was broadening, hair was sprouting around the hardness in his groin and he knew from the night juices of his dreams that he was a man. His voice was changing, the quavering of childhood mellowing into the deeper trill of adolescence.

As he rolled to the other side of the mat, he heard Ali's regular breathing close by. The other occupants of the tiny house, the wizened fishermen and his crew, were also asleep. It puzzled Mohamed why, just when he needed rest after a long day at sea and with the hard work of the voyage the next day, he could not fall asleep easily. He had slept away from home before, when he visited the neighbouring island of Baarah, the capital of the northern atoll. Usually he did not feel nervous with strangers or having to sleep in a strange place.

He tightened his thighs together and held himself, letting the warmth of his touch flow through him. He thought back to what Ali had been telling him before supper with his simple lesson on geography. In the dim light from the lamp, Ali had drawn a line representing the course he proposed to take to Male'. He had explained how they would have the protection of the waters of the atolls until they crossed the deep channels between them. He had warned of the unpredictability of the ocean and how at sea he must always be alert.

"The ocean can be your brother, Mohamed," Ali had said. "Respect it, trust it, and it will never let you down. You must get to know it because, just like a brother, it can be contrary."

What did Ali mean? Mohamed rolled onto his stomach and pressed himself into the mat laid across the sand floor. *Am I contrary?* Sister Fathimafaan said he was not like other boys. Even younger brother Hassan complained that he liked to sit and read the Holy Quran when all the other boys were enjoying themselves in games or at the beach. Was he different because he liked to be alone?

To Mohamed, he wasn't being contrary, just preparing

himself for life. His hand raced faster and his breath quickened as he surrendered to his dreams.

◆ ◆ ◆ ◆ ◆

Someone was shaking his shoulder. Mohamed blinked, wondering where he was. Ali's voice came softly to him from the gloom. "It is prayer time. Dawn has come. Rise and prepare yourself."

He shook himself awake and glanced around. There was nobody else in the hut. He realised he had slept too long and let people move around him, even in the dark, without him being alerted. He would not let that happen again. He had to be the first awake, the first to greet the new dawn. It shamed him to think that Ali had to wake him, just as though he were still a child.

He pulled his waistcloth tight as he followed Ali out of the hut.

"After prayers, you must go to the boat. We have fish to load."

Mohamed nodding, wiping the sleep from his eyes and casting aside the mellow feeling that held him. *Was there a note of mockery in his brother's voice?*

"Wash your face at the well and come." Ali pointed behind the hut. "We don't want to sail without you."

Mohamed was furious with himself. What had happened? Even the cold water splashed over him did not alter his vexation. He felt he had let down Ali by waking so late. Yet Ali had let him lie there, probably watching him while he dreamed. *Yes*, he thought, *brothers can be contrary.*

There was a looking glass by the well and he caught sight of himself in the faint light of daybreak. He was surprised at the peevish face that stared back at him. He took a deep breath, then another, willing himself to calm down. His grumpiness vanished and he saw a pleasanter image staring back at him from the glass. He nodded to himself, remembering that he should keep his emotions private and not let his face betray his feelings.

His was a bright, earnest face. His brow was broad, his ears small, not protruding like Ali's. There was a downy line of hair beginning on his upper lip, marking his emerging manhood. His brown eyes stared back at him, reflecting their boundless curiosity. As he caught himself dreaming again, he quickly put down the looking glass. Then he ran along the path to catch up with Ali striding out to join the others for prayers.

CHAPTER 4

It was late afternoon when they approached Male'. Mohamed stood in the prow of the boat, holding onto the curved post at the boat's bow that distinguished it as a boat from the Maldives. He gazed in amazement at all he saw ahead of him.

The deep channel running along the northern coast of the capital island was ink dark, not the turquoise blue of the lagoon that fronted Utheem. There were several open-decked vessels, *odis* like theirs, anchored off the beach, and also some much larger boats anchored in the deep offshore. They had masts taller than a palm tree and shelters made of boards at stern and bow.

Mohamed asked the crewman standing close to him where those great ships came from.

"M'bar." The man said nothing more, continuing to coil the anchor rope he was readying for their arrival.

Malabar! Mohamed was thrilled. That was the coast he had heard about, of the great land, India, to the east. He was thrilled at the mere sight of a vessel that had sailed such a vast distance.

He had heard that the Malabaris were great seamen, crossing all over the ocean to trade. It was the monopoly held by the Malabaris that the Portuguese coveted. He waved gaily to the men on deck watching them as their tiny boat sailed close to those great houses on the water. One of the men shouted something lewd in response, which caused his companions to laugh coarsely.

Mohamed didn't have to glance back at Ali to know his brother would be scowling his disapproval. He stared ahead instead, ignoring the ships sharing the approach with them, and looking at the coast. The best approach to Male' was the course they were on, from the north. The deep channel flowed almost to the island's beaches, enabling even the large vessels from Malabar, Arabia and Africa to anchor close to the shore.

Ali steered almost to the beach before ordering the crewmen to drop the anchor rock. They were so close, Mohamed could see the features of the people gathered on the shore. There was every colour of man, and of clothes, there. Merchants from overseas were easy to recognise by their turbans and robes. Most of the Maldivian men were bare-chested and barefoot, dressed modestly with a cloth around their waists. Some wore more elaborate clothes; a tunic and a waistcloth reaching their ankles.

The men handling crates and jars and bundles of coir rope looked much darker than the others. Some of them had short hair like a skullcap of dark curls, a contrast to the long locks of the Malabaris. The glistening ebony of their skin intrigued Mohamed and he looked to Ali for an explanation.

Ali was busy making the sure the vessel was secure and exchanging greetings with friends who were watching from the beach. They were shouting questions to find out what cargo he was carrying and whether this time he would sell to them.

"If you pay double," Ali called back in reply, beckoning Mohamed to his side. "We'll go ashore, to the Sultan's palace," he said brusquely. "It is our duty to inform him of our arrival from Utheem, what cargo we are carrying, and to request his permission to trade." He indicated that Mohamed should climb into the skiff that had been rowed out to meet them by a black man like the ones Mohamed had seen carrying cargo.

"Is this the colour of men who inhabit Male'?" he asked softly, not wishing his curiosity to be overheard.

Ali laughed, "Yes, indeed, Mohamed. They inhabit Male' and work here too, though they come from Africa. You will see plenty of Negro slaves in the capital. And Maldivian slaves too. They are the ones who have borrowed from the nobles and are working to pay off their debts."

As he stood in the skiff beside Ali and was rowed the short distance to the shore, Mohamed wondered at the new and surprising things he was learning. Male' was so big and busy compared with Utheem. According to Ali, there were about two thousand people living there.

From the shore he could see paths of sand leading through palm trees into the interior. There was none of the undergrowth that overran the shores of other islands. Everywhere seemed so clean. There were legions of coconut palms tretching inland and broad trees forming shady glades.

"Come," said Ali, catching him by his elbow and pushing through the group of men who were clustering around to greet him. Ali returned their salutations by rote, politely but firmly making his way up the beach and onto the strand that paralleled it. He glanced back at the boat, saw it was secured and safe, and directed Mohamed up the short lane that faced them.

At its end was a stockade of wooden posts where two sentries lounged in front of an archway with a half-open gate. They returned Ali's greeting casually and let him push open the gate. Beyond it was a courtyard of swept sand and a venerable banyan tree spreading its branches over it. At its two opposite sides were low houses of wood with thatched roofs extending beyond their walls; supported by wooden pillars these created an awning of shade over their front verandas. Several men were seated there in groups, engaged in soft conversation. Some of them nodded at Ali as he strode through.

At the southern side of the courtyard was a building of blocks carved from coral. It had wooden shutters open to reveal vertical wooden bars at the windows, and a huge door filled its arched entrance. The door was open. A man beckoned Ali to come forward.

"That is Lord Meedhoo," whispered Ali to Mohamed. "He is one of the Sultan's advisers."

Mohamed saluted politely, watching the man from under his lowered eyes. He was fat with an obsequious manner that must have developed from constant fawning and flattery of those in power. His eyes glinted with greed and Mohamed felt himself being appraised as though he were an object of trade, not the son of Katheeb Hussain of Utheem.

"The Sultan is expecting you," said Lord Meedhoo with an oily smile. "You have been long in coming."

"The currents were not in our favour to come to the Sultan's installation," said Ali. "We hastened here as soon as conditions were right."

"Ah, yes," said Lord Meedhoo, his eyebrows raised in mockery. "That means you waited until you had sufficient goods to make your voyage a venture of great profit."

Ali ignored the insult but it made Mohamed realise the small-minded meanness of the man. He wondered what percentage of those profits he would demand from them.

He followed in the wake of the fat man as he and Ali progressed into the gloom of the palace's interior. Although outside was hot, the large hall, with its high thatched roof and curtains hanging down from it, dividing it into sections, was cool. There was a pleasing fragrance in the air, sandalwood incense, which was like a soothing balm to Mohamed's intense curiosity. He gazed quickly around him, hoping he would not cause offence by his eagerness to see everything. Ali was being embraced by another man, a tough-looking character with a no-nonsense manner. Mohamed liked him instantly.

The man quickly dispensed with the formal greetings and, drawing Ali to one side, started an animated conversation with him. Lord Meedhoo was scowling at being left out. Mohamed decided that this must be the reception chamber of the Sultan. People were sitting around on mats quietly talking among themselves. The silk curtains hanging over doorways leading off the chamber probably led to the Sultan's private quarters.

Where, he wondered, *does the Sultan sit?* He looked in vain for a throne and then he noticed a much larger doorway at the rear of the chamber. A silk tapestry hung in front of it. This seemed to lead to the main audience hall so the people sitting around were probably waiting to be summoned into the Sultan's presence.

Slowly Mohamed raised his eyes and observed how the

walls were covered with tapestries and even the thatched roof had a tapestry ceiling hung with tassels. The floor, which was wooden like a boat's deck and raised off the ground, was covered with mats of dyed reeds woven in colourful patterns.

Mohamed had heard that it was the custom for the nobles of Male' to attend the Sultan every afternoon. Sometimes they would be called into the Sultan's chamber for an audience. On other days when the Sultan did not have time to see them, he would send them dishes of fruit and betel nut, after which they would withdraw and return to their homes.

Mohamed wondered how many afternoons they would have to wait for the Sultan to grant them an audience. He knew that Ali wanted to sell their cargo without delay so that they could return to Utheem in time for Ramazan. He wanted to ask the fat lord when the Sultan would come, but instead kept quiet, watching Ali and his friend talking.

Suddenly he realised that Ali was beckoning him. He went forward, aware that Ali's faced was grave with a look that was intended to warn him to conduct himself politely. So he lowered his eyes to the ground and stood obediently by his brother's side. Ali put his hand on his shoulder.

"So you are Katheeb Hussain's son?" the man said in the patronising voice uninterested elders use for children.

"Katheeb Hussain is my father." Mohamed answered, to show his independence, He felt Ali's hand squeezing his shoulder tightly.

The man laughed. "He has your father's spirit."

Ali's hand seemed to be forcing Mohamed to the floor. "This is the Sultan," he hissed in his ear.

Mohamed immediately fell to his knees, touched the floor with his finger, kissed it, and raised it to his forehead in the traditional salutation of respect. "God is my Lord; Mohamed is my prophet; I am a poor, ignorant being."

Mohamed felt another hand on his shoulder and glanced up to see the Sultan was bidding him rise. He did so, assured by the warmth of the man's eyes that he was not offended by his conduct. He noticed, though, the mettle in the Sultan's manner and guessed it was only because of the friendship between Ali and the Sultan that he was spared a rebuke.

"You and my old friend, your brother Ali, are welcome to my court." Suddenly the Sultan sighed, as though suffering immense pain. "I remember when I was young and innocent and full of fresh confidence like you, Mohamed," he said sadly. "Now I fear those days are gone." He gestured at the people sitting around the room.

"Everyone attends the Sultan, but will everyone attend to their duties when the time comes? You know, of course," he said to Ali, lowering his voice, "the Portuguese will return even though we have repelled them twice."

"News of your valour in battle, how you personally drove the Portuguese away, is known throughout the islands, my Sultan."

Mohamed looked up swiftly. Ali's tone made him sense that something was wrong. He had never heard his brother trying to flatter someone. The Sultan noticed it too. He sighed.

"Ali, I know you and your father are traders, not fighters. Save your sweet talk for the women of Utheem. Have no fear, you can do your trading without hindrance." He patted Mohamed's shoulder again, seeming almost reluctant to release him. He frowned, then turned away abruptly, striding off to the inner chamber.

Mohamed tried to understand what had happened; it didn't make sense. He felt the Sultan had created a bond between them both, as though he were in some way being favoured. He followed Ali out of the hall and through the courtyard, his mind bursting with questions.

"Does the Sultan have children?" he blurted out when they reached the lane in front of the palace and he could no longer contain his curiosity.

"Yes," said Ali. "Two daughters, one of them but recently born."

"He must love his family very much. Then why is he so sad?"

"Sad? How do I know? You should be sad for the disrespect you showed him."

"I didn't know he was the Sultan. He seems so natural, he

doesn't have the dignity of our father even."

Ali grinned. "Our Sultan is a brave man, Mohamed. He fought off invaders for the sake of this country. If the Sultan smiles on you, all those in Male' will recognise you. If he does not, then you do not exist. I'm glad he likes you, although what he saw in you I cannot fathom.

◆ ◆ ◆ ◆ ◆

What Ali said about Sultan Ali, seemed to be true. Mohamed discovered he was accorded the respect of a young prince, as the word became known that he and his brother enjoyed the Sultan's patronage. They were lodged by the Sultan's command in a house close to the palace and were sent meals from the Sultan's table every day. Each afternoon, Ali and he would wait in the anteroom of the audience chamber to see if the Sultan wanted to talk to them. While he acknowledged their presence on two occasions, he ignored them on two other days.

"It matters not," said Ali when Mohamed asked him why. "We have his shelter and dine on food from his table. It is the way."

Mohamed learned that Sultan Ali was respected because of his ruthlessness. He had been the mastermind of the resistance to Sultan Hassan, which had driven Hassan to the Portuguese in India where he had become a Christian. He had only recently succeeded to the throne, his presence there hastened by his bravery. He had personally led the islanders in repelling two violent attempts by the Portuguese to establish themselves in the Maldives.

His conversations with his nobles, which Mohamed witnessed during his visits to the palace, showed he was convinced that the Portuguese would try again. All the able-bodied men in Male' were armed with knives, which they lay wrapped in cloth on the floor of the audience chamber when they visited the palace.

Mohamed heard them boasting loudly of what they would do when the Portuguese next tried to invade, but he wondered how effective they would be. They seemed more interested in haggling over trading deals than in preparing themselves for a battle to repel invaders. The Sultan's guards looked impressive but Mohamed sensed their motivation was the Sultan's table rather than his welfare.

It was little concern to him, however, and he busied himself exploring Male'. He was told the island was four leagues in circumference and he was able to walk around it in a morning by keeping to the shore. The southern part was marshland and difficult to cross. The interior was thick with coconut trees that were harvested by some of the inhabitants, just as on Utheem.

There were more dwellings than on Utheem. Between the hamlets of thatched huts and some coral stone shelters, there were tracks of sand lined with coconut and payaya and mango trees. While some of the islanders were fishermen who went to sea every day except Friday, most of the inhabitants were engaged in trade, or professions like carpenters and goldsmiths, or were attached to the Sultan's court and assisting in the governance of the islands.

Male' was much more prosperous than Utheem and the nobles owned big compounds containing wooden and stone huts housing their families. On the waterfront trading was so hectic, with Ramazan drawing close, it was often difficult to find a way through the throng of people buying and selling coir, dried fish, cowry shells and local produce.

Mohamed observed everything keenly, soon discovering how the nobles profited from the efforts of the poor. Commission changed hands on every deal, with the producer being the one who made the least out of the trade, and the middleman the most. Ali's ploy of selling direct to visiting vessels would not have been possible if he did not have his own boat. Thus he could visit vessels and conclude deals without going through a broker on shore.

Mohamed accompanied him on some of his trading visits, and met mariners from countries he had never heard of. There were Malabaris from Barcelor, Cannanore, Calicut and Cochin; Gujaratis from Cambaye, Surat and Chaulk; Arabs, Persians, men of Bengal, St Thomas and Masulipatam, Ceylon and Sumatra.

Through his visits to the huge vessels of the traders from faraway, Mohamed overcame his awe of the ships and their crews. He found the vessels were basically the same as his father's own boat, only larger with cabins built on them to shelter the crew and to store provisions for their long voyages. So when he rose early one morning and glanced out to sea, he was not worried by the sight of more big ships sailing into view.

It was an impressive fleet of three huge vessels, sails billowing and flags fluttering in the wind. They tacked along the northern shoreline with such precision, Mohamed marvelled at their seamanship. Then he noticed the cannon protruding from the ship's side and called Ali from where he was resting to come and have a look.

Ali was tired. Trading had finished and he was anxious to leave Male'. He hoped that by the afternoon he could get permission from the Sultan to return home to Utheem. He emerged from the house, rubbing his eyes, muttering to himself about being disturbed so early.

"See those fine ships, elder brother," Mohamed called out with delight. "Can we not trade with them too? I would like to visit them, they are so grand."

For a moment Ali was speechless. Mohamed turned around to see him staring in disbelief.

"Oh, can't we visit them, elder brother?"

"We must pray we live to see the sunset," Ali said ominously. "Look at those flags. We are in great danger, Mohamed. Those ships are not merchant vessels. They are the galleons of the Portuguese, come to invade."

CHAPTER 5

Mohamed stared at the three ships-of-war without fear. They were an impressive, awesome sight but he knew from his previous visits to the other big vessels in the roadstead that inside those fearsome ships were men and boys just like him. Since they had not arrived with guns blazing, although their gun ports were open and men were on deck, they seemed more curious than aggressive. They did not seem to be preparing for an attack, more like an expedition, perhaps for water and provisions or to reconnoitre.

Because he had no experience of the Portuguese, Mohamed wasn't scared. Panic, however, was spreading through the town. Men were hurrying to the Sultan's palace and the waterfront was suddenly deserted. Some of the Maldivian boats that had crew on board were hauling up their anchors and unfurling their sails, hastening to get away. The Portuguese vessels ignored them even though they were anchoring close to the shore broadside on, in a formation that Mohamed could see might be threatening.

Ali warned him to stay in the house while he hurried to the palace. He wanted to seek the Sultan's permission to leave at once, yet — he told Mohamed –- he expected it to be refused since the Sultan would want every able-bodied man to take up arms to repel the Portuguese.

The Portuguese threat to the Maldives had begun with an incident that happened in 1503, fifty-five years before. Mohamed heard the details from people he met during his stay in Male'. He had asked why there was so much fear of the Portuguese when the islanders happily traded with foreigners from other nations.

It was because of this trading. The Portuguese began to wreak havoc on the traditional trading routes of the Indian Ocean by signing a treaty with the Rajah of Cannanore, to tax and thus control all the merchant seafaring along India's western coast. This gave the Portuguese an excuse to attack the ships that avoided paying tribute to the Rajah of Cannanore.

The Viceroy representing Portugal at the time was Vasco da Gama, the same man who had led the Portuguese into India. He used the treaty to control trade as well as to persecute his enemies. He instructed Vicente Sodre, his captain of the Indian Ocean, to demonstrate to the Rajah of Calicut, arch rival of the Rajah of Cannanore, by sheer ruthlessness that the Portuguese would not tolerate defiance.

Captain Sodre sailed with some caravels to wait off the coast by Calicut, which was a major entrepot for the Indian coastal trade. There he encountered four sailing ships, which he arrested on discovering they were from the Maldives, intent on trading in Calicut instead of Cannanore.

Each vessel was loaded with coir rope, dried fish and cowries, and also exquisitely fine silks that had been woven by the womenfolk of the islands. It was a large and valuable cargo that the merchants from Calicut who were on board had acquired in exchange for rice, salt, cooking utensils and silver.

Sodre was unable to determine who on the vessels were from the Maldives and who were from Calicut, since all were Muslims and all were dressed alike. He ordered their captains to hand over the Moors from Calicut as they were enemies, otherwise he would burn their ships. He transferred the cargo of one vessel to his own, emptying the vessel to show he was ready to do what he threatened.

The Maldivian islanders, being peaceful people, failed to understand the possible consequences. They identified the Moors from Calicut as ordered. They then watched in horror as the Moors they had surrendered were bound hand and foot and thrown into the empty vessel. Oil was poured over the ship and over the helpless merchants inside it. Sodre flung a flaming torch onto the boat, setting it ablaze. It burned quickly because it was made of boards already soaked in oil to make them waterproof.

One hundred of their fellow Muslims were burned to death that terrible day. The Maldivians were forced to sail their ships to Cannanore where the cargo was seized. Sodre warned the islanders never to trade again with Calicut or they and every vessel from the Maldives would be burned too. People in the islands still talked about it with fear. If the Portuguese could do that to innocent merchants, what would they do to their foes?

The Maldivian traders and merchants, hoping to preserve peace with the Portuguese, tried to enter into an alliance with them, undertaking to render them tribute and to trade through their nominees. This was to avoid having to trade with a pirate called Mamalle, who was the self-proclaimed Regent of the Seas and the real controller of the trade route to Cannanore. The Portuguese took advantage of the fears of the peaceful islanders and began to plunder the Maldives at will.

In 1517, the Portuguese opened negotiations with the

Maldives when they perceived an advantage to be gained from organised trade with the islands. Dom Joao de Silveira was despatched from Cochin by the new Viceroy to enter into an agreement with the Sultan, Kalu Mohamed. The Sultan had no choice but to agree to what the Portuguese wanted, to build a warehouse in Male' for them to use as a trading post.

A flotilla was despatched to the Maldives under the command of Joao Gomes, whose nickname 'Cheiradinheiro' meant 'one who sniffs money'. It consisted of four vessels with a crew of one hundred and twenty ruthless cutthroats. They plundered many of the islands north of the capital before anchoring in the Male' roadstead.

The Portuguese announced they had come to set up their warehouse under the treaty. They chopped down trees and fenced themselves in behind palisades by the shore. While some of them sailed to the outer islands where they forcibly seized trade goods, the others stayed ashore and constructed the warehouse, known as a Factory, to store their plunder until it could be shipped. The factory was well protected with cannon from their vessels, and served as a fort for the marauding invaders. Cheiradhinheiro made himself Captain of the Fort.

Sultan Kalu Mohamed and the people of Male' were in despair, unable to do anything about the Portuguese settlement on their island. They sent delegations to the Viceroy in India pointing out that the settlement was more than agreed to by the treaty. Nothing happened until four years later when a merchant from Cochin, whose ships the Portuguese had seized, decided to seek revenge by helping the islanders.

In 1521 twelve ships, well manned with buccaneers from the Indian coast experienced in sea battles, sailed without warning into the Male' roads. Six of them battled the Portuguese pinnaces while the other six tackled the caravel. Using firebombs and hand-to-hand fighting with cutlasses, they killed all on board and burned the caravel. They then assaulted the factory fort from the seaside where it was undefended. Those Portuguese who escaped into the jungle where happily hunted down and hacked to death by the

Maldivians.

The buccaneers were rewarded with the goods they captured from the Portuguese warehouse while the Sultan kept their two cannons. With their partial and unexpected thraldom to the Portuguese ended, the Maldives settled down to an uneasy peace, only interrupted by occasional forays to the undefended outer islands by Portuguese in the guise of pirates.

Emboldened by their success in driving out the Portuguese, even though it could not have been done without help, the Maldivians became more active in resisting foreigners. In 1540 they killed some Portuguese when they tried to rob a vessel of the cowries it was carrying for trade. A Portuguese captain, Gonzales Vaz, took prompt revenge by landing on an island close to Male' and seizing the chief whom he tortured to death.

Sultan Hassan's defection stirred up the Portuguese interest in having another settlement in Male'. An expedition of ships-of-war arrived in Male' supposedly at the behest of the Sultan Hassan. A force led by Abu Bakur and the current Sultan Ali, attacked the ships, destroyed three of them and killed many of the Portuguese, preventing an invasion.

Mohamed, when he heard those tales of the recent past, felt proud of his brave countrymen. They had resisted foreign occupation even though they were powerless to stop the Portuguese robbing the outer islands and restricting the islanders' trading voyages. As he watched the Portuguese vessels so close to the shore he wondered if Sultan Ali would use their arrival to negotiate a treaty to keep them at bay. Maldivians wanted only to be left alone in peace, not to fight. They were children of the sea, not warriors.

◆ ◆ ◆ ◆ ◆

Mohamed was bored, staying by himself in the house; he wanted to know what was happening. He could see the Portuguese galleons riding at anchor, but no one had come ashore. Perhaps the Portuguese were waiting to see the response of the Sultan to their presence. If the Sultan's guard fired the cannons from the palace, then the Portuguese were certain to return the fire. They would annihilate Male'.

Although he realised how serious the situation was, Mohamed was not alarmed. But he wanted to know what was going on. It was odd of Ali to leave him in the hut when he could easily wonder around and see things for himself. So he wouldn't attract attention, he took off the bright raiment of the Sultan's house and dressed like a village lad in a white waistcloth. He smoothed down his hair, which was growing long now he was a man. At the doorway of the low-roofed house he paused, wondering whether he should go to the palace or to the deserted waterfront.

There were many people on the town's tracks, hurrying hither and thither or huddled in frightened groups. It was clear that no one knew what would happen or what to do. It was too late to leave Male' and flee to another island. The only shelter from the ship's cannons would be in the mangrove swamp on the southern side of the island. People were already hurrying there. They had experienced the perfidy of the Portuguese before and did not trust their apparently peaceful presence.

He paused by a group of men gathered warily in the shade of a mango trees and heard them saying that Sultan Ali did not expect to negotiate a peace. The Portuguese didn't want peace, people said, they wanted war and they would not stop until they had occupied Male' and conquered all the Maldives islands. It was a terrifying prospect. Yet although he knew the stories of Portuguese cruelty he found it hard to believe anything bad would actually happen.

Relying on the adults being too preoccupied with their worries to notice what he was doing, Mohamed made his way nonchalantly towards the waterfront. It was ominously quiet. The Negro slaves, who were usually unloading cargo and carrying goods on their heads to the stockaded warehouses, were sleeping unconcerned in the shade of mango trees.

Their masters, the merchants and boat owners, seemed to have fled to the swamps, or perhaps they were congregating at the palace. Mohamed noticed one man, almost hidden by the undergrowth, digging a hole in the sand of his compound. The man dumped a sack in the shallow hole and hastily covered it over. The man's pathetic attempt to bury his treasures, as though he had already accepted defeat, annoyed Mohamed. If everyone gave up so easily, the Portuguese would take Male' without firing a shot.

Determined not to be afraid like the others, he walked boldly along the shore to where his father's *odi* rode at anchor. It was deserted. The two crew members who should have been on board guarding the vessel and its cargo had obviously abandoned the boat and swum ashore. Mohamed looked around cautiously. The Portuguese man-of-war vessels were anchored at the edge of the channel, out of range of any cannon that could be fired from the shore, but close enough to raise sail and tack into the open harbour if they were to launch an attack.

He sat on the narrow stretch of beach to think. He looked across at the huge ships. They were taller even than the Sultan's palace, which was the highest building in the Maldives. As he stared at them it gradually dawned on him that the Portuguese were not planning to attack Male'. If that was their aim they would have done so as soon as they arrived. taking the island by surprise. By revealing their presence so openly, the Portuguese must surely have come in peace.

That knowledge made him feel bold and, without thinking of the consequences, he made a decision. He stood up, rolled his waistcloth tightly around his sinewy thighs, and waded into the sea. It would be a long swim to the nearest Portuguese ship but he didn't care. He wanted to get close enough to see these strange, feared foreigners for himself.

He swam effortlessly to reach the anchor line of his father's boat and there he paused, hanging onto the rope to catch his breath. The boat was filled with sacks of rice and salt, ready to take to Utheem to sell to the islanders. He wondered if the Portuguese would let them leave, even if the Sultan gave his consent.

He pushed away from the boat and struck out with strong, confident strokes towards the Portuguese ships. After a few minutes he became aware of a small boat being rowed towards the shore to his right. He ignored it, concentrating on his own course, raising his head from the water from time to time to see how close he was to an *odi* anchored near the Portuguese vessels. He planned to board that, since it seemed empty, so he could sit in its bow and observe the ships without being noticed.

A sudden blow on his head stunned him. He opened his mouth in shock and water filled it. He spluttered, struggling to stop going under. He shut his mouth, held his breath, and bobbed back to the surface, thrashing out with his arms and legs to escape whatever had struck him. He was not fast enough for the oars of the rowing boat that closed in on him. The last sound he heard as he dived frantically to avoid capture was a shout of triumph.

◆ ◆ ◆ ◆

"Mohamed? Where are you?" Ali's voice echoed through the empty house. He called again. "Mohamed, come quickly, we have the Sultan's permission to sail to Utheem."

Ali strode into the house. He saw Mohamed's mat rolled up in a corner. His bundle with his clothes and the provisions he had bought in Male' were also on the floor. Thinking he must be at the well, Ali looked outside. The yard was deserted and there was no sign of splashed water on the sand to indicate that Mohamed had bathed recently.

Ali was puzzled. He had expected his young brother to obey him and wait until he returned. He glanced down the track to the sea front. All the Portuguese vessels were there and it seemed that no landing party had come ashore. So they had time to leave, but where was Mohamed?

Perhaps he had gone to the Sultan's palace to look for him? Ali had to find him quickly so they could sail that evening while the tide was right. He asked some of the people passing the house if they had seen a boy wondering along the track. Most of them were too busy carrying valuables to hide, or to find a safe place to hide themselves, to listen to him. Only one old man, who sat calmly on his swinging seat in the compound of his house near the beach, answered him.

"Do not worry," he said, scratching his beard. "I have seen that one. He is a smart boy. He will be all right."

Ali grabbed the man by his shoulders, bringing the swing seat to an abrupt halt. "When did you see him?"

The man brushed Ali's hands off his shoulders and set the swing into motion again. "Conserve your passion for your enemies, my son, not your friends." He paused, as though showing that he was not afraid like the other islanders. "The boy went to the beach. I saw him swimming."

Ali turned and was about to hurry off to the shore when something about the old man's calm manner made him pause. He turned back and lowered his face to the old man's. "What else did you see?" he asked softly, fearing what he might hear. "Tell me!"

"Some men, in a boat. They took him."

✦ ✦ ✦ ✦ ✦

"Your name what is?"

Mohamed opened his eyes. He had been pulled into the boat which was rowed by two men, both black like the Negro slaves he had seen carrying cargo in Male'. There was a white man in a jerkin at the stern of the tiny boat, another man with a pistol in his belt was sitting beside the man who had addressed him. He frowned, trying to understand the question. It had been asked in Dhivehi, but the man's odd way of speaking the islanders' tongue confused him.

He took a deep breath to gather his senses and calm himself after being fished out of the water struggling like a barracuda. "Mohamed, master," he said slowly, realising that humility was called for. "I am a poor ignorant being—"

"Of course you are," said the man, reaching forward and touching Mohamed's cheek, letting his fingers crawl slowly down to his jaw. He cupped his chin in his hand and raised Mohamed's head, looked directly into his eyes, as though reading his mind.

Mohamed felt his flesh tingling but he stared back without a blink. He saw the man's eyes were the colour of the Utheem lagoon, a blue green, and set in a face that was lined with concern. His nose was long, like a heron's beak. He had a goatee of greying hair and a sallow complexion. Mohamed guessed that he wasn't a seaman or even a soldier, although he had the animal smell of a man who had not bathed for a long time. The stale aroma of essence of sandalwood the man had dabbed behind his ears did nothing to disguise his disgusting odour. Mohamed had been told that these white foreigners had their own peculiar, unpleasant smell and now he knew it was true.

"Scared not you are?" The man asked the question in his curious manner of speaking Dhivehi. Mohamed wondered where he had learned the language of the islanders. He quite forgot that he should appear to be frightened, even if he wasn't. He found the man was so strange, even fascinating.

The man removed his fingers slowly from his chin and ran them up the side of his face, pinching his cheek as though assessing him. Mohamed shook himself, spraying the man with droplets of seawater from his hair. The man seemed to smile, his eyes ranging over his body, from head to toe. He leaned forward and squeezed his thigh, then slid his hand slowly under his wet loincloth and cupped him. Mohamed held his breath, keeping his eyes on the man without flinching.

The man withdrew his hand slowly and pursed his lips as though thinking. Mohamed glanced beyond him and saw the boat was being rowed to the shore, not to the Portuguese ship, so his swim had been in vain.

"Brave young boy, you are."

Mohamed looked back into the man's eyes which were suddenly bright, his pale face flushed. He returned the man's gaze guilelessly, even though he was puzzled by the man's behaviour. It was like some kind of bonding ritual rather than something he should be concerned about.

"Brave? What have I to fear?"

The man nodded as though satisfied before saying, in his strange way of speaking, "I killed you could have."

Mohamed saw that the other two white men in the boat were taking no interest in the conversation so he guessed they did not understand what was being said. By the man's attitude and his dress, he judged he must be someone of importance. He was wearing a high-necked tunic tightly laced at the waist, and drawers a deep scarlet colour fastened below his knees. Stockings held up with garters covered his legs and he wore shoes tied with leather laces. It was the strangest outfit Mohamed had ever seen.

"Why so much on my person you gaze, Mohamed, my boy?" the man asked with a smile. "A Portuguese nobleman never have you seen?" He leaned forward again and chucked Mohamed almost playfully in his crotch.

"No, my lord," answered Mohamed suddenly sensing he had nothing to fear from this strange man. The rowing boat was nearing the shore and he knew he could jump out and run away if the man looked like he was going to detain him. He had forgotten the other two men had pistols.

"Aren't you hot dressed like that?" he asked cheekily, wriggling away from the man's probing fingers.

"Of course!" The man chuckled. "Your Sultan I am to see so dress properly I must. You, my native little, so little wear." He paused as though reminded of something important. "Why to us you swim?"

The man's tone had hardened and Mohamed was warned by it not to trifle with him. Undoubtedly, the man's importance had been earned at the expense of others. If he was the commander of the fleet, as Mohamed suspected, then he held life or death in his power.

"I wanted to see what ship is that," Mohamed answered truthfully. "I have never seen one so grand."

"A carrack of His Majesty the King of Portugal it is," the noble said. "Over one thousand men aboard the ship are, and a burthen of two thousand tons it has."

"Where did you learn our language?" Mohamed asked without considering that the man might think him rude.

"Good it isn't, I know." The noble smiled ruefully. "To speak it better I will learn." His expression changed, as though he was remembering his status now the rowing boat was running onto the sand. He turned to the armed officer beside him and said something sharply in a strange language, the first time Mohamed had heard Portuguese. The other man nodded and put his pistol back in his belt. It was only then Mohamed realised it had been aimed at him the whole time.

"Release you I do," said the noble, his face now stern with authority. "Bright and young you are. From our ships keep away. Next time my soldiers kill you will."

Mohamed thanked the man with a bow of his head and pushed himself quickly over the side of the boat into the shallow water before the man changed his mind. As he splashed up onto the beach, the enormity of what he had done struck him. He had been fished out of the sea by the Portuguese and returned safely to the shore. Yet he could have been held as a spy.

He wondered about the strange man who had captured him, fingered him in that interesting way, and then let him go. Who was he? More important, what did he plan to do in the Maldives?

CHAPTER 6

Sultan Ali swept out of the audience chamber without a word, the grand raiment of his rank flapping at his ankles, reflecting his rage. He had dressed elaborately to emphasis his authority to his courtiers. A cotton cloth of royal blue reaching to his knees covered the broad band of his under garment. Over that he wore the traditional long cloth, like a sarong, draped down to his ankles, belted with a silk scarf decorated with golden embroidery. Another cloth of fine material reached mid thigh, held in place with a sash and tassels. A dagger of silver was sheathed in the sash. He clasped its shaft tightly as he tried to contain his fury.

He strode through the salons to his private quarters with Lord Meedhoo waddling in his wake, wringing his hands with anxiety.

Becoming aware of being followed. he stopped abruptly and turned, raising his hand, forbidding Lord Meedhoo to move closer. He glared at him. "You wish to enter the Sultan's private chamber?"

"The Portuguese –" Lord Meedhoo was forced to cut off his whine of discomfort as the Sultan ducked through the doorway and entered his quarters.

Inside, the room was hung with silk curtains; the bed on which he slept on a dais raised off the floor was a symphony of silk cushions. He threw himself on it in despair, burying his head in his hands. A soft rustle of silk signified a woman's approach and he raised his head reluctantly.

"What ails my lord?" Aisha, the woman he had made his queen, stood in front of him. Gently she placed her hands on his, drawing them away from his face. She looked at him calmly, waiting for him to speak.

"Am I not Sultan?" he asked peevishly. "The people were happy to have me when no Portuguese sails cast shadows on Male'. Now they ignore their sultan and try to flee, instead of heeding my call to take up arms and fight."

"The Portuguese have come too soon," said Aisha, holding his hand reassuringly. "More time would have helped you consolidate power and oust your enemies and the weak. Most of your ministers are from the court of Hassan. When the Portuguese say they come in the name of Hassan, his followers have no will to fight them, only us."

"Aisha, he is no longer a Muslim. He has become a Christian and calls himself Dom Manoel. He has lost his right to the throne of the Maldives, and to the loyalty of those who were his lily-livered sychophants I have inherited as courtiers."

"There are those of his family who want the throne, believing it is theirs by blood."

"You are his blood relative too, Aisha!" He withdrew his fingers from her grasp.

"Which is why you took me as your queen, my lord, to unite our houses."

The Sultan rose from where he lay on the bed and heaved a deep sigh. He raised his hand to Aisha's shoulder and touched her gently, sighing again. He reached down for her hands and took them in his. It was like a farewell. He looked into her eyes, marvelling at the unblemished beauty of her ivory skin, and the strength behind her delicate appearance. There was silence, a peace of understanding between them.

"Your blood mattered not," he said, dismissing her comment with a rueful smile. "I did not marry you to become Sultan."

"My lord, I married you because I knew you would!"

Whether she spoke the truth or not, her remark restored his confidence, banishing the sadness that threatened to overwhelm them both.

"You are the Sultan," she added in a firm tone. "You will lead the people and defend Male' from those tiresome infidels."

"Tiresome? They could be worse than that. Lord Meedhoo sees them as his way to power. He is your kinsman and of Hassan's house. He wants me killed. Already he sees himself as Sultan in my place. He can't wait to enter this chamber and install himself here, in my bed... and to take what's mine."

Aisha made no reply.

Did she understand? He sighed and looked at her intently. "I know what the future holds for me, my dear Aisha. It is a joy to me to know."

Her expression changed to one of alarm.

"Yes," he nodded as though to himself. "The future will bring success or martyrdom. Men will join me if there is to be a fight, others will scurry away like rats." He paused and looked beyond Aisha to where a little girl was standing at the entrance of their chamber. He beckoned her to him.

Sitti was his daughter. Her young face promised fine beauty and her eyes, like precious opals, were large and concerned as she watched them keenly. Her head was shaved in the manner of the times, with a tiny fringe of hair remaining over her forehead. He called her to him and her face brightened. He released Aisha and stooped down to lift her above his head, smiling at Aisha, making them both partners in his decision.

"You must not be frightened, dear Sitti. All will be as Allah wills. Ask your mother."

The girl looked away shyly as he set her down on the mat beside the bed.

"How like your mother you are," he said glancing proudly from her to Aisha. "You know when to keep silent, and when to talk. I pray you will grow as wise as your mother and give good counsel when it is required by your husband."

He knelt down and hugged her. "Yes, Sitti, if you find a

youth who is willing to defend our country against the Portuguese infidels, make him yours. Encourage him, stand by him as your mother does by me. Love him."

He stood up and nodded at Aisha, indicating he wanted to be left alone. She led Sitti out of the chamber and he watched with sad resignation as they left. The girl's bright innocence and trust bolstered him, adding strength to his faith. His anger was spent, his spirit renewed. He would return to the audience chamber and motivate his wavering courtiers. His duty was clear.

◆ ◆ ◆ ◆ ◆

Mohamed darted away from the beach, walking swiftly. He didn't want to run and let the Portuguese think he was scared. He wasn't. But he waited until he reached the screen of trees and undergrowth across the road from the waterfront before he turned to see what was happening.

The nobleman and his companion-at-arms were being carried ashore on the backs of their slaves. The other white man waited in the boat. Mohamed wondered if he should go back to the house in case his brother was looking for him. He decided to delay for a little while so he could watch what the nobleman would do.

The foreigner was taller than Mohamed had imagined when he was seated opposite him in the rowing boat. The plume of feathers in his hat added to his height and he carried himself as though he was used to being obeyed. He had an arrogance in his stance, which Mohamed had not noticed when he sat with him. It amused him how this white man's character was easy to fathom from the way he walked.

He seemed confident, and familiar with Male'. Without waiting for his companion, he set off at a brisk pace along the trail leading to the palace. The other man had to hurry to catch up with him so Mohamed guessed he was no more than an armed attendant. Two long boats were being rowed ashore from the Portuguese vessels and in them were soldiers with pikes and firearms. A man of apparent stature stood at the bow of one of them, sweeping the island with his eyes as though searching for hidden fortifications.

If he stayed watching, Mohamed might be held again so he snaked his way deep into the undergrowth. Looking back he saw the soldiers beach their boats and fan out to form a guard around them. The men made no move inland towards the palace, and even their commander stayed on the beach, using a telescope to scan the trails into the interior.

Mohamed's wet loincloth dried quickly in the heat of the morning. As he fought his way through the undergrowth to regain the path, burrs and leave stuck to his loincloth and thorns scratched his legs and chest. When he regained the path he was dirty and sweaty like a ragged urchin, looking like a slave boy, not the son of an island chief. He glanced back to the beach and was relieved when he saw he was a safe distance from the men and hadn't been observed by them.

He had penetrated the woods deeper than he intended and had emerged onto a narrow path at the side of the palace, not in front of it. There were people in a group, talking nervously among themselves. He overheard them refer to the strange noble as Dom Gaspar. He was known to the islanders as the one who had escorted Sultan Hassan when he decamped to India four years before. That explained why he could speak some of their language. The opinion of the courtiers was that Dom Gaspar had come to Male' as an envoy from the Portuguese Viceroy.

Mohamed lurked at the edge of the crowd until he became bored with the speculation about what would happen. Dom Gaspar himself had told him his ship carried a thousand men. Perhaps he should find Ali and tell him that so he could tell the Sultan. As he thought about it, Mohamed found it curious that a man of such importance should have revealed such a secret to him, a boy he had plucked from the sea. There must be a reason for him having done so.

Of course! He was surprised at his thoughts. *The Portuguese want the people of Male' to know that they number one thousand soldiers. It's a threat to intimidate the Sultan to surrender!* It shocked him to realise that he was being used as a messenger by the stranger's ploy. He decided not to tell Ali about his encounter with the cunning old heron. He was not going to be manipulated by the Portuguese, nor by anyone. The white man's trick to have him start a frightening rumour would fail.

"Boy!"

A woman's voice disturbed his thoughts as he sat on his haunches at the edge of the jungle. He looked up the path, away from the crowd and saw a woman beckoning him. She was dressed in a robe of fine cotton reaching to her ankles, where it was bordered in red and blue. It was open at her neck and fastened with gilt buttons. Bracelets of silver adorned her arms from her wrist to her elbow, so he knew she must be someone rich and important.

"Yes, my lady?" he said, rising to his feet.

The woman seemed to assume he was a slave for she nodded at him to follow her through the side door into the palace. He went cautiously, hoping he wouldn't bump into Ali. He found himself in an antechamber where several women were twittering away like startled birds. The woman who called him pointed at two heavy bundles and told him to wait with the other boys and carry them when they left. He bowed his head without speaking, too fascinated by what was happening to think of protesting. He realised how bedraggled he must look for the woman to mistake him for a slave. He sensed it would be wisest to keep quiet and do as he was told.

"The Portuguese envoy has given our Sultan an ultimatum," one of the women said loudly as she burst into the chamber.

There was a sudden hush amongst the frightened women. "How do you know?" demanded one.

"I was listening behind the curtain until Queen Aisha called me to help her."

"What is an ultimatum? Is it a rare gem?"

Before Mohamed could hear the answer, a very grand lady of sheer beauty and graceful bearing swept into the room. Two women accompanied her, one holding the hand of a young girl, and the other carrying a baby. It could only be the queen. Mohamed averted his eyes quickly, but no one took any notice of him and the group of boys waiting patiently.

The Queen began to usher the women out of the chamber and through the side door into the lane. "We must hurry," she said. "There's not a moment to lose."

Mohamed picked up the two bundles assigned to him and followed the other boys. The jostled each other to push through the door after the women. They trailed after them into the interior away from the palace, in the opposite direction to the beach. Mohamed felt sorry for the little girl who was being dragged along by the Queen as she kept on looking back at the palace. She caught his eye and he was touched by her bewilderment. He longed to tell her she would be all right, but then he remembered he was supposed to be a slave and must keep quiet.

The Queen, who was leading the group, turned east where the path met a wider avenue lined by coconut palms. The women had stopped chattering and were sweating in the morning's heat, even though the trees provided some shade. The woman who was carrying the baby walked on bravely, setting an example to the others and conscious of her dignity. Mohamed guessed that she must be the second of the Sultan's wives.

The unmistakable shape of Lord Meedhoo loomed ahead of them as he brushed aside the undergrowth with a sword and stepped into the avenue. He seemed to have been expecting them for he took the lead, urging the Queen and the others to make haste. For a fat man he was surprisingly agile and swift, although Mohamed suspected that it was fear that made him move fast. It was lucky that his nervousness prevented him from seeing or recognising Mohamed in his torn loincloth

At Lord Meedhoo's urging, the gaggle of women turned into a fenced compound set in a palm grove. A boy about seventeen years old greeted Queen Aisha with exaggerated respect and stood aside, bowing deeply, to let her enter the house.

"You should be safe here," Lord Meedhoo said. "My son will take care of you. I must return to the palace to hear what Dom Gaspar is saying."

"I'm sure you will find out *everything*." The mocking tone in Queen Aisha's voice was not lost on Mohamed. He sensed immediately that she did not trust Lord Meedhoo but was obliged to seek shelter with him in case the palace was attacked. She was obviously not happy with the arrangement.

"If Captain Andrade, whom we call Andhiri Andhirin, is in that big ship, we have much to fear," she said, reaching for her daughter's hand and drawing her close. "He is a ruthless murderer. Even here he could find us." The fear in her voice communicated itself to the other women. They twittered even more nervously than before, clutching at each other in dismay.

Lord Meedhoo seemed to quake too, his flabby arms shaking like jelly. He hitched at his robe and almost pushed Queen Aisha over the threshold into the house. Whimpering with fear, the other women crowded in after her. Mohamed, acting the role of slave, put the bundles he was carrying onto a pile of belongings by the door. The other boys took advantage of the confusion to scamper off away from the house without waiting to see what else they should do. Mohamed hunkered down in a corner of the compound. He observed Lord Meedhoo, his jowls shiny with perspiration, come out of the house and scuttle off down the road back to the palace.

"Hey, you, what are you doing here?"

Mohamed looked back at the house to see Lord Meedhoo's son was watching him from the doorway. He was about to reply as rudely as he had been addressed, when he remembered he was supposed to be a slave. He quite liked playing the part.

"Oh noble prince, to see if my lady, Queen Aisha, requires my services."

"You dolt! Go to the palace and carry a sword for the Sultan. There is to be a big battle."

"Yes, oh noble prince." Mohamed's curiosity got the better of him. "Oh great prince, who is this Captain, Andhiri Andhirin, of whom my lady, Queen Aisha, speaks?"

The youth looked at him arrogantly, but was clearly impressed at being addressed as a prince. "You ask a question of me?"

"Oh great prince, you are wise and all knowledgeable," said Mohamed, stifling his merriment at the fellow's pomposity. "Andhiri Andhirin is a name this unworthy slave does not know."

"You will," said Lord Meedhoo's son, his face spreading with a smile of menace. "Wrong him and you will rue the day you were born."

"Oh yes, great prince," said Mohamed with a bow. "I am a poor ignorant being—"

The youth laughed. "Tell that to Andhiri Andhirin. He is the one who will be Sultan soon."

◆ ◆ ◆ ◆ ◆

Mohamed felt disconsolate as he wandered away from Lord Meedhoo's house. He was upset by his son's obvious delight at the possible downfall of Sultan Ali, and suspicious by his lack of fear at the arrival of the Portuguese. It was unpatriotic for the son of a noble so close to the Sultan as Lord Meedhoo. He needed to speak to his brother and ask why that was.

Ali was not in the house when he reached where they were lodging. Mohamed used the time while he waited for his brother to bathe at the well and change into his proper garments so he no longer looked like a grubby slave. Then he settled down to recite verses from the Holy Quran. It gave him comfort in the midst of such confusing times. He was so engrossed he did not hear Ali approach.

"I have been searching high and low for you, Mohamed. Where did you go?"

"For a closer look at that big ship," he said, scrambling to his feet. "I met a Portuguese noble called Dom Gaspar."

"Did you indeed?" Ali appeared flustered, perhaps wondering whether he was to be believed. "Well, because you went missing, we are to remain here."

"Did the Sultan decline permission for us to sail?" Mohamed frowned so his brother wouldn't see that he was actually pleased to be staying in Male'.

"He granted it, Mohamed. You weren't here when we should have sailed. Now the Portuguese have forbidden any vessels to leave Male'. They think we might seek reinforcements from the outer islands."

"Then it is surely right for us to stay. There are many cannons on that carrack, and we could have been sunk at sea by their guns."

"You know a lot about this affair?"

"I know nothing." He hung his head, biting his tongue to keep from blurting out about his encounter with Dom Gaspar. Fortunately, Ali was not as taciturn as usual and wanted to talk about the situation. It was clear he was relieved to find Mohamed safe and that perhaps made him talkative.

"The Portuguese noble, that Dom Gaspar of whom you speak, is the Vedor da Fazanda," said Ali, as though reading the question in Mohamed's mind. "He is an important man in the court of the Portuguese Viceroy in India. He advises the government there and supervises trade and the collection of taxes. He has told Sultan Ali that we must accept the Christian Hassan as our ruler and pay taxes to the Portuguese. They are here to collect the taxes on his behalf."

"In a ship with one thousand soldiers? They must expect to carry away a lot of cowries."

"Where did you learn that, Mohamed?"

"I was told." He lowered his eyes. "What will Sultan Ali do?"

"He is discussing strategy with his ministers. He told Dom Gaspar he will give him a reply in three days."

CHAPTER 7

Captain Andre Andrade was thirty-three years old, and it rankled. From the poop deck of the carrack he had watched Dom Gaspar da Fonseca, who was ten years his senior, being rowed to the Male' shore. If he, Andrade, were older, the mission to interview the Sultan would have been his. Andrade spoke Dhivehi fluently and knew the mentality of the islanders. Instead, with dismay and disgust, he had witnessed Dom Gaspar divert his boat and fish a boy out of the water. He would have put his sword through the urchin in case he was a spy and thrown his body back into the sea.

Andrade regarded Dom Gaspar as a pompous bugger

who, because he was older and a senior official of the Viceroy's court, had been able to overrule him. He was an impediment to the glory that should rightly be his at this conquest of the islands. It infuriated Andrade that he was obliged to wait for such a stickler for protocol to have an audience with the Sultan. Action was needed, not negotiation. There was nothing to negotiate, their orders were clear.

He scowled as he saw the two long boats leave the carrack's side and bear the fleet commander, Dom Manoel da Silveira da Arajau, towards the shore. Dom Gaspar wanted to play the diplomat and appraise the Sultan of their presence; Dom Manoel wanted to be cautious and assess the island's defences. As far as he, Andre Andrade, was concerned, both men were wasting their time. They should have taken Male' by surprise and attacked at dawn. Nothing that old goat, Dom Gaspar, could do would convince the Sultan to surrender. And Dom Manoel would soon see there were no defences to consider. Male' was theirs for the taking.

Andre Andrade slammed his clenched fist down on the ship's rail. He had waited a long time for this chance to avenge his father's murder and he was impatient to get on with it. He turned away from gazing at Male', his fury unabated by the tranquillity of the scene around him. The translucence of the lagoons surrounding the ring of small islands, their powder-white beaches glistening under the sun and the refreshing green of umbrageous trees meant nothing to him.

He did not share Dom Gaspar's delight in engaging in intrigue in the Maldives again. He knew the islands too well to be thrilled by such a mission. For him this was invasion, not persuasion and one could only be successful through force. The trouble with Dom Gaspar, he reflected with a bitterness inspired by their former encounters, was that the sanctimonious apology for a man had convinced one Sultan to join the Portuguese, so he thought he could do it again.

Andrade strode the poop deck to contain his fury. He noticed the crew stiffened nervously as he approached them; he was pleased they feared him. They knew what he could do to hapless mariners of no consequence, especially when he was in a rage. It was rage that had driven him this far.

He leaned on the taffrail again and glared at the sea. If only Dom Gaspar and Dom Manoel knew what he had been through, they would have listened to him.

He let his thoughts wander, since there was nothing else to do. The sun didn't trouble him; he had been born at noon when the sun was at its highest. For the first fifteen years of his life, he had lived as a Maldivian on an island in the south, almost on the Equator.

If he closed his eyes, he could hear his mother calling him. "Mohamed, come for your lesson. It's important that you speak Portuguese, my child. It is the language of your father and his father. Some day you will have vengeance, and you will go to Portugal and claim what is yours."

He grunted bitterly. He had never been to Portugal and, if ruling the Maldives was to be his inheritance, his father must be turning in his grave. Vengeance, however, he would have, and he would not be thwarted by Dom Gaspar's pious meddling.

"Mohamed!"

The sound of his mother's sweet voice came to him again across the years. She had been so patient with him when he was a boy. Determined that he would know his birthright, even though he had been born in the Maldives and raised as a Muslim. She called him Mohamed when others could hear, but when they were alone in the house or sitting together on the swing in the shade of the compound, she would whisper "Andre" into his ear and talk softly to him in Portuguese.

He could still see her in his mind, even as he gazed across the lagoon to Male'. She had long black hair that she would brush for hours while he played at her feet. She would wear it hanging loose to her waist. Although she was obliged to dress in the ill-fitting garment of the island women, she always moved with dignity, like a princess. Her eyes were brown, her skin the colour of sunshine, and her smile as radiant as the stars. The island women never smiled at her and they eyed her jealously because she was in the Sultan's circle.

He had been three when the Sultan died. It was that

same Sultan who had caused his own father's death, and the same Sultan's patronage that kept his mother alive. He knew the story from his mother's whispered words but it was only when he escaped from the Maldives and got to Goa that he discovered his father was a greater man than his poor mother ever knew.

Simao Andrade was one of the greatest Portuguese captains who ever lived. He devoted his life to the King of Portugal, sailing with his brother Fernao throughout the Indian Ocean to conquer new lands, subdue recalcitrant natives and establish Portuguese rule. He helped in the capture of Malacca and in the opening up of Canton to trade. He was ruthless: he would string up his own men and hang them from the yardarm if he thought they were contemplating disobedience, and his determination helped the Fathers bring Christianity to the heathens of India.

In 1522 he had been appointed Commander of Chaul, north of Goa, and shortly afterwards captured two Turkish galleys and gained a victory in Dabhol that brought that city under Portuguese influence. He was at Chaul to welcome the legendary Dom Vasco da Gama when he arrived there in September 1524 to be Viceroy for the second time. On Vasco da Gama's death a few months later, he retired with honours. In a ship loaded with treasure, Simao Andrade sailed for Portugal with his new wife, a Christian mestizo woman, the daughter of a Portuguese official and a native woman of India.

Fortune left him as he sailed from the scene of his triumphs. Commander Andrade's vessel was blown by a storm on to a reef at the edge of the treacherous South Equatorial channel. Although the ship remained afloat, he and the crew were forced to abandon it to save themselves. The Sultan at the time was living on an island in the same atoll and as soon as he heard of the wreck, he demanded that all its treasure be salvaged and sent to him, as was the Maldivian tradition. Simao Andrade refused so the Sultan ordered one of his nobles to gather his best warriors and seize it.

The Portuguese were taken by surprise. There was a battle and Simao Andrade and his crew were slaughtered. Only his wife, who was six months pregnant, was spared.

The noble took her as one of his own wives and accepted her son when he was born as his own, as was the way of the Maldivian people. He was named Mohamed and raised as a Muslim although his mother kept the memory of Simao Andrade alive, telling her son the name his father wanted him to have was Andre. In time she gave birth to another son, a boy called Mathukkala, but she never failed to remind Andre that he was her real son, a child of Portugal, and a Christian.

For fifteen years, Andre Andrade lived a lie as a native of the Maldives, although his head was filled with stories about his great father. His mother's whispered tales nurtured hatred in his heart for what the Sultan and his step-father had done to his blood father. She urged him to go to Goa, claim his birthright and return with a fleet to conquer the Maldives, to recover his father's treasure, and to bring Christianity to the islands.

His chance came when a Portuguese vessel, under Captain Gonzales Vaz, raided the Maldives in search of islanders who had robbed and killed the Portuguese he had sent ashore to plunder. Andrade saw the ship's long boat on its way to the shore. He had no time to run and tell his mother of his plan, so he asked his brother – who had been playing with him - to take the message.

Mathukkala refused, clinging to him, pleading with him not to leave and join the Portuguese. Andrade pushed him away in a rage, seized a rock and flung it at his brother's head. So great was the force of the frantic blow, the boy's head burst, his brains fell out and he died on the spot.

Andre Andrade was given a hero's welcome in Goa. He was schooled in Christian precepts, baptised and given military training by the Portuguese. He was soon in command of his own vessel and engaging in private expeditions to raid islands of the Maldives in search of trade goods, and in pursuit of his personal vendetta. He told the islanders his name and then forced them to watch as he chopped off the heads of his hostages. He wanted the Maldive islanders to know that he, Andre Andrade, the son of Simao Andrade, was avenging his father's death.

His exploits filled the islanders with terror. Nothing

could stop this Portuguese pirate who spoke Dhivehi and urged the islanders to become Christian even as he slaughtered their chiefs. As news of what he was doing was passed from island to island, his names became distorted in Dhivehi until the islanders knew him not as Andre Andrade but as Andhiri Andhirin.

◆ ◆ ◆ ◆ ◆

"The Sultan asks for three days." Dom Gaspar was sitting at the head of the table. As the Viceroy's representative he had demanded the chair although that was the right of Dom Manoel da Silveira, the Fleet Commander.

It was another slight to irk Andrade. He thought the commander was weak, he should not let Dom Gaspar, a civilian, chair the meeting so he could dictate strategy. He glared across the table at the ships' captains who had been summoned for the meting, assessing where support lay for his idea of an immediate attack.

"We should not give him three hours, let alone three days!" Andrade's harsh voice cut into the silence as the officers considered Dom Gaspar's proposal. "We know what happened before. Dom Sousa de Ataide, the father of Sultan Hassan's Christian wife, died here four years ago because he gave the islanders time and didn't attack at once." He thumped the table with his fist.

"It is a disgrace for Portugal that on two occasions expeditions have been unable to capture these islands with their weak and very stupid people."

Dom Manoel da Silveira held up his hand, his fierce expression demanding silence. Andrade looked at him scornfully but nevertheless stopped speaking. Until Male' was taken and handed over to him, he was obliged to obey the Fleet Commander.

"I understand your frustration, Captain Andrade," the Commander said softly. "However weak and stupid these Maldivians appear, this is their home territory. If we assume we can occupy these islands without any resistance, we will be making the same mistakes as our predecessors. The Maldivians could be difficult to defeat."

"By the Blessed Virgin Mother! This council does not need such timid talk!" Andrade's oath and his implied insult to the Fleet Commander brought da Silveira to his feet. "Let's hear some productive talk to advance our cause," said Andrade with a sneer, pleased he had managed to rattle the Commander's composure.

"In three days – " began Dom Gaspar.

"In three days they will have had time to prepare for our attack!" Andrade shouted. "I'm surprised at your generosity in giving such a gift."

Dom Gaspar sighed in a way that infuriated Andrade since it implied he was incapable of mature thought. "My dear Captain," he said in a patronising tone that made his remarks rankle even more. "Do not misunderstand me. I am all for striking against the Maldivians if it is necessary. However, it will cost us less in lives and munitions, and be less of a strain on the Viceroy's war chest, if they accept us willingly."

"Trust you to think of the Exchequer!"

Da Silveria resumed his seat and chuckled ironically at Andrade's remark. "That is Dom Gaspar's duty as Vedor, my dear Captain," he said with a wry smile. "Finance propels or defeats us all."

Dom Gaspar acknowledged the compliment with a nod. "We have nothing to lose by giving them a grace period. I am fully aware of their internal situation, perhaps more so than Captain Andrade, since I deal at the diplomatic level and not at the level of ..." He paused, letting discretion govern his words, thereby depriving Andrade of a further challenge.

"Sultan Ali has no more than a dozen supporters in court, the rest in the government are of the house of the former Sultan, our – shall we say – guest. Most of them are concerned only with easy living, with a chance to trade peacefully and to fill their coffers. They are weary of the petty raids by such as you, Captain Andrade. They want peace. They will submit without a fight."

Andrade narrowed his eyes as he glared at Dom Gaspar, unable to work out whether he had been insulted or praised.

"So Captain Andrade's ventures have brought the people to their knees! You are to be thanked, Captain."

Andrade ignored the sarcasm in the Commander's voice, choosing to hear only the praise. It was what he expected. "You have given them three days, Dom Gaspar," he said knowingly. "Even though I am to be in command when Male' is occupied, I am bound by my oath to the Viceroy to heed your advice as though he himself is counselling me. This I will do, but I have my spies close to the Sultan's court too." He tried to make it sound like a threat, as a means to undermine the Commander's confidence in the Vedor.

"Very well." Dom Gaspar beamed. "We shall see. Perhaps we could arrange a picnic, an outing for the soldiers. They could visit the beaches and the uninhabited islands close by. It would do them good to relax and enjoy this place."

Andrade gulped. He could not believe what he was hearing, especially when Dom Gaspar's ridiculous suggestion was accepted by the Commander. "But we are at war!" he shouted, thumping the table.

"Yes, yes!" said Dom Gaspar, rising to his feet to indicate the matter was closed. "We are always at war. Let us have some pleasure too, now we have a chance."

◆ ◆ ◆ ◆ ◆

Andre Andrade slept for barely an hour that night. It was not the noise of his men partying and sending fire rockets into the sky that kept him awake, but the nagging suspicion that something was wrong. He could still think like a Maldivian. He did not know Sultan Ali, except by repute, but he knew him to be courageous. By putting himself in the Sultan's position, he knew that the request for three days to consider the Dom Gaspar's ultimatum was simply a ruse.

The Sultan would be thinking that the battle was already lost. The presence of the carrack with its one thousand men-at-arms was enough to ensure that. He would be planning to do something in those three days, whether it was to escape or to defy them. *Defiance!* The answer came to him as though he could read the Sultan's mind. *The unexpected? Attack! That's what Sultan Ali would do.*

Andrade's hammock was slung on deck. He stumbled as he leapt out of it in haste. He ran to the taffrail and leaned over, listening carefully. Daybreak was still a couple of hours away and he could see only darkness where the ocean and the night were one. There was the sound of waves slapping the boat's stern, and the gentle creak of the rigging as the ship swayed at anchor. He thought carefully, wondering what he would do if he were the Sultan threatened by the presence of Portuguese ships.

He recalled hour by hour all that happened since their arrival. He gasped aloud as he remembered the sight of the boy being fished out of the water by Dom Gaspar the previous morning. *Of course! He was a spy!* He gave a grunt of satisfaction now he knew what he would do if he were Sultan. Maldivians were good swimmers. A team of them could swim out to the ships under the cover of darkness and sever their anchor lines. The tide would wash the vessels onto the reef, even beach them on the shores of Male' itself.

Hastily he roused some of the crew and had them post extra lanterns in the bow. He woke Commander da Silveira and told him what he thought could happen. He asked permission to launch a boat to patrol around the carrack until dawn's early light ensured they were safe from the possibility of a night attack.

When it was done, he stationed himself at the ship's rail, watching for any movement of swimmers in the dark. By daybreak none had come and the rowers on guard duty were weary. He waved them away and watched them row for the nearest stretch of beach. The sailors were clearly delighted at this chance to have time off and splashed happily into the surf as the boat reached the shore.

With the sun rising, the sailors settled themselves on the sand to dry in its early morning warmth. The Commander joined Andrade on deck and raised his telescope to scan the beach. It seemed so peaceful.

"I can understand why you like the Maldives, Captain Andrade. You are fortunate in being promoted to govern these islands."

Hearing those mollifying words, Andrade was touched by pride at his success. The Commander was right. He liked the whores and the wines of Goa but the sight of the islands where he was born and raised did have a strange effect on him. He nodded at the Commander as a noise like a fire-cracker rebounded across the lagoon. He and the Commander gazed in disbelief at the shore.

Two fishermen, wearing only their waistcloths and carrying cane fishing rods, had been walking along the beach, past the sailors. By their gestures, they were waving and laughing happily at them. One of the sailors had a musket in his hand and it must have discharged, causing the sound of a shot. There was another shot, and one of the fishermen fell to the beach, writhing in agony. The other stood still, frozen in shock. Swiftly, a second soldier raised his firearm and smote the fisherman on the head with it.

The rest of the sailors jumped up from the sand where they had been resting. They surrounded the two fallen fishermen and danced around them, shouting with delight. As Andrade watched, powerless to do anything, he saw the bushes around the beach spring apart and a group of angry men rushed out, brandishing swords. They charged at the sailors, cutting them down before they could reach for their weapons. It was over in seconds and all the Fleet Commander and Andrade could do was watch in horror as the Maldivians took their revenge.

"You see what your weak and stupid Maldivians have done, Captain!" said da Silveria angrily. "We cannot wait for the Sultan's answer now. We must attack at once."

CHAPTER 8

Mohamed helped his brother wash the cut on his arm. It was a deep wound, but clean, as though a sharp knife had tried to carve a slice of flesh from his upper forearm. He tore up a cloth and bound it tightly. This time he asked no questions, tending to Ali quickly from the moment he had burst into the house, hot and sweating from running. Ali was too restless to sit quietly, but he was exhausted. He had been out all night and Mohamed had been awake waiting for him since dawn prayers.

"There were ten of them," Ali said, his eyes still ablaze with the fire of the fight. "We were hiding in the woods by the beach in case the Portuguese launched an attack in the night. They were in one boat." He shook his head, the horror of what he had done overwhelming him.

Mohamed sat at his feet. "You want to rest? I will stay here and watch over you." Outside the sun was climbing, beating down on the coconut groves, on the sandy trails, and on the thatched houses of the capital. The steady throb of drums being beaten to summon the people reverberated over the island.

"I can't rest when there is a battle to fight."

"You should rest so you can fight."

Ali nodded as fatigue and pain seized him. He swung around and let Mohamed raise his legs onto the dais as he lay back, his head on the cushion Mohamed placed there for him. "It was all so quick," he said, his voice losing its energy. "They came ashore...some were in the water, swimming, and others lying in the sun on the beach. Then two fishermen walked along the shore to greet them ... a gun was fired...the man fell..."

"Did the fishermen do anything to provoke them?"

"No." Ali's long wail showed his anger at what he had witnessed. "We couldn't let the Portuguese kill innocents. I chased after one of them but he turned and cut me."

"Did you kill him?" Mohamed held his breath in shock.

"It was the will of Allah," whispered Ali, as he closed his eyes and succumbed to exhaustion.

Mohamed took a fan made from the plaited leaves of a screwpine plant and gently fanned his brother, watching his gaunt, troubled face give way to the bliss of sleep. He stayed by him for the whole morning, listening to the sound of drums, and then cannon fire as the palace guns boomed. He went to the entrance of the hut and looked along the trail to the sea. The cannon balls fell short of the carrack, the only ship remaining. Its gun ports were open as though ready to fire on the town as soon as the cannons fell silent and the ship could manoeuvre within range.

Mohamed looked at Ali on the dais. His wound and the

loss of blood had weakened him. Sleep was the best medi-
cine. Even though the noise of fighting at the palace reached
Mohamed's ears, he doubted that it would disturb Ali. The
Portuguese obviously had invaded, just as the Sultan said
they would.

For an hour, Mohamed listened to the shouts of men
drifting over to him from the west of the island. Gradually
the noise lessened. He longed to see what was happening.
It would be too dangerous to go to the palace but wouldn't
Ali want to know about the battle on the shore? He was
still asleep, and surely wouldn't miss him if he went away
for a few minutes. He could run to the beach near the Eid
Mosque, stay a few minutes to watch, and then run quickly
back.

Even as he slipped into the undergrowth to work his way
through to the trail heading westwards, he knew he was
taking a risk. There was no one on the trail when he gained
it, and all the huts along it were shuttered. He ran as fast as
he could until he reached the mosque. Hiding behind it he
peeped around the shelter of its wall to look along the lane
to the shore.

To his dismay all he saw at first were bodies of islanders
strewn across the path. At the end, where the trail touched
the beach, he saw three men standing alone, their swords
raised. He recognised the man in the centre as Sultan Ali.
A group of Portuguese soldiers in breastplate armour were
walking in close formation up to the beach towards him.
The Sultan turned and gazed down at the bodies of his
guards strewn along the lane back to the palace.

He must have realised then that his choice had been made.
Mohamed willed him to lay down his sword and surrender.
Instead, Sultan Ali raised his sword in the air, shouted Allah's name, and charged down the beach into the approaching wall of Portuguese soldiers. He flayed at them with his
sword until a soldier's spear brought him down. Even on
the ground, he sliced at the legs of the invaders crowding
around him. Then a man pushed his way through the soldiers and stood over him. He spat upon the Sultan, drew his
sword and brought it down, cleaving his head in two.

Mohamed felt his legs buckle and he fell to the ground,

faint with terror and shock. The Portuguese were braying with triumph and their shouts brought him back to reality as they rampaged along the lane, hacking at the corpses in their way. He knew he had to flee before they found him. He dragged himself to his feet and dived into the jungle at the back of the mosque. He felt he would be safe if he kept to the trees since the Portuguese seemed more interested in carnage and plundering the shuttered huts than searching the jungle for fleeing islanders.

He came to a trail and cautiously peeped up and down it. There was a gang of soldiers heading to the eastern side of the island, so he couldn't go that way. The palace seemed to be surrounded by them. He saw a few yards up the trail a compound he knew. He darted across to it and shook the wooden gate. It was secured with a heavy wooden bar.

"Let me in! Let me in!"

No one responded to his desperate cry so he placed his hands on the cross post and vaulted up to grab the top of the gate. He hauled himself up and somersaulted over the top, landing on his feet in the compound. He caught his breath and glanced around anxiously.

Some of Queen Aisha's servants and Lord Meedhoo's slaves were crouching in an open-sided hut, paralysed with fear. He brushed himself down and walked over to them. He recognised one of them from the day before when they had carried bundles from the palace. He greeted him gravely.

"What is happening?" the boy asked, making a space for him in the hut. "We hear only cannon fire and screams. Are the devils coming?"

Mohamed quickly told them what he had seen. The servants began to moan in despair at the news of the Sultan's death.

"Why are you crying? Is the battle lost?"

Mohamed stopped his tale and looked up to see Lord Meedhoo's arrogant son had come out of the house. He remembered in time that the youth thought he was slave and, since he was bedraggled through having run through the jungle, he could keep up the pretence.

"Yes, my lord, the Sultan is dead."

The youth grabbed him by the shoulders and pulled him

to his feet. "How do you know this?" His eyes were bright with excitement.

Mohamed repeated the story of Sultan Ali's brave death, fighting to the end when he was alone, even when he could have surrendered.

"The man with the sword. Describe him to me."

Mohamed thought for a moment. "It was so quick, my lord. He was cross-eyed...and left-handed."

"No, not him. Was there a tall man there, his hair shaved short?"

"Yes, my lord. One like that came and inspected the Sultan's body."

"Ah!" he gasped. A cruel, satisfied smile spread across the youth's face. "Andhiri Andhirin is here."

"Is that true, my lord?" Mohamed knew he must be careful what he said, but he wanted to know more. "I am a lowly slave. I am unsure."

"I know Andhiri Andhirin, boy. He is as you describe."

"Oh, great lord! You know him?"

"I have met him once, when he spoke with my father." The stupid youth was too thrilled with the news, and his own self-importance, to keep his treachery secret. "Come, boy. You shall have the honour of telling Queen Aisha and my father your great news."

"Please, oh lord, I am a poor ignorant being –" Mohamed was worried that Lord Meedhoo might recognise him. He sensed it would be prudent to remain an anonymous slave for the time being. And he was anxious to return to Ali and tell him what had happened, and ask him what they must do.

The youth was regarding him with disgust. "Yes, you are right. You have no cause to address your elders and betters. Stay here in case you are wanted. I shall bear the glad tidings." He strode away without a further glance at Mohamed.

Mohamed waited a minute then crept up to the door of the main house, which was ajar, and slipped inside, crouching down on the floor out of sight. The room was dark as all the shutters were closed so he knew no one would notice him in the confusion. Lord Meedhoo was seated in a corner, clutching his arms around his body, his heavy jowls twitching nervously.

"Father," said the youth excitedly with an air of triumph. "Sultan Ali is dead!"

Lord Meedhoo groaned.

"Why should you be unhappy?" His son laughed, mocking his father's fear. "It was you who told Andhiri Andhirin that Male' could be his. Now you must go to him so he can make you the Sultan, and I shall be next in line to the throne."

Lord Meedhoo continued to hold himself firmly, as though frightened by the news. He shook his head. "If I go now, the Portuguese soldiers will cut me down and kill me. I must wait until Andhiri Andhirin himself sends an escort for me."

"I am disgusted!" A woman's voice rang out over the keening of the servants, surprising them all into silence. Queen Aisha had been sitting in the darkness, listening to what was being said. She rose grandly to her feet and stalked over to Lord Meedhoo, towering above him as he cowered on the ground. Her face showed no trace of the sadness that must have been in her heart. She spoke with a voice that was strong and steady.

"Lord Meedhoo, have you given me and my daughter, Princess Sitti, shelter just to betray us? During the reign of the last two Sultans, you skulked at the palace, eagerly grasping every favour that came your way. I know you have no courage of your own, for you can walk only in the shadow of the Sultan's parasol. Now, as there is no royal parasol to protect you from the burning rage of the sun of Portugal, you must stand alone." She paused, letting her words sink into Meedhoo's befuddled brain.

"Save Princess Sitti and myself and you could save yourself, for she is the daughter of a great Sultan and could become the next Sultana." She looked at Meedhoo's son who was listening intently, his eyes shrewd and calculating.

Lord Meedhoo's expression of abject terror softened slightly. His eyes, which had been wide with fear, narrowed as he sensed a solution in Aisha's words. He relaxed his grip on himself, but kept his arms folded across his vast chest. "I must wait," he said. "What else is there to do?"

"Go, go!" said Queen Aisha with the strength of authority in her voice. "Meet the Portuguese. Negotiate!" She turned her back on him, reflecting her exasperation at his weakness.

Lord Meedhoo frowned and glanced in despair at his son. The youth turned away, shrugging his shoulders, showing the contempt he felt for his father.

From his hiding place, Mohamed sensed the fat man's indecision. He watched him half rise, sit back, then wipe his face with the palm of his right hand, as though hoping to mop away his fear. Then he sighed and hauled himself to his feet.

"Where are you going?" his son demanded.

"I shall seek an audience with Andhiri Andhirin," said Lord Meedhoo nervously. "I have, I have...a plan!" He did not look very confident as he waddled slowly towards the door.

"What, boy! You are here in our house?"

Mohamed had been so engrossed in studying Lord Meedhoo's face, trying to guess what he was thinking, he had not realised that his son had caught sight of him in the shaft of sunlight as he pushed the door open for his father.

"Oh yes, in case you need me, my lord," he said, rising to his feet but keeping his face in the shadow so Lord Meedhoo would not recognise him. Lord Meedhoo, however, was too full of his own uncertainties to take notice of anyone else.

"Then stay here and be of assistance to Queen Aisha," he said, adding pompously, "We go on state business."

◆ ◆ ◆ ◆ ◆

As soon as he was outside the compound, Lord Meedhoo turned in the direction that would take him away from the Sultan's palace. With an irritable wave of his hand, he tried to send his son away.

"Where are you going?" He grabbed his father's arm.

"To hide from the Portuguese, you fool." Lord Meedhoo jerked his arm free and began to waddle down the trail. "Got to hide...The Portuguese will seize us for helping the

Queen to escape." He turned onto the track that would take him to the wooded interior of the island, his short, fat legs churning desperately as he hurried along it. He intended to find somewhere to conceal himself until the crisis was resolved, then he would decide whose side to take. He ignored his son striding at his side.

As he reached the last hut beside the track before the welcome cover of the lush undergrowth and trees, he was dismayed to find his way barred by a woman standing with her arms akimbo, a stern expression on her face.

"My lady," he said with a whimper. "I am in a hurry, let me pass."

"Why!" she exclaimed. "Are you really Lord Meedhoo? I have never known you to be in a hurry."

"I am now. Let me pass, this instant." He tried to dodge around her but the trail was too narrow and he shrank from stepping into the high grass at its side.

"Now? At this moment? Why, when you can save us all?"

Lord Meedhoo wheezed to a halt, realising he could not pass this formidable woman, renowned for her stinging tongue. One shout from her could bring the Portuguese to arrest him. He caught his breath and stared at her. "I can save us all?"

"If you do as I suggest," said the woman with the wink of a sorcerer, "you could become all powerful."

His chest heaved as he stared at her in surprise.

"Rally the people! You must move around the island as swiftly as your fat carcass will carry you. Your son can go with you and rally the youth. Tell the people to stop all resistance to the Portuguese. Tell them to go fishing, gathering wood and coconuts, and to behave normally." She paused to see if he had understood.

"Then you must go to the Portuguese. Stand before them and declare that the people welcome them. Tell the soldiers they must stop the killing and looting and let the people work and bring wealth and profit to our new rulers. Emphasise the riches to be gained here through peace, for that is what we – and they - want."

"I cannot...do that." His voice was like a whimper. He looked longingly at the cover of the woods. He felt drained of energy and hope.

"You must, if you are to become Sultan! Demand to see the leaders of the invaders. Go to the square in front of the palace. Shout to our people to stop fighting. It doesn't matter, they are too scared to fight anyway. Let the Portuguese hear you welcome them to our shores...in the name of Allah."

To Lord Meedhoo it was a scheme fraught with danger. What if the Portuguese fired on him before he could speak? He glanced at his son and saw a look of contempt on his face. Then he remembered Aisha had said something similar. "Sultan?" he whispered. "I can become Sultan?"

"If you act now." The woman stared at him almost hypnotically.

His spirit soared suddenly. He nodded, turning to son. "And you shall be Crown Prince. Very well, we shall do as you say."

◆ ◆ ◆ ◆ ◆

It was uppermost in Mohamed's mind to flee from the house as soon as possible. He had no wish to remain in the potentially dangerous company of the Sultan's widow. However, when he saw Queen Aisha call her daughter, Sitti, to come to her from where she was waiting with her handmaiden, he was touched by the young girl's bravery and soulful beauty and decided to remain.

Her eyes were red from crying and she ran quickly to her mother's side, grasping her around the legs. Queen Aisha, however, held herself aloof, waiting for the child to behave appropriately and not show fear. Little Sitti must have felt her mother's wish, for she drew herself away and looked wide eyed around the room. She frowned with surprise when she saw Mohamed and then looked at him curiously, apparently wondering who he was. He smiled to encourage her.

"Little Sitti," said Queen Aisha, ignoring Mohamed's presence since she thought him a slave of no consequence. "Our Sultan, your father, has gone. You will be brave, won't you?"

Sitti nodded doubtfully.

"You must never let anyone see fear or doubt in your eyes since that conveys your inner feelings. Those feelings are for you alone, not to communicate even with a gesture to others." She put her hand on the Sitti's shoulder and squeezed it.

"You are a special child, destined for greatness as the daughter of a brave Sultan. You will have enemies, but never let them see your eyes are red from weeping. They will think you weak."

Sitti's hands flew to her eyes as though she wanted to rub away the evidence of her tears. Her face, though, was tense and her childlike features shadowed by uncertainty. Mohamed wanted to reach out and hug her to him so she would feel strong. His heart flowed with pity for her.

There was a shout at the gate. A heavy hand rattled it, and a bellowing in Portuguese resounded through the compound.

"Boy!" Queen Aisha addressed Mohamed calmly. "Please open the gate."

"It's the Portuguese soldiers, my lady."

"I know." A vague smile of satisfaction played over her lips. She turned to her daughter. "Lord Meedhoo has not let me down. He has betrayed us to the Portuguese, Sitti, in return for his own life. I knew he would." This time she let her daughter cling to her legs without brushing her away. "Open the gate."

As Mohamed left the hut he heard the queen consoling her daughter with words that puzzled him. "Do not worry, Sitti. The Vedor will take care of us. I have made sure of that. We are too precious to the Viceroy for the Portuguese to let us follow your father to death."

Mohamed raised the wooden shaft that secured the gate, and stepped back. He was not quick enough. A detail of soldiers pushed through, banging the gate in his face and knocking him to the ground. As he struggled to get up, a soldier grabbed him, twisting him around and pinioning his arms behind his back.

"Aha!" he exclaimed to his comrades. "Here's a pretty one."

CHAPTER 9

Even Captain Andrade was surprised at the ease with which his men took Male'. In that, at least, the Vedor was right. The will to fight had long left most Maldivians. Few had supported their Sultan in his last stand.

"I told you they are feeble!" Andrade glared at his two colleagues, challenging them to dispute his word. He was seated at a table in the tent the soldiers had erected for him in front of the palace compound.

The Vedor was sitting in a chair at the other side of the table. "We must be grateful to our Commander, Dom Manoel, for prompt implementation of the invasion plan."

"Oh yes, of course!" Andrade did not bother to conceal his sarcasm. "Attack on two fronts to weaken the enemy? A fine strategy! What resistance did you meet coming from the south to attack the palace? None at all! There was only the Sultan on the western shore and my men despatched him."

The Vedor's long nosed twitched. "Our moment of glorious victory for Portugal need not be one of recrimination."

Andrade's face remained fierce but he was pleased the old bugger accepted that he was right. He could tell by the way Dom Gaspar tugged at his beard that he was upset. *Good! He was in charge now.*

"Captain Andrade!" Dom Manoel, the Fleet Commander, standing at the side of the table, also seemed unsettled by the situation. "My mission was to install you in Male' so you and the Vedor, Dom Gaspar here, can govern the Maldives on behalf of the Viceroy. That is accomplished. I would like to withdraw the carrack and my men as soon as possible. We need only to provision."

"You are so anxious to leave?" Andrade wondered what Dom Manoel had in mind. "Do you intend to seize some merchantmen on your way back to Goa and say they are the spoils of our invasion?"

Dom Manoel swallowed but did not respond to the jibe. "We cannot let a thousand men loose on this island. Already some of your own soldiers who are to be garrisoned here have started pillaging property. That will add to your problems of governance. I intend to sail tomorrow, to lessen the burden put upon you."

"You will await my orders!"

"With respect, Captain, your authority does not extend to me and my fleet. The Viceroy's instructions are clear that you are to govern the Maldives, once delivered to you, and to be counselled and audited by the Vedor da Fazenda." He nodded at Dom Gaspar.

Andrade sighed, his anger etched on his face. It was so. Even at his moment of triumph, he was stuck with the Viceroy's orders, and the Vedor's presence to see he obeyed them. He was aware of the emphasis the Commander had placed on the word *audited*. It was a rebuke all right. The only merit he could see in the arrangement was that if there were any shortcomings in the administration, he could blame Dom Gaspar.

"Of course, of course!" he said impatiently. He stared blankly at the chart of the atolls on the table in front of him, wondering what should be his next move.

"May I suggest," said Dom Gaspar slowly in that patronising manner Andrade hated, "that the Fleet Commander makes a patrol to the south? Let him show the Portuguese flag there. He could carry some important Male' personages with him to convince the islanders that the Maldives is firmly under Portuguese rule." He paused. "And that all trading must be routed through Male'."

"Aha! Your eye is on tax opportunities to help the exchequer." Andrade tried to sound scornful but the old goat's plan made sense.

"You must stay here, of course," Dom Gaspar continued. "I propose going to the north to impose our rule there."

Andrade gaped with disbelief. Was he going to get rid of the Vedor so easily? "Why would you do that?" he demanded, his voice edged with suspicion, his eyes hard as he tried to gaze into Dom Gaspar's mind.

"It is the most practical proposition. See from the chart." He pointed with his finger and Andrade was obliged to look down where he indicated.

"The islands to the north are the most prosperous, and

the closest to India. I need to monitor the trading from there as well as to win over the islanders to the Portuguese way. By staying here you, Captain Andrade, can counter any lingering ambitions of the Sultan's house. By staying there, I can counter the influence of any who may plot to usurp you."

Andrade was worried, but he was careful not to show it. The Vedor's plan sounded so plausible, he could not fathom what was the real reason for Dom Gaspar wanting to be based in the northern islands. There had to be an ulterior motive; he trusted no one or anything on its face value. Yet it was to his advantage to have Dom Gaspar out of the way so he could rifle the Sultan's treasury and garner what was due to him from his lost inheritance. It was time to suggest his own plan.

"I must have some native minister to assist me while you are auditing the resources of the northern islands, and converting the populace." He smirked.

"I agree." Dom Gapsar smiled with such smooth understanding it raised further suspicions in Andrade's mind.

"Your fluency with the language and culture, such as it is, makes such an idea most propitious. It is always politic to involve the conquered in the beneficial governance of the conquered."

The feeling of being out of his depth returned to Andrade. Why did the bugger always make him feel inferior even when he appeared to be agreeing with him? "Very well," he said, seeing no alternative but to stick to his original plan. "I shall take that noble we have detained who was shouting slogans, telling the people to accept us and return to their homes in peace."

"Ah, yes...Lord Meedhoo." Dom Gaspar nodded knowingly.

"You know him?" Andrade stared uncomfortably, and then smiled, remembering his own alliance. Dom Gaspar would not be so smug if he knew that Meedhoo was his informant about conditions in Male'. They had been in constant touch since he had spared Meedhoo's life when he captured him and his son on an outer island that he had raided months before.

"He has always been close to the Sultans. He is a good

choice." Dom Gaspar stroked his beard and sat back in his seat, evidently satisfied. "Having him at your right hand will bond the Sultan's house to you."

"I shall make him my Finance Officer!" Andrade spoke before Dom Gaspar could change his mind. "His son can be his deputy."

"Excellent."

"You agree?" Andrade scratched his head, wondering what the old goat was planning by this unexpected show of support.

"Why not? You must involve the island hierarchy in all your decisions. The only way we can obtain the cooperation of the islanders is to treat their nobles with respect. It is the culture, is it not? We come as conquerors but if we want to govern effectively, we should do so in partnership with the people. And their nobles."

Andrade scowled. He had never heard such drivel.

"That is surely why the Viceroy himself entrusted you with this onerous task, Captain Andrade." Dom Gaspar was making a speech, sounding like a Father. "It's because of your unique knowledge of the Maldives and of the mind and the culture of the people. And, of course, your prowess in battle."

Andrade relaxed, deciding Dom Gaspar was right. "I have done rather well, haven't I?" He nodded, pleased with himself. "You said my little expeditions in search of profit had made the people weary of resistance."

"By your good governance and example, Captain Andrade, you will convince the islanders of the virtues of accepting Portuguese authority and religion. And taxes." He smiled broadly.

"If they don't, I'll hang them, by God!"

"I hope that won't be necessary." Dom Gaspar leaned forward and tapped the chart. "I shall base myself at Baarah, from there I can control the whole of the north. If you have no use for her here, since you will have Lord Meedhoo and his son to advise you, I will take Queen Aisha with me. If the Queen is with me, the people will be ours too."

He was an old goat, this bugger! Andrade knew he had been tricked - but what an unexpected development. He had not thought Dom Gaspar's penchant was for island women. He was lustful for the queen! "Well, well..." he muttered, for a moment bereft of an appropriate comment.

"I beg your pardon?" Dom Gaspar looked puzzled.

"Well...it is an idea." Andrade tried to recover from his surprise by turning to the Fleet Commander. "Has the Sultan's wife, Aisha, been found?"

"She has been escorted to her chambers in the palace. She is under guard. She has her young daughter, Sitti is her name, with her."

"I will take the daughter too," said Dom Gaspar, a little too quickly for Andrade's acute sense of suspicion. "She must be removed from Male'."

"And why is that?" Andrade had really lost the thread of what was happening. He never cared for and deeply suspected the intrigues of court life and politics.

"Because, Captain, marriage to Sitti, the Sultan's daughter, would be a judicious ploy for any noble who harbours an ambition to be the new Sultan."

"Really? Perhaps I should marry her myself. Is she pretty?"

"Indutibly so."

"Hmm! The ploy sounds interesting."

"However, Captain, she is not yet ten years old."

"Take her!" Andrade realised he had been made to look foolish.

"I propose making an inventory of everything in the palace so that it constitutes a record of what we find and thus own here. The Commander can deliver the inventory when he returns to Goa. The property of the Sultan, of course, becomes the property of Portugal."

"It does?" Andrade scratched his head again, this time in frustration. Then he saw a way to rile the Vedor. "Does that include the Sultan's wife, Dom Gaspar?" He charged his voice with as much insolence as he dared.

"Of course!" The Vedor's smile was annoyingly condescending. "I shall merely be her custodian. She, as part of the Sultan's treasure, will remain intact with me as, I trust, the rest of the treasure will remain safe with you."

Mohamed squatted on the ground with a group of other prisoners outside the tent. He had been brought there together with Queen Aisha, her daughter and the womenfolk. When the queen and Sitti were directed to go inside the palace, he struggled to follow them, but a soldier had knocked him to the ground with an oath and a decidedly unpleasant leer. He had waved to Sitti as she followed her mother, but she seemed too frightened to notice.

He felt sorry for her, not for himself. Sitti was old enough to understand this great tragedy and must be feeling very alone. He was also worried about his brother and the pain he would be in because of his injury, and the concern he was causing him by not being at his side. It didn't occur to Mohamed to worry about his own fate. The men and boys he had been forced to sit with were slaves. They were keeping quiet, afraid to raise their eyes or look around in case they were bludgeoned by the soldiers.

Mohamed decided to wait quietly. It would be foolish to try to escape at that moment with that foul-smelling soldier continually eyeing him. The soldiers seemed alert for trouble, as though they would welcome the chance to smash someone's head. He reasoned they were acting like bullies because they wanted to make an impression. If he was quiet and slipped into the background, he hoped they would forget about him and he could steal back to the hut to find Ali as soon as night fell.

There was a rustle of activity at the entrance to the tent, a jangle of arms being presented, and men saluting. He peeped up and saw two white men standing in conversation. Both wore bonnets and although the sun was going down, patches of sweat under their arms stained their uniforms. The men shook hands and one strode off, followed by a troop of soldiers. The other man looked around him keenly, taking in the scene before him.

He seemed relaxed, talking with the soldiers in an easy manner. Mohamed sensed that they liked him. Since the soldier who had captured him was distracted, he took a longer look, wondering if the man was the feared Andhiri

Andhirin. Then the man turned and Mohamed saw he had a grey beard and a long nose. It was the one who had fished him out from the sea. He lowered his eyes to the ground hastily and hoped he hadn't been noticed.

The man finished inspecting the soldiers and began to walk over to the palace compound. Mohamed sighed with relief. Then the man paused in his stride, asking a question of the officer accompanying him. He was pointing towards the group of slaves. Mohamed wished the sand would open up and swallow him. He edged behind the back of a broad Negro and bent his head down almost to his crossed ankles. He was worried that the man intended to select slaves and might choose him. Oh, how he longed to run back to Ali and return home to Utheem, away from this predicament.

His assumption was right. The man was looking over the group with interest. He said something in Portuguese to the officer and then, in Dhivehi, addressed one of the slaves. "Up you stand!"

The young slave didn't move. The officer shouted at him in the strange tongue that was Portuguese and prodded him with his sword. It was obvious what he was expected to do and the boy scrambled quickly to his feet. The man's eyes surveyed the boy's near naked body and he nodded with satisfaction. The officer waved the slave out of the group. Mohamed tried to be as small and as unnoticeable as a sand fly.

"It you is?"

The oddly asked question, in Dhivehi, could only be directed at him. Mohamed raised his eyes slowly. He found himself looking into the piercing eyes of the Portuguese nobleman. He was frowning.

"What you are here doing? Slave you are?"

"No, oh great and noble magnificence." Mohamed scrambled to his feet and quickly bowed low, ignoring the soldier raising his sword to strike him. He spoke rapidly, hoping the stranger understood. "I am the son of the most honourable Katheeb of Utheem..."

The man held up his hand and Mohamed lapsed into silence. But the gesture was meant for the soldier who lowered his sword with a scowl at Mohamed. The man nodded to him to continue.

"I was in the company of our gracious Queen Aisha when a soldier kidnapped me and brought me here...to lie with this trash." Mohamed hoped he had not misjudged the situation or misread the noble's need to show his power.

"Indeed?" The man pulled at his nose, saying nothing, but his eyes appraised him keenly.

His silent inspection alarmed Mohamed. He sensed, rather than heard, the disapproval of the slaves squatting beside him. He looked like a slave so why should he pretend otherwise. If the Portuguese were angry with him then they would all be punished.

"Who I am, you know?"

"Oh most merciful, wise and just, noble lord, I do not," His extravagant reply brought a smile to the man's lips and caused his eyes to twinkle with an unexpected intimacy.

"Dom Gaspar, the Vedor da Fazenda, I am. Mohamed your name is?"

Mohamed nodded, surprised that this heron-like foreigner should remember that.

"Utheem? In the north, is it not?"

Again, Mohamed nodded agreement, thinking that this time silence was preferable to effusive flattery. Since the foreigner seemed to be well disposed towards him, he decided to risk a request.

"With your permission, my lord Dom Gaspar, noble Vedor, may I return to my island? I do not belong here."

"And how to your island of Utheem do you go, my fair stripling?"

"Elder brother Ali is here with my father's *odi*."

"Indeed?" Again a trace of amusement filled the man's eyes. Mohamed was relieved he had earned the man's favour. Because they spoke in Dhivehi none of the white men understood. The soldier who had captured him swiped his hand across his own throat as though that was what he was going to do to him as soon as the Vedor left.

"Too valuable you are here to stay." Dom Gaspar turned and spoke firmly to the officer beside him who gestured to Mohamed to step out of the group. He stroked his beard slowly as he considered something, his eyes raking over

Mohamed's limbs and face again. He opened his mouth to speak then, becoming aware of the Maldivians around him who would understand, closed it.

Then he said hastily, "Release you are. Again we will meet." He gave a slow wink and turned back to speak to the soldiers.

Mohamed waited no longer. With a bow to Dom Gaspar and to the officer, and an impudent grin at the soldier who had held him, he took to his heels, running down the trail in search of Ali as dusk closed in.

♦ ♦ ♦ ♦

Since he expected Ali to be angry with him for disappearing so long when he was wounded and needed care, Mohamed kept his peace. He said nothing while his brother berated him for his absence. He would probably have been beaten too, if Ali's arm didn't hurt. Instead, he had to put up with a sustained tongue lashing about his lack of responsibility. He bore it patiently, knowing Ali was right.

He was relieved when Ali's anger died down and he ordered him to go to bed. He did as he was told, dwelling on the strange incidents of the day as he lay on his mat on the *ashi*. He pretended to be asleep so he could see what Ali's was going to do. He was not surprised when, at the call to evening prayers, Ali slipped out of the hut.

When he awoke at dawn the next morning, he saw that Ali was already up, preparing to go to the mosque. Mohamed wondered if he had been out all night.

"How is you arm, elder brother?" he asked, hoping to find Ali in a better mood. He grunted in reply. Mohamed tried again. "Will we sail home today?"

Ali paused in his preparations and looked at him crossly. "The Portuguese will not let us go."

"Why not? The Vedor has given his consent for us to sail to Utheem. He told me so himself. In front of his officers." Mohamed bit his lip after the words spilled out. He had not intended to say anything about his encounter with Dom Gaspar.

Ali shook his head in despair. "You are living in a fantasy

world, Mohamed."

"What I say is true!" He got up from the *ashi* and went to Ali's side. "I must tell you what befell me yesterday." He prayed that Ali would be patient and hear him out. He spoke about being taken to the palace and held with the slaves and how Dom Gaspar had released him so he could return home to Utheem.

"You believe me, don't you?" He looked up at Ali, pleading silently with his eyes for his brother to accept what he said.

Ali's face was expressionless. "There was talk in the town last night that the Vedor is going north to govern. He is to leave that devil Andhirin in command here."

"If that is so," said Mohamed as an idea came to him, "let us offer our services as pilot. Let us cooperate with him. We will be protecting our own interests and our father will be pleased if we build up a relationship with the new commander of the north. It could be of help to us."

Ali sighed, patting Mohamed on his shoulder. "You are too young to understand, brother. Why should we offer help to the Portuguese? We don't need anything from them."

"In time, we might want our freedom."

Mohamed spun away from his brother, seized with a sudden excitement. Outside it was still dark but what had to be done was as clear as daylight to him. "If we offer our friendship and the Vedor accepts, we will be able to influence him. He is unfamiliar with our atoll. He is well disposed towards me though. Through this contact we will govern, not he."

CHAPTER 10

Mohamed lay the bolt of bright blue silk on the mat at Katheeb Hussain's feet. He bowed his head in respect. After a few seconds, he raised his eyes, expecting to see some sign of delight on his father's face. The frown of displeasure that met his eyes caused his spirits to sink.

"What is this?" The Katheeb ignored Mohamed and looked

at Ali, his grim expression demanding an explanation.

"It's a gift from –" Mohamed stopped the instant he saw his father's hand raised in protest. He knew he should not have spoken anyway but so much had happened in Male'. He couldn't contain himself. He had wanted to run home and tell his father all about it the moment their *odi* had reached Utheem. Ali had restrained him.

He lowered his head again and took some steps backwards, wishing he could blend into the gloom of the house and remain unnoticed by his father. The great excitement at being home and at all that he had witnessed in Male' became unimportant without his father's approval. He understood then why Ali had been so reluctant to agree to any plan to assist the Portuguese however advantageous it seemed. He had been aware of how their father would react.

Ali's strength and self-assurance appeared to diminish in their father's presence. Ali was brushing back his long hair nervously and looking at the bolt of silk as though he were seeing it for the first time. Katheeb Hussain coughed impatiently.

"The Portuguese – " Ali began an explanation but his father raised his hand a second time and stopped him.

"Is that object something that should be in my house?" His voice was calm but carried the threat of anger about to erupt.

It was the first time Mohamed had seen his father so upset. He was appalled at having committed some terrible breach of etiquette, even though he did not know what it was. He darted forward, picked up the bolt of cloth, and hastily carried it out of the house. He looked around for a place to hide it.

"Here." Fathimafaan beckoned him from the swing, indicating the space beside her. His brother Hassan was playing with a ball of coir at her feet.

"He won't even listen to us that it is a gift from the Vedor, the new atoll chief." Mohamed laid the cloth on the swing, disappointment shining moistly in his eyes.

Fathimafaan patted his shoulder, her expression full of affection and concern. "Our father is a man of conventions, Mohamed. He does not care for routine to be disturbed. He was anxious that you and Ali would return before Ramazan so you and Ali can properly observe the fast. We must look for the new moon tonight.

"Is that why he won't hear of our adventures, of the great Dom Gaspar, the Vedor of the Viceroy of India himself, sending him that bolt of silk as a gift? I told him our father is Katheeb of Utheem. It is a token of his respect."

"Let Ali report to him about the voyage. We have heard of the Portuguese invasion. Some boats returned to the atoll before ours. That was a cause of concern to father."

"We delayed so we could offer to guide Dom Gaspar's great vessel to Baarah."

"Did the Portuguese force you to do that?"

"No. It was my idea."

"Let father remain ignorant of that, Mohamed." Fathima-faan sighed. "You have grown while you were away."

He rubbed his hand over his head, pleased that his hair was growing long like Ali's. It was the sign that his manhood was recognised.

"I didn't mean like that," said Fathimafaan with a laugh at the gesture.

He looked at her doubtfully, identifying her remark as one of those pointless things that elder sisters sometimes say. "I brought you a present too."

"Did you bring one for me?" Hassan had stopped playing and tugged at his arm impatiently, wanting to be noticed.

"Yes, of course I did."

"From your Portuguese patron?" Fathimafaan sounded doubtful.

He grinned. "He did release me from slavery."

"What!"

The doubt in her voice changed to anxiety and that made him regret teasing her. He caught up her hand in his, clasping it firmly while he told her the story. Hassan crouched at his feet. It was the story he had been rehearsing on the voyage home to tell his father, but he understood now that it would be more tactful to let Ali tell it.

He came to the end of all that had happened in Male' and then concluded: "We left the capital ahead of the Vedor's vessel. There were two *odi* from Baarah at Male' and he requested them to pilot him. He plans to stop at many islands on the way, to meet the Katheebs and their people. He gave an audience to Ali and told him we should return to Utheem in advance and present his compliments to father."

It was the longest narration Mohamed had ever made. He was out of breath and took up a half-coconut shell and scooped water with it from the large jar kept in the shade outside the house. He drank slowly, hearing from inside the house the drone of Ali's voice as he recounted his version of events.

"If all you say is true, Mohamed, you and Ali are heroes."

"I did not mean to be boastful."

"I know." Fathimafaan smiled at him. "It is so strange to us."

"Do the devils breathe fire when they talk?" asked Hassan, his head on one side as though trying to decide whether to believe what Mohamed had said.

"No. But they do drink blood."

Fathimafaan shuddered.

"Well, it looks like blood. It makes them hot and hearty and gives them the strength of ten devils."

Fathimafaan slid off the swing and stood up. She gathered the bolt of silk in her hands and aimed a mock blow with it at Mohamed. "Keep such tales for Hassan, not for me. Do we say Ali drinks sea when he sips toddy? The Portuguese wine is not blood, just because it is red."

"You made it up!" Hassan jumped to his feet and shouted. "You didn't do any of those things. You never saw a beautiful princess or spoke to the Queen!"

"I did!" He wanted to catch Hassan and slap him but his sister's hand on his shoulder kept him back.

"You see, Mohamed. It is prudent to keep to yourself things that others would not understand. It is difficult for us to grasp the meaning of what you have seen. Father is wiser and knows more than we do, but even so your story will make him worry even more about you."

She held the silk at arm's length with an air of regret as she bore it away from the house.

♦ ♦ ♦ ♦ ♦

Ramazan brought tranquillity to Utheem and a sense of spirituality to Mohamed. His strict observance of the month of fasting, going without food or liquid during the daylight hours, helped him put his experiences in Male' into proper perspective. He recited the Holy Quran, attended the mosque, and carefully observed the rituals of bathing and fasting as he had been taught by his father.

The month served to reduce the impact of the Portuguese arrival on the people of Utheem. They heard that in Baraah, the Portuguese had commanded that a residence be built worthy of the Portuguese Vedor and of Queen Aisha. Many people forsook the traditions of Ramazan to work under the Portuguese soldiers. It was said that some even drank the blood wine.

Katheeb Hussain's expression grew more sombre as each report of what the Portuguese were doing was heard in Utheem. For Mohamed, every time he saw his father looking at him, he thought he was rebuking him, as though holding him personally responsible for this menace in their midst. Mohamed found solace in the Holy Quran and in the peace of Utheem as people prayed and meditated. No one questioned him about events in Male'.

In fact, so few people spoke to him, Mohamed realised he had become a pariah in the community. He missed the excitement of life in Male', of being close to the centre of things, of the luxuries of court and of the brave swagger of the Portuguese. He even missed the ridiculous boasting of Lord Meedhoo's son. With the appointment of Lord Meedhoo as Finance Officer to Captain Andhirin, his son's arrogance had soared to new heights. Because of his airs, he soon became known throughout the atolls by his nickname of Crown Prince.

Mohamed recognised that the way of life in Male', which he missed, was shallow but full of intrigue. It surprised him that it seemed an appealing alternative to the quiet days in Utheem during Ramazan. He tried hard to expunge such thoughts from his mind, and the discipline of Ramazan helped him. When he could he walked to the beach and sat in his favourite spot watching the birds. However, he no longer tried to catch them. He thought instead of the world he didn't know, of the Portuguese and their power.

The Portuguese had sailed in their huge ships into their

ocean from the east, around the great continent of Africa. His father's largest boat, a two-masted *batteli* of over ninety feet in length, which he used for voyages to India, was like a minnow to a shark in comparison. The extent of what the Vedor must know of the seas, and of the world, intrigued him. Despite the peace of mind Mohamed had gained from his observance of the rituals and rules of Ramazan, there remained a gnawing at his soul, a quest for knowledge to be answered.

He felt no different when Ramazan came to an end and the people joined in the celebrations of Eid. He and Hassan helped Fathimafaan every day in the preparation of special festival foods. He was aware that Ali had gone to sea again but even Fathimafaan did not know where. His father's attitude was unchanged; he was aloof and remote, ignoring him.

It was Hassan who brought him the news of a change in his father's bad humour. He was on the beach as usual, scuffing his toes in the sand in boredom when he saw his brother running towards him, calling his name with excitement. It was sweet to his ears to hear Hassan's voice uncomplicated by any reserve.

"Ali has returned," Hassan burst out, panting as he reached Mohamed. He threw himself down on the sand, laughing. "He has been to Baarah. He says Queen Aisha and Princess Sitti have arrived there and are in the good hands of Vedor Dom Gaspar. He brought a message to our father asking him to continue to serve the Maldives as Katheeb."

It was though a weight had been lifted from Mohamed's shoulders. He reached down and grabbed Hassan by his wrists, pulling him to his feet. "How do you know all this?"

"Fathimafaan bade me bring the news to you."

He ran with Hassan to the water's edge, dragging him into the sea. They laughed happily as they romped together before falling exhausted in the sand, lying there letting the sun's caress dry the sea's spray from them.

That evening, as Mohamed expected, his father summoned him into the house. Katheeb Hussain was seated cross-legged on the dais. He put aside the sheaf of parchments he had been reading as Mohamed entered. A lamp burned in the corner, its flickering flame exaggerating his father's shadow so it seemed to fill the room. Mohamed waited silently for his father to speak, feeling his eyes studying him intently.

"You are growing," his father said, as though seeing him for the first time after several weeks. "You are almost a man."

Mohamed nodded happily.

"However, a developed body and two hundred moons do not make a man. Experience gained through disappointment; wisdom through folly; bravery through fear; faith through despair; these help make a man."

Mohamed prepared himself for the lecture that was coming. His father must have sensed his impatience.

"All that you know, Mohamed. You know so much and yet so little. You knew that one day I would commend you for thinking ahead, for charting a course between myself and the Portuguese who have occupied our country. Yes, yes, I support you for your courage to do what you believed was right. You believed the Vedor was a good man and could be useful to us."

Katheeb Hussain paused, as though he had difficulty in addressing his son as a man and not as a boy. "If you believe something is right, does that make it right? You have no knowledge, no experience, of the world to say what is right. It is honourable to be hospitable and kind to strangers. It is also honourable to be heroic and resist strangers if they come with ill intent. You saw in the Portuguese Vedor a quality you could trust, and you trusted. Fortunately, your judgement was not at fault. Perhaps mine was. It seems Dom Gaspar is an honourable man.

"My cousin, the Kathheb of Baarah is pleased with him. He says the Vedor does not intend to change the way we govern ourselves. He seeks only to see that we pay tribute when it is due and for that he wants our trading to continue profitably."

He raised the parchment that he had been reading. "Dom Gaspar has begged me in most civil terms to remain as Katheeb. He has written lavish praise about your intelligence and spirit, and says you have brought me honour by your behaviour, and that you are a credit to me."

His father sighed, shaking his head in bewilderment. "This Vedor is said to be a wise man. What he sees in you I know not. You are a puzzle to me, Mohamed."

His father dismissed him with a wave of resignation, as though accepting events were moving beyond his control. Then as Mohamed reached the door, his father told him to wait. He rose slowly from the dais and stepped down with difficulty. It was the first time Mohamed had seen his father less than agile. Perhaps he had not noticed before that his father was showing his age.

He waited stiffly as his father came to him. Side by side they both realised that he had grown almost the same height as his father.

"I have arranged for you to go away," said his father, placing his hand on his shoulder. He paused, searching his eyes with his. "Aha," he said, pleased. "I see your eyes brighten, that sparkle of spirit must be what the Vedor recognised."

He took his hand from Mohamed's shoulder. "You have more to learn than we can teach you here. You have to learn to see, to think, to fight and to guide. I do not want the Portuguese, this Dom Gaspar, to have the pleasure of bringing you to manhood."

"Father?"

His father turned away, and sniffed. His voice was thick when he began to speak again. "You will sail with Ali to Nolivaranfaru to meet your uncle. He will introduce you to a great teacher who is visiting him. You will sail with this Master to Beydali. That is a small port close to Calicut controlled by Muslim traders, beyond the influence of the Portuguese. You will do whatever the Master tells you. In Beydali, under him, you will learn. You will become a man, my son."

His father's tears, as he embraced him, wet his cheeks. He was to feel them on his face for the four long years he was away.

————⊕————

PART TWO
Utheem, Northern Atolls, Maldives
1562-1568

————⊕————

CHAPTER 11

Standing in the crow's nest of the ship carrying him from Beydali, Mohamed could see a ten-league circle of ocean. The sky was a clear blue, brushed with strands of cloud, like the hair of a beautiful woman trailing in the breeze. The sea flowed with gentle rhythm, as though propelled by his passion to reach home. The sails were full and the wind swept the ship along, the Malabari helmsman steering skilfully to take advantage of the ocean's race.

It was a voyage of some ninety leagues from Beydali to the Maldives. For Mohamed, the voyage had been longer; it was four years since he had set out from his island. In his mind he still held the memory of that morning. He had left with a heavy heart, wondering if he was being sent away by his father as a punishment. The Katheeb did not come to the beach to see him go; only Fathimafaan and Hassan were there, both pretending to be unconcerned. Neither of them waved, and he had turned his back on them quickly, prepared to face his destiny.

He looked back on his innocence with a sense of shame for his irresponsible behaviour. He knew now how wise his father had been. Had he stayed on Utheem he would probably have become the favoured playboy of the Vedor, as arrogant as Lord Meedhoo's son, the crown prince.

Beydali was close to Calicut; seamen from there, who made frequent voyages to Male', kept him informed of life in the Maldives. Andhiri Andhirin was proving himself an inept but ruthless administrator who left the governance of Male' and its dependent islands to Lord Meedhoo and his son. In the northern atolls, however, the Vedor's sway was more enlightened and people were allowed to continue with earning their livelihood without interference.

As he gazed at the horizon watching for Kelaa, the first island in the atoll where Utheem was located, Mohamed wondered if his father, sister and brothers had changed. He knew they would have difficulty recognising him. He had left as a scrap of a boy, oh so proud of himself, but in reality feeble both in body and mind. He had added six inches to his height and gained the muscles – and guile – of a warrior.

He stood upright in the crow's nest, rolling with the vessel's movement, his knees dipping with each plunge and stiffening with each climb. His long, black hair, which he wore gathered in a knot at the top of his head like a Nayar warrior, showed flecks of gold where the sun and salt sea air had bleached it. He was dressed like a Nayar, covered only from the waist down with a large cloth of fine, white cotton that reached to his knees and passed back between his firm thighs.

He favoured the Nayar style because of the awe with which Nayars were regarded in India. They were lords who meddled with neither handicraft nor trade, nor any other exercise but arms. They were renowned as the best soldiers in the world; hardy and courageous, exceedingly adroit in the use of arms.

He had learned their skills at a school of Nayars in Kerala. He could carry a shield in one hand and a sword in the other - or else a javelin, or muskets, or matchlocks and pikes - and he could fight with the best, and win. He had learned how to train his body in such dextrous suppleness of limb that he could bend in all possible postures while lunging at any antagonist. He had become a master in weaponry and earned the respect of the great Nayar teachers.

The Nayars, however, never went to sea and were fearsome only on land. For his skills as a navigator and master mariner, he was sent by his teacher to train with the sons of some renowned Malabari ship owners. They considered themselves men of honour, and none would do any toilsome or vile thing. With them he studied the finer points of seamanship.

After such vigorous training, he and his companions were capable of becoming merchants or corsairs, esteeming one profession as highly as the other. With them he sailed the Malabar and Coromandel coasts, to the southernmost atolls of the Maldives, Suvadu and Addu, and from there on the trade routes to Galle in the island the Portuguese called Ceilao.

He had sailed in storms and wild seas that battered and tossed the vessel until he thought he would never see land again. He had sailed deep beyond the Equatorial Line and was the only survivor on a vessel becalmed for weeks in a desolate and lifeless sea. With neither water nor food, he had survived by eating raw fish and collecting dew to drink. He had comforted crazed men and cradled the dying in his arms. During his months adrift at sea, he became hardened by the cruelties of mankind and of nature. The experience charged him with the spirit of a visionary who knew all the ill-fortune Allah could conceive.

His vision and humility were developed through the teaching of the learned master of Beydali. This great man of wisdom encouraged the streak of individuality and impatience, which had caused his father such distress, by honing it to become his inner strength. Guided by the discipline of Islam as explained by his master, he learned to control the fire that raged within him so it became a soft and radiant glow that could inspire others.

He was too active a person to reflect much on the spiritual qualities his teacher believed were his. To Mohamed it was enough to know that he had pleased his teacher so much that he was permitted to return home. He was looking forward to joining his father and his brothers in sailing the Indian Ocean as traders, and in leading a useful and honourable life. His days of adventure were behind him.

With one hand clinging to the mast while he gazed at the horizon, Mohamed stroked his beard with the other. He was growing it in the style favoured by Katheebs and those who have made the journey to Mecca. It was already long for he shaved only under his throat and above and below the lips. He had no hair around his mouth because of the traditional belief that hair, if it touched food or drink as it was being consumed, was a disgusting pollutant. He regarded the other style of beard popular in the Maldives, short and trimmed to a point, as being more suited to a pirate than to a true son of a Katheeb.

He was happy as he watched the horizon. His years at Beydali had been hard. For the first year he was without friends and he needed them, not like the days when he chose to wander alone on Utheem. This was a time of remorse, of chiding himself for his unfortunate lot; it was also the time he found comfort in the Holy Quran due to his teacher's patience with his constant demands for clarification. Then as the months passed and he felt himself changing, he gained confidence that led to the enjoyment of every day. He sought, and found, the best in everyone and in everything.

"Land ahoy!" he shouted with delight. Since the islands were but a few feet above sea level, the coconut palms, which were their tallest feature, could be seen only when the ship was almost upon them. He had been watching keenly for the white ripples of surf that heralded the outer ring of coral reefs around every atoll. In the distance he could see a trace of contrasting water and then there, in the haze of sea and sky at the horizon beyond, was the low silhouette of Kelaa.

At his shout, he felt the helmsman begin to change course to a more southerly direction which would take the ship down the eastern ring of the atoll, past Filladu to Baarah. It was there he would disembark, since the ship was bound for Male' with salt and rice and other goods of trade. No one knew he was coming home; he would have to wait in Baarah until he could find a *dhoni* bound for Utheem. Yet it would only be a few more days before he would see his father and family again.

◆ ◆ ◆ ◆ ◆

Mohamed strolled out of the surf onto the beach, his bundle of belongings slung over his shoulder. He paused, the afternoon sun behind him warming his bare shoulders. He looked ahead at the hamlet of thatched huts that lined the shore. Behind them was a larger building, built of bleached coral stone, set in a compound. It was separated from its neighbours by a low wall. To his surprise there was a youth, whose skin was so fair he could only have been Portuguese, sitting outside it, eyeing him with hostile curiosity.

Mohamed was intrigued. He walked over to him nonchalantly. "Peace be with you!"

The youth frowned and studied him. "Dressed like a Nayar you are, but Dhivehi you speak."

"So do you. I took you for Portuguese."

"Portuguese of course I am." The youth's tone conveyed muffled pride, but whether it was because Mohamed had complimented him on his ability to speak Dhivhei or because of his birthright, wasn't at first obvious.

"Do you live here?" Mohamed gestured at the island, his face conveying agreeable surprise.

"Until to Goa I return. From Malabar you come?" The hostility was fading from the youth's stare.

Mohamed nodded, studying the youth. It was part of his training: to appraise an unexpected acquaintance thoroughly with a single glance, lest he become an enemy, or a friend. A person's weakness or strength could be crucial. He sensed the youth was comfortable with his surroundings, even though he was a foreigner. He decided that by giving information, he could gain some in return.

"I belong to Utheem," he said. "I am returning home."

The youth nodded but said nothing. He wore a loose tunic and breeches with stockings and shoes. He was sitting in the shade, on the trunk of a fallen palm tree. He gestured at his side, inviting Mohamed to sit with him.

"It must be lonely here without fiends?" Mohamed sat down on the trunk, hoping by his question to discover if there many other Portuguese people on the island. He put his bundle on the sand in front of him.

The youth looked stern and Mohamed realised he had gone too far. The lad was no simpleton, even if he looked so guileless.

"How do you know friends I have not?" His voice was hard.

"I mean friends from Portugal."

"Valet to the Vedor, Dom Gaspar, I am. For nothing I want."

"I see." Mohamed sighed, hoping to ingratiate himself with the lad before it was too late. "You must forgive me. I left this atoll before the Vedor arrived." He paused to see if the lad would say anything. He didn't but his eyes searched his face intently. Mohamed grinned. "My name is Mohamed. What is yours?"

"Joao, I am." He nodded as though satisfied with what

he saw in Mohamed's eyes. "Changes many there are." He relaxed and seemed happy to talk. He began by telling Mohamed what a good man the Vedor was to everyone. The Vedor respected the Maldivians and believed they should learn a better way of life freely from the example of the Portuguese, not by being coerced. He was using his presence to demonstrate to people the benefits of being subjects of the Portuguese Emperor. He had encouraged the people to build more boats and engage in fishing and commerce and coir production.

Mohamed listened carefully, nodding his head to show his appreciation of what Joao was saying. "Does the Vedor live alone?" he asked as his curiosity got the better of him. He was wondering if the Vedor had taken a local wife, as the Portuguese were accustomed to doing in India.

"Really, a long time away you are!" Joao stretched out his legs lazily in front of him and smiled. He then explained that the widow of the former Sultan, Queen Aisha, and her daughter, were living in the house with the Vedor. "Under his protection they are. Under his blanket not."

It was Mohamed's turn to smile, amused by Joao's insistence about the propriety of the relationship. When he lived at Beydali and was under instructions from the Nayars, smiling and levity were forbidden. Maldivians did not smile much anyway, preferring to keep humour to themselves for they despised melancholy. He knew the people of Baarah would be intrigued, and perhaps puzzled, by the domestic arrangements of the Vedor and their former Queen.

"The daughter, the little princess, is she happy?"

Joao raised his eyes from contemplating his own limbs in front of him. He pulled himself upright and regarded Mohamed with greater curiosity than before. Mohamed sensed that somehow the question disturbed him.

Then Joao relaxed and shrugged his shoulders. He said that at first Princess Sitti was withdrawn and spoke little, unless addressed directly. One day, he related, the Vedor had heard the Queen rebuking Sitti about her apparent indifference to everything around her.

"'Madam,' he told her, 'you are not a befitting person to rebuke your noble daughter, even though she is your own child, she is destiny's child too. You and she are different. She is of a very gentle disposition.'"

Mohamed tugged his beard, uncertain what to make of this report, although flattered that Joao had shared the story with him. He remembered Sitti's wide, frightened eyes. She must be nearly fourteen years old now.

"Happier now she is," said Joao with another shrug.

Mohamed wondered what she looked like and whether Queen Aisha would remember how he helped her and Sitti to flee from the palace. He knew he would not be able to see them unless there was some reason for their appearance in public. "The Vedor," he began quietly, not wanting to worry Joao with his questions. "Is he here in Baarah?"

"Here I am, so here he is." Joao stood up quickly, brushing the sand from his breeches. "Too much with you I have spoken. Now go, before guards I call."

Mohamed stood up too and saluted gracefully, which seemed to appease Joao, who nodded his head slightly. The heat and monotony of island life had made him less alert than he should have been, in his position. Mohamed bowed, hoping to reassure Joao by his benign expression that he need not worry. He hoisted his bundle on his back, saluted again, and strode off along the beach without looking back.

◆ ◆ ◆ ◆ ◆

Fathimafaan clung to his arm. He was taller than her now and she seemed frailer and much younger than he expected. She had set up a howl of shock when he walked casually into the compound where she was seated on a log, grating coconut to use in the evening meal. He put his arm around her, urging her to be quiet.

"See," he said with a trace of a grin. "I am not a ghost."

Her fingers left specks of grated coconut on his sunhued, sinewy arm. She drew away from him quickly. "Mohamed!" she said regaining her composure. "Is this really you?"

His grin broadened as he stepped back from her and opened his arms wide. His head, held high, drew the sun, which made his eyes glint and the golden streaks in his hair sparkle. His young beard could not disguise his handsome countenance, not hinder the aura of dependability he radiated.

Fathimafaan clucked her tongue. "Why are you dressed like a beggar?"

It was not the welcome he expected. He looked down at his broad, naked chest, covered in a crescent of thick, tight, dark curls, to his lean thighs wrapped around with his Nayar loincloth. His feet, as always, were bare. He owned neither slippers nor tunic. His bundle contained only two cloths, a comb and a bunch of palm leaf parchments on which he had written verses from the Holy Quran. His grin returned.

"As always, dear sister, you are right. I am a beggar of life. I beg of you to forgive me."

"I'll box your ears. Coming here unannounced and frightening me! You must bathe and dress and prepare yourself to meet the Katheeb."

He was happy to be told what to do by his sister. Whatever he had done, whatever he had learned, would not change her attitude towards him. He nodded. "I will do as you say. How is father?"

"You have come in time, Mohamed. He grows old and tired. He is weary of his duties." She looked at him shrewdly, then sat down again to continue scraping the flesh of the coconuts. "Say nothing of that to him."

It had never occurred to Mohamed that he would ever dream of commenting on his father's behaviour to his face. He must have changed greatly if Fathimafaan saw him as likely to do so. "Do you have a robe for me to wear? I must not rouse in him the anguish my appearance has caused you."

She dismissed him with an irritable wave of her hand. She at least remained as moody and as unfathomable as ever. He picked up his bundle and walked around the house to the well, finding it odd how everything appeared smaller than he remembered. He unknotted his hair, letting it fall down to his shoulders, and began to draw water from the well. He doused himself energetically, as though washing away the past four years, becoming again the simple son of a respected island chief.

As he combed his hair carefully, letting the sun dry the drops of water on his body, he became aware that he was no longer alone. He continued with his toilet. If he were at Beydali, instinct would have made him reach for his sword for he was trained to be prepared for the unexpected. He sensed, perhaps through smell, perhaps intuition, that he was being observed. By his brother.

"Hassan," he said, turning slowly. "Why do you hide yourself behind a palm tree?"

"You hide yourself behind a mane of hair and a mass of muscles." A boy stepped out from the trees and stood, his hands on his hips, gazing curiously at him.

"If that is indeed you, Hassan, you have grown strong and shrewd without having to endure four years away from home as did I." He was impressed by Hassan's build. The boy had matured in body, and his face no longer had the harried, inferior look of a doubtful younger brother. "Father must have been well cared for with you at his side."

Hassan handed him some clothes without comment, his eyes drifting downwards from his long hair to his naked loins. Mohamed shrugged, indicating that he had indeed grown. He observed that Hassan too had developed. He wore his hair short in the manner of boatmen. He was about four inches shorter than Mohamed, with broad shoulders and sturdy, mariner's legs. His muscles had developed from years of loading and unloading cargoes on the Utheem beach. He was showing signs of discomfort at being in Mohamed's presence, slipping without being aware of it into the role of junior to his brother.

Mohamed wrapped the cloth Hassan had brought him around his waist and pulled the tunic on over his head. It was Hassan's and too tight for him. He grinned ruefully and shrugged again. Taking a ribbon from his bundle, he tied it around his brow so that it kept his hair away from his cheeks. He smoothed his beard dry. "Now I am all right to meet father?"

Hassan looked happy at being asked his opinion. "No, you are not. You are four years older."

"I am not a stranger, though."

"You are, Mohamed, you are, but then you always have been, haven't you? You will see that so much has changed since you went away." He led him to the outside door of the house.

Mohamed noticed that the walls had been repaired with new boards and there was new thatch on the roof. "You have worked hard, Hassan," he said. "The house looks so much better than I remember."

"At last you have come!" The voice that called out to him from inside the house had an edge of pleasure in its rebuke.

Mohamed ducked through the doorway and went in, his eyes swiftly adjusting to the gloom, taking in the sight of his father standing up to greet him. He would not have recognised him had they met by chance. The Katheeb had grown old.

Mohamed knelt on the floor in front of him as a mark of respect and his father touched his shoulder in acknowledgement.

"Come," he said, drawing him onto the dais so he sat with him on his mat. He beckoned Hassan to join them too. "Ali is married and at his wife's island. I shall have you for myself for a few days. We have much to talk about."

Mohamed expected his father to question him about Beydali and all he had learned there. Instead he spoke to him of his own concerns, as though anxious that Mohamed should understand the situation in the islands before setting forth to discover for himself. He spoke of Male' and the rule of Captain Andhirin, which had degenerated into lawlessness and licentiousness after its promising beginning.

"No man is more self-righteous in his actions than a convert," his father said. "Andhirin is worse than the Portuguese he serves and whose religion he has adopted yet he was raised as a Muslim. He despises our religion and our traditions. He permits every form of vice in Male' and gives no heed to what Lord Meedhoo and his son, whom every one mockingly calls Crown Prince, do in his name. Fortunately Dom Gaspar is more astute. Have you seen him?" The question had a hint of reproach to it.

"No, father." Mohamed, hid his smile. "I landed in Baarah but I would not consider paying the Vedor a visit until I had seen you."

His father was satisfied. "Very good. We must not be in a hurry. Dom Gaspar has his ways, Andhirin his. They are both under orders to possess us. The Portuguese are here to colonise and to convert, but commerce is the wind in their sails. We are that wind."

He paused then said quietly, "Perhaps, my son, one day the wind will become a monsoon and blow the Portuguese away?"

CHAPTER 12

It was not easy for Mohamed to adjust to the routine of being at home. Nothing he had been taught prepared him for the indifference of people to what he had done. The experiences that were so important to him were irrelevant to his family and neighbours. He had been away, seen the world, spent his youth, and that was that. Now he was at home and should play his part.

He recognised his father was growing weary. He no longer wanted to sail or trade, preferring to stay at home with his memories and his opinions. Mohamed observed how Ali and Hassan were conducting themselves and found he too was expected to conform to his father's wishes. After he made a voyage to other atolls under Ali's watchful eye to collect coir and dried fish, his father put him in command of a vessel of his own. He was pleased that Ali had evidently given his father a good report of his ability.

He shortened his hair. He also curbed his desire to tell everyone about how, in India, he always walked with a sword and a buckler, had become proficient with lance and pike, and was considered a master marksman. He concentrated instead on trading, in persuading islanders to sell to him at a rate lower than they intended, and to buy from him imported goods at a price higher than they wanted to pay. His charm was devastating, as Fathimafaan never ceased to observe.

He made a trading visit to Male', accompanied by Hassan. The three brothers never left Utheem at the same time. There was always one of them at home in case their father needed help. It had been his father's idea that Mohamed should sail with Hassan. He wanted his two sons to get to know each other now they were men. He must have sensed that Hassan might be resentful at Mohamed's return.

Mohamed, too, was aware of that possibility. He went out of his way to encourage his younger brother, forgetting he was his brother and regarding him as a friend. He found him agreeable company. His strength was his strength, although his vision was necessarily blinkered by his island environment. So Mohamed kept his worldly pronouncements to himself, unspoken, and enjoyed Hassan's simple, ingenuous personality.

In Male' they were obliged to sell their cargo of cowries to the Portuguese factors at a considerable discount. However, the system of factors enabled those without the resources of the big traders to benefit too. Fishermen were becoming entrepreneurs and there was a modest prosperity spreading through the capital. There was also an element of fear and lawlessness.

The capital no longer bustled with activity during the day. Only slaves worked hard when the sun was high, loading cargoes. People no longer flocked to the mosque five times a day. Officials and petitioners with projects to accomplish were obliged to solicit an audience with Andhiri Andhirin in the evenings. There were no daily consultations with courtiers and people as there had been in the time of the Sultans. Andhirin had installed a retinue of Portuguese guards, cohorts and concubines to attend and amuse him. Lord Meedhoo was his chamberlain and he governed through him and his scheming son, whom even he called the Crown Prince.

With nightfall, Male' assumed a different character to its daytime lethargy. The sunset being no longer the time for prayer brought shadows that shielded the nefarious nature of the night. It was the time when men took to the streets in search of wine doled out by the Portuguese. Nightfall was when women, heavily veiled, slipped from the houses of their absent husbands to the homes of their paramours, only returning at dawn, before the husbands did.

There was singing in the streets, boys chased and fought, women were molested and old men insulted. Gangs of Portuguese men, arms clasped in drunken embrace, staggered along the lanes in search of excitement, or passed out in a stupor on the beach.

Instead of being able to resist the loutish behaviour of the occupiers, the residents of Male' were obliged to accept it. Those whom the Portuguese favoured did well; others found it difficult, surviving only on the fish they could catch and the charity of their neighbours. Although there was no outright oppression and cruelty, the presence of so many lecherous and carousing Portuguese was changing the character of the capital. Since most Maldivians found it easier to do what the occupiers wanted, and certainly more rewarding, there was no will to resist.

Mohamed kept his views to himself, engaging in commerce during the day and then returning to the *odi* to sleep at night. He longed to counsel Hassan not to go ashore after dark but he knew this would only create unnecessary conflict between them. Instead, he sat in the bow of the *odi*, staying awake until Hassan returned. He was glad that he said nothing, for Hassan always returned early and without a whiff of wine on his breath.

It perturbed Mohamed that the people of Male' were drifting into a way of life so alien to their culture and religious beliefs. Even Friday was no longer a holiday. The Portuguese held a religious service on Sunday mornings and gave participants wine to drink, which enticed many Maldivians to attend, happy to forget the strictures of Islam.

Mohamed was relieved when their trading was finished and he was able to sail back to the sanctity and traditions that had been preserved in Utheem.

◆ ◆ ◆ ◆ ◆

Katheeb Hussain faced his three sons across the *bodu ashi*. Their evening meal had finished and they had washed their fingers in the basin brought for them by Fathimafaan.

During the meal, Mohamed had spoken of the visit he and Hassan had made to Male' and his concern that it was becoming a sinful place.

"With so many foreigners either living there or visiting to trade," Mohamed concluded, "it is not a fitting place to call the capital of our country."

"Perhaps it is," said Ali. "Let all the foreigners remain there and not visit the islands where the true Maldivians live."

"Are they true to Allah?"

"My sons," said the Katheeb, his voice hard with exasperation. "I have lived long and travelled far. It grieves me to see that in my twilight years when I should be blessed with peace, even my sons are arguing among themselves."

"Not an argument, father."

Mohamed, who was the only one who would dare interrupt the Katheeb, saw the look of anguish on his face and lapsed into silence.

"Yes, Mohamed, hear me out. "I feel I am no longer capable of being the Katheeb of Utheem. The world is changing but I am not. A man of Portugal is our atoll chief; an upstart who is a Christian governs us instead of a Sultan. We are Maldivians, as Ali says, but whether we are true to Allah, I no longer know. What is true?" He paused, although he did not expect an answer.

"I want the three of you, all my sons, to visit Baarah. It is the Eid festival season, time for you to pay respects to our atoll chief, even though he is from Portugal. It will be the opportunity for you to present yourself to him, Mohamed. He must have heard of your return and will think it amiss if you delay calling on him."

"As you wish, father."

"Ali, you will take with you a missive from me to the atoll chief. In it I ask him to relieve me of my position as Katheeb. My father was Katheeb before me, and I pray that one of you will be Katheeb after me."

"We pray you have many more happy years to guide us and be a leader and example of righteousness to your people."

Katheeb Hussain dismissed Mohamed's remark with a

wave of his hand and stood up. Ali, Mohamed and Hassan scrambled to their feet too. They waited as their father hobbled out of the house and then the three of them looked at each other.

"Do you always try to make people feel good?" Hassan asked, taunting Mohamed.

"It is a shame to hear him talk of giving up as Katheeb. He is not too old."

"His legs hurt him," said Ali. "He is right, one of us could replace him."

"You expect it to be you!"

"Hush, Hassan," Mohamed out his hand on his younger brother's shoulder. "Come, let us stroll on the beach. It is a pleasant night to consider the future. You too, Ali, come with us."

"He is thinking of his wife," said Hassan as they walked together down the avenue of palm trees to the beach. In the faint moonlight, the three ships of the Katheeb of Utheem could be seen bobbing quietly at anchor. There were several other *odis* and *dhonis* in the lagoon. The breeze as it embraced them on the beach loosened their tongues.

"I am keen to go to Baarah," said Hassan. "The Eid festival is a time when many young people from all the atolls north of Male' gather together."

"What they do," said Ali, "is not in keeping with our faith. The Vedor lets the revelry take place without considering its effect on the young. And he is the guardian of the daughter of the late Sultan."

Hassan interrupted him with a scornful laugh. "You forget we are going to convey our greetings to the atoll chief, at our father's command. It would be churlish to refuse."

He nudged Mohamed in his waist with his elbow. "What Ali says makes the visit sound promising. You and I are of the age to look for a wife. It should be easy to choose one from so many visiting Baarah for the festival."

"We must remember our status, Hassan," said Ali sternly. "Since the Portuguese came, girls have become so bold, they run after young men without shame. We have been instructed to make a visit, so we will have to stay there at least for the afternoon otherwise the Vedor will be displeased."

"Ali, you have become too respectable since you have married. We have to have fun, too, when we are there, don't we, Mohamed?"

Mohamed had remained silent, listening to the banter. He sympathised with Ali, whose wife lived on Thakandhoo, a day's sail from Utheem. While Ali spent much of his time with her, he was often away on voyages for his father, or visiting Utheem. This was one of the rare occasions since Mohamed's return when all three brothers were together on the island.

"Let us not quarrel," he said. "Ali is right. It would be unseemly for us as the sons of Katheeb Hussain to forget our position. We must not succumb to the blandishment of girls who have been encouraged by the Portuguese to believe they can behave immodestly."

Hassan whooped with mockery at this long-winded statement.

Mohamed caught him around his shoulders and hugged him affectionately.

"I, however, am also on the lookout for a wife. Perhaps I shall find one tomorrow."

CHAPTER 13

The island of Baarah had been favoured for settlement since people first chanced on the Maldives. By misfortune through shipwreck, or by design through a desire to quit their native countries, mariners and adventurers in ancient days discovered the Maldives because they lay at the crossroads of the Indian Ocean.

While most of the islands are circular or long, Baarah appealed to the early settlers because of its crescent shape. Its two arms embraced a bay where vessels could anchor safely; the outer rim of the crescent, with its rocky foreshore, was at the atoll's edge, battered by the waves of the Indian Ocean. Thus, from outside the atoll, the island appeared deserted and inhospitable, which enabled the island – and its inhabitants – to escape the attention of passing vessels intent on plunder.

An established and prosperous community of fishermen and coconut farmers had developed on Baarah across the centuries, the island's safe anchorage induced vessels to trade. Baarah became influential throughout the Maldives as its people travelled from island to island. They were renowned not just for their industry but also for their intelligence, part of the heritage of people descended from settlers of so many nationalities.

That Dom Gaspar should choose Baarah for his base was the result of his keen understanding of the Maldives, which he had gained through his years of visiting the islands from India on the business of Portugal. He saw Baarah as a rival to Male'. While it had neither the density of population or development, nor the strategic location of the capital, it was blessed with a natural harbour and resources of land and sea to make it self-sufficient. The people, with their mixed heritage, lived together harmoniously, bonded by the habit, if not the faith, of their religion.

As Vedor, Dom Gaspar wanted to capitalise on that. He had no intention of inhibiting the lifestyle of those over whom he ruled. He believed that, given time and a good example, people would pay less attention to their religion and more attention to profitable pursuits. Prosperous Maldivians would be malleable Maldivians, happy to accept conversion by missionary fathers spreading the joys of Christianity. Until that happened, Dom Gaspar was content to let the people of Baarah observe their traditions, as long as these did not lead to conflict with the Portuguese presence.

The fun and games of the Eid festival was an occasion he enjoyed. It was an opportunity to meet influential people from the neighbouring islands who, by tradition, paid their respects during the festival to him as atoll chief. He could discuss their problems and suggest solutions that were in the Portuguese interest. During the festival the islanders, who had escorted their chiefs joined in the celebrations and feasting, hosted by the people of Baarah.

After four years living in Baarah, Dom Gaspar's knowledge of Dhivehi had improved and he now spoke it fluently, albeit with a refined Portuguese accent. He flourished in

Baarah, enjoying the warm climate and developing a liking for a diet of fish and rice. He had returned once to Goa and obtained there a commission to remain at Baarah at the Viceroy's pleasure. This suited him well as he was of the age when he wanted less of the intrigue associated with being at the eye of the colonial cyclone blowing its way across Asia.

As Vedor, Dom Gaspar, who was not married, was content to be at the centre of his own small, tropical haven. He had no family to yearn for, nor to miss him, while he served his country far from home. He had a retinue of Portuguese militia and clerks who sailed to all the islands, and Male', collecting taxes. On his last visit to Goa, he had found a Portuguese boy to serve as his valet. In addition, he had the company of the Sultan's widow, Queen Aisha, and her daughter, whom he loved as though she were his own child.

It was to this idyllic setting of Baarah, with its enlightened and benevolent ruler, that Mohamed Thakuru and his two brothers came with Eid greetings from their father.

Dom Gaspar's valet, Joao, brought the news as the Vedor was relaxing after lunch on a swing seat in his garden. Queen Aisha and her daughter, Sitti, were sitting on a separate swing. He had abolished the custom of the women remaining in purdah in their own quarters. He enjoyed the stimulation of Aisha's company and the antics of her daughter, and encouraged them to spend time with him.

"A boat is being rowed at great speed towards the beach," reported Joao. "There are three men in robes standing in its stern."

"More well wishers," said Aisha when the Vedor translated for her. "Your reputation is spreading. Far more people are coming to visit you this year than before."

Dom Gaspar smiled. "You do not mind all this extra work? Without your guiding hand there would be no festival. I have no idea what to do. It's a relief to leave everything to you."

"It is my duty to serve you, my lord." Queen Aisha's smile was radiant, reflecting her contentment. "You could have left Sitti and me to the mercy of Andhiri Andhirin at the palace in Male'. You didn't. You shelter me here and show me every respect."

"As befits your majesty."

She chuckled happily at his response. Sitti was tugging at her sleeve. "Yes, child, you may go and see who these three grand gentlemen are. Come back quickly and tell us. We shall have to prepare for our guests."

There were scores of boats from other islands anchored in the bay. The beach and the trails leading to it were thronged with people who had come for the festival. Joao led the way through while Sitti followed closely. As people saw her coming and the word spread among the visitors that she was the daughter of Queen Aisha, they made space for her to pass.

At the shore, people in the crowd were speculating on the identity of the three new arrivals. They were all dressed elegantly in full regalia, with long robes of blue and white, and turbans. Only nobles were permitted to dress so grandly. They were barefooted and stepped ashore smartly, avoiding the wash of the surf.

One of the men addressed their crew. "There is no need to anchor. Remain in position at your oars. Do not leave the boat unless my brothers or I call. We will return immediately after paying our respects to the Vedor, our atoll chief."

"Who is that man?" Sitti asked Joao. "He is very handsome with his fine beard and commanding manner."

Joao scratched his head. "Him before I have seen. From India he comes."

"He is a Maldivian noble, Joao! You know nothing." Sitti giggled. "Who are these men?" She addressed a woman in the crowd.

"Princess, those are the three sons of the Katheeb of Utheem. It is the first time they have come to Baarah for the festival since you have been here. It is strange that the Katheeb himself is not with them."

"Is it?" Sitti giggled again. She liked the look of the three sons of the Katheeb because they were so dashing. Judging by the murmurs of the people in the crowd, they were well known. "Let us tell Dom Gaspar who his guests are," said Sitti, beckoning Joao to follow her back to the house.

The news meant little to the Vedor but Queen Aisha was

impressed. "The Utheem brothers are renowned for their skills; they are masters of the sea and adept at trading."

"Then we shall receive them properly." Dom Gaspar swung himself off the swing and looked around the compound. "Joao, you may bring them here when they arrive at the gate."

"If that is so," said Queen Aisha, aware that letting strangers enter their private compound was yet another breach of etiquette, "then Sitti you must prepare drinks for our guests. Bring sherbet and betel, seven leaves for each person." She composed herself on her swing, spreading out the many folds of her dress around her. "I am looking forward to meeting these three famous brothers. You see that Sitti was quite excited by their appearance."

Joao led the trio up the path. They walked briskly, their robes fluttering behind them. Dom Gaspar rose to his feet to welcome them. For a moment they faced each other without speaking then the Vedor uttered the traditional greeting. "Peace be with you."

"With you be peace."

◆ ◆ ◆ ◆ ◆

Mohamed stood on one side of Ali, Hassan on the other. His quick eyes took in the scene and he was pleased. Queen Aisha sat with much more decorum than when he had last seen her in Male'. He was sure that he had glimpsed a pretty young girl in the doorway of the house as she peeped out. He glanced again, but she was gone.

"We come to convey Eid greetings from our father, the Katheeb of Utheem," began Ali in a serious tone. "He wishes through you to convey greetings to the Viceroy's representative in Male'."

While Ali was speaking, Mohamed studied the Vedor. He was plumper and his goatee greyer but his blue eyes were bright and still held a sparkle of interest in what was happening. He was listening carefully to Ali in case he missed any nuance in his address.

"Our father sends his regrets at not being able to visit you personally. He has sent a written message – "

"Yes, yes," said Dom Gaspar, departing from the usual formalities and avoiding having to accept the roll of parchment Ali was about to hand him. "We will speak. First, some refreshment. Please enter my humble abode."

For Mohamed it was strange to hear traditional Dhivehi phrases correctly uttered by a man he thought of as a foreign heron who had plucked him from the sea. He spoke slowly but his voice contained the element of amusement that Mohamed remembered. It was as though, being anxious not to cause offence by saying something incorrectly, he wanted everything to be received in good spirit. His personality put them at ease, and even Ali succumbed to his charm.

Dom Gaspar ushered them into the reception hall and walked over to the *kuda ashi,* the wooden platform reserved for dignitaries on the western side of the hall. He invited Ali to join him there, which confused Ali. He hesitated and then declined, as he knew his place was with his brothers on the *bodu ashi,* the guest platform opposite.

"As you wish," said Dom Gaspar. "The elder son of the Katheeb of Utheem is welcome by my side."

Mohamed observed Queen Aisha smile to herself, obviously used to the Vedor's skill in making people feel at ease. She had slipped into the hall with them and settled on the platform behind Dom Gaspar, thereby lending her support to whatever pronouncements he made. Mohamed looked beyond her and saw Princess Sitti watching from the shadows. Her eyes were no longer wide with fear but bright with amazement and curiosity, radiating from a face of unblemished beauty. He hoped she would remember him.

Queen Aisha beckoned the girl forward to serve the drinks and Joao followed with a tray. She went to Dom Gaspar first but he waved her away to serve the brothers. Mohamed looked straight into her eyes and she blinked in surprise and lowered hers quickly. Whether she remembered him or not, he sensed he had made an impression on her. Joao did remember him and smiled conspiratorially as he proffered the tray of drinks.

Ali was too concerned with the importance of his mission to touch his drink, Mohamed had to gesture with his head to indicate that he must sip it to avoid causing offence. Ali was flustered. Even Hassan noticed and smiled at Mohamed behind his hand.

Dom Gaspar had used the serving of the drinks as an opportunity to study the three of them. Mohamed wondered if he remembered him but he kept his face expressionless when he felt the Vedor's eyes on him. He had no wish to upset protocol; they waited in silence for him to speak.

"Please convey my thanks to the Kathheb of Utheem for the chance to welcome his three fine sons to Baarah for the first time since I have been atoll chief. I trust your father is well?"

"He is indisposed," said Ali. "He has sent us with this, to explain his absence." Ali held up the roll of dried coconut leaf on which his father had inscribed a message. Joao stepped forward to take it over to the Vedor.

"No, please read it aloud. There should be no secrets between friends and brothers, and our Queen."

The remark intrigued Mohamed because it was definite affirmation of what he had heard. The Vedor was using the authority of Queen Aisha to bolster his own, while ensuring her wellbeing was linked with his, and thus to Portugal. It was a clever ploy, particularly as it made the odious Portuguese representative in Male' appear less important while the Queen was in Baarah.

Ali unrolled the parchment, coughing in embarrassment at the attention thrown on him. It was obvious he wanted to be no more than a messenger and politely take his leave. Mohamed on the other hand, was fascinated and quite happy to gaze on Queen Aisha and her winsome daughter. Hassan seemed to be enjoying it too.

"Our father writes," said Ali, his voice strained, "Greetings to Atoll Chief. I have become weak with old age. Therefore I would like to request you to look into the possibility of transferring my position as island chief to one of my sons."

Dom Gaspar nodded. "Please convey to your father my concern for his good health and thank him for the honour he does me in recommending one of his sons for his post. I will convey his message to Captain Andrade when I am next in Male'." He smiled, evidently deciding the formal part of the audience was concluded.

"I recall," he said, "meeting a youth in Male' who told me the chief of Utheem was his father. He was most helpful to me. Yet I see him not." He looked at Hassan and smiled encouragingly, and then at Mohamed. He was puzzled; he frowned, pulled his nose, and looked again.

"I am he, oh great and noble magnificence," said Mohamed with a bold smile. "I have but recently returned to the Maldives after four years of study in India."

He was aware of Queen Aisha looking askance at the mischievous way he had addressed Dom Gaspar. Quietly she rose to her feet, beckoned to Sitti, and together they walked to the door of the hall.

"You are a great asset to your father," Dom Gaspar was saying, but Mohamed's eyes followed Sitti and he caught her glancing back at him.

"Ah, I see you are anxious to join in the games," said Dom Gaspar as though he understood. "You must spend the night with us! You can return to Utheem tomorrow."

"My lord," said Ali uncomfortably. "Our father is ailing. Since the three of us are here, there is no one to attend him. We should return to Utheem before nightfall."

"But if it is your lordship's wish..." interrupted Mohamed diplomatically, with a glare of reproof at Ali.

"Of course," said Dom Gaspar with a sigh. "How thoughtless of me. You must attend your father." He turned away from Ali and stared into Mohamed's eyes, then looked away with a smile of recollection.

"I hope there will be an opportunity for me to make better acquaintance with you all. I know of your reputation as honest, pious sons of a noble father. I wish him, and you, well. Go in peace."

CHAPTER 14

It was traditional at the time of the Eid festival for islanders to dress in their finest clothes to socialise with visitors from other islands. There would be games, competitions and refreshments. Young men would take part in team wrestling and young women, under the pretext of playing a kind of tag, would chase and touch the men they fancied. It was a time of great hilarity, a welcome break from the routine of hard island life.

Queen Aisha liked the games as much as any of the simple islanders did. She was disappointed, therefore, when she left the Vedor's house to find that the games had stopped. Instead the island women were gathered in groups gossiping outside the house. They were speculating about the three Utheem brothers, discussing how fine and proud they looked, and wondering about the purpose of their visit.

"What a shame!" she said when she saw them idling. "Are the people of Baarah so timid there is no girl with courage enough to make a pass at these handsome men who have come for the Eid celebrations?"

The women stared back at her in silence. She called over one of them, Hawwa Fulu of the Baarah Katheeb's house, and asked what was wrong.

"Our island girls are shy," Hawwa Fulu said. "They are not like the women in Male' who have more experience in these games. There they do not mind touching strangers."

Queen Aisha looked around. "Baarah girls are pretty enough. This is a good time for a real game. Can't we find someone to make a pass at one of the Utheem boys? I will reward whoever is bold enough to do it."

The women seemed shocked at her suggestion. Even when Queen Aisha called some girls by name to take part in the tag game, they lowered their eyes modestly, shaking their heads. "Is this the way Baarah girls get their men, by staring at the ground! It's a game, that's all. Won't anyone play?"

Sitti was embarrassed by what her mother was asking the girls to do. "They are not in the mood," she whispered. "Leave them be."

Queen Aisha caught sight of a girl on the outside of the group. She was dressed in a torn and dirty chemise, the clothes she wore every day. She was one of the poorest people on the island and nobody took much notice of her. She was of age, though, and her head was no longer shaved, although her hair was bedraggled and dull with dust.

Queen Aisha had an idea. "Rehendi, come here."

The girl ducked behind a group of women to hide but Queen Aisha told Sitti to take her by the hand and bring her to the front of the group.

"Rehendi, can you save the womenfolk of Baarah from humiliation? These girls do not want to tag one of the Utheem brothers in sport. If you do as I say, I'll reward you with jewellery. I want to show these fainthearted girls how to play at our Eid festival."

Rehendi was not shy, and she knew she was being picked on as amusement for the Queen's pleasure, not to preserve the tradition of the Eid games. "Madam," she said politely. "What you are asking is beyond the aspirations of a poor girl like me. I will do what you ask for the honour of Baarah, not for reward." She looked at the others.

"Perhaps the girls are shy because they fear the consequences of annoying the great Thakuru brothers. What could happen to me? Only death, and we all have to face that sometime."

Queen Aisha laughed. "Rehendi, the others may be shy but they are not frightened. They are too proud and haughty. They are thinking of the disgrace if the Utheem brothers spurn them. I will dress you in fine clothes so you look like a princess. You will surely win the heart of the one you tag."

The villagers greeted the Queen's plan with excitement. The Utheem brothers were famous throughout the atoll and the idea that Baarah's poorest girl would try to tag one of them was a delightful scandal. Yet later, when they saw how attractive Rehendi looked after bathing at the Queen's well and dressing in clothes belonging to Princess Sitti, they were surprised.

Although Rehendi was fifteen, older than Sitti, she was small. As she stood on one side of Queen Aisha with Sitti on the other, she could have been the princess's sister.

"Now you are pretty enough for any man!" Queen Aisha was delighted by the transformation. "When the brothers come out, you must run after them. The one you should tag is Hassan, the youngest. Ali is married and the other one,

Mohamed, is surely best avoided."

The crowd grew as women came from their houses to watch the sport the Queen had organised. Some of the girls cast jealous glances at Rehendi, regretting now that they had not volunteered. Hawwa Fulu and the other women wondered what would be the outcome of the ruse. Sitti, too, was concerned and felt it was a pity to tease Rehendi, although she did look nice in the clothes borrowed from her. She would have liked to join in the game herself but being the princess she couldn't. Rehendi would play for her.

◆ ◆ ◆ ◆ ◆

Dom Gaspar with Joao at his side led Mohamed and his brothers out of the house to bid them farewell. He had spoken long with Mohamed, asking him about his experiences and at sea. He was interested to learn that he had visited so many ports in the Indian Ocean, as well as the southern islands. He questioned Hassan too, and was amused by Hassan's frank replies. Mohamed felt that the three of them had made a good impression.

At the gate to the compound Dom Gaspar slipped his arm around Mohamed's shoulder, a gesture everyone noticed as a sign of the Vedor's approval. He hugged him briefly then nodded in the direction of the crowd. "All of Baarah has turned out in your honour. Won't you at least take a walk to witness the wrestling, even if you cannot stay long?"

Mohamed looked at Ali and beyond him to Joao who was grinning broadly as though trying to make him agree. "It would be a shame for us to leave without some sport." He winked at Joao and then linked his arms in those of his two brothers and walked with them on either side, down the avenue of people who waved and shouted greetings at them. They all sensed the excitement in the air.

Suddenly Mohamed heard the rustle of someone creeping towards them from behind, but he sensed no threat and took it as part of the fun. He felt a soft blow on his back and then a girl's voice cried out.

"This knock is intended for an Eid head!"

The crowd shrieked with laughter and amazement.

Mohamed's reaction was too quick for the girl to escape. He twisted around, seized the pretty young thing who had tagged him and hoisted her onto his shoulders. The crowd whooped with delight, so he decided to give them something more to talk about. He strode away from his brothers with the girl balanced on his shoulders. Even the youths who had been wrestling stopped to watch.

"Why have you stopped wrestling?" cried Hassan. "Are you so weak you pause for breath when a girl tags someone? Hah! My brother Ali and I will show you the true art of wrestling, so you won't be distracted by the tag game anymore."

He walked onto the field followed by Ali. There were shouts from the crowd at this unexpected development. While some wanted to see what Mohamed would do with the girl on his shoulders, they soon forgot about her as the wrestling erupted into a fierce contest: the youths of Baarah versus the two Utheem brothers.

Mohamed was grateful to Hassan for creating the diversion, drawing attention away from him and the girl. He trotted gently down the lane away from the wrestling, with her on his back. From the corner of his eye, he saw that Princess Sitti was watching him, her face flushed. Queen Aisha leaned forward to reassure her. He hoped she was telling Sitti that the sons of the Katheeb of Utheeem were honourable and she need not worry about her friend.

He decided it was time for some sport of his own. He sensed the girl wasn't frightened and he liked the warmth of her thighs around his neck. He broke into a run, carrying the girl easily on his shoulders since she weighed no more than a sack of cowries. He trotted with her along a lane, past festival revellers who watched him with astonishment, to the other side of the island where waves dashed on the rocky foreshore. He waded into the sea, spray splashing them both.

He expected the girl to beg him to release her but she was laughing with joy. "What are you going to do with me?" she said when he paused with the water up to his waist and swirling around her ankles where they dangled from his shoulders.

"I intend to throw you deep into the sea so you will

drown." He tried to sound fierce although he was oddly elated.

"That will be a happy event."

"What?" Her reply puzzled him. Why wasn't she frightened? Any other girl would have begged him to put her down and let her run back to her family. Then he had a doubt. Even though this was only a game, by carrying her off he must have shamed her family and compromised her. He hoped the people of Baarah would take it in good spirits, as part of the fun of the games.

"Why will your drowning be a happy event?" he asked, pretending to be angry with her for her boldness in tagging him.

"Because I am not the rich girl you think I am from my clothes and my jewellery. I am a poor, destitute child with an invalid mother to look after. Drowning would be a happy end to my miserable life."

He turned his head and looked up at the girl on his back with astonishment. Her young face was the picture of heroic innocence, her eyes bold and fearless as they met his. Then she lowered her lashes modestly.

"Queen Aisha said I must tag you as the younger of the Utheem brothers, because none of the eligible island women were brave enough to do so."

He was amused the Queen had arranged this, especially as the girl had made a mistake. That was surely to his benefit. "What is your name?" He softened his voice so it was not so intimidating.

"I am Rehendi. If you drown me my name will be preserved for posterity. I have one final request. These clothes and these ornaments do not belong to me. You must let me remove them before you drown me and then return them to the Princess Sitti, for they are hers."

Mohamed wondered if she was deliberately calling his bluff or really believed he would drown her. Her story sounded plausible enough but her courage seemed improbable. Remove her clothes and let her die? What sort of girl was she? If she was actually prepared to die because she believed it honourable to do so, she was remarkable and courageous. A girl to value highly. On the other hand, was this her way to trap him into marriage?

"You offer a weak excuse for insulting me by tagging me – instead of my younger brother. Don't you know who I am?" He tried to sound threatening as he stood with the waves crashing around his thighs, splashing her dress as she clung to his back.

"No." She was unperturbed by her mistake. "People told me you are one of the three sons of the Katheeb of Utheem."

"Hah!" He laughed mockingly at the girl. "You tagged the wrong one, and disobeyed what you were told to do by the Queen. I really will have to drop you in the sea now."

"I have already said that I have no care what you do to me. My only concern is that you return to Queen Aisha and Princess Sitti this now very wet dress and her pretty jewellery that they lent me so that I would look worthy enough to tag one of the Utheem brothers." She smiled nonchalantly. "Even if I did tag the wrong one."

This was incredible. She was unfazed by her plight and really was more worried about her borrowed clothes than the possibility of death. He was impressed. Surely destiny had played some part in bringing her to his notice.

"Rehendi, I will grant your request on one condition," he said, lowering his voice so she had to lean forward to hear against the sea's roar.

"What condition is that?" Her breath tingled his ear.

"That you promise to marry me."

She gasped.

"You must. To save your honour, and mine. I have compromised you by bringing you here where no one can see or hear us. It means we must marry."

Her expression changed and he saw fear in her eyes for the first time. She was dismayed. "Please don't mock me. You are a son of the Katheeb of Utheem. You could marry even Princess Sitti. Why do you shame me by asking such a thing of me, the poor wretch that I am?"

"Now I understand!" he said. Determined he would not be rejected. "You are a woman who likes to talk. You are talking so that I will let you stay on my shoulders and not plunge you in the sea." He swooped down so the water washed them both up to his shoulders. "Say Yes or No to my condition. If you do not answer now, I will toss you beyond those breakers."

"Did I climb on your shoulders? Why should I want to stay here? Put me down as you will." She was silent for a moment as she gazed at the waves crashing around them.

He had been trained as a warrior to wait patiently for prey, and he did so now.

"Very well," she said when he did nothing. "If you were to send a person to ask for my hand in marriage, I am prepared to name my dowry. But I have a condition too."

Her spirit amazed him. He was offering marriage instead of death yet she was feisty enough to toy with him.

"You want to bargain! Tell me the condition." He was expecting her to ask for some bauble for herself.

"If I am to be your wife, please do Princess Sitti the honour of asking her to be your wife too."

The time for words had passed. Somehow this simple island girl had divined what lay in his heart. He walked out of the surf back to the beach and gently lowered her to the ground. He turned his back on her and walked away without a word. She would understand. There were certain proprieties to be observed now that she had agreed to marry him.

The wrestling game was still in progress but as soon as Hassan saw Mohamed striding up from the shore, he shouted at Ali. Together they charged the defenders of the opposing team and wrestled their way past them. The crowd cheered their victory. They continued running until they reached the beach where Mohamed waited. He helped them aboard and told them it was time to leave. Ali was relieved. Together they faced the shore and saluted Dom Gaspar and the watching crowd.

He waved back enthusiastically, apparently delighted with the afternoon's activities. Joao, who was standing at the Vedor's side, pretended not to notice Mohamed's extra gesture of farewell, although it was clear he knew it was intended just for him.

◆ ◆ ◆ ◆ ◆

Queen Aisha was pleased. Her efforts had turned the day into a memorable one for Baarah. She waited patiently for Rehendi to return, ignoring the speculation of the village women about what had happened to the girl. Hawwa Fulu accompanied her on her walk back to the house. Although she badgered Rehendi to tell her what Mohamed Thakaru said, the girl kept silent.

The women waiting with Queen Aisha set up a wail of joy when they saw Rehendi was unharmed, even though she was wet and dishevelled. The Queen was surprised at their reaction.

"Rehendi was never in danger," she said, gesturing at them to be quiet. "You are good at imagining the worst."

Rehendi approached and stood obediently before her.

"Tell us what the Thakuru brother said to you!" demanded Hawwa Fulu.

This was too much for the Queen. "I am surprised that you expect Mohamed Thakuru to have said anything to Rehendi. Does a man usually speak to a girl when she tags him? Is that the custom here? It was a game, that's all."

"I asked her that," said Hawwa Fulu with a sniff of hurt pride, "because with my own eyes I saw him speaking to her."

Queen Aisha smiled down at Rehendi. "Child, do not reveal a secret to so many gossipers, lest you be turned to stone."

Rehendi tossed her head back proudly. "I cannot reveal what was not said. Therefore I cannot be turned to stone."

The Queen was pleased with the girl's response. She may be poor but she had a tongue that was a match for any of the island women. Queen Aisha realised that unwittingly she had made a good choice in the girl. She was happy about the outcome, even though the girl had tagged the wrong brother. She had thought that Hassan, being close to Rehendi's age, would have been more inclined to join in the game.

"Go to your home, Rehendi," she said. "You are the prettiest and luckiest girl in Baarah, after Princess Sitti, of course. By your dedication you have added to today's enjoyment, preserved the honour of our women folk, and made yourself rich. You may keep the dress and the jewellery as your own."

As she studied the girl's face, Queen Aisha became aware of a glow of self-confidence about her that she had not seen before. It was something more than the fine, although now damp and spoilt, clothes she had been dressed in. The Queen knew that look.

She guessed that something had indeed happened to Rehendi on the beach. Mohamed Thakuru, she thought with a sigh of satisfaction at the outcome of her idea, would be returning to Baarah soon.

CHAPTER 15

Dom Gaspar liked beautiful things, being fussed over, and a simple life. He knew that he had been virtually pensioned off into a backwater by Dom Antonio, the new Viceroy in India. There were those in Goa who were pleased to see him assigned to the Maldives since he could no longer investigate their own corrupt affairs. For him, it was not a punishment to be in Baarah, but a pleasure. He had achieved a certain stability and a warm, if sisterly relationship, there with the Queen.

Standing on the deck of the vessel bearing him towards Male', Dom Gaspar recognised he had found contentment. He gripped the rail and gazed out at Big and Little Bandos, the two islands they were passing as the ship approached the capital. In Baarah he felt he had family in Queen Aisha and her daughter. He had taken the Queen to Baarah with him as a strategic move, as a hostage for his own safety and to consolidate his position in case of a feud developing with Captain Andrade.

Over the years, Queen Aisha had become a companion. He had improved his Dhivehi through conversing with her, and recognised her strong character and individuality. Watching her daughter, Sitti, grow into a girl of poise and beauty was an education for him. Having spent his whole life exclusively in the company of men, to have charge of two women was a new experience that gave him a feeling of satisfaction.

His old friends in Portugal and Goa wondered how he would survive on a small island with native fisherfolk, and no Portuguese company of his own quality. For him, however, island life was preferable to the long and uncertain voyage back to Portugal and a quiet retirement. He was happy instead to remain on Baarah. He was well looked after by the Maldivians and had his valet, Joao, with whom he could converse in Portuguese if he felt lonely.

Joao was on the voyage with him to Male'. He was a robust lad who was sensible enough to enjoy the advantage of serving the Vedor in Baarah, rather than continue as a cabin boy on a carrack. Dom Gaspar liked having him as his shadow. He looked around and saw that Joao was by the helmsman, watching him alertly. He beckoned him to his side.

"Master?"

"My box. Is it ready?"

Joao thought the question was unnecessary and didn't answer.

"We shall be arriving soon."

Again Joao said nothing, waiting for the real reason why he had been called to the Vedor's side.

"I have not been to Male' for several months," Dom Gaspar said thoughtfully. "Captain Andrade has made the island his own. I hear it is a place where every vice is available for a young man with a few pieces of gold."

"Indeed?" Joao sounded uninterested.

"It is also an island of treachery. Captain Andrade thrives on intrigue, on pitting his courtiers against each other so that they will not be a threat to him. You should be aware of false friends there. It is not like Baarah."

"I understand." Joao nodded and looked at the skyline of Male' as the ship tacked for its approach.

They could see clusters of palm-thatched houses among the coconut trees. Behind the trees was the high wall of Captain Andrade's stockaded fort. The Portuguese flag flew over it, highlighted by the afternoon sun. It reminded the Vedor to fly his own pennant so he told Joao to arrange it.

There were several merchantmen anchored in the roads off the northern shore, which Dom Gaspar noted with satisfaction. He suspected that Andrade was falsifying the trading reports for Male', so that he could accumulate some of the Portuguese-imposed tax for himself. However, as long as there was sufficient commerce to keep the island going, to remit taxes to the Viceroy's representative in Ceiloa and the traditional tribute to the Rajah of Cannanore, he was prepared to overlook Andrade's fiddling.

Although Captain Andrade was not liked in Goa, he was valued for keeping the Maldives within Portuguese influence. The Vedor was under instructions not to antagonise him, and at the same time to exert some check on his excesses. By living out of Male', Dom Gaspar ensured there were not two swords in the same scabbard, and that a cordial working relationship between the two was maintained. He was wondering what would be the outcome of this meeting, their first for nearly a year.

The welcome augured well. In the stern of the boat being rowed to meet him, Dom Gaspar could see the rotund figure of Lord Meedhoo, between two Portuguese officers in full dress uniform. He was glad he was being accorded an official welcome. Joao handed him his hat; he adjusted the plume and put it on.

He climbed down the rope ladder into the eight-oared boat before there was a chance to invite Lord Meedhoo aboard. He acknowledged him, returned the salutes of the Portuguese officers, and then flattered Lord Meedhoo extravagantly in Dhivehi. Meedhoo beamed with pleasure, his lips and gums bright red through chewing betel leaf, adorning his chubby face with the wide grin of a clown.

An armed guard of honour waited on shore. He inspected the men briefly and then walked with them as his escort to the fort. He was pleased by the smart looking sentries on duty at the entrance, and by the work that had been done to fortify the stockade. At least there was proof that Andrade had spent some of what he claimed on improvements.

It was a delight for Dom Gaspar to go through the formalities of the public meeting with Andrade. This was held in the presence of both Portuguese and Maldivian officials.

After they had saluted and embraced one another, Andrade invited the Vedor to sit beside him on the formal swing seat. The Maldivians, who were keenly watching the encounter to see if they could spot a rift in the relationship between the two men, would have taken anything less as a slight to the Vedor.

Dom Gapsar was aware of the attention being paid to his every utterance by the courtiers, and played up to it.

"Greetings my brother, Andhiri Andhirin," he said in Dhivehi, repeating it in Portuguese for the benefit of the soldiers. "Andre Andrade, you are my brother."

Andrade was taken aback by this effusiveness. He blinked, but rapidly entered into the charade, praising Dom Gaspar as his partner in governing the Maldives. They each enquired about the other's health, about the other's household. Andrade asked about the voyage, and Dom Gaspar enquired about the weather in Male'. They agreed, as old friends would, that they had waited too long for this reunion. They toasted each other's good health and long life in a token glass of wine.

It was a superb performance, which satisfied Dom Gaspar and the Maldivians in the courtyard. He was almost disappointed when Andrade called a halt to the public proceedings and invited him to his chamber for a private meeting. Making sure that Joao was in close attendance, he followed Andrade out of the courtyard into the fort. He noticed that Lord Meedhoo and his crown prince were following them but at the entrance to his chamber, Andrade stood aside to let Dom Gaspar pass through. He said something harsh to Lord Meedhoo and his son then closed the door firmly in their faces.

"Well, Dom Gaspar, that was quite a show."

"It is I who must thank you for arranging it. I feel it important to create an impression of solidarity, don't you? And, of course, to maintain etiquette; to set an example. That is the way to show the natives to see we are united in extending to them the benefits of Portuguese colonisation."

"Hah! You'll find Maldivians could beat us when it comes to the formalities of ceremony and small talk."

"I bow to your superior knowledge and experience."

"Yes." Andrade sounded doubtful, wondering if Dom Gaspar was insulting him with his patronising tone. "Let's get down to business."

"By all means." Dom Gaspar sat in a chair away from the open window. He realised that they could certainly be overheard by anyone listening at the window or door, but since they were speaking Portuguese, what they said would be incomprehensible to the islanders.

"The annual tribute?" he asked, dispensing with his usual courtesy.

As he expected, Andrade wasted no time in making an excuse to direct blame away from himself because the tribute hadn't been paid. "Lord Meehoo informs me it is two years since we sent the last payment of dues to Ceiloa. We are supposed to send half from Male' and half from the area you govern. Is your half ready? The Viceroy will not pleased if payment is further delayed."

Although Andrade appeared angry, there was something else on his mind. "Portugal is losing interest in me, in the Maldives," he added unexpectedly.

Dom Gaspar composed his expression into one of compassion so he could learn more about Andrade's state of mind. It was curious that he felt Portugal was neglecting him.

"I have never been to Portugal." There was a note of despair in Andrade's voice.

It was a strange remark and it indicated how Andrade felt inferior as a Mestizo.

Dom Gaspar seized on this weakness. "Then I shall certainly suggest in my next despatch to the Viceroy that you make a visit to Portugal to report to the Emperor in person. You could acquaint him with the prosperity and pleasing aspect of Portugal's possessions here."

His smooth tone hid his conviction that Andre Andrade would never be invited to Portugal. He was Andhirin Andhirin, born in the islands, and that was where he would remain.

"Regarding the tributes," Dom Gaspar said, his voice taking on a severe tone. "It is not for Lord Meedhoo to advise you about payments. That is my responsibility. The cargo to cover payments for two years, including your share from Male' and mine from the atolls, is ready. The delay was necessary while I sought a suitable Maldivian captain to put in charge of the tribute vessel."

Andrade sighed with exasperation. "You will never find a Maldivian you can trust."

"I believe I have. My choice is one of the Thakuru brothers from Utheem."

Andrade sniffed, considering the implications. "We could send any local captain and crew with a detachment of Portuguese soldiers on board. That's the only way to see the Maldivians don't rob us."

"Can you spare soldiers? They could be killed and the tribute stolen if you can't trust the appointed captain. The Utheem brothers, on the other hand, are honest and dependable and totally reliable."

"Can they navigate?"

"Yes, indeed." Dom Gapsar smiled. "One of them, Mohamed Thakuru, has returned from four years in India. I have spoken with him and he has an extensive knowledge through his travels and training of Ceiloa and of the Malabar and Coromendel coasts."

Andrade yawned with the air of a man much bored by debate. "You must take the responsibilty. I am aware of your recent association with the Utheem brothers. Many here are jealous of them."

"Of course! No one can match their success as traders, and their father is an honourable man and a well-respected Katheeb. Look at your native courtiers. Is there anyone you can really trust among them?"

"You are always showing me my weaknesses, Dom Gaspar. I know the reason why some people court and flatter me. Lord Meedhoo informs me of everything."

Dom Gaspar pursed his lips so he didn't have to give vent to his opinion about Lord Meedhoo. "Quite so. He surely has told you that any danger to Portuguese rule would come from the north. That is why I consider it important to have the most influential people in the north supporting us. The only way to keep capable people in our service is to see they are treated fairly and well rewarded."

Andrade grunted, throwing his hands up in the air. "You know as well as I do that our treasury is bare. We cannot afford rewards."

"Status, which costs us nothing, is seen as a reward by people who already have money."

"Status?"

Dom Gaspar sensed he had Andrade trapped. "During the last Eid, the three brothers came to Baarah to deliver Eid greetings to you. They also brought a message from their father containing a simple request. If you grant it we will bind them to us. And it will cost nothing."

"You always were cunning, Dom Gaspar. What is this request of me?"

The Vedor smiled. "Their father feels he is old and would like one of his sons to be appointed Katheeb in his place."

"Good Lord! That's easy enough." He paused as a thought struck him. "Why don't we make all three of them Katheebs? You've got so many islands in your atolls, give them one each."

It was Dom Gaspar's turn to be surprised. The proposal caught him off-guard. He stared at Andrade wondering why he had suggested it. "You know these brothers?"

"If I do not, it matters not. I rely, Dom Gaspar, on your recommendation."

Andrade's smile was oddly menacing. It made Dom Gaspar feel he wasn't in charge of the conversation in the manner he had thought. Was there some depth, some guile, some implication, that he had missed in this interview? He got up from his seat and walked away from the window, stroking his beard.

"Do not think you are the only one with an agenda, Dom Gaspar," Andrade said with a chuckle. "I had reports about Mohamed and Hassan of Utheem when they were in Male' last year. I know they are uncorruptible. Such men are dangerous to us. As Katheebs, with authority, they will become identified with us. Their threat is removed."

"I admire your sagacity." Dom Gaspar meant it. Andre Andrade had learned a shrewdness in Male' that he had not expected of him. Perhaps he had become more Maldivian in personality during his time back in the islands.

"I will see you have the letter of appointment for them as Katheebs, when you return to the north." Andrade brought the meeting to a close with a signal to Joao to open the door. Dom Gaspar turned and walked out with a swagger to disguise his sense of foreboding.

◆ ◆ ◆ ◆ ◆

Dom Gaspar was resting in his room. The previous evening he had been obliged to join Andrade at a dinner party, ostensibly in his honour. It was really an excuse for the captain to lavish hospitality on his Maldivian cohorts and concubines, and to enjoy his favourite Portuguese wine. He became repulsive the more he drank, and ordered the whipping of a hapless servant boy who displeased him. Dom Gaspar wanted to protest but it would have caused an unnecessary scene in public. He had retired soon afterward, pleading fatigue from the journey.

He was gradually aware that Joao was moving around the room, tidying up his clothes. He was making a more commotion than usual, as though trying to attract his attention.

He yawned. "Very well, Joao, what is it?"

"I'm sorry to disturb you, master. If you care to come with me you might hear something interesting."

"What do you mean?"

"There are two nobles arguing in the ante-chamber. I do not understand what they are saying but I heard your name mentioned, and that of Utheem and Katheeb."

Dom Gaspar rose from the bed immediately and slipped his arms into the gown that Joao held up for him. He felt exhilarated at a having a chance to learn what Andrade's nobles were saying. "Good." He patted Joao on his back. "Perhaps we shall learn from them. Show me."

Joao led him from the guest chamber through the doorways hung with silk curtains until they reached the outside of the ante-chamber. They could hear the voices of two men in heated argument inside the room.

"One of them is the fat man who came to meet us when we landed," said Joao in a whisper. "I think the other is the Crown Prince, who acts a secretary."

They heard a high-pitched shouting and Dom Gaspar strained to understand what was being said.

"You must do what Andhiri Andhirin has told you! Write the letter of appointment for the three of them."

Dom Gaspar frowned at the sound of the whining voice of the man he instinctively disliked. "That's Lord Meedhoo," he said softly to Joao.

"It will be bad for us if the Utheem brothers have such power. Three Katheebs can do a lot against our interests." The voice was that of a younger man, probably the Crown Prince.

"Our interests? It is you who lusts for power, boy, not I." By his outburst, Lord Meedhoo sounded hurt.

"You should have opposed this appointment!"

"How can I oppose everything Andhirin wants to do? He would soon dispense with me. Only as his confidante can I know all he is planning. Please write the letter, my son."

"How does it help if we know what he is planning - and do nothing to prevent it when it is against our interests?" The youth sounded bitter. "The Thakuru brothers are from the north; they are allies of Dom Gaspar and he of them. That is why he has persuaded Andhirin to make all three of them katheebs."

Lord Meedhoo bleated in in exasperation. "You worry too much! I know what is going on, you don't."

"I cannot wait for you to do something. I will become Sultan one day, even without your help. I will crush these Utheem brothers, and anyone else who would oppose me."

There was a rustle of curtains being pulled aside. Joao hastily pulled Dom Gaspar away, guiding him back to the guest chamber.

CHAPTER 16

Even though he had long known he should be wary of his Portuguese colleagues, Dom Gaspar was reluctant to admit he had under-estimated the cunning of the Maldivians. His visit to Male' had confirmed his suspicions of potential treachery by the half-blood upstart, Andrade, or Andhirin as he seemed more appropriately known. He saw that as part of the rivalry typical of those who craved the Viceroy's approval. He had not expected treachery from the cohorts Andhirin trusted. The plotting of Lord Meedhoo and his deranged son was dangerous since it could affect the hold of Portugal on the Maldives. Treachery of a colleague was nothing compared with this unexpected treason.

What he should do to stop this spread of rebellion was foremost in his mind on the voyage northwards home to Baarah. His preoccupation with how to influence events blinded him to the incredible beauty of the lush green islets fringed with golden sand set in the heavenly blue of trans-lucent lagoons, although it made the voyage pass quicker. He was aware of Joao's concern about his state of mind since the boy watched him constantly as he sat by himself on deck gazing out to sea for inspiration. He deliberately ignored the presence on board of the four Portuguese sol-diers Captain Andhirin had insisted accompany him 'for security'. He didn't trust them. It made him more apprecia-tive than ever of Joao's loyalty, an adoration he needed to boost his resolve.

He made a decision. "Joao!"

The boy rushed his side, balancing himself to absorb the rolling of the ship in the choppy seas of the channel. The outline of islands marking the southern rim of the northern atoll was ahead of them.

"Joao, tell the helmsman to change course for Utheem. We will go there before returning to Baarah." Dom Gaspar eyed the lad intently to see his reaction to the order. He was gratified by his slight nod of agreement before he turned away to instruct the helmsman. Dom Gaspar sighed. There were so few he could trust and so much intrigue. The only way to contain these pesky flies was to spin his own web.

He did not expect a reception committee at Utheem since there was no advance notice of his arrival. However, the sight of a Portuguese vessel bearing down on the island would not be ignored. He had the Portuguese flag and his pennant run up and a crowd quickly gathered on the beach. He was flattered to see that the rowing boat sent to meet him was under the command of young Hassan Thakuru, a delight indeed as well as an honour. He admired the youth's well-honed physique and beaming smile; it was a pleasure to gaze on such unassuming grace after the ugly undercurrent of treachery at Andhirin's fort.

He disembarked on the beach helped by Joao and clinging keenly to Hassan's proffered arm. He was surprised to see the old Katheeb and his sons were there to greet him. He acknowledged the customary salutations of the Thakuru brothers and nodded at the crowd. Then he strode up to greet Katheeb Hussain Thakurufaan who was seated on a bench at the crest of the beach.

"I have been most concerned about your health, Katheeb," he said. "I felt I should come here straight from Male' to visit you. How are you feeling?"

Dom Gaspar knew that this public display of respect would impress the family, as well as the islanders. Gossip and spies would carry the news to the other islands. He wanted his support for the Katheeb and his sons to be known among the atolls of the north.

The Katheeb responded with the expected pleasantries and then invited him to his house. While the eldest son, Ali, helped his father walk, Mohamed and Hassan flanked him as they strolled to the Katheeb's house. Dom Gaspar told the two armed soldiers who wanted to accompany him, to wait on the beach. He wanted everyone to see he felt safe with the Thakuru brothers. Joao padded after him across the sand carrying the small wooden box he had entrusted to his care.

At the Katheeb's house he was invited to sit on the main platform, the *kuda ashi*, as guest of honour. He recognised the compliment and liked it.

"Before taking my seat, Katheeb," he said at once, breaking the tradition of showing respect for his host with platitudes of courtesy. He wanted them to realise the urgency of his mission, "I have this document of appointment from Captain Andhirin."

Joao stepped forward with the box. He opened it and removed the scrolled parchment inside. With his right hand he handed it to the Katheeb who received it with his right hand, transferred it to his left and held it close to his chest as a sign of respect.

Satisfied, Dom Gaspar sat down cross-legged on the mat placed on top of the dais. He waited for the Katheeb to unroll the scroll, but the old man seemed reluctant to do so.

"This is the answer to your request," Dom Gaspar said, trying to conceal his impatience with the niceties of convention demanded by the situation.

"Oh, Lord Vedor, Dom Gaspar, we are greatly honoured that you personally have brought Captain Andhirin's reply to us."

"I could do nothing less, Katheeb."

While this exchange of mutual admiration took place, Dom Gaspar observed the bearing of the three brothers sitting opposite him on the lower dais, the *bodu ashi*, with their father. In Mohamed's features he could see the lack of fear and the youthful enthusiasm that had enchanted him five years before.

"The letter," he said, when the Katheeb still seemed reluctant to read it, "is the appointment of your sons as Katheebs."

"My sons?" The Katheeb blinked at him from rheumy eyes, his gaze showing his concern that Ali, whom he expected to succeed him, had not been singled out. "I asked for one of them to be appointed in my place."

"I considered it better," Dom Gaspar said carefully, "for you to remain as Katheeb and be able to call on each of your sons should you need assistance. Captain Andhirin was happy to agree to this." He had become so used to lying, he barely noticed that what he said was not true. He felt it unnecessary to give Andhirin the credit for the idea of appointing all the brothers as Katheebs. It served his own purpose as well as Andhirin's.

He looked directly at Mohamed, who would be addressed throughout the islands by the name of Thakurufaan now he had been appointed as Katheeb. "I have another reason for my visit. I have a favour to ask of you." He was pleased by the glitter of willingness that lit the young man's eyes at the prospect of a challenge.

"Allow me to ask what the request is?" Mohamed spoke

with a glance at his father who was still clutching the rolled up parchment as he stared into space.

"You know the seas well." Dom Gaspar permitted himself a slight smile at this private reference to how he had first met Mohamed. "I would like you to captain the ship I must send to Ceylon with the annual taxes."

Mohamed answered without hesitation. "I am honoured by your request. If my father does not object, I am willing to serve you."

Dom Gaspar's smile broadened. "I knew I could rely on you. You must organise everything yourself. There is a vessel in Baarah in need of repair before it can make the crossing. You must inspect it, repair it, and choose your crew."

Dom Gaspar expected his request to fill the old Katheeb with pride. Even if he wanted to refuse to allow Mohamed to sail under the Portuguese flag, after accepting the appointment of his sons as Katheebs, he could not. Dom Gaspar knew the family's prestige was above any petty criticism that they were assisting the Portuguese. He was rather pleased with the way he had arranged everything. Now he could send the outstanding payments to the Viceroy's representative in Ceylon. No one could justly accuse him, as Andhirin had tried at Lord Meedhoo's behest, of failing in his duty as the Vedor.

◆ ◆ ◆ ◆ ◆

The garden pavilion of Vaaruge, the house where Dom Gaspar lived in Baarah, was his favourite retreat. It was cooled by the breeze that wafted in through open louvres of wood and privacy was created by silk curtains hanging from its roof beams and at its entrances. Varuuge had none of the grandeur of the fort that Andhirin had built for himself in Male'. Dom Gaspar was content with a modest abode, with guestrooms and a garden for entertaining, and a separate pavilion as his quarters. There he was tended by Joao who slept on cushions on the mat beside his bed, always close to him when needed.

He was reclining on the swing seat inside the pavilion pondering what should best be done in the interests of Portugal when he became aware of someone brushing aside the silk curtains and standing in the shadows watching him.

"Joao?" He was suddenly alert at the silence, knowing no one else would dare to disturb him when he was relaxing.

"Not Joao!" It was Aisha's voice and from its sharp tone, he knew she was upset. He sat up as the queen settled herself on a cushion beside the swing. "You must be tired after the voyage?"

That the queen should come to see him in his personal pavilion without informing him first was unusual. He parried her question, ignoring its facetiousness, while he tried to guess what was amiss.

"Why should I be tired?" He leaned back on the swing seat and studied Aisha. Her composed countenance gave no clue but he knew enough about her to sense the anguish she was concealing behind that mask of complacency.

"If not tired, my lord, perhaps worried?"

He glanced around the pavilion for Joao and was relieved to see his outline beyond the silk drapes. He frowned at Aisha. "Have I reason to worry?"

"I was merely wondering about your visit to Utheem in such a great hurry, even before returning here, which protocol required." The queen sounded peeved. "People do talk, you know."

"Then you, too, must know the reason by now. It was to hand over the letter appointing the three Utheem brothers as Katheebs. Now they will each be addressed as Thakurufaan."

"So I heard. Is it wise to favour them so much?"

"If I am helpful to them, I expect they will be helpful to me."

"Of course." Aisha smiled and arranged her dress around her on the mat. She was trying to appear unconcerned. "When you were in Male', did you happen to meet Lord Meedhoo and his son?"

"Yes." He was alert now, suspecting this was the real reason for her coming to his pavilion unannounced. "Why do you ask? You have closer relatives for you to be concerned about."

"I will explain. I have received a letter from the Crown Prince. It was brought by someone on the vessel on which you sailed from Male'."

He pulled himself upright in alarm, steadying the swing and stared at her in disbelief. "I was not informed!"

"Here is the letter." Aisha produced it from the folds of her dress. "The Crown Prince announces his intention of marrying Princess Sitti. You can read it yourself."

He brushed it aside, feeling the anger boil inside him. This was a move he had not anticipated. "I will not read such a letter. If that so-called Crown Prince sent this letter to you without my permission, on my ship, sailing under the Portuguese flag, it is a deliberate insult. I am surprised you even brought it to my notice."

"I must do so, my lord, out of respect for you – to inform you what is afoot."

"And what is that?"

"The Crown Prince knows that if he marries Princess Sitti he is assured of becoming the next Sultan. I am worried. He and his father are people of consequence and could do me, you – us - harm if we refuse their request."

Dom Gaspar tried to control his rage. He tore the letter from Aisha's hand and flung it to the floor. He was angered by the thought of that pompous jackanapes even thinking of marrying Sitti. *What the scoundrel would do so blatantly in his lust for power!* "Have you told the child about this?"

"It was my duty so to do."

"And what did she say?" He bit his lip. Sitti would not understand what lay behind this proposal. It might even sound desirable to her to move to Male' as the wife of the prospective Sultan.

"Sitti says that it is the custom for Muslim girls to wait until they are of age before marrying. She says that since you are her father now, she will do whatever you decide."

He calmed at hearing those words. "You see what a sensible girl she is. I am not the one to break her heart and go against her wishes."

"We will have to reply to the letter."

"Why? It contains the ravings of a madman. We will ignore it." He folded his arms across his chest and looked at her with defiance in his eyes.

"I know what devilry is abroad in Male'. Even some of our Portuguese officers have succumbed to lavish bribes from the Crown Prince. They report to him all that Captain Andhirin decides. He and his fat-bellied father have too much influence over Andhirin." He tugged at his beard. "And now they are trying to worm their way into the bosom of my adopted family. Sitti is right, she is my daughter now. It grieves me to think how the Crown Prince intends to use her."

He watched Aisha rise to her feet and leave the room without a word. It was then he became aware that Princess Sitti had been sitting in the shadows, listening to every word.

◆ ◆ ◆ ◆ ◆

Marriage in the Maldives was an easily contracted partnership. Youths married at will; a man was permitted four wives by law, as long as he was able to support them all. However, a girl without a father had to be 15 before marriage was possible and even then the consent of a magistrate had to be obtained. A girl with a father could get married at 11 and fathers were usually keen to see their daughters married, even at such a young age, as the result was one less child at home to feed and clothe.

Thoughts of marriage had been on Mohamed's mind ever since the Eid games at Baarah. He remembered that Rehendi told him she was without a father, so he would require permission from the magistrate. The Vedor's visit to Utheem and the appointment of him as Captain of the tribute vessel was the excuse Mohamed needed to visit Baarah. However, he was not keen on requesting his own father's blessing for the marriage as he sensed it would be withheld.

Instead, he discussed with his father the necessity of one of the sons going to Baarah to repay the courtesy of the visit made by the Vedor. Since Ali was married and was spending most of his time on his wife's island, either he or Hassan should make the courtesy call. It was not difficult to convince his father that he should be the one to go.

The pinnace was prepared and a week after the Vedor's visit, on a Friday after the noon prayers, Mohamed was ready to set out.

Hassan accompanied him to the beach. "Why do you go alone?" he asked, barely able to conceal his envy.

Mohamed ignored his mood. "You know I must go alone even though I would prefer to have your company. Someone has to stay here with father."

"While someone has fun with all those unmarried girls in Baarah?"

"Hassan! I go to pay my respects to Dom Gaspar. It is a duty visit."

"Then why do you leave Utheem so late in the day? You will be unable to row there and return before nightfall. You will have to stay the night in Baarah."

"Exactly! Do you recall how Dom Gaspar was disappointed we could not stay for dinner on our last visit? This time I will not have to upset him by refusing his invitation."

Hassan hummed knowingly to himself. "You learned more than navigation, martial arts and religion in India, my brother. You developed a taste for girls too, didn't you? Perhaps I should prepare betel leaf as a welcome for your return?"

Mohamed shrugged, amused by his brother's sharp intuition. Betel leaf was exchanged at important events like a wedding. He clasped Hassan affectionately on his shoulder. "Do as you please," he said with a grin as he climbed aboard the boat. "Betel is always welcome for its welcome. Women like it especially." He shouted at the oarsmen to start rowing, leaving Hassan standing on the beach watching him quizzically.

He considered Hassan's words as the boat rose and fell in the sea, spray slapping his face whenever waves splashed its side. The eight oarsmen struck out boldly and he let them row at a good pace until they were in sight of Baarah. Then he bade them row slower. "We shall anchor off the beach and after my visit to the Vedor we shall try some night fishing."

In his mind was Hassan's remark about betel leaves,

something he had forgotten. An exchange of betel leaves was essential for what he intended. He had already learned before setting out that Dom Gaspar was not in Baarah, which was why he was anxious to make his visit that night. He had another matter to pursue and would be obliged to find betel leaves to accomplish it.

The dark carpet of night draped Baarah by the time the boat reached the island, and Mohamed steered it in close to the beach. He jumped into the surf and made his way silently across the beach to Vaaruge, the Vedor's residence. He expected a guard there to inform him that Dom Gaspar was not in residence, and that was exactly what happened. However, he did not expect to meet Fulu, one of Queen Aisha's handmaids. She was standing under a tree talking to friends and called to Mohamed as he was moving away from the guard's flaming torch.

"I remember you from your visit for the Eid festival when you were tagged by Rehendi," said Fulu boldly. "The girls never stop talking about when you will return for her."

"Please keep my return as your secret, Fulu," he said, wondering how much he could trust her. "I was hoping to pay a courtesy call on the Vedor."

"Why is that a secret, pray?"

"Others might think I am here for another reason."

Fulu, who was a pretty girl with a winning smile, was well used to repartee, having learned much from her mistress. She giggled at his answer. "What other reason could you possibly have, Mohamed Thakurufaan, to be strolling in the dark of Baarah at night?"

"I am returning to my boat to go fishing."

"If you are hoping to land a good catch, Mohamed, there is one whom I know would take your bait."

He looked at her in surprise, but kept his face in the shadow so she did not see how embarrassed he was at the reason for his presence being so apparent. "I was not aware that fish are so foolish in these waters."

Fulu stifled her giggle. "Mohamed, even that which you are aware of is not what it seems. My dear friend Rehendi, whom you carried off on your shoulders, is not a princess as you might think. There are, as some of us know, other fish in the Baarah lagoon."

"A better catch, you mean?"

"A better princess, I mean."

Mohamed chuckled thoughtfully. "Now I know you are casting your own line." He bid her farewell, disturbed by her remark yet convinced that what he was going to do was the right course to take. As he reached his boat, he called for one of the oarsmen to bring his box. He told the rest of the men to wait for him so they could go fishing after midnight.

He made his way to the house of a friend of who had been expecting him, since he was the man who had sent the message about the Vedor's absence. The friend escorted him and the boatman with the box to the house where Rehendi lived. It was no more than a shack of dried palm leaves in the jungle at the very edge of the village, but he had no eye for the miserable poverty of the place.

He went up to the shack's entrance blocked with a screen of palm leaves and called Rehendi by name. There was no reply only a sudden silence, like a sigh, in the night noise of the forest. After a pause, the chirping chorus of crickets resumed. He uttered Rehendi's name impatiently until he saw the flickering of a candle being lit, and the screen was pushed aside. A girl, with her frightened mother standing beside her, peered out. Mohamed's heart leapt when he saw her wide, trusting eyes, and that confident but modest smile. His gaze dropped to the taut nakedness of her breasts, like polished bronze in the glow of the candle light.

"Rehendi," he said, trying to keep his voice steady. "Here are two honest citizens to bear witness to my proposal. Here in this box," he took it from the oarsman and laid it at her feet, "is your wedding dress and ornaments. Name your dowry for our marriage, as you promised."

To Rehendi's credit, she recovered smoothly from the shook of seeing him, and of his proposal. She smoothed her long tresses over her breasts with both hands and then ventured a slight, braver smile. "I did promise."

She lowered one hand and he caught sight of a plump, dark rose nipple as she reached for her mother's arm. Whether this was to give her surprised mother assurance or to gain it for herself, Mohamed wasn't sure.

Rehendi spoke softly, toying with her hair flowing across her bosom in a way that stirred Mohamed so much he scarcely heard what she was saying. It never occurred to him that she must have been practising this speech while he was languishing in Utheem wondering how to approach her.

"Gold equivalent to seven dinars would be my dowry. However, I am without a father so you must first seek permission from the magistrate, as my official guardian, for his consent to my marriage."

She gazed at him with a boldness that hit him in his heart. The challenge in the depths of her charcoal black eyes sent his spirit soaring. He reached out to hold her and then realised, as her mother shifted nervously, that he must remember protocol. He coughed, confused.

"Alas, I have no betel leaves in my humble home for this occasion," Rehendi said simply, showing more self-assurance than he did.

"Oh yes, I mean no." Mohamed tugged at his beard in anxiety. "I forgot. I will arrange something. We must do this properly."

It became a night of hectic activity. Mohamed, who considered himself brave and resourceful, wondered why he felt out of his depth. He hurried first to the house of a neighbour and asked him to sell some betel leaves. Although it was night, the man lit a flambeau and went to his garden and cut his biggest creeper of leaves. He refused payment because of the respect he had for the Katheeb of Utheem and his desperate son.

To fulfil the formalities properly, Mohamed returned to Rehendi's house and presented the betel leaves to her in the presence of his friend and the boatman as his two witnesses. Next he rushed to the house of the magistrate and roused him from sleep, requesting his permission to marry Rehendi. The magistrate tried to dismiss him, saying he was temporarily lovesick and should not disturb him so late at night. Only when he saw how determined Mohamed was and the two witnesses affirmed the girl was willing, did he give his consent.

As Mohamed approached Rehendi's house, he was amazed to see the crowd of neighbours that had gathered there. He paused in the shadow of a coconut grove to watch, while keeping out of sight. Rehendi's mother had gone to Vaaruge, at Rehendi's request, and informed Queen Aisha and her daughter that if they wanted to see her just this once, they must hurry to her house. Her mother repeated the same message to everyone she met. The neighbours rushed to the shack expecting to find the girl in her death throes. Instead she was looking radiant as she greeted them in the dress given her by Queen Aisha. They soon caught her mood of excitement, and only Princess Sitti seemed subdued.

"We must get more betel leaf prepared," said Queen Aisha, clapping her hands. "And let us send to Vaaruge for more lamps to brighten this wedding house."

Fulu, the Queen's handmaid, was despatched for the lamps.

Sitti sat down on the mat beside Rehendi. "How lucky you are to be married," she said in a low voice. "Why didn't you tell us before, instead of surprising us with this late preparation?"

"I sent for you the very minute I myself knew."

The twittering excitement of the women in the house died as the deep voice of a man was heard outside. Mohamed spoke huskily so no one would recognise his voice. "Rehendi, step out and see your husband!"

Rehendi swallowed, her eyes filled with tears of joy but mingled with sadness as she saw Sitti's crestfallen gaze. Her friend looked as though she might faint.

"Take these," said the Queen, pushing her way to Rehendi's side and pressing the prepared wedding betel leaves into her hand. "You must present these to your new husband as confirmation of your betrothal."

Rehendi stepped out into the night, walking beyond the rim of light thrown by the coconut oil lamps. She passed into the glade of palm trees where Mohamed, unseen by the crowd, waited in the shadow's depths. He held out his hands for her and accepted the betel. At the touch of her fingers on his he felt incapable of controlling himself. He grabbed the betel leaf, put a sheaf in her hand, and turned away, anxious that Rehendi should not see the bright light of desire burning in his eyes. He plunged hastily deep into the forest's ferny gloom.

Behind him he heard the cries of women asking each other who was this mysterious husband who had fled into the night. He glanced around and saw Rehendi and Sitti holding hands as they peered into the jungle. He waved slowly, but it was too dark for them to see him.

He hurried back to the beach, his heart light that at last he had a wife, although his body was afire. The oarsmen heard him coming and were ready as he hauled himself aboard. Without waiting for his orders, they rowed the boat swiftly out into the open sea.

"Now," he said like a shout of glee, "it's time to go night fishing."

CHAPTER 17

At sunrise the next day Mohamed returned to Utheem. He let the oarsmen row slowly homewards, stopping occasionally to fish by dangling lines over the boat's side. He himself held a line as the boat ploughed through the water. He had no interesting in fishing, though, as he contemplated what would be his father's reaction to his marriage. The thought of it drove away his proud moment of joy at the sight of Rehendi... and knowing that she was his.

He sat silent and thoughtful in the boat's stern, staring at the dark and ceaseless rushing of the waves illuminated by the grey light of the moon. He noticed only by instinct when there was a tug on his line. He pulled in his catch and tossed it on the pile of flapping fish in the boat's hold. The oarsmen were puzzled by his change of mood, especially as the one who had accompanied him ashore told them in an excited whisper what he had witnessed.

Katheeb Hussain was walking on the beach, aided by a neighbour, as they rowed up to the island. He was on his way home from dawn prayers. Mohamed jumped out of the boat as soon as it scraped the sand and waded ashore. He saluted his father and held his arm, telling the neighbour to go, and walked with him towards their compound. His father's breathing was as laboured as his gait and Mohamed was saddened at how feeble his father seemed.

"Fish?" his father asked softly, starting the conversation.

"Yes, father." Mohamed wondered how to explain what had happened. He didn't want to upset him so decided to wait until later. "The Vedor was away from Baarah, so we did not stay. I let the men fish on the way home."

"You must be tired." His father withdrew his hand from his arm and walked on ahead unaided. "I shall let you sleep and then you will tell me about your visit."

Mohamed sighed. When his father made even a simple command like that, there was no defying it. He wasn't tired; he was in love. However, he went into the house, spread his mat on the *bodu ashi* beside Hassan, who was still sleeping, and lay down. Within minutes he fell asleep, even as he realised that the oarsman who had accompanied him to Rehendi's house would soon be telling everyone about his betrothal.

He woke after the noon prayer to the sound of his father and Hassan preparing to have lunch. He joined them as his father uttered the traditional words to begin the meal: *In the name of Allah, the Most Gracious, the Most Merciful.* Hassan helped himself to rice and started to eat. His father served himself shakily, slowly raising a handful to his mouth. Mohamed took a portion of rice and some fish, dipping his fingers listlessly in and out of the food on his plate. Strangely he lacked appetite, in contrast to Hassan's ravenous enjoyment of the meal.

His father coughed, addressing Hassan. "I hear from everyone in Utheem that last night Mohamed went to Baarah and married the poorest girl there. He has left her there, considering we are not worthy to receive her, or even to be informed of this event."

He turned his head to address Fathimafaan who was standing behind him. "See how our brave Mohamed eats. I find it difficult to swallow food myself. The young today are a peculiar lot."

Mohamed was stunned by the rebuke. He put down the handful of rice he was about to raise to his mouth and stared at his father. His heart was full of sorrow for what he had done to the old man. He had tried to spare him anguish but his father had found out before he could explain. In shame, unable to speak, he scrambled to his feet and walked out of the house.

He went to the beach at the far side of the island where he played as a child. Birds still patrolled the scrub and the beach, but he took no notice of them. He sat on a patch of grass and stared out to sea, losing his mind in the churning waves climbing higher and smashing down, then rushing up to the sand and retreating. He became absorbed by the motion of the world turning, losing his consciousness in deep meditation. His body hardened, rigid with love for poor Rehendi, thrilled by her obedience to him and inspired by her innocent trust. He longed for her.

◆ ◆ ◆ ◆ ◆

Queen Aisha was having her long, dark hair brushed by her maid, Fulu, when one of the village women came to the gate of Vaaruge. Aisha could hear the woman asking the gateman to let her pass and sent Fulu to see what was amiss. She hoped nothing had happened to the Vedor who was visiting other islands in the atoll. He was a good man, dedicated to his work. He showed her every respect and was so fond of Sitti.

When he returned she would have a lot to tell him about the betrothal of Rehendi to Mohamed Thakurufaan. It worried her a little that, since the betrothal, Sitti seemed downcast. It could be because she was losing her friend, or perhaps simply because the Vedor was away. Sitti was normally quiet, difficult to encourage to high spirits so she wasn't too concerned.

Aisha looked up at the women who were approaching from the gate. She rose quickly in surprise, her hairbrush falling from her lap to the floor. Hawwa Fulu of Baarah Katheeb's house and another woman she did not recognise accompanied her handmaid. Only when she came nearer did she realise the woman was Fathimafaan, daughter of the Katheeb of Utheem.

"Come, come," she said warmly, pleased to have a visitor. She was wondering whatever had occurred to bring Fathimafaan to Baarah, but she had to wait until the usual pleasantries were exchanged to find out. To her delight, it did not take long for Fathimafaan to start speaking in hushed tones of the extraordinary events at Utheem.

"You must have heard how Mohamed is such a determined person. He takes after our father in that way," she said. "Mohamed did not tell father of his marriage to Rehendi before father heard it from others. So father reprimanded Mohamed. He just stopped eating and walked out of the house."

Queen Aisha sucked in her breath with an admonitory hiss to disguise her apprehension at what scandal Fathimafaan might relate, since she herself was responsible for the start of it.

Fathimafaan was not to be silenced. "He has been away from the house for a week, sleeping on the beach, not even coming home to eat. Yesterday father called for Hassan and me. He told us he realised that by his actions Mohamed had married the girl he loves. He said that since Mohamed had not brought her home, Hassan and I must come for her. So here we are."

Aisha clapped her hands with relief. She liked a good love story and here was one that she had herself created. She told Fulu to run to Rehendi's house and make the girl prepare, and to come to Vaaruge for a farewell party.

"We should not stay long," said Fathimafaan. "Hassan is waiting with the boat."

"I understand. You can leave after sunset. It is not fitting for a noble person's new wife to be taken home in broad daylight, even by sea." She sighed. "If only I could accompany her but the Vedor is away so I am obliged to remain here."

While they were waiting for Rehendi, the Aisha gave instructions for refreshments to be served. She also sent word to some of the women of the island to join her so that Rehendi would have a proper farewell. She was aware that

Sitti was watching the preparations with doleful eyes.

"Don't be so downcast," she said. "Your friend Rehendi will be close by, on Utheem, so she can visit us often."

Sitti said nothing.

"It's her age," Aisha whispered to Fathimafaan. "Young girls are often moody."

Rehendi entered the compound accompanied by Fulu and some of the women who had been at the games and refused to tag the men. They were chirruping like birds in their excitement.

"This is a happy moment for us because we began this process which has resulted in such a romantic marriage," Aisha announced in the manner expected of a queen. "Your luck has changed, Rehendi."

From the corner of her eye, she saw Sitti turn away sadly. It made her wonder if there was more to her daughter's moodiness than a passing phase. She shrugged away her concern to concentrate on Rehendi. "Are you ready to go to your husband's island?"

"Yes." Rehendi wasn't in the least bashful. "However, I am sad at leaving my mother behind."

Aisha took her hand and squeezed it. "Don't be saddened by that. Living obediently with one's husband fulfils a woman's purpose in life. Your mother is always welcome with us, we will treat her as our sister and she won't be lonely."

Even she was impressed by the dignified way that Rehendi conducted herself. She found it astonishing how borrowed raiment could change a chit of a poor girl into a beautiful, hopeful bride. She felt proud of what she had done for the girl.

"Doesn't she look pretty?" she said to Sitti, hoping to encourage her to be cheerful. "Won't you say goodbye to your friend?" She watched as Sitti embraced Rehendi, wondering what words of nonsense she was whispering into her ear. Rehendi said something in return and then the two girls embraced again, with more affection than before, as tears started to stream down their cheeks.

"Come, come, come!" Aisha said, urging the two girls to walk towards the beach. Dusk had fallen and it was time for the farewells to finish.

Even Fathimafaan was weeping. "These are tears of joy," she explained. "Now everything will be all right at home between Mohamed and our father. He is old and he is sick and in pain, that is why he has been difficult. I am sure he will be happy when he sees Mohamed's bride. It is time for life to return to normal at home."

♦ ♦ ♦ ♦ ♦

After seeing Rehendi and Fathimafaan board Hassan's sailing boat for the voyage to Utheem, Queen Aisha walked back to the house. She clasped her daughter's hand in hers and walked with a light step. She was thrilled by the events, especially as it had turned out so well.

"You must be happy for Rehendi," she told Sitti. "Such a fine husband too. Just because we gave her one of your old dresses to wear for that silly game of tag!"

She heard Sitti's sob and felt her pull her hand away. "Ah," she said with a sense of relief. "Now I know what is wrong with you. You want a husband too! Well, perhaps we shall arrange something with that noble lord from Male'. Would you like that?"

Sitti's reaction frightened her. The girl went a deathly pale and her eyes rolled up, showing only the whites.

"Child, what is wrong?"

Sitti slowly slipped to the sand without a sound.

"Fulu, come quickly!" Aisha clapped her hands loudly. "Our dear daughter has fainted."

The women carried Sitti's seemingly lifeless body into Vaaruge and placed her on the swing seat in the middle of the queen's room. No one knew what to do. Queen Aisha asked for some charmed water that had been blessed by having verses of the Holy Quran recited over it. Fulu tied a necklace of charmed leaves around the girl's neck.

"It must be the excitement and the heat," said Aisha, glad that Dom Gaspar was not at home to see Sitti looking as though she were at death's door. He would surely blame her for the girl's condition. He would think she had shouted at her, or demanded too much of her sensitive nature.

She found it difficult to understand Sitti; she was so submissive and gentle yet she, her mother, was so strong in mind. Sitti's real father, Sultan Ali, had been strong in body so she was sure Sitti must have some strong qualities. The thought of her dead husband delivered a sudden shiver of passion through Aisha's body.

"You must not get sick too," said Fulu, thinking the queen was feeling cold.

"That is nothing. Quick, sprinkle the charmed water on the child's face."

There was such a keening of women in distress, all crying with sympathy at the likelihood that Sitti was dying, Aisha soon found it tiresome. She hated displays of false emotion and blamed her daughter for being the cause of it. She leaned over and slapped Sitti's cheek vigorously.

What a relief it was when Sitti promptly opened her eyes. Aisha gestured to the wailing women to keep quiet and leaned down again to hear what she was saying.

"Who sprayed me with water? What are these things around my neck?" Sitti sat up, taking in the sight of the women crowded into the room.

Aisha tried to put her arms round her shoulder to comfort her, but Sitti shrugged her off, making her wonder why her daughter was so cool towards her. Sitti tore of the necklace of leaves around her neck.

"You should wear the leaves, dear child." Aisha's voice was tearful with concern. "You are not yourself."

Some of the women began to speculate that a genie had possessed Sitti, or that an evil spirit had been cast on her to make her collapse - only to revive in such a petulant mood, so unlike her gentle spirit.

"Mother, please ask these people to go."

Sitti looked desperate so Aisha did as she requested and ushered everyone out of the room. "Dearest Sitti," she said as soon as they were alone. "What ails you? Is there anything I can do?"

"No, mother." Her voice was soft with melancholy. "Leave me alone."

Aisha was at a loss to explain her daughter's behaviour the next day when the Vedor returned. "We have sprinkled her with charmed water when she was asleep, and put charmed leaves all around her mat to keep away evil influences. I myself put a magic unguent on her forehead. She just wiped it off."

She allowed Dom Gaspar to peep through the curtain of the chamber where Sitti was lying on her bed, so he could see the condition she was in. He wrinkled his long nose at the smell.

"Is that the magic you are using to make her recover?'

"It is what the healers recommend."

"Oh Aisha!" he said, sounding disappointed. "Sitti has suffered some kind of shock. None of your black magic will cure her. She will recover her normal good spirits by herself. Leave her alone, don't nag her, let her reflect on her situation, and she will understand what is troubling her. We cannot help."

Queen Aisha followed the Vedor back to the main chamber. She sat opposite him and scratched her ear thoughtfully. "Perhaps Sitti needs to be married. She has seen Rehendi blooming with happiness. Perhaps we should consider again the proposal from the Crown Prince?"

She saw the rage light up in Dom Gaspar's face and immediately regretted raising the subject. He had arrived that morning by a sailing ship which had come from Male' with some Portuguese officers. She had sensed he was agitated but had ignored the warning signs because of her anxiety over Sitti. Now she feared she had set off his wrath.

"Crown Prince!" He spat out the words, his pale face turning puce with anger. She wondered if he had been drinking the Portuguese wine she had heard so much about. He was even clenching his fists.

"Please do not upset yourself. I was only thinking about Sitti. My concern confused me."

"Yes, yes." He took a deep breath, his face gradually returning to its normal pallor. "I know this is not of your making. You do not know what I have heard."

"What is that?" She was agog with curiosity. "Is it news from Male'?"

He nodded, frowned, and then sighed again. "Your choice of a husband for Sitti continues to plot against me. You take a cobra to Sitti's bosom and yours if you ever let him come near her."

She caught her breath. "What have you heard?"

"Your dear crown prince seems to know everything that happens here. He even knows I threw aside his letter of proposal. He is in a rage that we spurn him. The puppy thinks he can marry Sitti and that Lord Meedhoo will marry you, and then together they will rule the Maldives."

She felt the flush of anger burning her cheeks. "That is nonsense!"

"At last you understand."

"How can they rule if you and Andhirin are here?"

"My spies tell me Lord Meedhoo and his whelp have a scheme worthy of the devil himself. They are turning Captain Andhirin against me. I am the only one stopping their plans of taking over so they want me out of the way, somehow."

"Since you know of this, why don't you challenge Andhirin? Couldn't you have him dismissed and take his post yourself? Then you could exile Lord Meedhoo and his son."

"Ah, my dear Queen, we no longer live in the days of the Sultans. I do what the Viceroy commands. Captain Andhirin is sure to pick a quarrel with me if he thinks it would make me leave Baarah, or even condone my death if he thinks I will try to oust him."

He took the glass of water from Joao who had slipped into the room and was standing silently as though waiting instructions. "Do you want some refreshment, my dear?" he asked.

Aisha shook her head. She was thinking. "I know Meedhoo very well. His object in life is to amass riches. He lacks the will to connive with his son the way you suggest. He would not want to rock the boat he rows so happily through the coffers of Andhiri Andhirin, and Portugal."

She watched the Vedor's expression harden. It was difficult to understand him at times. He applied his foreign notions to Maldivian society and came up with odd conclusions. She had thought that her daughter's marriage to the Crown Prince would be a consolidating move but, if what the Vedor said was true and she herself was to be part of the bridal package, she must change her plans.

CHAPTER 18

Mohamed scanned the sky carefully, noting the wisps of cloud scattered in ragged patches as though cast into the heavens by an angry hand. He raised his head and sniffed the air, the breeze tugging at his hair as he stood by the tiller of the sailing boat. He stroked his beard thoughtfully.

Hassan, who was standing by the mast, noticed his concern. "Don't worry, Mohamed, the weather will hold. You'll soon be back with your wife."

Mohamed answered only with a nod of his head as he gazed again at the sky. *How like Hassan to be the optimist*, he thought. He had chosen this course home from Male' between two atolls because he suspected the weather would be capricious. Their voyage to and from Male' had been successful and soon they would be back in Utheem. He was glad.

He had found Male' rotten with intrigue. Friends on the waterfront told him of rumours about the Crown Prince and his jealousy of the Utheem brothers. They warned him repeatedly to beware of him. It mattered not to Mohamed. He was interested only in conducting his business and doing what was required of him.

The news that he was to captain the tribute boat to Ceylon with taxes for the Portuguese gave him a status he felt he did not deserve. Even Hassan had suggested that he make a courtesy call at the court of Andhiri Andhirin. He had no time for such niceties saying they were in Male' to trade, not to petition for anything. He explained to his friends that he must sail back home as soon as possible to catch a fair wind and current. And to see his wife, they responded.

In truth, he was disturbed by the attitude of the Portuguese occupiers of Male'. Protocol and routine appeared to have been jettisoned in favour of a very casual approach to tradition. Captain Andhirin no longer received petitioners in open session at his fort. He surrounded himself with his cronies and had little contact with the people, except through Lord Meedhoo and his son.

Mohamed heard how Lord Meedhoo had taken another wife. She was the grandmother of the daughter of Sultan Ali's second wife. Mohamed had seen that child being carried by her mother when he helped Queen Aisha and Princess Sitti flee the palace years before. The mother had died while the girl was still young and the child's grandmother raised her. She was Sitti's half sister while her grandmother was a daughter of a former Sultan. It seemed to Mohamed that Lord Meedhoo was using every strategy he could to retain a royal connection, as well as influence over Captain Andhirin.

He was shocked when he heard how both Lord Meedhoo and his son had abandoned the discipline of their faith and no longer attended prayers at the Friday mosque. Not only that, the Mudin's call to prayer had been silenced and people were forgetting the customs of the religion that had sustained them for four centuries. Under the influence of Captain Andhirin, greed for money and a lust for pleasure had become the new order in the capital.

This distressed Mohamed so much that he deliberately ignored the customary courtesy of paying respects to Captain Andhirin, as he would have done to the Sultan. Why should he, since he did not respect him? Compared with the Vedor, who was a man of compassion and understanding, Andhirin was no better than a pirate. Mohamed felt that if he were to call on him voluntarily, then he would be condoning the dreadful things Andhirin was doing to rip apart the fabric of Maldivian culture and society.

As if sharing his dark mood the sky as he gazed at it was deepening to gloom. He looked around, taking his bearings again. Malos Madulu was to the east and Miladu Madulu to the northwest. He calculated the storm he sensed was brewing would break on them within a couple of hours.

◆ ◆ ◆ ◆ ◆

"Why are you changing course, Mohamed?" Hassan shouted from where he was crouched on a thwart baiting a hook. "Don't you want to hurry home to Aiminafaan?"

"With father in such poor health, Hassan, it is for him

we must hurry home." He didn't want Hassan, or anyone, to know how much he missed his wife. He had given Rehendi the name Aiminafaan when she came to Utheem. She had become a joyous companion. Her willingness to do anything for her new family made her a treasure for them all. She was a great help to his sister Fathimafaan, especially in caring for the old Katheeb who could no longer walk. Most of all, she was a gentle presence that softened his heart.

"We may have to delay our return by a night, Hassan. That would be better than being away for ever."

"You worry too much, Mohamed. It's just a passing cloud." Hassan gestured contemptuously at the sky, dismissing the clouds as being of little concern. "We have bartered enough in the islands. Let us use this strong wind to take us home speedily."

Mohamed said nothing. He was watching the sea, feeling its growing impatience in the way the swells lifted the bow of the boat and slapped it down again. The boat was their father's thirty-one-feet *bandu odi*, ideal for sailing between the islands but not reliable in a sudden storm in the channels. He had made many voyages between the atolls since Aiminafaan had become his wife and his father had slipped into decline. With Ali looking after the administration of their enterprises, he and Hassan were entrusted with trading, the buying and selling of goods throughout the atolls.

He had learned a lot about the local waters from Ali and, through his training in seamanship, was able to recall every mark and sign. His knowledge of the islands was unrivalled and he would sometimes make detours simply to discover characteristics of different atolls and their islands. He had been trained to be prepared and he knew that even the smallest scrap of knowledge could become the greatest help in an emergency.

"We will make for Ugoofaru," he said, naming the major island community of that atoll.

Hassan brightened. "They say the girls are very willing there."

"I agree the people are very lax in morals. They have no religious leader. He was driven out by the Portuguese."

For an hour, Mohamed steered the vessel, trying to gain

more speed from the wind, but nature was against him. Although the boat was making course westwards there was no northwards advance. The waves were growing in size, battering the boat as it climbed up each one, to pitch down on the other side. Hassan and the two boat boys who were the sole crew had given up fishing and were clinging to the mast. Mohamed tied a rope around his waist and secured it to the mast so that he would not be swept overboard.

It was a relief when the rain came because it lanced the sea's fury. Huge drops splattered his head, streaming down his eyes and making it difficult to see the run of the waves. The rain hammered his bare shoulders and chest, drenching his loincloth, so he was cold and soaked where seconds before he had been warm and dry. Hassan and the boat boys shielded themselves with mats, relying on him to steer them out of the storm.

He saw the telltale rush of white ripples beyond the screen of falling rain and knew a reef was close. He could not see what island lay beyond it because visibility was so poor. He braced himself for the unexpected and watched the bow rise, felt the boat being lifted up as though in the palm of Allah, and then fall into the heaving waters of the lagoon the other side of the reef.

The reed mat sail was sodden with rain and the wind clapped against it as though it were a board. The boat was in calmer waters but the giant rollers of the channel had been replaced by skittish waves that, aided by a boisterous wind, tossed and thrust the boat onwards. Mohamed felt exhilarated; the danger had passed and ahead lay the unknown. With difficulty, he steered towards the lighter blue of shallow waters that he glimpsed through the rain.

Experience told him they were closing fast on the shore of an island, even though the driving rain prevented him from seeing it. He ordered the boat boys to bring down the sail and told Hassan to be ready to throw out the anchor stone. He peered into the rain until he saw a jungle of tall coconut trees suddenly leap out of the lagoon ahead of the boat. He shouted at Hassan and flung the tiller over to keep the boat from running onto the shore. The anchor stone dropped, held, and they succumbed to the surf.

Shaking off the rope halter, he grabbed a rope from Hassan and looped it around his chest. He dived into the water and swam swiftly with the tide, using strong strokes to propel him to the shore. As he put down his feet, the surf dragged him back. He waited for a wave and swam with it, closer to the beach. He stumbled ashore and pulled the rope with him, making its end fast to a tall coconut tree. He looked up at the sky to give silent thanks to Allah, as he saw the rain was easing.

◆ ◆ ◆ ◆ ◆

Although the storm rolled on, leaving them drenched to the skin and shivering, it was followed by nightfall. Because no one had seen them arrive in the heavy rain, Mohamed decided they should spend the night on board the boat, in case it drifted. They all stripped off their wet loincloths wrapped themselves in blankets and huddled together for warmth. With sunrise, Mohamed set the crew to clean up the boat and dry out the sails while he and Hassan dressed in sarongs and walked ashore. He judged that they had made a landfall on Dhuvaafaru, an island south of Ugoofaru.

The chill rain of the previous day was replaced by glorious sunshine. Mohamed relished the warmth after the cold lashing of the storm. An old woman sweeping the fallen leaves and debris from the sand in front of her hut confirmed the island was indeed Dhuvaafaru.

"Why should we stay longer?" said Hassan. "There is nothing here for us."

"Perhaps you are right." Mohamed turned and began to walk back to the beach. A movement in the glade beside the woman's hut caught his eye. He gestured to Hassan to look.

A boy in a skimpy loincloth was walking towards them from the beach. He had a handful of coconut and dried fish which he raised to his mouth to eat, while with his other hand he scratched a rash of sores on his body, in between swatting at the flies that swarmed around him.

"Look at that boy," said Mohamed softly.

"A worthless urchin." Hassan sniffed. He was still sulking at being wrong about the storm, even though Mohamed had not upbraided him for his lack of caution.

"He's hardly worthless. See how he is dong so many things at once. He is walking, eating, scratching and chasing away flies. Most people are so idle they do only one thing at a time. He is the kind of active person we need?"

"He is?"

"Yes. If I am going to be away taking the Vedor's boat to Ceylon, we need an extra hand at home and to sail with us on our trading trips."

"Not him!" Hassan shook his head firmly in disagreement. "Look at the boy. Take him home and you will add a useless extra mouth for us to feed. What a poor wretch!"

"So was Aiminafaan when she was Rehendi, until Queen Aisha bathed and clothed her for the Eid festival. Look at what that poor wretch is now. No one is more helpful at home."

"That's because you took her as your wife."

"I have a mind to take that boy. Bathe, clothe and train him and you will see that with Allah's good grace, he will become a clean and useful person. Think, Hassan, what you and I would be without our father's help."

"You want to be his father?" Hassan shrugged his shoulders, keeping his thoughts to himself. "Shall I go and pay our respects to the island chief?" he suggested, clearly anxious to have nothing to do with Mohamed's soul-saving.

"I hadn't thought of that!" He was relieved that Hassan was taking the village courtesies seriously, even though he had scorned them in Male'. "I'll wait for you on the boat."

As Hassan turned to walk inland again, Mohamed beckoned to the boy. The lad marched over eagerly. His breakfast finished, he was using both hands to swat the flies and scratch his sores.

"Boy," said Mohamed with a sympathetic look in his eyes to reassure him he meant well. "Do you have a father or mother?'

The boy looked at him as though Mohamed were stupid. "If I didn't have a father and mother, I wouldn't be."

"That's not what I meant." Mohamed scratched his chin, unconsciously imitating the boy's action. "Are they alive?"

"If they were, I wouldn't be in this state."

Mohamed was amused by the boy's frankness. He seemed to be about fifteen years old. He was obviously used to hard work since he looked strong, if undernourished. His rash was minor, a result of poor diet and dirt. In the islands there were many lads like him whose parents were dead or who came from homes so poor they had to rely on the charity of neighbours. They slept on the beach, lived on coconuts and fish they begged, scrounged or stole, and worked for anyone who could pay or feed them.

Mohamed liked the bright look in the boy's eyes. He made his decision. "If you want to improve your life, would you sail with me and work on my boat?"

"If you want to improve your life, would you feed me so I can work? Without food I do not work, I pray."

Mohamed laughed. *The boy has spirit!* "Follow me," he said. "I will give you food."

"Then I will work."

On board, the boat boys had prepared a meal prior to sailing. Mohamed gave the boy rice, banana, and a sweet mixture of coconut and sugar. He watched him gobble it up like a hungry shark. When he had finished, the boy dipped his fingers in the sea to clean them, and then turned to face Mohamed.

"The food I have." He patted his stomach happily. "Where is the work?"

"First, you shall bathe!" Mohamed pushed the boy on his chest so he toppled over the side of the boat with a shout of surprise. Mohamed leaned over to see he was all right and watched the boy break the surface of the water, shaking water from his matted locks.

He spat water from his mouth. "You are a strange master," he said, spluttering. "If this is the work, the pay is too much."

Mohamed told him to enjoy his sea bath and while he was bathing, he rummaged through the boxes of supplies. He found an unguent and a new loincloth. When the boy pulled himself up onto the stern of the boat, Mohamed made him stand naked while the sun dried him. Then he took the unguent and applied it to his body, rubbing it in fiercely. The sores closed.

"I see you are a man," he said, chucking the boy playfully in his crotch.

"It sticks out, doesn't it?"

Mohamed laughed and tossed him the cloth and a cap and told him to dress.

There was a shout from the shore as Hassan returned. "Who is that stranger on our boat?" he called out.

Mohamed realised he did not know the boy's name so he decided to give him one, more in jest than in earnest. He chose the Maldivian word for an officer in charge of boats. "This is Dhandehelu of Dhuvaafaru," he said, delighted that Hassan at first did not recognise the boy he had called a worthless urchin.

"Dhandehelu," Hassan shouted. "Bring the boat nearer so I can board." He pointed to the bow rope that had been tied around a coconut tree by Mohamed the night before.

The boy grabbed the bow rope and hauled on it, bringing the boat closer to the shore. But at the same time, the anchor rope in the stern was strained taut, so after a few pulls, the boat could move neither forwards nor backwards.

"What a Dhandehelu you are, boy!" Hassan was laughing. "You don't pull the shore rope until you have extended the anchor rope. With your strength, if you pull like that the anchor rope will snap."

"If you had told me what to do before, I would have done it," the boy said eagerly. "I always do exactly what I am told."

Hassan boarded the boat and studied the youngster. He turned to Mohamed who was chuckling to himself while watching the performance. "Is this really the same boy?" he asked in amazement. "For keenness and strength he will certainly serve us well."

Dhandehelu had been named in jest but Mohamed was pleased how quickly the boy took to seamanship. Obviously it would take time for him to be the officer in charge of their boats, but he would certainly be useful as a watcher and helper. Since he had no living relative and no ambition beyond his next meal, he considered the boy a lucky find for them. *Perhaps*, he thought, *this is why Allah with the storm took us to Dhuvaafaru.*

With the calmer sea Mohamed resumed the voyage to Utheem. On the way he began to instruct Dhan, as he nicknamed the boy, teaching him how to coil ropes in readiness for landing, and how to maintain everything shipshape in such a small vessel. The boy's bright chatter and pithy comments kept them all amused and the hours at sea passed quickly.

Only when they were in sight of Utheem did Mohamed's heart sink. Instead of being happy at seeing his wife again, he had a premonition of doom. The sight of Ali's ship tied up close to the shore heightened it.

"Our brother is here," he told Hassan as they sailed into the bay. "He must have brought his family as he has sailed here in his *odi* instead of rowing in his dinghy."

"Is that bad?" asked Dhan who had more than his share of inquisitiveness.

"Did I say so?"

"Your words did not, but I listened to your heart as well. It is sorrowful."

Mohamed looked at him intently. It seemed that Dhan was going to be more of an asset than he had realised. The boy's blithe innocence enabled him to see and sense what others missed.

As soon as they reached the shore, he and Hassan hurried to the house, leaving Dhan and the two boat boys to secure the vessel and start unloading. Ali's wife and Aiminafaan were outside the house with women from the village. His wife had tears in her eyes, which she tried to brush away as he drew closer. He understood. No one said anything as people made way for him to pass.

"Mohamed and Hassan are here," Fathimafaan exclaimed in a voice full of relief. His father was lying on a mat on the *kuda ashi*. He uttered a bleat of recognition as Mohamed stared at him in dismay.

"How long has he been like this?" Mohamed demanded.

"Three days." Fathimafaan dabbed at her face with her fingers, wiping away a tear. "He waits only for you and Hassan."

"His time is near," said Ali in a whisper. He put his hand

on Hassan's shoulder to restrain him from falling to the ground to embrace his father. "There is nothing you can do."

Mohamed kneeled down and took his father's hand in his, squeezing his fingers to comfort him. "We have come from our voyage in time, father. Hassan and I and Ali and Fathimafaan are here with you."

"Yes," said the old man with a tired grimace. "Only a short time remains and I will go on my voyage. The pain, my legs..."

Fathimafaan placed a cloth soaked in rose water on his brow. "Don't talk, father."

"My children..." he spoke with difficulty and the others had to sit beside him on the dais to hear what he was saying. "I am proud of you, my children. You have the qualities I taught you. When I am gone, do not quarrel among yourselves and always be kind to people. Carry on with the business honestly...in cheating there is no honour." He paused, his rheumy eyes searching for Mohamed's. He tried to pull himself up so Mohamed crouched by his side, lowering his head to hear his words.

"Everywhere I see Islam is losing to the rage of the infidels. Mohamed, do not let people give up our religion. There are only a few left who remember the ways and rituals. You have been schooled by the Imams of Calicut; you must practise our religion to the best of your knowledge. Preserve it for your children and their children."

"I will, father. I will. We all will."

"Then I shall rest in peace."

Two days later, Katheeb Hussain of Utheem died. He was buried with traditional rites next to his father outside the mosque in Utheem, where he had prayed throughout his life on the island.

CHAPTER 19

All those of Katheeb Hussain's house observed the traditional mourning period of forty days. Mohamed was impatient to start on the trip to Ceylon as the northeast monsoon had passed and the winds and currents were favourable for the trip. However, he remained in Utheem out of respect for his father's memory, and because of convention. Ali and his wife stayed as well. Since Aiminafaan was nearing childbirth, the presence of Ali's wife was welcome extra company.

Mohamed used the time to instruct Dhan in seamanship. He also taught him how to use a sword and buckler and they sparred together often. In resourcefulness he could teach the lad nothing. He was sturdy youth who quickly filled out with food from the family kitchen. As he grew, Mohamed realised he was older than he original thought.

Dhan himself had only a quip to describe his age: "Two good dinners and too many moons." This was typical of his pleasing manner. His dark, sunburnt features were usually brightened with an ingenuous smile, except when he furrowed his brow to concentrate on a task.

Hassan had been wrong in describing him as an extra mouth to feed; he was more like two mouths, always seeking a second helping of rice. When Mohamed made a comment about the amount of food Dhan consumed in a single sitting, he merely shrugged and said: "I collect water whilst it rains."

It was impossible to begrudge Dhan his extra ration of rice and fish since he was so energetic. Any task assigned to him was accomplished speedily and he was ready for more. He would work for hours in the hot sun without complaining, returning home in the evening to sit quietly with the family, speaking only when spoken to and performing little tasks for Aiminafaan without being asked.

The sadness Mohamed felt at the passing of his father was dissipated by the birth of his son a few weeks later. Aiminafaan recovered well, thanks to the presence of his sister and sister-in-law who supervised the bed warming – the placing a pot of fire under the bed to make her strong again. A few days afterwards, word came from Dom Gaspar that Mohamed should visit Baarah to prepare the large *odi* for its voyage to Ceylon.

After waiting so long, Mohamed was reluctant to leave home when his son had just been born. He asked Hassan to go instead.

"See the boat is made ready for the voyage. Provision it and take on crew. As soon as it is ready to sail, inform Dom Gaspar so that he can load his goods. Check the inventory well. Send for me when all is loaded and I will come at once."

Hassan listened to his instructions, clearly pleased to be active again after the period of mourning. It occurred to Mohamed that his younger brother probably had other reasons for being pleased about going to Baarah. It gave him an idea.

"Take Dhan with you. He will be useful."

Hassan scowled. "Whatever for?"

"You do not want to spend all your time attending and guarding the tribute ship, do you? Dhan is like our brother, he can be trusted with all that we trust ourselves with."

"You think of everything," Hassan said with a grin of appreciation.

Mohamed stroked his beard, wishing that were so. "You, of course, will stay at our Uncle Katheeb's house. You will want to relax after the work is done. See that Dhan has his meals at Dom Gaspar's house."

"That's a good idea. He eats so much, let the Portuguese support him."

Mohamed smiled. "See that he sleeps on the *bodu ashi* in the outer sitting and sleeping room of Vaaruge. By dwelling in the Vedor's compound, no one will disparage him."

Mohamed called Dhan, who was plaiting a mat sail in the shade on the beach, to join him and Hassan in the boathouse. He instructed the boy about the trip to Baarah, and added some tips on how to behave.

"You should be sure to get the first serving of food from the Vedor's kitchen. Be the first to go to sleep, and the first to rise. You should sleep with one eye open and one ear alert. If the Vedor or Queen Aisha should enter the room, you must rise at once and pay them due respect."

Dhan cocked his head on one side as he considered the instructions. "It seems I am to be your eyes and ears inside the Vedor's residence."

Mohamed ignored the comment, even though it pleased

him. "The Vedor, Dom Gaspar, has a Portuguese valet called Joao. He can be a knowledgeable friend."

"A knife is beautiful if the blade is sharp."

"He is sharp enough. By the way, the Queen has a daughter called Sitti. She is my wife's friend; they are about the same age. If you see her, enquire about her health. She has been sickly of late, I hear."

"I shall wish her well on your behalf."

"Hmm." Mohamed wondered what Queen Aisha and Sitti would make of Dhan. He hoped they would be as amused by him as were the women of Utheem. Dhan's baby-face good looks and enchanting disposition would surely win their hearts. He was going to be more than just an officer in charge of boats,

◆ ◆ ◆ ◆ ◆

Dhan was a chameleon. He had learned when he was very young that if he became what people expected him to be, he could survive. They accepted him, trusted him, and fed him. On his home island of Dhuvaafaru, after the death of the fisherman who had raised him as his own son, he was obliged to seek charity from other villagers. He had no false pride and was happy to do whatever job was required. If wood had to be hewed, he was an axe man; if yams had to be dug, he was a farmer; if a man wanted to talk, he would listen.

Despite his apparent independence after living alone for so long, Dhan liked to be liked. He discovered that when he said something funny, people laughed. If he made people happy, they rewarded him. So he adapted his personality to suit the occasion. His new master, Mohamed Thakurufaan, expected him to be his Dhandehelu, and so he would be. He would also be his eyes in the house of the Vedor, since that was required.

It was a task he enjoyed. Doing what Hassan told him to make the boat ready to sail was an easy job. He did whatever he was told and then asked for more to do. Everyone liked him; he was happy.

At the end of the first day's work after he had arrived in

Baarah with Hassan, a servant came from Vaaruge to conduct Hassan and him to dinner. Hassan declined, asking the servant to tell Dom Gaspar that his uncle had prepared food for him, and he could not eat meals in both places. He apologised for not eating the meal prepared from him at Vaaruge.

That gave Dhan a nice idea. The servant showed him into the *bodu ashi* saying he would bring his meal there. Dhan went instead to the kitchen and served himself. He finished, and served himself again.

"Boy, why twice you eat?"

He looked up in the middle of scooping rice form the banana leaf that was his plate. A stranger with pale blue eyes and a pale skin was watching him from the doorway of the kitchen. He was too young to be the Vedor, so perhaps this was his son, for he was dressed in breeches and tunic and wore his long hair tied with a ribbon at the back.

"Oh, master," said Dhan with his mouth full, not pausing in scooping up food in case the plate was snatched away from him. "My master cannot eat so I must eat for him. It would show disrespect for the rice, and the cook, if I did not enjoy it."

"A little rascal you are." The foreigner spoke Dhivehi in a strange way, but Dhan could understand him.

"A bigger one I may become with such good fare." He gobbled down the last mouthful, nodded at the youth, and washed his hands quickly.

"In the outer room sleep you must. My instructions are. Wrestle you?"

Dhan was puzzled for a moment. Was this youth challenging him to a fight? "If master wishes me to wrestle, I will."

"Good. Tomorrow morning, let us meet. Exercise I need. My name Joao is, master not." He smiled, eyeing Dhan as though judging his physique and whether he could throw him. For Dhan it seemed strange to be asked to sport with a white boy. It would be unwise to win.

As Mohamed told him, he put down his mat on the *bodu ashi* and was the first one to sleep. In large homes the sleeping platform was used by houseguests for sleeping at night as well as for sitting and eating during the day. He fell asleep easily but woke as soon as he heard someone slide open the door and enter the room. He rose immediately, startling the man who was crossing the room. It was another foreigner.

"*Meu Deus!*" the man said in Portuguese, pulling back. "I didn't know anyone was here. Who are you?"

"I am the Dhandehelu of the boats of Mohamed Thakurufaan. I came here with his brother, Hassan, to get the big boat ready for the voyage to Ceylon."

"Indeed? I am Dom Gaspar, the Vedor, and you are enjoying my hospitality as this is my house."

"I am in your debt, my lord." In the flickering light from a candle, he could see the man looked tired, as though carrying too many cares.

"Where is Hassan Thakurufaan?" Dom Gaspar asked, glancing around the room.

"He sleeps in the house of his uncle."

"Then why are you here?"

"I have no relatives on this or any island. If I had, I would be there."

Dom Gaspar's smiled kindly, a glint of amusement livening up his tired eyes. He touched the boy's chest lightly. "You may consider me your relative."

"My lord, you are the Vedor, the father of everyone in this atoll, myself included. I took that into consideration before deciding to sleep here."

"Boy, you speak well! Even the adults here do not understand I am what you say, nor know the problems I have. But why do you sleep so early? We could arrange amusements for you." He put his arm around his shoulder and Dhan felt his hand drifting down his shirtless back, until it rested on his tightly muscled rear, squeezing him through the thin fabric of his sleeping cloth.

Dhan raised his face to look into Dom Gaspar's eyes, composing his features into a picture of youth and innocence. "I sleep early to work early."

"Then we must meet earlier than this tomorrow? To share what you are made of."

"My lord, I am but flesh and bones…and a large appetite."

Dom Gaspar reached across and rubbed his palm against Dhan's crotch. "So I see. We must assuage that need."

"If master so wishes..." He stood without moving as Dom Gaspar raised his cloth and fell to his knees in front of him.

◆ ◆ ◆ ◆ ◆

The next morning, when Dhan was at the boathouse caulking the hull of the boat with tar made from shark oil, he looked up to see the youth he had met the evening before standing at the entrance watching him. He placed the brush of palm bristles in its cup and stood up.

"Boy, I think hiding from me you are." Joao shook his fist at him in mock fury.

"Should I stool in my feeding plate?" Dhan uttered the proverb without thinking. Joao looked at him blankly. "I mean, I would surely be unwise to hide from you, were it possible." He walked out onto the beach, assessing Joao's weight and size since it was obvious there was to be a contest. It would be easy to rush the youth and up end him on the sand while he was still preparing his opening move.

Joao, however, put his arm around his shoulder in a show of affection. "Ten minutes we wrestle? I know work you must."

"Can a fisherman work after fighting a barracuda?"

What he took to be a compliment made Joao smile with pleasure. He drew a large circle in the sand with his foot. "There we wrestle. I shall put you out first." He unbuttoned his tunic, hung it from the branch of a palm tree, and slipped off his under-tunic so he was bare to the waist.

Dhan gasped at the sight of a livid blue-red scar running across his white, hairless chest.

Joao flexed his muscles proudly. "Many fights I have." He traced the length of the scar with his finger, and then he turned around, showing Dhan his back. It was etched with badly healed welts of a furious whipping. "A gift from my countrymen," he said. "The Vedor rescued me. A good man he is."

Dhan shuddered. If the Portuguese could be so cruel to each other, especially to a boy who was not even old enough to be a soldier, how did they behave to their enemies? He was wearing only a breechcloth so he stepped warily into the ring Joao had drawn in the sand. He stood, not entirely sure of himself, with his arms akimbo, waiting to see what would happen.

Joao was clad only in black silk breeches, his feet bare. Strands of his long hair fluttered free from the ribbon that bound it at the nape of his neck. He crouched, extending his arms, waiting for Dhan to make the first move.

It seemed to Dhan that Joao, who was older by a few years and taller, had the advantage. He decided to let Joao think that was the case. He feinted to the right, which Joao ignored, then attacked on the left, seizing Joao by the arm and trying to swing him around. Joao immediately brought his right forearm across his throat, forcing Dhan to let go.

Dhan pretended to stumble back and Joao leaped for him, unable to stop himself as Dhan stepped smartly aside. He fell face down in the sand, but still inside the ring.

"A thousand apologies, oh master." Dhan said contritely, kneeling beside him.

Joao looked up, grinning beneath the sand that smeared his sweating face. Dhan relaxed, thinking it was all over. Suddenly, he felt a hand clasp around his ankle with the bite of a vice. Joao somersaulted from the ground, pulling Dhan's feet from under him sending him flopping backwards onto the sand. Joao landed with a thump on his chest, pinning him so he couldn't move.

"I win?" Joao was grinning so Dhan made no attempt to move. Then suddenly Joao began to tickle him.

Dhan tried hard not to give way to his shrieks of laughter but he couldn't. He begged Joao to stop, trying to pull himself away. Joao followed and together they tumbled out of the ring, rolling down the beach and into the surf. There they lay, side by side, exhausted.

"You I like," said Joao, cuffing Dhan fondly on his chest. He jumped to his feet and ran laughing into the sea.

"You I like too," said Dhan, splashing after him.

◆ ◆ ◆ ◆ ◆

Dhan's stay at Baarah became the happiest time he had ever known. For the first time in his life, he had a friend. Joao respected him instead of looking upon him as a beggar or a slave. Joao visited him every day when he was at the boathouse working on the *odi*. He spoke in his fractured Dhivehi and told him about the Portuguese presence and the Vedor and Queen Aisha. In the evenings, as they sat together on the swing seat in the garden, Dhan tried gently to correct Joao's Dhivehi, while Joao taught him some words of Portuguese.

Sometimes Dhan had glimpses of the women who lived in the house. Joao told him who was who. The one who interested him most was the Queen's maid, Fulu, a girl of his own height and age who was often to be seen bare-breasted as she dressed the Queen's hair. He saw little of Princes Sitti and was not able to pass on the message Mohamed had asked him to give her. Instead, he told Joao, and the boy managed to speak on the matter to the princess when he was accompanying her on a walk one afternoon.

That evening, as he was lying on the *bodu ashi* preparing for sleep he heard the swish of a curtain and the rustling of skirts in the room. He rose immediately and coughed so his presence would not surprise the person who had entered the room from the women's quarters. It wasn't Dom Gaspar.

"Who is that?" a voice asked timidly.

"I am Dhan from the Utheem boat." He said, longing to ask who wanted to know. As the woman moved across the light, he got a better view, as well as a hint of scent. He had never seen anyone quite so beautiful. Her hair lay in tresses down to her bosom, framing a pale face with eyes a soulful amber. She was hesitating, like a nervous butterfly.

Dhan was tongue-tied, perhaps for the first time in his life. His mind raced as he wondered what this vision might require of him. "Are you a dream?"

"I was in a dream," she said with a sad smile, clearly relieved to be talking. "Then Joao said that you brought an enquiry about my health from Mohamed Thakurufaan."

"He is my master."

"Would I your mistress be."

"Madam?" Dhan had no answer to such a riddle.

"Go you with him to Ceylon?"

"To the edge of the world if he so demands."

"You will see him before he sails?"

"Oh yes." Dhan was pleased to give the answer she obviously wanted to hear. "I will be accompanying Hassan Thakurufaan tomorrow to deliver the big boat. She is loaded now and ready to sail."

"Then give him this." She placed something in his hand and made him close his fingers over it. "This is the sacred ring my father was wearing at the time he was slain by the soldiers of Andhiri Andhirin. It is more precious to me than my own life. Take care of it."

"As I would your life, princess."

CHAPTER 20

Mohamed sat alone inside the wooden cabin built amidships of the big boat. The voyage to Ceylon had been a success and he was thinking about the report he would make to the Vedor. The southwest monsoon winds had favoured him, filling the lateen rigged sails on the ship's two masts, powering them onward, so he had been able to complete the voyage in the fifteen days he had set himself.

On the horizon, as the vessel approached the channel between Kelaa and Dhaffaru islands, he could see Hassan's fishing *dhoni* waiting to escort him home. It was unusual to make a voyage without mishap or delay and Mohamed wondered if his new talisman, as well as Allah, had helped. He turned his attention to the box he held cradled on his knees. Carefully, he unlocked it and slowly raised the lid, thrilled by the tense anticipation he was creating where none really existed.

Yes! he said happily to himself as he saw the sachet lying in the box. It was made of the red velvet he himself had sewn for it during the voyage to Ceylon. Beside the sachet was the packet of letters addressed in embroidered characters to the Vedor, sent from the governor of the Portuguese territory in Ceylon.

Mohamed reached into the box, ignoring the letters, and took up the sachet. He unlaced its drawstring and into his right hand shook out her father's ring that Sitti had given him. It lay glistening brilliantly against the scuffed amber of his palm; an unexpected declaration of Sitti's devotion and a poignant reminder of her father's bravery. He felt a flush brightening his cheeks and a throb of hardening desire as he looked at it. He glanced up quickly to make sure none of the crew could see him through the open door. He lowered his left hand, slipping it under the waistband of his loincloth.

Sitti's gift of the ring was a talisman that had spurred him on throughout the voyage. He felt honoured, doubly blessed to have the dutiful Aiminafaan as his wife and the affection of the Princess. It had been fifteen nights since he had lain with Aiminafaan and now his thoughts were constantly of Sitti, whom he thought he would never have. The ring in his palm signified his life was going to change.

He closed his hand, making a fist of determination around the ring. When Dhan had delivered it to him, as he was about to leave Baarah in command of the tribute boat, he had locked it in the document box. He needed time to consider what he should do. His thoughts raced faster and faster, until he fell back with a sigh of ecstasy. Now he knew. He returned the ring to its sachet and slipped it into his bundle of belongings. One day he would wear the ring, but only when he was married to Sitti and worthy of it.

He looked around the confines of the small cabin. Everything was in order. He smoothed his ebony black hair away from his tanned face and caressed his beard. It had grown thicker. He was mature now, confident and strong, unlike the young prodigal he had been on his return from India. He would be a good husband to Princess Sitti, as well as to Aiminafaan. He had not forgotten her request about Sitti when he first proposed marriage, although it seemed impossible then.

As he emerged from the cabin he saw that Hassan's *dhoni* was drawing alongside. He gestured to him, unable to make himself heard above the rush of the wind and waves, indicating that they must continue to sail to Baarah and not land at Utheem. His first duty was to report to the Vedor, as it was he who had commissioned the voyage, and the vessel was his.

Mohamed told the crew to decorate the masts with flags and coloured ribbons and Hassan had put some streamers flying from the curved prow of the *dhoni*. The two boats made a fine sight as they sailed into Baarah's bay. People were gathering on the beach in welcome. Mohamed surveyed the crowd carefully but he knew the girl he wanted to see would not be there.

A rowing boat put out from the beach. The Vedor stood in its stern, dressed in his uniform tunic; at his side stood Joao. Mohamed observed the boy was waving excitedly at Hassan's *dhoni*. He looked over and saw that Dhan was in the *dhoni's* bow, waving back in acknowledgement. He was pleased that Dhan had made himself so agreeable to everyone.

He welcomed Dom Gaspar aboard and escorted him into the cabin where he handed over the box with its letters, and the key. He left Dom Gaspar so he could study the box's contents in privacy, and went to greet Hassan who had also come aboard. They embraced, and then he enquired about his wife and child. Joao and Dhan were clasping each other as though they were old friends who had not met for years.

Dom Gaspar emerged from the cabin holding the letters. "The governor is full of praise for you, Mohamed. He acknowledges that he has received the presents and tributes for three years for forwarding to India." He looked around at the crew on both boats, making sure everyone heard his words. "I thank you for doing this difficult job so well, just as I wished and expected. Now, will you be my guest and come ashore to Vaaruge?"

There was nothing Mohamed would have liked more at that moment since it would give him a chance to see Princess Sitti. "Forgive me, my lord," he said. "Hassan brings news of my wife and son. I must return with him to Utheem."

He ignored the look of surprise on Hassan's face. Luckily, Hassan didn't protest that he had done no such thing and that everything was all right home, and there was no need whatsoever for him to return to Utheem in a hurry. However, Mohamed wanted to go home and speak to Aiminafaan before seeing Sitti. What he planned to do must not be hurried.

"I thank Allah that He has favoured me and I have been able to carry out your mission satisfactorily." Mohamed bowed his head in respect before Dom Gaspar. "I hope you will not be offended if I return home urgently. I shall leave Dhan here to supervise the unloading and to see the vessel is pulled on to the shore and is well sheltered. He can receive the wages and rations of the crew from you and will pay them accordingly.

Joao nodded his encouragement at Dhan who was standing stiffly to attention as the Vedor swept his heron's eyes over him.

"Dhan is as welcome as you are in my house, Mohamed. And in my kitchen." He smiled knowingly at Dhan. "His company much pleases us."

After the Vedor and Joao had left the boat, Mohamed called Dhan into his cabin. He gave his bundle with the ring inside and his mat to Dhan, telling him to put them in his brother's *dhoni*, as he would return with him to Utheem.

"Wait," he said as Dhan was about to leave the cabin. "You heard what I told Dom Gaspar, so you must do what is required. Then you can return to Utheem. However, there is another matter also."

"I expected that. The rat gnaws into the young coconut; the bat drinks the water."

Mohamed was too stunned by the lad's intuition to be angered by his remark. "If you are successful, I shall indeed profit by your labours," he said. "Yes, I want you to thank Princess Sitti for the ring. Tell her I carry it close to my heart and it was a talisman that kept me comforted during the voyage."

He raised his hand to silence Dhan who was about to make another clever remark. "Your duty is to pay my compliments to Queen Aisha. In the course of conversation, see what she would think if I were to ask permission to marry Princess Sitti. If she agrees, it can be arranged. Otherwise, consider the matter closed and let no one else know about it."

"Hello, Dhan!" Joao hailed him as he was about to finish his work for the day. The sun had already set and the sky was aflame as night rolled in. "You are always busy. Why don't you for a walk with me come?"

"I am too tired from being always busy. I must bathe and eat and sleep so tomorrow I can be busy again."

"You must have some fun."

"Fun does not fill my belly."

"Very well. You will miss me."

"Why? I can see you."

"Now you can, but at dawn I am to sail with Dom Gaspar."

Dhan hurriedly finished what he was doing and joined Joao for the walk to Vaaruge. He would miss his new friend's company but his own work was nearly finished and he would have to return to Utheem. "Have you given Princess Sitti the message from Mohamed Thakurufaan?" he asked.

"It is done," said Joao looking at Dhan with a deep fondness in his eyes.

"Did she say anything?"

"Alas, no. She could not. Queen Aisha flies too close whenever I am there."

"Parrots, even if speechless, can bite hard," said Dhan promptly.

"She is hardly speechless, that one."

Dhan laughed at Joao's quick retort and then sidestepped as he aimed a punch of affection at his chest. He ran off to the well to bathe while Joao returned to the compound. When he returned, Joao waited for him in the kitchen while he finished dinner, and then beckoned for him to follow. They walked hand in hand to the beach, where it was dark and only the stars could see them.

The absence of the Vedor from the island the next day was the opportunity Dhan had been waiting for. Conversation with the Queen or Sitti was difficult during the day because of the presence of various nosy women around them. Yet, once before when the Vedor was away, Sitti had sought him out on the *bodu ashi*. Perhaps now she would come again?

That night as he lay on his mat, he did all he could to indicate that he was awake and couldn't sleep. He coughed a few times, turned noisily on the platform, and even muttered to himself as though in distress. He could hear the large swing in her parlour in motion, so he knew the Queen was there.

After some time there was a rustle of garments and he opened his eyes to see Queen Aisha standing in the doorway, holding open the curtain. Her voice had a slight edge of annoyance as she said: "Dhan, can't you sleep?"

"No, madam," he replied respectfully, knowing it would not help to joke until he had assessed her mood.

"Why is that?"

"I have things on my mind. Perhaps they are keeping me awake."

"I have too. Come into the parlour. We can while away your sleeplessness by talking."

This was better than he expected. He entered with appropriate hesitation and quickly looked around. Then he lowered his head with embarrassment, a rush of blood spreading across his cheeks. Standing by the swing, her full bosom bare, was the Queen's maid, Fulu. He raised his eyes again and met hers, seeing there a glint of invitation.

Looking away shyly, he realised there was another person in the room too, lying on a swing bed concealed by long silk curtains. The perfume that came to his nose reminded him of the night Princess Sitti had given him the ring for Mohamed. It was she who was on the concealed swing bed.

Queen Aisha asked him to sit on the log seat beside her swing. He could see Fulu where she stood behind the Queen, gently rocking the swing. He glanced at her again and she seemed to be aware of his interest judging by the warning in her eyes not to stare in case the Queen noticed.

"Dhan, you must know this is most unusual, for me to invite you to talk with me," said Queen Aisha outlining the terms of the conversation. "But we live in unusual times."

"The cooking pot may be bad, but the rice boiled there in is good," Dhan said eagerly.

Fulu put her hand to her mouth to stifle a giggle.

"I do not talk of food, madam," he said to excuse himself

for being flippant. "I mean that out of bad can come good." He averted his eyes from Fulu, disturbed by the sight of her breasts bobbing as she suppressed her laughter.

"You are right, Dhan." The Queen seemed unaware of what was happening behind her back. "Thanks to Dom Gaspar my daughter and I have been safe here. Were we in Male' we would be at the mercy of the uncouth Portuguese there. I think it is fear of that which drives Sitti to such melancholy."

Dhan saw the chance to deliver his message. "Pain and sorrow can be the companion of a healthy young lady who has no companion."

The Queen smiled sadly. "You speak of matrimony? That might be true, but who is here worthy of marrying my daughter?"

"That brings to my mind, madam, that I have a message from my master, Mohamed Thakurufaan. Will you permit me to give you the message?" He was aware of a stirring sound from the bed behind the screen as Sitti sat up and listened.

Queen Aisha didn't seem very interested. "So what did Mohamed say?" She yawned.

"He asked me to find out whether you would give your blessing for a marriage between him and your daughter, Princess Sitti."

There was a loud gasp from behind the screen, which even the Queen must have heard.

"He also said that if you do not like his proposal, treat it as though it has not been mentioned."

The Queen's face darkened with annoyance, beads of perspiration breaking out on her brow. Dhan was devastated by her reaction. He waited, biting his lip as she took a deep breath to control her own emotions.

"This is preposterous! Since he has become the captain of the Vedor's vessel, Mohamed Thakurufaan's ambitions are growing beyond his station. Does he think that because my daughter and I are living humbly in Baarah, we could contemplate an island trader as the Princess's husband? His marriage to that poor girl, Rehendi, was one thing, quite appropriate. We have not descended to such a level."

To stop her flow of outrage, Dhan clutched at his stomach and began to moan.

"Oh madam," he cried. "Now I know why I could not sleep." He rose to his feet, holding his waist, his face screwed up in pain. "Those mangoes I ate this afternoon. Too green!" He darted for the door.

"Wait!" Aisha was dismayed at his rudeness. "Where are you going?"

"To relieve a pain." As he glanced back he saw Fulu was doubled up with laughter and not, like him, with a feigned stomach ache.

He did not see the Queen or Fulu again before he returned to Utheem the next morning. He did see a lot of activity at Vaaruge with village women visiting the house. He was keen to leave after suffering from the Queen's wrath the night before and so he did not enquire what was wrong. The Vedor had previously arranged for him to be rowed over to Utheem in one of Baarah's boats. He took trading goods, spices and medicines to Mohamed and Hassan as presents from the Vedor.

As soon as he arrived in Utheem, he went to the house where Mohamed was sitting in the shade in his garden, mending a fishing net. Aiminafaan was sitting on a swing seat, nursing her baby on her lap. It was such a happy, domesticated scene that Dhan had no wish to spoil it, so he had to be careful the way he spoke.

After exchanging the customary greetings, he said as casually as he could to Mohamed, "We shall have to consider it as something not said."

The look of dismay in Mohamed's eyes showed his message had been understood. Before Mohamed could ask questions, he left his side to greet Aiminafaan and to look at the baby.

Aiminafaan regarded him reproachfully. "I heard what you said, Dhan. In this atoll we say that something is not said when a girl turns down a proposal. Is that your message to Mohamed? You see, if it is the girl's parents who don't agree, we say something different." She smiled sweetly but Dhan thought he had had enough of this business.

"Just because women wear their hair in a bun, they think

they can poke their noses into other people's affairs."

Aiminafaan giggled, which took the edge off his vexation. "I am not mature enough to wear my hair in a bun, Dhan. I am Sitti's friend. I know her mother's impatient temperament and I know Sitti's patient one. In a year or so I am sure she will be here as my sister. I shall rejoice on that day."

◆ ◆ ◆ ◆ ◆

Although Aisha rose early on the morning that Dhan left Baarah, she was unable to find him at the *bodu ashi*. He had already gone to the beach so she decided to leave matters as they were and not bother with him. She was still upset by the conversation of the night before and wanted to give the boy a piece of her mind so he could tell Mohamed Thakurufaan what she thought about his precociousness.

She was still feeling incensed by the effrontery of the Utheem brothers when she returned to the parlour to prepare for the morning. It was sometime before she realised that Sitti had not woken up, although the sun was high. She went to her swing bed and raised its curtain to call her. Her heart stopped. The girl was lying face upwards with her eyes wide open; she was as motionless as if she were dead.

She screamed. Fulu burst into the room, took one look at Sitti, and joined in the keening. The noise attracted the other women in the compound and soon a crowd gathered around the bed to stare at Sitti. The gentle rise of her young, smooth bosom showed she was still alive, but perhaps only just. Aisha frantically poured her best rose water from Hyderabad on her forehead while Fulu fanned her vigorously with a bunch of vetiver grass, sending its sweet fragrance wafting around the room.

Aisha was relieved when Sitti's eyes showed some movement. She seemed to be awake, but in a trance. The women helped raise her upright, and Aisha poured a few drops of syrup in her mouth so revive her. She collapsed back on the cushions and stared morosely at the ceiling.

Aisha knew that if anything happened to Sitti, Dom Gaspar would be consumed with fury. Since that could be dangerous for all of them, she ordered a sailing boat to be sent in search of him.

When Dom Gaspar returned a few days later, Sitti had still not spoken, although she had taken some liquid as refreshment. She was lying listless on her swing, alternating between sleep and consciousness. She seemed too distant to hear anything.

"I have asked everyone in Baraah to help with cures," Aisha told Dom Gaspar quickly, anxious to stall his wrath as he stared down at Sitti. "We have written verses of the Holy Quran in ink on pieces of paper and dissolved them in water for her to drink. We have offered sacrifices. She has been bathed in purified water. We have put those bangles of herbs on her wrists and ankles. What more can we do?"

Dom Gaspar gazed thoughtfully at Sitti. Her pale, still beauty made her look like a statue sculpted from pure alabaster. He sighed. "You are an important woman in these islands, Aisha, even though you are no longer queen. If there is a cure to be found, you will find it. Try your cures and see if they work. If not, if our dear Sitti leaves us, then you will know the bitter truth about your faith."

It was a challenge Aisha accepted. For days she supervised different regimes of oils, herbs and unguents, and diets of vegetables and fish and turtle eggs. Incense sticks were lit around Sitti's bed and braziers of scented charcoal were placed in corners of the room so their sweet smoke would kill any malfeasance in the air. During it all, Sitti remained as though her mind had left her body. She would rise and walk when urged to do so, and allowed Fulu to bathe her and dress her hair. But she spoke to no one. Her radiant beauty clouded as she became a creature of the shadows, the recluse of Vaaruge.

Aisha was forced to swallow her pride and admit that she could not do anything to help her daughter. She sought an audience with Dom Gaspar, threw herself on the sand in front of him and begged him to do something. "I have exhausted all possibilities. Sitti's cure is beyond my powers."

"I am not of your country, or of your religion." Dom Gaspar replied, sounding callous. "My knowledge of what should be done in such cases is negligible."

Aisha scrambled to her feet, upset by his attitude. "When

you have to make a decision of importance, I know you consult various people about it. It seems our daughter's health is not so important to you otherwise you would consult – "

"Aisha!" he said sternly. "That is not correct. Sitti is my biggest concern. I have done everything you have asked of me to help you cure her. Supposedly you, as her mother, are the one who knows best."

"So I thought! If you cannot help me, then perhaps we should return to Male'? But without your protection I fear the worst."

"The protection of Portugal will be with you and Princess Sitti as long as I live!" He gestured for her to sit down on the swing beside him. "You are distraught to speak in such a manner."

Aisha sighed, loath to accept defeat. "I can turn only to you."

"Very well. You have asked people in the atoll for help, yet you did not ask the Utheem brothers. They have wisdom and skills from their father, and from their own broad experience. Do you have any objections if I ask them about this matter?"

The fight had left Aisha, at least temporarily. She still regarded the brothers, especially Mohamed, as impertinent in his request for Sitti's hand. However, she was willing to forget her objections for Sitti's sake.

"What ever you do, I will accept." She hung her head sadly, resigned now to Sitti being dead within days. There was nothing the Vedor, nor the Utheem brothers, could do to change that.

CHAPTER 21

The rain heralded its arrival with a howl. It swept the trees and thatched houses of Utheem with a rush of menace. The tops of the coconut trees bowed before its fury and loose branches crashed to the ground. The rain struck with the relentless beat of a crazed drummer, thudding on the rooftops and pounding the grey swirl of the sea with its heavy presence.

The season of the northwest monsoon was always a contrast, with sultry days followed by vicious cloudbursts and curtains of rain that descended on the world and closed off the next island from view. For Mohamed, the wind and the rain were a challenge; he knew the sea's moods and its currents, and he enjoyed coping with its wild furore.

He stood alone on the beach, heedless of the rain. He had sensed the rain was coming long before the rush of wind set the trees dancing. Before the skies opened, he had caught sight of a rowing boat heading towards the island from the east. He raised his hand to shield his eyes from the rain and peered out to sea. He had lost sight of the small vessel but was not alarmed. The sea had settled under the rain's onslaught and the current of the incoming tide was sure to bring the boat straight to the shore.

He looked back to see Dhan had taken shelter by crouching under the bow of a small boat drawn up on the beach. Hassan was watching from the entrance to the boathouse. He folded his arms across his chest, refusing to give way to the rain's insistence that he take shelter too. His eyes were almost closed by slaps of rain but he squinted out to sea. He had been waiting since the beginning of the monsoon season, since Dhan had returned to Utheem from Baarah, for this visit.

The rowing boat suddenly emerged from the gloom, soaring in on the crest of a wave that brought it flying up to the beach. Dhan and Hassan ran to join him as he hurried to secure the boat. The oarsmen jumped out and ran with the boat pushing it up the beach beyond the sea's grasp. Mohamed leaned in and took hold of the man crouched in the bow and lifted him out. Ignoring the man's protests, he carried him up the beach to the boathouse, only letting him stand on his own feet when they were out of the rain's drive.

Dom Gaspar coughed with embarrassment at his unceremonious landing before he spluttered his thanks. Dhan burst into the shelter, dragging Joao with him. Hassan and the boatmen crowded in too.

"The r-r-rain," stuttered Dom Gaspar, still catching his breath. "By surprise it took us. The sky was clear and the sea calm when Barah we left."

"Your mission must be important to put to sea in this season when every day's weather is deceptive. Is everything all right in Baarah? Queen Aisha is well...and her daughter?" Mohamed was careful to keep his anxiety within the realms of politeness.

"How clever of you to divine the reason for my visit." Dom Gaspar fussed, plucking at his wet clothes. A drop of water hung from the end of his nose. He gazed at Mohamed standing tall and confident beside him, clad only in a wet loincloth. He gasped audibly at his rippling physique and then said hastily, diverting attention from his stare, "Your strength, your body, prodigious it is. You carried me as though I were no heavier than a child!"

Mohamed nodded modestly, but was thinking to himself: *How simple are these Portuguese, so easy to impress.* He looked for Dhan and saw he was helping Joao to dry himself. Hassan gave Dom Gaspar a towel and he wiped his face and nose with it, regaining his composure with each stroke. He was, Mohamed reminded himself, a man of experience and stature who must have been in worse scrapes than a sudden cloudburst.

He looked out and saw the sky was clearing. "It will pass soon," he said. "We must go to the house so you can dry yourself. I will lend you some clothes."

"You honour me by your hospitality, Mohamed." Dom Gaspar's face betrayed his dismay at the thought of having to wear a loincloth like Mohamed. "We shall doubtless be drenched again, so I shall remain as I am." He turned his attention to Hassan and Dhan, greeting them fondly.

"Dhan," he said with a note of censure in his voice. "Since you put the boat to
shelter and left, we in Baraah you have seen not."

"You will see me when you need me. Is the boat exposed?"

"Am I to expose it you to see? Come for our entertainment, Dhan. Mohamed, the season for the next voyage will soon be with us. Then send Dhan you will?"

"As you wish." Mohamed was wondering when the Vedor would broach the reason for this unexpected visit. The rain was easing so he again invited Dom Gaspar to accompany him to the house. "Dhan, run along with Joao and see that refreshments are prepared. Hassan, will you look after the crew?"

The gloom sipped away and the sun reappeared, its rays warming Mohamed's shoulders. He stepped out onto the path and suggested that Dom Gaspar remove his tunic so he could dry himself in the sun's rays, but the Vedor was too conscious of his status to do that. Mohamed sensed that he wanted to talk privately, so he fell into step beside him as they walked slowly under the dripping canopy of trees to the house.

Dom Gaspar began with a sigh. "Mohamed, I have known you long and trust you. You are my captain and I want you to take the tribute ship to Ceylon early next year, as soon as the weather is right. I do not want to have comments about tardiness from Lord Meedhoo."

"I will serve you in any way I can."

Dom Gaspar cleared his throat, clearly uncomfortable at what he had to say. "Perhaps you can help me in the matter of Princess Sitti?"

"I beg your pardon?" Mohamed almost faltered in his stride at the unexpected request, wondering what it implied. Fortunately, Dom Gaspar was too wet and worried to wonder about his reaction.

"She has been in a decline for months. She's wasting away. There seems to be no one who can restore her interest in life. All the Queen does is enlist charlatans who pretend to work spells. There is nothing physically wrong, I'm sure, no rheum, no pain. She won't tell us what ails her, and barely speaks at all. It's as though she has put herself into a trance."

Mohamed was guilt-stricken wondering if, through some misunderstanding, he was the cause of Sitti's melancholy. He loved and yearned for her. Was it because of this that she had taken sick? He had heard she was confined to Vaaruge and was said to be unwell, but this was the first news he had how extreme was her distress. Dhan had told him about the Queen's reaction to his message and it caused him anguish wondering what Sitti felt. He fretted, wondering how they could ever be together.

The sun's rays helped clear his mind as well as restore his strength. "You want me to help?" he asked as casually as he could, his heart beating faster at he saw a way to be with Sitti.

"That is why I have come here today. You are a man of principles, strong in your beliefs. You might know some way to remove the curse that has struck dear Sitti."

"A curse?" Mohamed nodded, smiling to himself because he knew it wasn't a curse at all. He thought of the ring she had given him and its unspoken message. He would use the opportunity to remove this so-called curse and cure Sitti according to convention. He saw this as a chance to prove the importance of prayer and Islam to the people of Baarah, instead of their black magic spells.

"I am grateful that you have come to me. The respect people had for my father was because of his trust in God. We must organise prayers for Sitti's recovery."

"Prayers?" Dom Gaspar looked doubtful. "Will you do that?"

"If you help me. There are certain rituals."

Dom Gaspar waved his hand impatiently, as though brushing away the objections his own principles were about to raise. "Tell me what you require."

"Can you gather forty people who can recite verses from the Holy Quran? Also, give alms to forty destitute people," he added as an afterthought so that some poor islanders too could benefit from the situation.

Dom Gaspar shook his head wearily. "In all the northern atolls, from Male' to here, who still follows Islam? You know Captain Andhirin forbids people to go to the mosques. In Utheem you can be devout because you are in my fief and I believe my task is good governance and commerce, not suppression of one religion and conversion to another."

His deep sigh so betrayed his fears about Andhirin that Mohamed was overwhelmed with sympathy for him. He vowed to himself that he would do whatever was right for Dom Gaspar, come what may.

◆ ◆ ◆ ◆ ◆

A few days after the visit of Dom Gaspar to Utheem, when the weather had cleared, Mohamed set out for Baarah. He left Hassan at home to look after the house and family, promising he would return after forty days. He took Dhan with him, aware that the boy would be useful as a go-between for what he had in mind, as well as a cheerful influence. He was confident that his prayers would succeed and Sitti would regain her robust health and vitality. He knew in his heart that Allah was guiding him, and he wanted others to see that too.

He instructed that two pavilions be built on the shore of Baarah facing the open sea, the same coast where he had run with Rehendi four years before. The pavilions were to be ninety paces apart. One was where Princess Sitti was to stay for the forty days of prayers. It was furnished comfortably and there were always to be people on hand to tend to her needs and keep her company. Ambergris was to be burnt as incense and flowers were to be strewn daily on her prayer mat. The second pavilion was to be similarly provided with incense and flowers as well as prayer mats.

He was pleased on arrival at Baarah to find that Dom Gaspar had done as he requested and two tented pavilions erected. The only problem was that he had been unable to locate forty people who could recite correctly from the Holy Quran. He had found only nine willing to do so.

Mohamed told Dom Gaspar that it was enough. He explained that eleven was an auspicious number too and the nine who had volunteered, together with himself and Dhan, would make up that number. If Dom Gaspar had any doubts about the efficacy of what Mohamed was planning, he said nothing. Queen Aisha kept out of his sight, as though deliberately spurning him.

He declined Dom Gaspar's invitation to stay at Varuuge, saying he would dwell in the prayer pavilion instead. Although he longed to gaze on Princess Sitti, his instinct warned him that it might defeat his purpose if she saw him too soon. He had learned enough to understood the reason for her catatonic state and wanted to draw her out of it gently, while subtly assuring her of his presence and keen devotion.

He sensed it would be necessary to remove Sitti from her mother's inhibiting presence if she was to recover voluntarily from the shock she had suffered. So Sitti was installed in the pavilion with her attendants while Queen Aisha, on Dom Gaspar's insistence, kept away. The nine who were to join him and Dhan in reciting verses of the Holy Quran set up camp in the other pavilion. They had with them, laid on a bed of red hibiscus petals on the sand, a scarf belonging to Sitti. They sat around this and began to recite the Holy Quran from memory, each helping the other if he faltered.

At the end of the first day of recitation, Mohamed gave Dhan the shawl to take to Sitti resting in her pavilion. Dhan bore it reverently to where the Queen's maid Fulu – who had come to see what was happening – was waiting at the entrance. He chanted in Dhivehi *Amaanaathuge amaanaai amaanaathey amaanaai* meaning that he was bringing with him an object entrusted to him to be delivered. Fulu accepted it and took it inside for Sitti.

The scarf was sent back to the praying pavilion the next day and Mohamed again gave it to Dhan in the evening to return to Sitti. Dhan shouted the same phrase as on the day before outside the pavilion and was surprised when, instead of Fulu, Queen Aisha herself emerged. He presented the scarf to her and was astonished to hear Sitti call weakly from inside the tent asking whether it was Dhan's voice she could hear.

"Dhan!" cried the Queen in delight. "Did you hear that? She recognises your voice. What magic word did you say?"

"It was not a magic word, madam." He lowered his head apologetically. "I used the wrong phrase. I should have said *Avahaara! Avahaara!* Because that's what Mohamed told me to use when giving something to a royal person."

"Your words worked, Dhan. I'm so relieved."

He reported the conversation to Mohamed who smiled knowingly. "Tomorrow, say the same words. She will get better because she knows I am here. Your voice alerted her."

A few days later, after the recitation was over, Mohamed gave Dhan the scarf to take back, adding a small knife with a handle made from fish tooth that he had carved himself.

He had wondered for a long time how to match Sitti's gift to him of a ring. If the ring symbolised her love for him, a knife to penetrate its circle would signify the strength of his devotion.

"Give this to Princess Sitti, hidden in the scarf. But say nothing to her, lest the Queen overhears."

Aisha, her attendants and the village women were amazed by Sitti's recovery. Each day, as Dhan returned the scarf, she registered more progress. The soothing sound of the daily recitation coming from Mohamed's pavilion, to which she listened avidly every day, had a healing effect, revitalising her. After two weeks she was reciting the verses herself in her own pavilion.

When her attendants weren't watching, she withdrew to a corner and took out the knife. She toyed lovingly with it, rubbing her fingers gently along the shaft fashioned by Mohamed's own hand, squeezing it to her bosom in rapture. Gradually her appetite returned and she began to eat more, taking an interest in her surroundings and even smiling occasionally at her servants. Yet she spoke very little and said nothing to her mother.

Her recovery was reported daily to Mohamed by Fulu and Dhan but Mohamed refused their request that he should himself pay Sitti a visit. That, he told them, must await Allah's will. On the fortieth day, as he soon as he completed the ritual recitation, Mohamed abruptly left Baarah.

Although he made no attempt to see Sitti, he longed to gaze on her again, to embrace her as he had done in his dreams every night of those forty days. It was painful to be so close to her and yet, because of custom and his respect for the Queen and Dom Gaspar, be obliged to keep his distance. Better, he decided, to be at home in Utheem than on the beach in Baarah within sight of her beauty. Dhan, who seemed half in love with her himself, spoke glowingly of her looking like a forest sprite.

Mohamed left Dhan on Baarah to prepare the Vedor's boat for the next voyage to Ceylon. He was content, as he returned to Utheem, that Sitti now understood there was hope and that, if Allah so desired, eventually they would be together.

The people of Baarah regarded Sitti's return to good health as a miracle. People from other islands in the atoll found reasons to visit Baarah and see Sitti for themselves. The household staff, as well as Sitti's friends, told the story of her illness and cure by prayer. Queen Aisha found that she was the centre of attention and that people were generous in praise of Mohamed Thakurufaan as a noble scholar and man of faith.

This development caused Aisha to think about what had happened. She had always wanted the best for Sitti, even though at times she did not understand her daughter. It was obvious that she should be married but because of her illustrious background, it was hard to find someone of suitable standing. With the Portuguese occupying the islands and controlling all the positions of power, they rendered the hereditary nobles worthless as potential suitors.

As she lay on her swing bed at night, preparing for sleep, Aisha thought often about a husband for Sitti. Dom Gaspar didn't understand the importance of the right background for her husband because he was a foreigner. He was set against the Crown Prince and, from what she heard about that young man's scandalous debaucheries in Male', it was fortunate she had not pushed his suit.

Aisha prided herself on her adaptability. She had been raised in a strict religious background and was happy with established conventions. However, there was no longer an establishment; the Portuguese had usurped the throne and destroyed respect for religion. She recognised how fortunate the people of the Northern Atolls were in being ruled by Dom Gaspar, and having Mohamed Thakurufaan to keep the religious rituals alive. She was aware of the irony of the situation. The very man she had rejected as a husband for her daughter was the one who had cured her, and whom everyone admired.

In the room where she sat on her bed in the evenings, swinging backwards and forwards, as she puzzled about what was best to do, she could sometimes here Dhan on the *bodu ashi* next door. She had observed how diligent he was in preparing the boat for the voyage to Ceylon. If he passed her when she was relaxing in the garden, he was courteous but she sensed his attitude of innocent respect had changed. He and Joao were firm friends, always in each other's company, otherwise the boy kept to himself.

One evening, hearing Dhan enter the apartment and throw himself onto the *bodu ashi* with a moan, she went to the curtain and peeped through. His eyes were tightly closed and he seemed to have fallen asleep. She called his name softly, but there was no response. *How he has changed,* she thought, remembering when he first came to Vaaruge nearly a year before, no one could enter the room without him jumping to his feet.

The next night, she tried to rouse him again, first peering around the curtain to see if he was there, and then calling his name. He didn't stir. Two days afterwards, Dom Gaspar and Joao left Baarah for a visit to another island and that night Dhan entered the sleeping room earlier than usual. As soon as she heard him, she went to the curtain and called his name. There was no reply. She called him louder, and repeated his name again. He rose up with exaggerated reluctance from the *bodu ashi*, rubbing his eyes, but she knew he couldn't have fallen asleep in such a short time.

"Dhan, are you deaf when I call you now?"

"If a hen crows, it is not dawn."

"Are you so in need of sleep, you ignore my cry! I would talk to you, Dhan. Please come."

He came reluctantly but Aisha sensed she had stirred his curiosity. She sat on the swing and indicated the log seat at her feet. He was gazing around the room as though looking for someone. "My daughter sleeps in her own chamber now she is well. We have Mohamed Thakurufaan to thank for that."

"Your maid Fulu attends her?"

"Why, yes." The question puzzled her. She wondered how to steer the conversation to the matter she wanted to discuss. "Thank you for keeping me company. As you know, Dom Gaspar is away. One does need company sometimes. You said that once yourself."

"I did?" He fidgeted.

"Yes. About Sitti when she was in decline."

"I did not understand your views then. It is a matter best left unsaid."

"I speak about Mohamed Thakurufaan."

Poor Dhan seemed entrapped by embarrassment. He almost rose to his feet, remembered his manners and sat down again, twisting his hands.

"Well?"

"Yes, quite well, madam. I am well. He is well. He leaves for Ceylon next week. The boat is nearly ready." He paused in his babbling. "May I return to the *bodu ashi*, madam? I feel better if I am asleep."

"My dear daughter Sitti was asleep until Mohamed Thakurufaan's prayers awakened her. Do you remember what you told me the last time you were here to repair the boat?"

"You push me when I am falling, madam."

"Hush now, do not misunderstand me. I am not teasing you. You told me that Mohamed wanted my opinion regarding a possible marriage between him and Princess Sitti."

"Words not said, madam."

"Then say them now. Ask me my opinion and you shall have it." It was the first time she had seen him stuck for words. "Fie, Dhan! Sometimes you are more stupid than a fish."

He gaped, stunned by her use of the kind of phrase that he liked to utter.

"Even though words were not said, now is the time to say them, Dhan." She paused, surprised at what she was saying. "Circumstances change and we must change. I wasn't then but now I am in favour of Mohamed Thakurufaan marrying my daughter. I am sure Dom Gaspar will approve. You must help arrange this before Mohamed leaves with the tribute ship for Ceylon."

"Allah be praised!" Dhan's shout of astonishment resounded through Vaaruge, causing the Aisha to reel back in surprise, setting the swing rocking. Then as he calmed down, he blurted out something that really surprised her.

"Madam, there is another marriage I have been asked to arrange."

She nodded her head for him to continue, wondering

what calamity was to come.

"Hassan Thakurufaan is keen to marry Kamana of Baarah Katheeb's house."

◆ ◆ ◆ ◆ ◆

Queen Aisha was relieved that she had organised everything to everyone's advantage. The betrothal of Mohamed to Sitti and Hassan to Kamana took place when the Utheem brothers came to Baarah in preparation for the voyage to Ceylon. Sitti was ecstatic and conducted herself with an unexpected vivacious dignity. Her joy at being married to Mohamed impressed all who saw her.

Aisha triumphantly announced to Dom Gaspar that she no longer feared what their enemies in Male' might do, now that Sitti was secure as a wife of a virtuous man. Dom Gaspar's nose twitched and he didn't say a word, but she knew he was happy for them both.

CHAPTER 22

The second voyage to Ceylon began so auspiciously for Mohamed that he wondered if he too had been blessed by the recitation of the Holy Quran. He was as devout as he could be in a country where religious values were torn asunder by the presence of brutal foreigners. He prayed five times a day even though he was unable to go to a mosque as they had long been closed.

Sitti was like a gift from Allah to him, especially as marrying her also fulfilled Aiminafaan's wishes. Not wanting to alarm her with the ardent craving of a husband on their first night together he took her gently, aware of her tender disposition and how she had suffered because of him. But she tore at him like a tigress, raking his back with her nails as she writhed beneath him. She begged for more, not letting him rest until she fell back exhausted, a sweet smile of fulfilment on her childlike face. At that moment, he knew he was truly blessed.

The voyage was successful and he returned to Baarah within seventeen days. He stayed there a week revelling in the strength and affection he discovered in Sitti, before taking her home with him to Utheem. Aiminafaan fell upon Sitti as soon as she arrived, embracing her and smothering her with kisses. Both women seemed delighted to be together again, not just as friends but also as his wives. Aiminafaan proudly showed off their son and, from the look in Sitti's eyes, he sensed her desire to bear him one too.

After a few days of bliss basking in the adoration of Aiminafaan and Sitti, Mohamed woke to find Ali and Dhan had arrived from their trading voyage to Male'. He soon noticed that while Ali had done well on the trip, he was more thoughtful than usual. He was always slow to reveal what was on his mind so Mohamed didn't ask him what was wrong, content to wait until he was in the mood to confide.

When he questioned Dhan about whether anything untoward had happened in Male', the boy's cryptic answer was: "Though the flying fish flies, the limpet cannot." From that he assumed that Dhan had not approved of what he had seen and heard there.

Ali's news, when he eventually revealed it, was unexpected. He waited until it was the eve of his return to Thakandhoo, his wife's island, where he had made his home, before speaking his mind. The three brothers had gone to the beach to watch preparations of the boat for Ali's voyage at dawn the next day.

"Our boats are old and slow, Mohamed," Ali said suddenly, gesturing at their vessels anchored in the bay.

Mohamed sensed he was at last to hear what was on his elder brother's mind. "They are our father's legacy to us," he said quietly to encourage Ali to talk.

"Our father was so wise," said Ali. "I often try to think what he would do in these faithless times."

"He said we must remain steadfast in spite of the Portuguese presence."

"That's right," Ali sighed. "I have seen how people have abandoned all that father held sacred. Some day we may have to flee even from Utheem so we can continue to worship and live religiously as he wanted us to do."

"What do you mean?" Hassan kicked a fallen coconut across the beach, showing he doubted his elder brother's understanding of affairs.

"What happens when the Vedor is no longer governing the Northern Atolls? He is old now and has many enemies, not just among the nobles close to Captain Andhirin but among Andhirin's Portuguese colleagues too. This I learned in Male'. If Dom Gaspar is replaced with a man as despotic as Andhirin then we and our families will be in danger."

"Ali is right, Hassan. It is well to think of the future." Mohamed put his hand on Hassan's shoulder to restrain him. "Ali, you have been thinking much lately. Do you have a suggestion about what we should do?"

"As I said, our boats are old and slow. We could not escape in those, or even trade with them for many more years. We must build a good sailing vessel of our own."

"That's a good plan!" Hassan bobbed around with enthusiasm. "We must find the right trees to fell and season the timber. It will take time."

"I have another idea," said Ali slowly. "Mohamed, you know that Dom Gaspar planned to build his own boat. He has gathered all the timber. Dhan has heard from his boy, Joao, that he has changed his mind. He told Joao he no longer wishes to leave Baarah and retire to Portugal so he has no need of a boat to sail to Goa. He plans to sell the timber."

"Then let him sell it to us!"

"Yes, Hassan, that was my thought too." Ali looked more relaxed now he had spoken of what was on his mind. "You are the closest to Dom Gaspar, Mohamed. Can you arrange that?"

"Ali, you always did plan wisely for the future. I will talk to the Vedor. He should agree since I have relieved him of the problem of delivering the taxes safely to Ceylon. Hassan and I would work under you if you will supervise the building of the boat."

Ali shook his head. "No, Mohamed, both you and Hassan have wives from Baarah and can stay there with them. My wife is in Thakandhoo. I shall be forty soon. I want to spend time with her while I can still appreciate her!"

Hassan was delighted and slapped Mohamed on the

back. "You see what a good idea this is, brother. We will have time ashore with our new wives too."

"I shall do this to build a boat for our future, Ali," Mohamed said gravely, hoping to calm Hassan's exuberance. "I shall find the best carpenters. Hassan can supervise one side while I do the other. I have ideas about vessel design from what I learned in India. We will make a boat that is sleek and fast, one in which we could spend months at sea in case it ever has to be our home."

He was as excited as Hassan about the project and lost no time in discussing it with the Vedor. Dom Gaspar gave his approval immediately and even offered to house, feed and pay the carpenters as well as to provide the timber. It was decided that Mohamed and Sitti would lodge at Vaaruge, and Hassan would stay with his wife at Baarah Katheeb's house. Aiminafaan and his son and sister would remain in Utheem where Mohamed would visit them once a week.

The four months it took to build the boat was a period that bonded Mohamed and Hassan in a way brothers seldom achieve. They worked together in such harmony, everyone knew that the boat would be a success. There was a tradition in the Maldives that a good boat could only be built by well-fed carpenters. Aisha and Sitti made sure their cooks prepared the best dishes for the men.

Construction went smoothly. Dhan became his namesake: Dhandehelu, the officer in charge of boats. He was meticulous in checking every detail, even making suggestions to improve some things that Mohamed and Hassan had already agreed on. Joao added tips too, based on his own knowledge gleaned from sailing on Portuguese ships. A crucial innovation was to build the hull of the boat with the smoother side of the timber facing outwards. Conventionally, the unhewn side of the boards formed the exterior of the boat. With a planed, smoother side the vessel would glide faster through the sea, however weak the wind.

The launching of the boat was an excuse for a feast that went on all night. Mohamed felt proud, not because he stood in command of such a beautiful vessel, but because of the teamwork that had gone into building it, and the camaraderie of the people who helped. He realised that the

Portuguese were destroying not only the people's religion but also the traditional spirit of cooperation that bound the islanders together.

He had little time to reflect on the breaking up of island society as he took the new boat on its maiden voyage. Hassan and Dhan accompanied him and he invited some of the carpenters to sail on the vessel they had built with such dedication. Joao was invited too and he and Dhan worked side by side as crew. The wind filled the sails joyfully; even the sea seemed to welcome the new vessel with a strong current that bore it gracefully through the waves.

As was his habit, Mohamed cast a fishing line to tow behind the boat. To his surprise, within minutes he caught a fish, a *kaluoh*, a kind of sailfish. Because of the boat's speed, the line pulled the fish so fast it jumped clean out of the water and landed on the deck.

Seeing that, Mohamed called Hassan to his side. "This fish has given our boat its name. You saw it jump? Let us call our boat *Kaluoh Fummi*."

Joao didn't understand the name so he asked Dhan to explain. Dhan scratched his head and tried to apply his small knowledge of Joao's language. "The jump of the fish?"

"Jumping Fish!" said Joao.

The mood of happiness touched everyone on board; Mohamed went to the bow and offered a silent prayer that the sunny days would continue. He was unable, however, to shake off a feeling of foreboding, that *Kaluoh Fummi* would bring tragedy as well as happiness.

◆ ◆ ◆ ◆ ◆

For Captain Andhirin the morning started badly. He was woken by the sound of children playing outside the walls of the fort. Even though he slept in a chamber deep in the interior, their incessant shrieks penetrated through the open windows and doorways. It was an annoying racket that nagged at his ears, causing his head to pound from having drunk too much wine the night before. He summoned the officer of the watch and told him to round up the children and give them twenty lashes each.

With satisfaction he heard their screams as the soldiers set about them. After their blubbing had died down, he lay back in bed thinking about the day's activities. There would be the usual crowd of petitioners hoping to see him. He would let Meedhoo and his son deal with them. He knew how devious the islanders were. They thought they could fool him but he remembered what he had learned from his mother: never trust a native. The Portuguese were honourable people; their word was their bond, except when dealing with natives, of course.

He wondered, as he did every day, when he would be transferred from Male' to Goa or even to Lisbon. Portugal was his fatherland, even if he had never been there. It was Portugal he had served loyally since he was baptised in Goa after escaping from the island where he was born and raised. There was a new Viceroy in Goa, Dom Luis de Atayde, so perhaps he should petition him for a transfer. He had done well in Male', secured trade and significant annual taxes for Portugal. Under him, governing the islands cost Portugal nothing. In fact, though his efforts, the Maldives was contributing handsomely to the Portuguese coffers. He should be rewarded for his loyalty by promotion and a new posting.

As he shaved, he studied himself in the mirror. He had preserved his lean looks, even though his eyes were dull and his liver angered by nightly carousing with his officers. They were good men. What else was there to do except enjoy the company of his compatriots, down a few jars of wine, and pleasure a comely concubine or two. Preferably in pairs.

He took his time to prepare and it was after midday when he was ready to attend to business. His servant had said that Meedhoo's crown prince, Tuffashana, was waiting to see him. Well, let him wait. That young man had an evil streak in him. Even though he was so pompous, there was ruthlessness to his nature that Andhirin had sniffed out long ago. His father was simply greedy; his 'crown prince' was ambitious, and dangerous.

At the entrance to the audience chamber, Andhirin drained in a single gulp the glass of wine his servant held out for him. He hoped it would soothe his hangover so he could deal with Tuffashana. It was time to put him in his place. He peeped through the curtain and saw him pacing impatiently up and down on the carpet in front his chair, his throne as the natives called it. He wondered what had agitated the scoundrel so much. Maldivians were usually content to sit as though in a dream and wait, instead of moving around unnecessarily.

Scowling with distaste at having to meet him, Andhirin strode into the chamber and mounted the dais to take his seat. Tuffashana stopped pacing and stepped forward but he didn't bother to show respect by bowing. Andhirin raised his palm and glared at him, halting him in his tracks.

"Allow me the courtesy, my dear 'crown prince' of Lord Meedhoo's house, to settle comfortably in this chair of state before we review what must surely be totally unimportant matters you have come to disturb me with." He snapped his fingers for the servant to bring another glass of wine and then instructed the boy to use a screwpine fan to direct some air at his sweating brow.

He glanced at the Tuffashana, enjoying his agitation. He observed that he was dressed in a more formal fashion than usual, with a new silk cloth hanging from his waist to his ankles, secured by a broad brocaded waistband. He wore a cap of many layers that must have come from India. It showed that he was undoubtedly skimming off taxes intended for the treasury as he was too well dressed – as though he was planning a voyage - for his income.

When the wine was presented, Andhirin took another large gulp, and felt himself cooling down in the air stirred by the fan. Only then did he signal that the 'crown prince' could approach.

"I wish you success and long life, Andhiri Andhirin." The young pretender's voice was oily with insincerity. "However, since you appear to be blind to what is happening, I fear it may not be so."

"Oh hell, Meedhoo's whelp! Is this going to be one of those difficult days? Please don't speak in riddles."

Stunned at being called a dog, he was nevertheless intent on speaking. This determination alerted Andhirin that this was indeed a matter of importance, although his instinct told him treachery was brewing.

"Go on!" He waved to him to continue while he drained his wine glass.

"I speak from my heart, Captain Andhirin. Could you tell me which is the capital of the Maldives? Is it still Male' or is it now Baarah?"

"Bloody riddles, boy!" He sighed, seeing the direction the conversation was headed. "I have discussed all this before, with your father."

"Before is not now. I am not my father. People are asking who rules the Maldives. Is it you, on behalf of our Christian Sultan and the Viceroy in Goa, or the Vedor Dom Gaspar on behalf of the three Utheem brothers?"

Andhirin yawned in his face. "Why can't you say what you want to say and then go about your business? You are jumping up and down like a puppy."

Tuffashana halted immediately, biting his lip. His eyes were hard, and Andhirin wondered if it was through hatred or simply his lack of comprehension that he was being baited. The game of taunting him was an amusing one. Andhirin leaned forward to so he could catch every nuance, despite giving the impression that he didn't care what was being said. He wanted to see how he could tease the dog.

"There have been changes in these islands of which you may not be aware," Tuffashana said with his smarmy arrogance. "Life is becoming uncertain for people close to you, such as me. And my dear father."

Andhirin took a sip from the glass that had been refilled by the servant without him asking. "Is it now? Uncertain for you? That's grave."

"I say that Dom Gaspar is ruling this country from Baarah under the influence of the three Utheem brothers. He has forced the last Sultan's daughter, Princess Sitti, to marry Mohamed Thakurufaan of Utheem. It is Mohamed Thakurufaan who takes the annual taxes to Ceylon. Who knows what illegal profit he and his brothers make from that?"

He licked his lips. "There has been a revival of Islam in Baarah. Dom Gaspar summoned people to the island to recite the Holy Quran and pray for forty days. In addition,

Dom Gaspar has reduced the number of Portuguese officers in the islands so people can worship if they like. Now I hear he has instructed the brothers to build a vessel so big that it can only be for one purpose."

"Really? What's that – something else you won't get commission on? Transporting goods perhaps?"

"To attack Male' and remove you as head of state."

"Are you aware of what you are saying?" Andhirin controlled his anger because he was curious about what the foolish fellow actually knew. "Are you accusing the Vedor, my noble friend Dom Gaspar, of disloyalty to Portugal?"

"You can chop off my head if you like. What I say is true. Don't you know that people are fleeing across the Equator to the southern islands where Portuguese rule is so weak and you can't collect taxes? Soon there will be two separate kingdoms, one south of the line in Addu and one in the north at Baarah. Male' will mean nothing."

Tuffashana paused dramatically, then added: "You should consider what is happening to my country, not just count the annual dues from coconuts, coir rope, seashells and dried fish."

"Nicely put. Profit has always motivated the Meedhoo house. Are you worried because you are losing your influence? I may disagree with Dom Gaspar at times but he is not a man to be disloyal to Portugal, or to me. You are up to something!" He waved him away and turned for another glass of wine.

"You should hear me out! I can prove what I say about Dom Gaspar. If you find I accuse him falsely, then execute me for treason."

"I don't need an excuse for that, do I?" Andhirin sniggered. "You can prove it?" He sat back and stared hard as Tuffashana shuffled his feet uncomfortably, perhaps aware he had pushed too hard.

"Very well." Andhirin smiled, calling his bluff. "How can you prove Dom Gaspar is disloyal?"

"Write him a letter telling him to come here in his new ship with the Utheem brothers. Tell him you have heard rumours of his disloyalty and want a meeting with him. If he doesn't come, I have proved my point. If he comes, my head is yours."

The answer was too quick, too pat. Andhirin threw his wine glass to the ground in disgust, startling the servant so much he dropped the fan, which only added to his rage. "Why am I plagued by this perpetual scheming by you and your fat father! You come here daily and make my life a misery with your machinations."

"Then I shall leave Male' – and join those in the south, my home."

"Oh no!" Andhirin wagged his finger in his face. "You have shit like a dog and it smells. If I allow you to go I will be relieved of your presence, but not of the shit." He glared fiercely until Tuffashana cowered his head and stepped backwards.

"I did not mean offend you, my lord, Captain Andhirin. I am thinking only of you. I will serve you loyally until I die."

Andhirin nodded, saying nothing. He would find a way to see that Tuffashana did not have very long to remain loyal.

He knew Dom Gaspar and if the old bugger were planning to oust him, he would present himself in Male' as soon as he was summoned. That would prove the tiresome dog wrong and he could remove him forever by accepting the offer of his head. It was most satisfactory. The puppy's mistake was not realising that the Portuguese were more cunning than Maldivians.

CHAPTER 23

The Vedor read the letter aloud. Mohamed watched him, sensing the turmoil Dom Gaspar was in. This was a crisis he appeared to have been expecting. It was an honour he did the three brothers by coming to Utheem to consult them but he was driven by necessity, not respect. The letter made that clear.

Mohamed and his two brothers, attended by Dhan, were sitting on the *bodu ashi* at home while Dom Gaspar sat on the *kuda ashi*. Joao stood close to his master. The escort of an officer and the boat crew, who had brought the Vedor to

Utheem, sat outside in the shade of the sea grape trees.

The letter called upon Dom Gaspar to hasten at once to Male' bringing the Utheem brothers and their new boat with him. This was necessary because of reports received in Male' that Dom Gaspar was plotting with the Utheem Katheebs to overthrow the Portuguese governance of the Maldives.

"It's a lie!" said Hassan as soon as the Vedor finished reading aloud.

"Of course it is," said Dom Gaspar. "However, Captain Andhirin believes otherwise."

"Has Andhiri Andhirin signed the letter?" Mohamed was wondering where such reports came from.

"Yes, it is genuine."

"Who brought the letter to you?"

"Two Portuguese officers with ten men. They are to escort us to Male'. Their boat has already returned."

"They are not known to you?"

The Vedor shook his head. "They are newly posted from Goa. What do you think? Will you come to Male' with me in your new boat?"

Mohamed looked at Ali and nodded, giving him the opportunity to speak for them all. "We do not plot against anybody," Ali said with a frown. "It is not our way. We are willing to do whatever you require."

"I am strengthened by your support." Dom Gaspar stroked his beard. "What do you think is the best course of action, Mohamed?"

"You have to go, of course. It is the only way you can confound whoever is creating this problem between you and Captain Andhirin. We shall come with you too. It will be an opportunity to test *Kaluoh Fummi*."

"With respect," said Dhan, falling into step beside Mohamed after they had bid the Vedor and his escorts farewell on the beach when he left at the end of the meeting. "With respect—" he began again.

Mohamed interrupted him sharply. "Respect should make you hold your tongue."

"I can wield a sword but not my tongue."

"A sword, is it?" Mohammed patted his shoulder, valuing Dhan's instant understanding of the situation. He never complicated his thoughts with tact. "All right, what is it that bursts to be said with respect?"

"The truth, of course. I asked Joao about these Portuguese men who brought the message to the Vedor. Joao says they are a suspicious lot, like murderous thugs he thinks. I think we should go to Baarah and kill them before they kill us."

"That would make Andhirin's letter a remarkable prophecy because the rumours would become true. We are Muslims, Dhan. The power of the sword is with us, but we do not use it first." He patted his shoulder again, hoping to reassure him, but Dhan had a look of resolution in his eyes. "Dhan, you must go to Baarah not to kill anyone but to prepare *Kaluoh Fummi* for the voyage. We shall sail in three days."

Dhan shrugged, twisting away from Mohamed's consoling hand. There was nothing Mohamed could do to convince him, but he knew he would not take on the Portuguese by himself.

◆ ◆ ◆ ◆ ◆

Mohamed had a chance of his own to observe the soldiers when they boarded *Kaluoh Fummi* three days later. To him they looked like all the other Portuguese who occupied the islands: sweaty, unkempt, loud-mouthed and foul smelling. He could see from Joao's attitude towards them that he did not like them. He wondered why those officers and men had come on *Kaluoh Fummi* instead of travelling back on their own boat. Was it to escort or arrest them?

His doubts slipped from his mind as he supervised the departure. He had said farewell to Sitti who was to stay at Vaaruge with her mother while Aiminafaan remained in Utheem with his son. No one seemed interested in their departure, a few children played on the sand while some fisherman sat idly in the shade of the boathouse, empty now that *Kaluoh Fummi* was in the water. This was an opportunity for him to demonstrate how fast and seaworthy she was.

Ali showed Dom Gaspar into the vessel's cabin. Joao was with him. Dhan was shouting at the soldiers, gruffly telling them where to sit so they did not upset the trim of the boat. Mohamed exchanged a glance of amusement with Hassan over Dhan's obvious dislike of the men. He would have to tell the lad to curb his feelings since the Portuguese were their guests on the ship, not their enemies.

Actually the Portuguese seemed a sullen lot and fortunately they kept to themselves, cooking, eating and sleeping in the ship's bow. Mohamed and his brothers were too involved to take much notice of them as they were crewing *Kaluoh Fummi* themselves. He had decided not to bring any islanders as crew in case they were delayed in Male'. He was apprehensive about what might happen there, since he thought Andhirin was not to be trusted. As for Dom Gaspar, it was difficult to know what he was thinking. When he was not relaxing in the cabin, he stood at the ship's side, staring out to sea, watched carefully by Joao.

Mohamed was thrilled by the ease with which *Kaluoh Fummi* handled. She was a magnificent craft, responding easily to the lightest touch on the tiller; the broad sails of woven coconut leaves caught the slightest breeze, sending her bow slicing through the water with brisk acceleration. The sea was calm and they were making good progress as they entered the Kashidhoo Channel on the final leg to Male'.

It was then that Mohamed realised that the muttering he had heard for some minutes was the Portuguese arguing among themselves. He watched one of the officers go up to Dom Gaspar where he was standing at the ship's side, and start to harangue him. The Vedor looked shocked; he raised his voice in anger and seemed to be ordering the officer to move out of his way.

Mohamed beckoned Joao. "What is he saying?"

The lad looked frightened, his usual self-confidence drained out of him. *"Meu Deus!"* he cried. "This is treachery. Be on your guard."

Mohamed handed the tiller to Hassan and gripped Joao by his shoulders, shaking him. "What is happening?" The other officer had joined his colleague and both were arguing loudly with the Vedor.

"They want to know why Dom Gaspar has let you live.

They say that the instruction they were given by Lord Meedhoo's crown prince was to bring your head to Captain Andhirin. They want to kill you now. Dom Gaspar has reprimanded them, saying you are under his protection. He says he cannot believe this is Captain Andhirin's order. The officer is saying that Dom Gaspar is a traitor if he defies their orders and he will kill him too."

"We have been tricked!" Hassan glared at Joao, reaching for him.

What happened next was to be etched in Mohamed's mind for the rest of his life. As he looked at Dom Gaspar protesting at what the officers were saying, his cheeks colouring with rage, a soldier who had been standing behind the officer drew his sword, pushed the officer aside, and plunged it straight into the Vedor's chest.

Joao broke away from Hassan's grasp and rushed screaming towards the soldier, drawing a knife from his belt. The officer who had been arguing with Dom Gaspar pulled out a firearm concealed in the full sleeve of his coat, pointed it at the charging Joao and pulled the trigger. Joao's head split into two, hair and brains splattered over the deck as he toppled across Dom Gaspar's dead body.

Hassan jumped onto the back of the soldier who had killed Dom Gaspar. He knocked him down with a single blow onto the deck and then scooped him up while he was struggling and tossed him over the ship's side into the sea. Dhan, seeing Joao was dead, went berserk. He grabbed the anchor with its rock lashed to a heavy wooden post, and smashed it wildly into the skulls of the soldiers gathered in the bow.

Mohamed seized the tiller and swung the vessel against the wind so it keeled over, sending everyone sprawling. He leapt on one of the officers and smoothly slit his throat while Ali hacked off the other's head with his sword. Some of the soldiers dashed into the cabin to get away from Dhan but he followed them in, roaring madly.

In seconds it was all over. Dhan emerged from the cabin, dragging the bodies of the soldiers with him and chucked them overboard. He raced back up the deck towards the bow, picking up those soldiers who were wounded and tossing them into the sea. He paused when he came back to Joao. He bent down to pick up his friend's body, and the fight drained out of him. He looked up at Mohamed with a strange calm emanating from his glazed eyes. He sighed heavily, cradled Joao's body in his arms and walked over to the ship's side.

"No, Dhan!" Mohamed shouted as Dhan stepped onto the gunwale edge, preparing to jump into the water with Joao's body. Hassan threw himself at him and caught him around his waist. They tumbled onto the deck together as Joao slipped from his hands into the waves.

"You can better avenge Joao and Dom Gaspar from this world, not the next," said Mohamed. He helped Hassan and Dhan to their feet. Ali had taken the rudder and was holding *Kaluoh Fummi* steady in the wind.

"Help me with Dom Gaspar," he ordered Dhan, hoping to distract him from his grief. "Take his legs."

He kept his own feelings hidden as they cast Dom Gaspar's body to the deep.

As he looked around the boat, the enormity of what had happened struck him. Dhan had acted quicker than anyone had and yet it was he, Mohamed, who was supposed to be trained to anticipate danger and act in an emergency. He looked up at the sky, trying to clear his mind of the carnage, but the image of Dhan charging down the boat, cracking open the skulls of all who tried to stop him, remained.

"Allah is great!" he shouted to the heavens.

There was a heavy silence on board, broken only by the tightening of the coir cords that bound the coconut timber masts. He listened carefully and surveyed the ocean, drawing comfort from the sea's swell and the air's clean salt tang. He walked over to Ali and took the tiller from him.

"The wind is changing," he said. "Let's clean up the boat. Every stain of this terrible moment must be removed."

Dhan's response was swift. He leaned over the side to fill a gourd with water and began sluicing down the deck. He was so engrossed in his work, Mohamed wondered if he really knew what he had done. He had changed their destiny.

"Ali, Hassan, we must decide what to do. Perhaps it is time to take our wives and leave the Maldives, just as you foresaw might happen, Ali."

"This is not the way I wished it. Dom Gaspar was a good friend to us all. The Portuguese will seek revenge as soon as they hear what has happened."

"That will take time, won't it?" asked Hassan.

"Joao said that the order to kill us came from Lord Meedhoo's crown prince, not from Captain Andhirin. When we don't arrive in Male' as expected, he will surely tell Andhirin that we are the ones responsible for the Vedor's death. We are outlaws now, whatever we do."

◆ ◆ ◆ ◆ ◆

Tuffashana drained his goblet of wine and signalled to the Portuguese boy to fill it again. He was rocking backwards and forwards on the formal chair at Andhiri Andhirin's dinner table as though missing the motion of the swing seat he normally sat in. He pushed away his stew of fish almost untouched.

"You do not like our food, Tuffashana?" Andhirin had been observing him closely, watching him get drunk, watching him command the Portuguese servants as though they were his own, listening to him boast of his wealth to the officers dining with them. He had taken the measure of the man and now, like a fisherman playing the line to land a big catch, decided it was time to give him a little more line to see what he would do.

"We are not like you Portuguese." Tuffashana belched happily. "We like to eat at the end of an evening, not in the middle."

"Eat then sleep, is that it?"

Tuffashana giggled. "Yes, Andhirin. Eat then bed – but not for sleep!" He guffawed, nodding at the officers to join in his crude laughter. Some did.

Andhirin joined in too but, despite his appearance of being drunk, his mind was ice cool. He had discovered by some judicious torture that Tuffashana was bribing some of his officers. To pay them, he was using gold sequestered from the treasury by his father, Lord Meedhoo, in the time of Sultan Ali. By rights, that was Andhirin's gold, his father's treasure stolen by the Sultan when Simao Andrade was shipwrecked more than four decades earlier. Andhirin could not forget.

"You should be careful who you share your bed with, Tuffashana." Andhirin observed which of his guests laughed at his joke; they were the loyal ones. "She devils can take advantage of a man in his cups, and cup his manhood."

In the gusts of laughter from all those at the table, Tuffashana's manner changed from heartiness to an attempt to be alert. It was a quality that had helped him survive with the Portuguese, which even Andhirin appreciated. He was able to sense the way the wind was blowing and to swing with it. Now he blinked as he made an effort to understand what was happening.

Andhirin smacked his lips, as though not recognising his guest's discomfort. "If she could find anything to cup, of course!" From half-closed lids he noticed from the twitch in Tuffashana's cheek that his insult had driven home.

Tuffashana, however, grinned broadly. "Ah yes, I have heard she-devils voice that complaint about the Portuguese."

Andhirin kept his anger in check and glowered at his officers to warn them by his glance that they should not show offence. He let the banter continue, watching the Tuffashana's reactions. He was undoubtedly involved in some complicated plot, but what was his objective? Clearly he harboured an ambition to become the next Sultan, which was how he earned his nickname. It was a joke the Maldivians enjoyed, but he had no support, no following beyond those he bought with gold. He couldn't start a rebellion among the islanders, so what was he plotting?

Andhirin knew that the soldiers sent to deliver the summons to Dom Gaspar had been selected by Tuffashana and were in his pay. He guessed that Tuffashana was trying to cover himself by making sure that Dom Gaspar and the Utheem brothers did not come to Male'. That would give credence to his tale that Dom Gaspar was a traitor.

Just before the dinner Andhirin had received a report that the bodies of some white men and some driftwood had been found washed up on the island of Kashidhoo, indicating that a vessel had sunk in the area. It could have been *Kaluoh Fummi*. That would suit the 'crown prince' very well.

Andhiri Andhirin stood up, signifying the meal was at an end. The officers scrambled to their feet. Tuffashana looked bemused and then stood up too. He was frowning, perhaps because Andhirin's parties usually went on until the early hours of the morning. There used to be occasions when Andhirin enjoyed carousing with Tuffashana. He was a rogue and it was sport to outwit him. The news of bodies being found might bring the scoundrel's plot into the open.

"Why don't you join me in my chamber, Tuffashana? A night cap, perhaps while we discuss matters of state?"

The 'crown prince' straightened up at this public boost to his prestige in front of the Portuguese officers. It was what Andhirin wanted. Tuffashana would feel privileged that he was being invited for a private audience. One of his Portuguese secretaries stepped forward to protest, but Andhirin waved him away.

"Tuffashana is our brother, our eyes and ears in Male'. We are comrades in arms, not of arms, eh, Tuffashana?" Andhirin crooked his elbow so that he was obliged to link his arm in his as they walked to his chamber. "I have some news for you, Tuffashana," he whispered into his ear. "I don't want my staff to know yet."

"What is that?"

"Make yourself comfortable. Another glass of wine?" Andhirin clapped his hands for a servant, who appeared from behind a silk curtain carrying a jug. He filled two goblets and glanced at Andhirin.

"Leave the jug here," Andhirin said. "See we are not disturbed." He wanted to create an intimacy, a feeling of trust so that the 'crown prince' would relax and perhaps divulge more of his plot than he intended.

"So what is your news?" Tuffashana said as soon as the servant had withdrawn.

"News? Ah yes. Bodies of some white men, presumably Portuguese, have been found. Washed up on Kashidhoo island. So near to Male'"

"I have heard that too. I was going to tell you," said

Tuffashana at once. "I wanted to wait until I was sure."

"Sure of what?"

"That *Kaluoh Fummi* has been wrecked."

"You are of the opinion that is what happened?"

"There were no other boats with Portuguese soldiers on board that were expected in Male'."

"Well, no boat of that size has been seen by our patrols. The bodies were found a week ago. I hope the Vedor was not among them. You said he would not come, so perhaps he was not on board that boat that appears to have sunk."

"If he was," Tuffashana said quickly, "and is dead, someone should go immediately to Baarah to take over before the islanders revolt."

"Why should they do that?"

"The Vedor's rule was lax. Sultan Ali's widow is there and so is his daughter, Princess Sitti. They could be a threat with the islanders rallying around them. I will go to Baarah for you and bring them here."

"It was my understanding that the Vedor removed those two women from Male' so they would not be a threat to us."

Tuffashana's eyes brightened, as though he saw the opportunity he was waiting for. "There is a way to solve this very simply. I will marry Princess Sitti and stay with her in Baarah as atoll chief, replacing the Vedor. That way the Northern Atolls will remain loyal, to Portugal. I will ensure it."

"Interesting." Andhirin smiled to himself. "If *Kaluoh Fummi* has been shipwrecked, that means the Utheem brothers who were sailing her must be dead too."

"Yes, yes."

"Then what is the threat to our rule? Who would lead the islanders against Portugal?"

For a moment Tuffashana was nonplussed. He sipped his wine. "The brothers are as much a threat dead as they are alive," he began, rethinking his strategy aloud. "They were well loved in the north. If they died coming here at your written request, the people could revolt in protest. By going to Baarah before that happens, I can secure the islands and there will be no threat to your leadership, Captain Andhirin."

Andhirin slammed down his glass and glared at him. "Get out! Your petty plotting bores me!" He dismissed him with a wave, disappointed that his scheming had not been more intriguing.

"I have your permission to sail for Baarah?"

"Do what the hell you like, 'crown prince'. You are a scoundrel and a stupid one at that. I should thrash you for insulting my intelligence."

He turned his back, furious at himself for allowing Tuffashana to manipulate him in such an easy manner. He sipped at his wine again as Tuffashana swept out of the chamber, apparently uncowered by what he had said. Andhirin reviewed in his mind what had happened and decided the outcome seemed promising. The 'crown prince' obviously thought that Dom Gaspar and the Utheem brothers were dead, otherwise he would not dare go to Baarah. And with him out of Male' the main obstacle to his own stranglehold on Maldives, and the treasury, had been removed.

PART THREE
Exile
1568-1573

IMHOTEP
QUO
VADIS

CHAPTER 24

A strong wind bore *Kaluoh Fummi* northwards. Mohamed decided they should return to Utheem before fleeing from the islands. He wanted to pray at the mosque and say farewell at the grave of his father and grandfather. They would also collect Aiminafaan and his son and their sister Fathimafaan to go with them. His brothers agreed.

"But what about our wives in Baarah and Ali, your wife in Thakandhoo?" asked Hassan.

"My wife has her family there to take care of her. Your wives, too, have relatives and friends in Baarah, We should only think of them when we have a secure place to stay."

"You speak well as always," said Mohamed. He returned to steering the boat. In the grim silence that possessed them as each dwelt on what had happened, he considered where would be good for them to seek refuge. The islands south of the Equator were havens for those opposed to the Portuguese. However, even with the speed of *Kaluoh Fummi*, sailing north to Utheem and then south to Addu would be fraught with risk. By then the Portuguese would be looking for them.

He decided instead to sail further north beyond the atolls of the Maldives to the island of Minicoy. He had visited there during his days of training at Beydali. The islanders shared language and characteristics with Maldivians, and at one time must have been part of the Dhivehi realm. Portugal had never invaded Minicoy and the people had been left in peace. The island was a refuge for Muslims from the Maldives who settled there to continue in their religion beyond Portuguese interference.

Among those refugees were two devout Muslims whom Mohamed knew: Ali Hajji and Hassan Hajji. They were so called because they had made the arduous pilgrimage to Mecca and Medina. It was after they returned from their pilgrimage and seen how the Portuguese occupation was destroying Islam in Male', that they fled – first to southern India, which is where Mohamed had met them, and then they set up home in Minicoy.

As soon as *Kaluoh Fummi* reached Utheem, Mohamed, his brothers and Dhan hastened to the mosque. There they performed their prayers and, in an atmosphere of calm after the dreadful slaughter they had witnessed, sat quietly on their prayer mats and reflected on the future.

"Can you counsel us, Ali?" Mohamed deliberately deferred to his brother since, being the eldest, all decisions should stem from him.

Ali heaved a heavy sigh, his face haggard with dismay at events. "Before embarking on any voyage, we should know the course we plan to take, and also why we are making the voyage. This is no different. We have decided to leave Utheem so we should each specify our aims and objectives."

Without waiting to be asked, Mohamed announced that his objective was to rid the Maldives of the infidels. "If Allah so wills!"

Hassan was not to be outdone. "My aim is to bring to an end the Portuguese occupation and restore an Islamic Sultanate."

They all looked at Dhan. He had been silent with his grief and anger for most of the voyage to Utheem. Now he spoke: "I will help you, my brothers, in whatever you plan, and to kill all the Portuguese in the Maldives."

Ali nodded, "It is my aim to achieve all your aims." He then stood up and clasped Mohamed by his hand. "Will you be our leader, Mohamed? Will you be the Maldives avenger? You are younger than I am and you have the benefit of the marshal training and religious learning our father wished for you. We will support you, even to martyrdom."

Hassan added his hand to Ali's handshake. "I will follow you too."

"And I!" said Dhan with a loud shout.

After another prayer in which Ali beseeched Allah for success, Mohamed sent Dhan to alert Aiminafaan and his sister for the departure at dawn. Then the brothers went to the grave of Kalu Katheeb, their grandfather, and of Katheeb Hussain, their father. Mohamed was overwhelmed with sadness at having to leave Utheem, his home, and his roots. Silently, he communed with his father's spirit, seeking his support.

A sudden gust of wind ruffling the tops of the palm trees as he stood by the grave seemed to be the sign of approval he sought.

♦ ♦ ♦ ♦ ♦

A Portuguese soldier left by the Vedor to guard Vaaruge reported to Queen Aisha that a boat was sailing towards Baarah. When he said it was not *Kaluoh Fummi* and was flying the Portuguese flag, she thanked him for the information and dismissed him. She went to her chamber and, in its gloom, sat in silence on the swing seat.

She had a premonition that whatever this Portuguese vessel was bringing, it would not be good news. She had heard of the disappearance of Aiminafaan and Fathimafaan from Utheem in the dead of night and no one had news of the Utheem brothers or of Dom Gaspar. She clasped her hands in her lap and waited.

When Fulu told her that a young Maldivian, dressed like a Portuguese nobleman in tunic and breeches with polished boots and a cap with a feather in it, was waiting for her in the compound, she guessed who he was. She prayed that the arrival of this man would not upset Sitti. She composed herself and went out to meet him.

"Tuffashana!" She greeted the 'crown prince' as graciously as she could. When he didn't stand up but continued to loll in the swing seat in the compound, she was immediately on her guard as his arrogance signified he was not afraid of her, or of Dom Gaspar.

He dispensed with the formalities of greeting with a wave of his hand. "I have been commanded by Captain Andhirin to send you to Male'. At once."

"You have been commanded? Is there not a letter of invitation?"

"I have come myself. I know what you did to my last letter."

"Do you? And where is Dom Gaspar?"

"He also wishes you to come to Male'."

"Does he? And what about Princess Sitti? Is she to stay here alone?"

"As the wife of Mohamed Thakurufaan her place is at home here in Baarah," said Tuffashana.

"You mean she needs the consent of her husband to travel? So, of course, I must wait here until Mohamed Thakurufaan comes to take care of his wife."

"No!" Tuffashana bristled with annoyance at having his orders questioned. "You must leave tomorrow. My boat will take you, and my soldiers escort you."

"Well," she said with a sigh. "Tomorrow is a long way off."

"It is not. It is near. You must prepare."

"Well, near or far, I am not leaving Sitti until Mohamed returns."

She tried not to show it but she was desperately worried by this turn of events. She guessed from Tuffashana's manner that something dreadful had happened to Dom Gaspar. The 'crown prince' was sprawled on the Vedor's official swing as though he had been appointed to the post. But what of Mohamed? Was he dead? If so, Sitti would be obliged to marry Tuffashana when he demanded it. As he surely would.

"Aisha!" The 'crown prince' spoke sternly. "It would be unwise for you to disobey an order from Captain Andhirin. He requires your presence in Male'. I am sure your daughter, the Princess Sitti, would not object to your visiting Male'. Shall we ask her?"

"You know her mind?"

As Aisha spoke, the 'crown prince' suddenly leaped to his feet, sweeping low in a bow that he had copied from the Portuguese. Aisha looked behind her to see Sitti standing in the doorway. She was dressed in her finest robe with the sun highlighting her flawless complexion and her hair glistening after its long brushing with coconut oil. She heard the Tuffashana catch his breath in admiration.

Sitti walked with grace to the other swing and sat on it calmly. She gazed at Tuffashana with the apparent innocence of a young virgin. Tuffashana's second gulp of desire echoed through the silence of the garden.

Aisha smiled to herself, realising that Sitti had decided the best ploy for dealing with this loathsome creature was for him to believe she was sympathetic to whatever he was scheming. It seemed a good idea, at least until they both knew what had happened.

"Please sit down, my lord," said Sitti in a husky voice. "We are honoured by your visit."

He gaped, trying to speak. "I, er, I, er, came to see how you are getting on."

"How kind of you. You must stay until Dom Gaspar returns. Naturally, my mother must stay too. If you are here as our guardian, a month can be regarded as one day."

Her smile would have melted the heart of an ogre. Tuffashana was mesmerised and could only utter weakly, "Yes!"

"Please rest here in the shade." Aisha beckoned to Sitti to leave the garden with her. "We shall prepare a meal for you."

Tuffashana could not take his eyes of Sitti as she deliberately passed close to him, letting a trace of her perfume waft in his direction. He breathed in deeply and lay back on the swing, fondling himself contentedly.

◆ ◆ ◆ ◆ ◆

Aisha supervised the preparation of a feast of rice, barbecued fish, bananas and coconut milk and sugar. She knew Tuffashana was as greedy as his father and hoped that after he had devoured so much in the midday heat, he would fall asleep. She sent a boy to fan him gently as he lay on the swing. She needed to keep him occupied and out of the way for as long as possible, so she and Sitti could decide what to do.

Tuffashana seemed to know that Dom Gaspar and Mohamed were not returning to Baarah. He wanted Princess Sitti and clearly thought it was his right to have her. Fortunately he seemed so enraptured with her and confident that she would be his that he was content to savour the anticipation. There was nothing they could do and their only hope was hope itself.

After a long and blissful siesta, Tuffashana awoke, and took a stroll around the island before entering the main pavilion in the evening to take the dinner that Aisha had prepared for him. He looked around expectantly.

"Where is Princess Sitti? I want her to lie with me after dinner."

Aisha sighed. If that was his intention, then Mohamed Thakurufaan really must be dead. "She is outside," she said firmly, conveying her disapproval.

"Then let her come inside. To me."

"Of course, my lord. She is performing her evening prayers. She will join you afterwards."

"Prayers!" He scoffed in derision. "How quaint. Such a virtuous woman. I shall wait." He made himself comfortable on Dom Gaspar's own cushions on the *kuda ashi*.

Aisha was flummoxed. She stared at Tuffashana, thinking of how honourable Dom Gaspar was. She was overwhelmed with loathing for this upstart who thought he could take his place. He was worse then the Portuguese. She would willingly kill him if it would help save Sitti from his clutches.

The voice of her daughter broke into her thoughts as she entered the room, smiling graciously. "Oh, my lord Tuffashana," Sitti said coquettishly, "you are not yet asleep? I will join you in a little while."

Turning to her mother, she said something that struck Aisha as very odd. "It is dark outside and there is no maid to be found anywhere. Could you accompany me to the *gifili*?"

The *gifili* was the open-air bathing area, surrounded by a screen of *cadjan*, coconut thatch, outside the pavilion. Why Sitti should want her to go with her, Aisha didn't understand. She said nothing, though, and left the room with her daughter, taking a coconut lamp to light the way.

Sitti held her fingers up to her lips in a warning gesture until they were close to the *gifili* and could not be overheard by Tuffashana.

"What is this about?" Aisha demanded, wondering whether Sitti was going mad again. Perhaps the thought of having to lie with the 'crown prince' was causing her to lose her mind. "You have never asked me to accompany you to the *gifili* before."

Before Sitti could answer a man coughed. "Oh my goodness!" Aisha nearly dropped the lamp in shock. "Who is that in the bathing area?"

Sitti giggled with delight. "It is Hassan Thakurufaan. He has come to take me away to where my husband is waiting."

Aisha watched in amazement as Hassan and Dhan emerged from their hiding place. "What are you doing here?"

"It will take too long to explain," said Hassan. "Mohamed sent us. He is making a new home in Minicoy for his wives and son. Princess Sitti will be safe with us there. I am taking my own wife too."

"Allah has answered our prayers!" Aisha was close to tears. "But you must leave at once. The 'crown prince' is about to plunder what is not his."

She embraced Sitti. Dhan slipped away to collect Hassan's wife from Baarah Katheeb's house. "Do not be sad, daughter, dear," she said, trying to control her own tears. "God has saved you, so be happy. I have brought you up well."

"What about you? Why don't you come too, I'm sure Mohamed will welcome you."

"Mohamed doesn't want his mother-in-law living with him in a new place!" She tried to sound light-hearted. "Besides, there is something I must do here. Go!"

She pulled her hand away from her daughter's grasp, and then wiped a tear from her face as she watched Hassan lead her off into the dark. Before he went, he said their boat was anchored off the ocean side of the island, away from the Portuguese ship in the bay. The darkness would help them but if the Portuguese were roused, they would surely chase them.

She went back to the pavilion. Tuffashana looked up eagerly as she entered, his expression changing when he saw she was not Princess Sitti.

"My daughter is not well," she said. "Perhaps the excitement of seeing you. She begs you to wait, sleep a little, until she is feeling better. You may not know, but women do have these difficult times. She will come later."

He grunted irritably, but seemed prepared to accept what she had said.

Aisha had no sooner settled down on her swing bed than she heard shouts and curses from beyond the compound walls. She sat, frozen in fear, wondering if the Portuguese guard had caught Hassan and Sitti. As she listened to the ruckus she realised it was coming from the tents where the soldiers were sleeping. She rose quickly and padded softly across the sand to the front of the compound to see what had occurred.

The beach was in an uproar. The Portuguese seemed to believe they were under attack. They were shouting for lights and were rushing around blindly, bumping into each other. In the vague moonlight, she caught sight of Fulu running towards Vaaruge.

"Come, child," said Aisha, catching Fulu in her arms. "Don't be afraid!"

"I'm not!" The girl seemed to be having hysterics. She was laughing so much that tears were streaming down her cheeks. She allowed Aisha to lead her inside the house.

"What happened out there?"

"It was Hassan and my dear Dhan," she said. "Hassan cut the posts supporting the tent where the Portuguese soldiers were sleeping. The beams crashed down on them, and when the 'crown prince' came rushing out, Dhan threw sand in his eyes.

Aisha shook her head. "Such games. They should have killed them."

"No," said Fulu. "There was no time. They had to leave quickly. They had two men with them, great warriors who have made the pilgrimage to Mecca. I spoke to them myself. They have sailed away from here. Dhan told me that no one will be able to catch them because he has sabotaged all the boats in Baarah. He removed the rudders and changed the masts. It will take a day to sort them out. By that time, Hassan and Sitti will be beyond capture."

"I pray that you are right."

A howl of rage like a cat in torment stopped their conversation. Fulu didn't stay to hear what was wrong; she fled out of the back door into the night, leaving Aisha to fend for herself. Taking a deep breath and drawing herself up to her full height, Aisha drew aside the curtain and walked into the room where she had so often seen Dhan sleeping peacefully. At the opposite doorway she saw Tuffashana groping his way in the gloom, shouting insanely for Sitti to come to him.

"You are too late, my foolish prince," Aisha said with a laugh. "She has gone!"

"Gone?" Tuffashana shrieked with rage. He still had sand in his eyes and peered around the room, as though expecting to find Sitti waiting for him. "Where has she gone? Bring her here now, I command you."

"She has gone to meet her husband. She is safe from you."

"Mohamed Thakurufaan was here? He is alive?"

"Why are you surprised? Did you plan it otherwise?"

"Witch! You have caused this trouble. Dom Gaspar would have lived if it weren't for your meddling."

Aisha bit her lip, it was what she feared. "This morning you said Dom Gaspar was alive in Male' and awaited me. Now you say he is not. Truth comes from the lips of cowards when they are provoked." She smiled scornfully. "It must be you who caused Dom Gaspar's death, since only you know of it."

She was ready for his fury. She watched him as though he were a child as he pulled his sword from its scabbard and advanced towards her. Coolly she stared behind his right ear and smiled.

"Ah, Mohamed Thakurufaan, you are here?"

"What!" Tuffashana swung around. There was no one there.

As he turned back in bewilderment, Aisha grabbed his arm, pulling him off balance. He stumbled and dropped the sword. She snatched it up before he could recover his footing and drove its blade down into his back. Pushing on it with all the strength her hatred could muster, she forced him down on his face until the sword was buried in him up to its hilt. He died skewered to the sand.

"I could not die at the hands of a traitor," she said to his body. "I have saved the Maldives and the children of the sea from you and your evil."

She turned as a Portuguese soldier burst into the room, his sword drawn. "Ah," she said, a smile spreading over her face. "I die at the infidel's hand. Allah is great!"

The blow was so quick, she didn't see it. She fell, her head cleaved from her body, beside the dead 'crown prince'.

CHAPTER 25

Minicoy, called Maliku by its inhabitants, lay thirty-five leagues from Baarah beyond the Eight Degree Channel. Depending on the season, it took two or three days for *Kaluoh Fummi* to make the voyage. The island was much larger than Utheem and, at some seven miles long by half-mile broad, bigger than Male'. The people were tough seafarers, making a living by trading with merchants from Bengal and the Malabar Coast.

Mohamed and his brothers found a warm welcome there. The islanders soon learned about the exploits of Hassan, Dhan and the two Hajji brothers who accompanied them to Baarah. While some islanders wondered whether the Portuguese might seek revenge by attacking Minicoy, others pointed out that Captain Andhirin had neither the vessels nor the men to launch an attack. Even if the Portuguese in Goa were to attack, they would first have to contend with the Rajah of Cannanore and his forces.

Ali Hajji and Hassan Hajji were respected in the community because of their devotion to their religion, combined with their strength and alertness as warriors. The support they gave Mohamed, especially in the raid on Baarah, convinced the people of Minicoy that Mohamed's cause was a just one. If the Hajji brothers were helping, everyone would.

A plot of land by the seashore, where *Kaluoh Fummi* could be careened on the beach, was found for them. Many of the villagers helped them build houses and loaned them cooking pots and other items until they could obtain their own. A well was built, and a *gifili*, and after a few weeks, they were settled in sufficiently to consider the future.

On Ali's advice they had brought with them all the money they had sequestered in Utheem, but their trading days were finished. To support themselves and obtain supplies, all three brothers worked as crew on local vessels trading with India. They sailed at different times so there was always one of them at home to look after Fathimafaan, the wives of Mohamed and Hassan, and Mohamed's son.

Their routine settled into an easy, simple pattern. At first they found it strange to be able to lead a normal life without the constant threat of interference from the Portuguese. Mohamed drew strength from the ritual of prayer five times a day, and he spent a lot of time in religious study with the Hajjis. However, he did not forget the vow they had all sworn before they went into exile: to rid the islands of the infidels. In this, Ali Hajji and Hassan Hajji supported him.

Many evenings, as he sat on the beach gazing at the stars and listening to the rhythm of the sea, Mohamed thought about the ways to achieve his aim. All he had was *Kaluoh Fummi* and his brothers, Dhan and the two Hajji brothers, in total only six brave men. Moreover, except for Dhan, they all had families to consider. It was one thing swearing an oath to wage a holy war, but quite another matter when it meant abandoning loved ones.

He discussed this with the others. Without hesitation, they swore they would do whatever he said.

"One of my concerns," he told Ali, "is to bring your wife and children here too. You cannot be happy separated from them."

"I must wait," said Ali. "We have news that Andhirin has sent more soldiers to Thakandhoo. He thinks we will invade there for my wife, just as Hassan did for his and yours in Baarah."

"We must do what Andhirin does not expect," said Mohamed. "If he is ready for us, there will be too many Portuguese for us to fight."

"It doesn't matter how many there are." Hassan looked fierce. "I will kill them all."

Mohamed nodded his encouragement. "That's the spirit.

We shall drive the foreigners out, but only if we have strategy. We must be like mosquitoes. Constantly biting them. We cannot be like a shark and eat them all up at once."

"What do you propose?" Ali seemed as eager as Hassan.

"We must prepare *Kaluoh Fummi* for a long voyage. Andhirin expects us to attack Thakandhoo to rescue your wife. He does not know of our vow to overthrow him. Let us strike at his heart. Lets us kill some of his men in Male'. That will worry him."

"He will believe people living in Male' have done that. He will take revenge on them and send to Goa for reinforcements."

"Ali, you are right. What do you suggest?"

"We need the people to support us. Let us visit as many islands as we can and explain our objective. We should urge people not to abandon Islam. Let us tell them that, with their help, we Maldivians can drive these foreign occupiers from our shores."

"I prefer Mohamed's plan."

Mohamed held up his hand to silence his younger brother. "Hassan, Ali is right. We cannot succeed alone. I have seen how our people have succumbed to the Portuguese yoke. We are a meek race; we want peace. Islanders have become accustomed to the Portuguese presence. They do what they are told and live without protest. We have to convince them to do otherwise and to join us."

Hassan snorted with impatience. "We can only do that by setting an example. Show them what it is like to regain and enjoy the freedom we are experiencing here."

They were sitting around a fire on the beach, away from their families for this talk about what to do. They had barbecued some fish, and the glow from the fire lit up their faces in the darkness. Dhan passed a banana leaf piled high with fish for them to eat, and then he coughed. Mohamed signalled that he could speak.

"There are many islands without Portuguese soldiers on them. But they have people who gossip, which is like talking directly to the Portuguese. Do something, gain something."

"What do you mean?" Hassan shook his head at Dhan's convoluted way of talking. Dhan, however, felt he had said enough.

Mohamed stroked his beard. "I see the point. If we go to such islands and tell people to resist and return to their religion, the Portuguese will soon learn about it."

"And if we kill some Portuguese on other islands," said Dhan, "Captain Andhirin will know it's us."

"We must visit as many islands as we can, north and south." Mohamed was excited by the new plan forming in his mind. "He will never know where we will strike next. He will believe we have several different boats and dozens of men. He is a coward, so he will be worried."

Ali was less enthusiastic. "I agree with what you say but we must know what is happening in Male'."

"How can we do that? We can't sail to Male' and ask." Hassan laughed at his own joke.

"Perhaps Dhan can go as a spy. He speaks a little Portuguese. No one knows him as one of us."

"Mohamed, I am your hands, not your ears. I have a friend, a boy from my island of Dhuvaafaru, who is living by his wits in Male'. I shall ask him to seek a job as a servant in Andhirin's fort. Andhirin always wants new boys and he will like my friend. I shall make occasional visits to Male' and he shall pass his news to me. But when the battle is to be fought, I must be at your side, Mohamed."

◆ ◆ ◆ ◆ ◆

Kaluoh Fummi glided through the water without a sound; in the light from the half moon, she was like a ghost ship. Mohamed had sailed her into the bay of the island over the reef, guided by the shadows of boats at anchor. He knew the waters of the island well and steered the boat close to the shore by the village. Dhan and Hassan Hajji took an oar each and rowed the last few yards so the others could disembark in the shallow water and wade ashore.

Each knew his task. While Hassan Hajji stayed on board, keeping the boat steady, his brother and Dhan swam quietly to the largest vessel in the bay. Dhan climbed on to it stealthily without rousing the Portuguese soldier asleep in the stern where he should have been keeping watch. He died without a whimper as Dhan swiftly cut his throat. In the dark, Dhan could not see if the cook asleep in the galley was Portuguese or Maldivian.

He shook him awake. "Do you speak Dhivehi?" he asked in Portuguese. The frightened man shook his head. Dhan's knife put him out of his misery.

When he was satisfied there was no one else on board the ship, Dhan dived back into the sea. Ali Hajji cut the anchor rope and together they swam behind the vessel sending it towards the angry waters beyond the reef.

Ashore Mohamed, Hassan and Ali made their way to the house of the island chief. Mohamed knew the Katheeb's house from one of his trading visits to buy coir. He had seen then that a tyrannical Portuguese officer was billeted with the chief. Since there was a Portuguese ship in the harbour, there could be other infidels on the island as well. When they reached the house, he and Hassan stationed themselves on either side of the doorway and tied a rope at ankle height across it.

Meanwhile Ali went to the kitchen at the back of the thatched hut and found a large copper cooking pot. He took it to the side of the house and at a signal from Mohamed beat on it loudly with his sword. As expected, the Maldivians stayed inside, too frightened by the noise to come out, but the Portuguese dashed out to see what was going on.

The first man tripped on the rope and sprawled face down on the sand. Before he could get up Hassan swiftly hacked off his head with his sword. The second man emerged and was speedily despatched by Mohamed. Hassan grabbed the third man by his throat, throwing him on top of his dead companions and stabbing him in the back.

The screams of the dying men and the noise of the copper pot created such a din, no one else inside dared to move.

"Katheeb," Mohamed called out. "Are you there?"

The answer was a muffled wail of fear.

"Come out. You will not be killed."

There was no sound of movement.

"I am Mohamed Thakurufaan of Utheem, Katheeb; I am not Portuguese so you can believe what I say. Come out. We have come to rescue you from Portuguese occupation. You have it in your power to rise up against the invaders. To lead your people back to Islam."

He listened carefully to the movement inside the house. Suddenly there was a rushing sound and he heard someone shout in Dhivei: "Mohamed, he has a firearm."

Two men burst out of the doorway, one with a sword swinging wildly, and the other with a pistol which he fired straight at Mohamed's head. But the warning from the Katheeb alerted him to duck, as Hassan's sword chopped into the soldier's shoulder, sending him spinning into the sand. Ali brought down the copper pot on the head of the other soldier and then stabbed him in his chest.

"Are there any more?" Mohamed shouted. "Will you come out now, Katheeb?"

The man was shaking as he put both hands out of the door in an attitude of prayer. He was mumbling for mercy.

"Come on, Katheeb." Mohamed was impatient with the man's fear. "We mean no harm. We want to show you what is possible for a Maldivian to do. Are you content to live under infidel rule? If so, you are an infidel as well."

"Mohamed, they force us —"

"You are living an unhappy and helpless life like this. Where is your faith? Tell your people to return to the mosques, to prayer, to Islam. Let them support us and we will rid these islands of the Portuguese for ever."

"And tell the Portuguese the Thakurufaan brothers said this!" Hassan glared at the frightened man. "They will not harm you. It is us they will seek."

"Come," said Ali, pulling Hassan by his sleeve. "We must go. We have done enough here."

They ran towards the beach where Hassan Hajji had *Kaluoh Fummi* ready to sail. Dhan helped pull Mohamed on board. He was laughing.

"When I heard the pot banging, even I thought the devil was abroad."

Mohamed didn't join the laughter. Like Ali, he was perturbed at the killings. He knew it was necessary to send a warning to Andhirin that his days were numbered, but that didn't make it easier for his conscience. He quietly went to the bow to pray.

The success of their first raid taught Mohamed many things. One was the ability of *Kaluoh Fummi* to bear them in and out of islands speedily. However, the ship needed maintenance. While they could anchor off an uninhabited island and go ashore for fresh water and to barbecue fish and boil rice when they wanted a meal, a base was needed where they could refit the vessel on their long voyages throughout the atolls.

Coconut mat sails were fragile; they succumbed quickly to the constant battering of wind and rain. If Mohamed was going to keep *Kaluoh Fummi* away from Minicoy for months at a time, he needed a place to get new sails. On their way north through the atolls after the first raid, he called at several islands where there were no Portuguese so he could meet people and explain the reason for their campaign.

He was gratified at the support he gathered. It seemed that people only needed leadership to encourage them to resist the Portuguese. Everyone he met was keen to return to the sacred values of Islam; even the youngsters were curious about the Islamic identity they had never known.

At Maroshi, in Miladu Madulu atoll, he met a toddy tapper called Raaveri. His job was to climb coconut trees to tap the sap from the flower spathes. This sap, called raa or toddy, made a refreshing drink when taken straight from the tree. Raaveri offered Mohamed and his brothers coconut cups filled with it as soon as they landed.

They drank the clear, semi-sweet liquid with relish. Raaveri was a simple fellow who had never left his island. He had spent his life tending his coconuts and harvesting their products, making rope from the coir torn from their husks, oil from the dried kernel of the nut, and mats and thatch from the leaves. He claimed that nothing was wasted from the coconut tree. You could eat its heart and cook with charcoal made from its shells. Its trunk gave timber for boats and building.

Meeting Raaveri gave Mohamed an idea. He explained what he was doing. Raaveri had no quarrel with the Portuguese since they rarely came to his island, but he was a devout man and saw the value in what Mohamed said. When Mohamed asked if he would help them, he was doubtful about what he could do.

"There is something," Mohamed told him. "Look at our boat. You see our sails. They need repair. We have spare sails on board but cannot repair the old ones when we are at sea." He looked up at the coconut trees growing all around them. "Could you mend our sails for us and supply new ones?"

Raaveri scratched his head, considering the matter. "What you ask will depend on you. My sons and I can supply you with any amount of sails. We will make a rack on the beach and store them there. Come when you want and take the sails and leave your old ones in their place so that the curiosity of the idle is not aroused."

Mohamed was touched by the man's willingness to help, especially when he added that he would leave a pot of toddy honey for them once a month. That would improve their diet after weeks at sea. Maroshi was an ideal base for them to visit occasionally since its great bay had two entrances. *Kaluoh Fummi* could sweep in at high tide and creep out from the other side when the tide was low. If a Portuguese ship came looking for them while they were visiting there, they could escape swiftly.

During the voyages of *Kaluoh Fummi* through the islands, Mohamed drew on the friendship of old acquaintances of his father as well as of Ali and himself. In the day time he sailed *Kaluoh Fummi* to the west far away from the atolls, braving the winds and waves of the deep ocean, returning only to the calmer waters of the atolls at night when they were unlikely to be seen by any Portuguese vessel on patrol. His friends welcomed his visits by night, providing food and water, and passing on information about the Portuguese. Some nights they raided islands where the Portuguese were living, killed them in their sleep, and told the inhabitants to say it was the work of the Maldives Avenger and the Thakurufaan brothers.

Captain Andhirin was enraged by Mohamed's exploits and ordered his men to bring him his head. He put vessels on permanent patrol to cover the area from Utheem to Male' while others circulated in the two northernmost atolls with a back up vessel and crew stationed at Baarah.

On his behalf, Lord Meedhoo issued a proclamation that anyone found helping the rebellious Utheem brothers would be hung, drawn and quartered. He blamed Mohamed for his son's death, even though it was Queen Aisha who had killed his Crown Prince. The Queen's deed inspired awe whenever the tale was told and her bravery became the envy of island women sick of the Portuguese and their collaborators.

The first voyage of *Kaluoh Fummi* up and down the atolls lasted four months. Mohamed was pleased as he steered the vessel out of the lagoon where they had sheltered for the night. They were on their way home to Minicoy. He congratulated himself not only for the havoc they had wrought whenever they found any Portuguese on the islands, but also for the support which the people gave them, heedless of the threats of punishment.

Perhaps his feeling of success made him careless, or was it his anxiety to see Sitti and Aiminafaan and his son in Minicoy? Whatever the reason, that morning he was so full of confidence, he sailed out of the lagoon without first sending Dhan to the other side of the island to see if any vessels were in the vicinity.

The first warning he had of danger was when Hassan Hajji, at the bow, shouted in alarm at the huge sails of a Portuguese man-of-war rounding the island just as they left the lagoon.

The captain of the ship seemed as surprised as they were. In the time it took to run out his cannons, *Kaluoh Fummi* had sped out of range. It was breezy day and the wind that caught the boat's mat sails also filled those of the larger vessel. With its superior speed, the huge ship was soon bearing down on *Kaluoh Fummi*. They could see the crewmen in its bow, all of them armed to the teeth, eager to capture them.

"What are we going to do?" said Hassan. "They will catch us soon."

"If they do, we will fight and die martyrs," said Mohamed. "But I don't think they can fly."

"What do you mean?"

"You know that island ahead?"

Hassan shook his head. "I don't know but it seems you want to put us aground. You are heading straight for it. Are we to land and repel them on the beach?"

Mohamed smiled grimly. He was watching for the break in the reef that he remembered from a visit to the island with Dhan on one of his trading trips. They had sheltered there for the night. He shouted at Dhan to go to the bow and guide him in. Luckily the tide was high, but the same tide would benefit the vessel chasing them.

Dhan saw the gap and gestured to show Mohamed how to steer through it. The captain of the man-of-war hove to, obviously uncertain about whether it was safe to follow.

"He doesn't need to follow us in," said Ali. "He has got us trapped. He only needs to wait until we try to come out of the lagoon."

"That's right," said Mohamed. "I hope he waits a month."

He swung the tiller around, following the path through the reef that Dhan indicated, avoiding the rocks in the shallow of the lagoon. They rounded the island inside the reef. Behind them, the Portuguese ship was no longer in sight.

"Now we fly," said Mohamed. "Can you see the channel?" he shouted to Dhan.

Dhan waved for him to steer more to the east. As he coaxed *Kaluoh Fummi* where Dhan pointed, Mohamed saw the gap for himself. What appeared from the sea to be one island was in fact two, with a narrow channel separating them. With the help of their oars they rowed and punted *Kaluoh Fummi* into the channel and guided her along it until they reached the lagoon at the other side. The wind took them again and they sailed quickly out into the open sea.

Mohamed laughed. "You see, Hassan, the Portuguese are sure they have us trapped in that lagoon. I'd like to sail past them to show we've escaped. Instead, let them wait there and wonder forever where we have gone. They will discover we have vanished. We have the sea for ourselves now."

"Allah be praised!"

CHAPTER 26

The days rolled by like the surf on the beach, each wave following relentlessly the one before, washing quickly onto the shore, then slipping away. When they were at sea, living on *Kaluoh Fummi* for days, weeks, months on end, time no longer mattered. Battling monsoon winds or drifting through the doldrums of becalmed seas, Mohamed and his followers were ceaseless in their harassment of the Portuguese.

No one knew where they would strike next. One night they would slip into an island in the north, the next they would attack a dhoni commandeered by the Portuguese in the south. Their hit and run operations were classic guerrilla tactics conducted at sea. They hid at islands with bays, like the one at Maroshi, where they could exit speedily if discovered, and be secure in inlets where no passing ship could see them.

The Portuguese were frustrated by their failure to find *Kaluoh Fummi*. Whenever they did sight her, she always outsped them or disappeared completely. The Portuguese junior officers who were drafted to islands as administrators fled with their soldiers back to the safety of Male'. With the Portuguese gone islanders began to pick up the pieces of their lives, but without a devout leader it was impossible to return completely to the rituals of their religion.

Mohamed's plan was to keep up the pressure on the Portuguese so that their frequent raids heightened the climate of fear in their minds. He did not let the weather deter him; even in storms he attacked, his boat looming out of the rain and thunder like an avenging angel on startled infidels seeking shelter from the elements. As he kept up the raids, the islanders began to support him, telling him where to find the Portuguese occupiers. The administration of the atolls was collapsing as Captain Andhirin and the Portuguese became isolated in Male'.

News of what was happening in Male' reached Mohamed from sympathisers. He built up a network of trusted friends who went to Male' and reported on what was happening.

Through Dhan, a youngster called Abdullah was recruited and trained on how to ingratiate himself with the Portuguese and what to watch for at Andhirin's fort.

Abdullah was an amenable, likeable lad, and with the help of Mohamed's contacts was able to infiltrate Andhirin's coterie of boy servants. A system was set up so he could send messages to Mohamed through traders and fishermen. Mohamed longed to go to Male' in disguise to see the situation for himself but his brothers advised him against it since the risks were too great. They feared that the momentum for the revolution would be lost if anything happened to him.

When it was learned that Andhirin had obtained reinforcements from Portugal, as well as hired mercenaries from Malabar, Mohamed avoided then by being unpredictable, by his superior seamanship, and – it seemed to the islanders – by divine intervention. He had become hardened to fatigue, to the unceasing slap of wind and rain on his face, and to the perpetual motion of *Kaluoh Fummi*. He no longer noticed the discomfort of living aboard for weeks with five other people in the small confines of the ship.

They all missed their families. The passing of time only registered with Mohamed when he returned to Minicoy and saw that his son had grown a year older. At least he and Hassan had their families to return to. Ali had no one and felt it badly. Several times Mohamed sailed *Kaluoh Fummi* close to Thakandhoo to see if there was a way for them to land at night for Ali to rescue his wife and children. Always there were extra vessels anchored off shore, indicating the presence of Portuguese and Malabari soldiers. Andhirin was using Ali's wife as bait to lure him in.

By 1572, it was three years since Ali had seen his family and he desperately wanted to see them again, even if it was not possible to take them to Minicoy. Mohamed was sympathetic and agreed to put Ali ashore secretly at night from the ocean side of Thakandhoo, which would not be guarded. Ali would make his way across the island to his house while Mohamed waited off shore with *Kaluoh Fummi*. If it seemed safe, Ali would bring his wife and children to the shore at an agreed time. If it weren't safe, he would return alone.

The plan worked well at the beginning. The night before landing Ali, the brothers launched an attack on the Portuguese in a neighbouring island. They expected that the next day, boats based at Thakandhoo would put out to search for *Kaluoh Fummi* and the watch on Thakandhoo would be reduced. It seemed that was what happened when *Kaluoh Fummi* did a quick round of the island and saw all was quiet. In case they had been observed, Mohamed then sailed westwards from the island to the open sea, giving the impression that he was leaving the area for good.

At night *Kaluoh Fummi* returned. Ali bid his brothers farewell and slipped into the sea, swimming with bold strokes towards the shore. As silently as she had come, *Kaluoh Fummi* sailed away.

Later, when Mohamed returned in the boat to wait for Ali off the ocean side shore as arranged, there was no one there. Daybreak was coming so he dared not wait too long. Suddenly two huge ships sailing side by side appeared out of the gloom of the dawn and bore down on *Kaluoh Fummi*. Mohamed could hear the shouts of triumph from the armed men lining the rails as they prepared to capture him. Realising he had no time to turn the boat and flee from the approaching ships, he tacked… and sailed straight towards them.

The Portuguese were confused. *Kaluoh Fummi* with the wind filling her sails, skimmed past the two ships, even before they could be fired on. By the time the ships managed to come around to give chase, *Kaluoh Fummi* was beyond their reach.

Later, Mohamed learned from Ali's wife what had happened. Ali had managed to reach the house by the main bay where she lived. It was unguarded and he swiftly gained admittance. His wife was overjoyed to see him. In whispers he spoke to his children and told them how proud he was of them. They were overawed at this strange man, smelling of the sea, who appeared in the night.

His wife warned Ali that the Portuguese were everywhere on the island and it would be impossible for her and the children to flee with him. She begged him to leave her immediately and return to Minicoy. She told him to come for her when the war was won.

Ali was always sentimental. He couldn't bear to leave without taking her and the family with him. But to do so would expose them to risk. They were not suffering any more than the other islanders under the Portuguese so it was probably safer for them to remain on Thakandhoo. Perhaps he was weary of fighting after months at sea; perhaps he was just tired and let emotion cloud his judgement. He took his wife in his arms and lay down with her, his sword at his side.

The Portuguese soldiers and Malabari mercenaries came with the dawn. They surrounded the house so Ali could not escape and then entered to arrest him. He rose up from the floor with his sword swinging, plunging it first into one and then another until a dozen men lay wounded or dead at his feet. He saw the deathblow coming and shouted praise to Allah as a soldier drove his sword deep into his heart. The soldiers cut off his head and carried it away in triumph, leaving his wife and children to bury the rest of his body.

◆ ◆ ◆ ◆ ◆

Captain Andhirin stared at Lord Meedhoo. The man was quivering with excitement. He had an escort of Portuguese soldiers with him and looked like a jellyfish surrounded by barracudas. It was early evening and Andhirin had just emerged from his siesta. He was in a foul mood as he had that morning received a most unpleasant despatch from Goa.

It was from the Viceroy himself. It questioned his ability to govern the Maldives and demanded to know why there were so many Portuguese fatalities in islands that for fourteen years had been perfectly peaceful. In a period of three years, not only had Dom Gaspar, a senior and respected administrator of Portugal been killed, but so had over two hundred Portuguese soldiers and officials.

It seemed to the Viceroy that instead of taking immediate action on the death of Dom Gaspar, Andhirin had prevaricated. The letter warned that the Viceroy would not tolerate the situation any longer and Andhirin must immediately crush this minor uprising. The threat of what would happen to him if he failed to take effective action was unstated, but Andhirin knew he would be in disgrace.

As soon as he read the letter, he had upbraided Lord Meedhoo, urging him to be more vigilant in pursuit of the troublemakers. "The people must take an oath of loyalty to Portugal," he told him. "If they do not, have them beheaded."

After that interview, he had slept fitfully during his afternoon nap. He hoped to find the situation resolved when he woke. He did not expect to see Lord Meedhoo so soon. He climbed wearily onto the platform and took his chair, eyeing the fat, wobbly Maldivian with dismay.

"What is it this time?"

"A victory, oh noble lord." Lord Meedhoo was so excited his voice squeaked. "Captain Andhirin, I have done as you commanded. The Utheem brothers are defeated."

"What?" He sat up and stared at the man. "What do you mean?"

"See what I have here. These brave soldiers of Portugal arrived this morning from Thakandhoo. They have brought you something. It is my gift to you." He waved one of the escorts forward. He was carrying something wrapped in banana leaves and offered it to Andhirin.

He eyed it suspiciously. "What the hell is that?"

The soldier, an evil glint in his eye, unwrapped the leaves. In his hand was a blood-soaked mess of flesh and hair.

"This is the head of Ali Thakurufaan!" Lord Meedhoo wheezed with delight. "Your enemy has been slain."

Andhirin was speechless. He looked at the object and thought that its lifeless eyes were staring back at him, promising revenge. "*Meu Deus!*" he said, leaping to his feet. "Get that thing out of here at once!"

"But it's the head—"

"I know what it is, you fat fool."

"I thought you wanted victory."

Andhirin swore loudly, stomping up and down the platform in anger. Lord Meedhoo bowed and tried to withdraw from the chamber. Andhirin halted him.

"This is not a victory, this is a disaster. Don't you know

what you've done? By having that head brought here, you've brought the curse of the Utheem brothers on us. Mohamed Thakurufaan is sure to attack Male' now. If he comes for nothing else, he will come for his brother's head."

"We are well defended –"

"Shut up! You must have that head buried at once, on another island. Not here in Male'."

"I will do it, Lord Andhirin. Whatever you say."

After Meedhoo had gone, taking the ghastly head with him, Andhirin sank back in his chair to think. He imagined he was Mohamed Thakurufaan planning what to do next. He was certain to want revenge in a spectacular way for his brother's death. If he were Mohamed, he would strike quickly, at the heart of Male'.

Andhirin bit his lip, trying to puzzle out his strategy. With one fishing boat and less than a handful of men, there was not much that Mohamed could do. However, if he had the support of the people of Male', if they were to rise up and join him as he attacked, Andhirin's forces could be in trouble. If the Viceroy heard there was an uprising in Male', even if unsuccessful, Andhirin knew he would be court-martialled and probably executed for not doing his duty properly.

He thought carefully. He had enough men to defend the island against an attack from the sea, but what about one that could come from within? People like Lord Meedhoo were naturally treacherous but their loyalty was secured by giving them power. It was the ordinary people of Male', the fishermen and toddy tappers, and goldsmiths and rope makers, who could help the rebels. They had to be forced into submission, brainwashed to be loyal to Portugal, before Mohamed Thakurufaan came at night to enlist their support, as he had already done in the out islands.

"Abdullah!" he shouted at the boy who was arranging cushions on the visitor's platform. "Tell my valet to bring me wine."

The boy bowed and silently left the room.

◆ ◆ ◆ ◆ ◆

Mohamed wept when the news of Ali's death was brought to him in Minicoy. He and Hassan joined in ten days of mourning and prayer. He resolved to draw strength from the tragedy so that Ali's death would not be in vain. He was intrigued to hear from his spies that Andhirin had been appalled at being presented with Ali's head and had it buried at Funadhoo, an island close to Male'. It showed that he considered Ali was still a force to be reckoned with, even though he was dead.

After the period of mourning had passed, Mohamed called Hassan, Dhan, and the two Hajjis for a conference. They had spent the monsoon season in Minicoy, in comfort and luxury compared with life on board *Kaluoh Fummi*. So Mohamed wondered if their resolve had weakened. They sat together on cushions in his house, passing the mouthpiece of the hookah pipe from one to the other as they spoke.

"My brothers," said Mohamed, looking around him, feeling pleased that they all looked fit and eager. "We could spend the rest of our lives here in comfort and safety. Already the Portuguese are in disarray, unable to govern in any of the atolls. Only in Male' do they hold sway. We can sail soon to begin again, or we can stay here and be content with what we have done."

Dhan was the only one who spoke, muttering a rude phrase that indicated Mohamed was mad if he thought that was what they wanted to do. Mohamed held up his hand to still his outburst, although he was actually gratified by it.

"Then we agree not to let down those who have helped us. We will continue the fight."

"We must attack Male'," said Hassan. "We have spent three years raiding islands. It is in Male' that the people are being forced to renounce Islam and drink the wine of the Portuguese."

"We should not be so confident, Hassan. If the Portuguese overcome the fear they have of us, and if the Viceroy in Goa decides to send a force against us, we will be defeated. We are only five men."

"We have the people of the Maldives behind us," said Dhan. "Abdullah reported that the citizens of Male' are falsely pledging their loyalty to Captain Andhirin only to save themselves. It is not genuine. They don't mean it and they will support us."

"If we can get there." The deep voice of Ali Hajji filled the room. "You will find Male' is well guarded. Impregnable."

"Then we must bide our time." Mohamed's own words set off an idea in his mind. "We must keep up the pressure on the Portuguese for the next few months. Andhirin will surely expect us to attack Male' soon, so we won't." He paused and looked around his companions, an enigmatic smile spreading across his face. "Instead, we shall disappear."

CHAPTER 27

For Andhirin each day was a difficult one. He would wake and listen to the sounds of the fort and people passing in the lane outside, wishing that none of this had happened. It was odd to think that all the time Dom Gaspar was alive he had only minor problems to deal with. The old bugger must have been doing something right. Since his death everything had gone wrong. Every morning, as he lay in bed, he tried to guess what would be that day's bad news.

Usually it was a report of another attack on his men on an island by Mohamed Thakurufaan and his damn fishing boat. His activities were becoming legendary; some said the boat could fly, that it could become invisible. What was more realistic was the inability of his men to stop the attacks. They had resumed as soon as the monsoon had lifted. Mohamed seemed in no hurry to avenge his brother's death by invading Male' although each week he visited another island, drawing dangerously close to the capital.

There was trouble, too, from Indian pirates operating under the protection of the Rajah of Cannanore. They swooped on merchantmen in the waters of the Maldives, damaging the lucrative trade where Male' was an entrepot for the ports of Malabar and the Coromandel coasts. Another problem was the payment of taxes to the Viceroy in Goa and to the Portuguese in Ceylon. It was four years since payments had been made and the authorities were pressing him to do something about it.

Andhirin was thoroughly demoralised. His occupation of the Maldives had turned into a never-ending nightmare. Although the first 10 years had passed agreeably enough, he had never found the treasure that had been stolen from his father. However, he had managed to cream off a percentage of the annual taxes for himself and had the loot safely stored in chests in his chamber. He had dreamed of retiring with it to Goa in triumph, with accolades showered upon him for his masterful governing of the country. Now for his return to Goa he might be in chains.

"What bad news today?" he demanded of his commanding officer when he finally rose from his bed, completed his toilet, and appeared in the ante-room of his chamber for the daily audience. "Where did that fishing boat from hell strike last night?"

"All was quiet, Captain. We have had no reports of any attacks on the islands for several days."

"You will. Just give them time. This is the season. I have studied the guerrillas' technique. They will seize every opportunity in this fine weather to harass us somewhere."

The Commander took no notice. "We have had vessels on patrol. The boat continues to elude us. When last sighted close to Male' she sailed off before we could catch her. She was probably reconnoitring, testing our defences."

"And what of our defences?"

"Captain, it is impossible for one ship and five men to attack Male'."

"Do you know everything, Commander? Have you ever seen this Mohamed Thakurufaan? Does anyone know what he looks like? Why, he could even be in Male' at this very moment."

"We are vigilant in checking strangers. We interview the fishermen and traders who arrive from the out islands."

"Interview, Commander? I hope you thrash a few hides to see none of them are hiding information. Only by terror can we stamp out terrorism, this rebellion. As soon as we have got rid of the Utheem brothers I shall take a vow of loyalty from every single person in Male'. I need to demonstrate to the people and to the Viceroy that we are in control."

He watched as the Commander saluted and marched off. He felt the man did not have enough respect for him. *If Portugal still had men of the calibre of his father, men who were inspired to rule, instead of being career soldiers, he would smash all resistance within a few days. Those Portuguese posted to the out islands only had themselves to blame for getting killed.*

Andhirin knew that he was a beleaguered man. He had looked in vain for companionship among the Portuguese who might understand him and what he wanted to achieve. He joined his senior staff socially in the cool of the night, but found them wanting in ambition. At times he preferred the company of Maldivians like Lord Meedhoo. At least Meedhoo shared his lust for money and pleasure, and he was not squeamish about having a few people beheaded to accomplish his aims.

He relied on Meedhoo not just for information but also for the truth. The man could lie better than the devil, yet he knew what was really happening in the Maldives, beyond Portuguese surveillance. The fat man had contacts everywhere. It seemed the only thing he did not know was the whereabouts of *Kaluoh Fummi*.

"It is so odd," Lord Meedhoo said one evening when he and Andhirin were sitting in the garden by the stockade fence, enjoying a flagon of wine together. "The boat has disappeared."

"What do you mean? Just because no attacks have been reported for a few weeks! Mohamed Thakurufaan must be holed up in some island where he has friends. There are over a thousand islands in the Maldives, how can we know where he is? He's preparing to attack us here, I'll be bound. And it will be soon, before the monsoon season begins.

Lord Meedhoo's jowls wobbled as he shook his head emphatically. "If Mohamed is on an island, be it in an atoll to the north or to the south of Male', I will know within a few days of his landing there. However, Lord Andhirin, it is not for my spies to capture him. I can only give you the information for your soldiers to do that. But I have had no news, that's what puzzles me."

"Could he have gone back to Minicoy? He might fear

an early monsoon and be seeking the safety of his refuge. There was a bad storm last week." Andhirin beckoned the serving boy to fill Lord Meedhoo's goblet.

"The storm? That is what's strange, said Meedhoo. There was a vessel in the roads that came from Minicoy. The crew were old fishermen, none of Mohamed's band. They were asking for news of Mohamed and Hassan of Utheem. It seems they fear that *Kaluoh Fummi* was lost in that storm. She has not reached Minicoy, that's for certain, and no one in the atolls has seen her, even as far south as Addu."

Andhirin cursed the boy who had spilt some wine while Meedhoo was talking. "Damn you, Abdullah. Be more careful when you serve your masters." He cuffed his ear with the back of his hand and sent him off for another flagon.

He reached for his goblet and leaned back in his chair, raising his eyebrows in surprise at Meedhoo. "Can it possibly be that God is helping us? Has he done what my brave Portuguese soldiers could not accomplish – finished off Mohamed and his cursed boat. Hah! I don't believe it. We must be vigilant!"

◆ ◆ ◆ ◆ ◆

The disappearance of Mohamed and *Kaluoh Fummi* became the talking point throughout the islands. Weeks without him being sighted became months; the monsoon season came and went; calm seas returned, and Captain Andhirin braced himself for more guerrilla attacks. But nothing happened. Then a trading vessel came from Minicoy and from its crew Meedhoo's spies learned that the wives of Mohamed and Hassan believed *Kaluoh Fummi* was lost at sea and her crew of five had perished. In Male' the inhabitants were in a state of despair. Mohamed Thakurufaan's daring in attacking and defying the Portuguese in the atolls had given them a glimmer of hope. Now they could only survive by doing what Captain Andhirin commanded.

Peace was curious. Andhirin found it exhilarating. No more did he wake up wondering what calamity had occurred during the night. He began to make plans for his future again. His first move was to re-deploy the Portuguese in the islands whence they had fled because of the guerrilla attacks. He urged them to punish those following Islam, as that was a symbol of disloyalty to Portugal. Everyone who refused to give up their religion would be executed.

He knew he must set an example. If he could present the Viceroy with a country whose people had publicly pledged loyalty to Portugal, he would be well rewarded. He could take his treasure and settle in grand style to Goa. By delivering a compliant Maldives to Portugal, he could regard the death of his father as being properly avenged.

The parties in the garden of the fort every night after sundown assumed a new mood. He and his officers, and the Maldivians who joined them, were no longer drinking in despair but in exultation that victory was theirs. Andhirin, however, was not completely convinced. After the uprising of the previous four years, he wanted a demonstration in public by the people of Male' that they truly accepted the rule of Portugal.

His scheme was simple. He outlined it to Lord Meedhoo, letting all those in the garden hear what he was saying. He wanted the servants to know too, since they would spread the word among the inhabitants. It would become a rumour that fishermen and traders would relate on their voyages to the other inhabited islands. Maldivians throughout the archipelago would soon hear what he was doing, and that he was their master and Portugal their conqueror.

"I shall issue a proclamation," he said. "This will require all the people living in Male', yes, every single one, to assemble outside this fort a week today, on Wednesday morning."

"We shall make every single one of them drink wine as a symbol of their loyalty to Portugal. While the people are here, Commander, you will take your men and search every house on the island. You will put to death any man, woman or child who does not obey my order and present themselves here. You will burn their houses too, and burn every mosque still standing, and smash every shrine. We will deliver the Maldives as a free and Christian country to the Emperor of Portugal!"

The drunken cheers of his men pleased him. He raised

his goblet at them and drank deeply. He was amused to see that at least one of his servant boys, Abdullah, took his message seriously. From the corner of his eye he noticed the boy slip out of the garden by a side gate, doubtless to spread the news among the islanders. There was nothing like gossip and rumour to unsettle people.

A week later, Andhirin, true to his word, instructed the town crier what to say. He told him to make his announcement loudest in the hamlets where people still thought they could defy him. He gave him a jar of wine to spur him on his way.

"Now," he said to Lord Meedhoo who, as always at night was by his side, "we shall celebrate. Tomorrow we will have to behead a few people if there are any disillusioned fools who want to be martyrs. The rest will be ours. The Maldives will be mine. And Portugal's, of course."

◆ ◆ ◆ ◆ ◆

Aboobakur raised his head slowly from the ground. He stayed on his knees, his palms open in front of him, as he gazed at the tomb of Abul Barakaath, the saint who had brought Islam to the Maldives. He was no longer disturbed by the proclamation he had heard from the town crier. The presence of thirty-nine men praying with him was enough; he was not alone. They were all prepared to die defending their faith.

The night that engulfed them was dark, their sole lamp throwing an eerie flame on the praying men. It was a night when evil stalked the sandy lanes. Aboobakur shivered, although it was not cold. He glanced back apprehensively at the praying men and caught sight of some men standing under the palm trees, watching them. His heart lurched with fear. Had the time to die already come? He turned back and resumed reciting, concluding with a loud and defiant "Amen!"

"Amen!" A voice from the trees echoed his.

He turned again, blinking with surprise. A tall man with a long black beard and a bandana around his brow holding back a long mane of jet black hair, stepped forward.

He wore only a white waistcloth, his naked chest gleaming with oil in the flickering lights, his muscles taut, and his gaze unflinching. He had a sword strapped to his waist, a dagger at his belt, and a musket in his hand. His companion was dressed in a similar fashion. A boy, whom Aboobakur recognised as Abdulla, Andhirin's servant from the fort, was beside them. They had been betrayed.

"Amen!" the man said again, with no trace of irony. "Your prayers have been answered." The stranger looked fierce although there was an unexpected benevolence shining from his eyes.

"Who are you?" Aboobakur said uncertainly.

"That is not important. You are important, you and these men gathered here with you. You have kept your faith. With God's help, we shall drive out the infidels. Tonight. For ever!"

All the men who had been praying sat up and swivelled round to see who was this stranger who came like an apparition in their midst.

The goldsmith gasped. "I know that man," he shouted to his neighbour as he leapt to his feet. "It's Mohamed Thakurufaan!" He rushed forward to embrace him. "Now we are saved!"

Mohamed raised his hand and the man halted in his tracks. "Save your energy for the fight. We must take the fort. I shall need your help. Those of you who are prepared to kill or die for freedom, go to the beach and wait there until you here the noise of the battle. Then hunt and kill every Portuguese you can find. Those who are not prepared, remain here and pray that we succeed."

"If not," said Hassan who was at Mohamed's side, "it is death for us all and the children of the sea will never be free."

Mohamed spun around on his heels and walked away. He did not want to get engaged in discussion of tactics. Hassan and Abdullah, the servant boy, followed him.

"Is Dhan with you?" the boy asked.

"Yes, Abdullah." Mohamed put his hand on his shoulder. "He is on *Kaluoh Fummi* outside the harbour. You shall see him after the battle."

"Andhiri Andhirin believes you are dead and your boat lost. He has grown even crueller from the time he was convinced you were no longer a threat."

"You were brave to spy for us and send me messages, Abdullah. You are free now, you need never go back to the fort again. Wait on the beach for Dhan to land."

"You cannot take the fort by yourself. There are over three hundred Portuguese on the island. Most are at the fort tonight preparing for tomorrow's celebrations – and executions. I am coming with you."

"We will succeed, Abdullah," Hassan said. "We have the help of two ships full of Malabar cut-throats."

"Pirates?" Abdullah sounded shocked. "Andhiri Andhirin has spoken of such a possibility with his commander. He said they would never raid here because we have cannon at the fort."

"We shall see, Abdullah." Mohamed patted the boy's shoulder again. "Now go. You have done enough by keeping us informed during these months we have been away. You kept the faith. Go to help Dhan."

"That I will do."

"We need more like him," Mohamed said to Hassan as the boy ran off. They walked together in silence, heading for the fort. They had already discovered, when they landed on the southern shore at nightfall, that only a few sentries were on duty that night. Everyone seemed to be at the fort for Andhirin's victory party.

Mohamed stopped suddenly and raise his hand in warning as he listened carefully. He gestured to Hassan to follow him into the undergrowth at the side of the trail. "Someone is running behind us," he said in a whisper. He poised like a panther and then pounced, bringing down the person on the path with a flying tackle. He held his knife ready at the man's throat.

"Where are you going?" he demanded.

"To the fort with you, Mohamed."

"It's you again, Abdullah?"

"I've come back to help you. I know a secret gate into the fort. I can get you into the garden without anyone noticing."

Mohamed replaced the dagger in his waistband and helped the boy to his feet. "You must have been sent by Allah."

"And nearly had your throat slit," said Hassan. "Come. We delay too long. Someone will give the alarm."

Mohamed and Hassan followed Abdullah, approaching the fort from the rear along a jungle path, and crept stealthily around it. Abdullah showed them a new gate in the wall. It had been built on the instructions of Lord Meedhoo so he could pass easily in and out of the fort without being challenged by the Portuguese sentries on guard at all the other entrances. It gave access to an inner courtyard where the party was in full swing.

"This time you must go," Mohamed said to Abdullah. "Go to the beach and tell Dhan we have entered the fort. He must come with the Hajji brothers and the Malabaris and finish off what we are about to start. Go with God."

He and Hassan peered around the garden for Andhiri Andhirin, using the trees at its edge for cover. Torches burned, lighting up half a dozen barrels of wine and platters of food laid out on trestle tables. Men were dancing together as an army band played Portuguese folk music. Others were singing raucously and staggering around, holding each other up. Everyone seemed to be drunk.

The sight fascinated Hassan. "These are warriors?" he whispered in astonishment. "These are our masters?"

Mohamed shook his head. "They are infidel devils incarnate."

He looked beyond the drunken revellers to the main entrance of the building, a group of Portuguese officers and some Maldivians were sitting in chairs watching a near naked belly dancer gyrating in front of them. A fat man in robes dangled a young girl on his knees.

"That's Lord Meedhoo!" Hassan aimed at him, preparing to fire.

"Wait," said Mohamed. "There is Andhiri Andhirin, sitting at the end of the row of his officers, watching everybody."

"Shoot him!"

"First we must find cover. Andhirin is a good shot. He'll

return fire immediately."

"You are afraid to be killed?"

Mohamed drew his dagger and stuck it at eye level in the trunk of a tree. "I am afraid to forget what father made it possible for me to learn." He rested his musket on the knife, using it to steady his gun. "We have only this one shot, then destiny." He fired, stepping quickly behind the tree's trunk.

For a moment nothing happened. The band played, the party continued, the noise of drumming and singing drowning out the sound of the shot. However, Andhiri Andhirin jerked back in his seat as though he had been punched in the chest. By instinct his hand raised his weapon and he fired into the trees. The ball struck the handle of the knife, close to Mohamed's ear. Then Andhirin's eyes glazed over, blood seeped across his tunic and he slumped forward. There was a pause before he toppled off his chair and collapsed in a heap on the ground.

Hassan let off a shot at Lord Meedhoo but the fat man scrambled to his feet as Andhirin went down. He flung the girl off his lap and dashed with surprising speed into the shelter of the inner courtyard.

The drumming and singing stopped, to be replaced by the sound of shouts, *Allah Akbar, God is Great!* filling the sudden silence.

As Mohamed drew his sword, the stockade gate crashed open and a crowd of Maldivians, led by Dhan, rushed into the compound brandishing weapons. From the fort's rear, the Malabaris mercenaries burst in at the same time, enthusiastically cutting down everyone in sight.

The Portuguese died within minutes where before they had been dancing drunkenly. While Mohamed and Hassan engaged the braver officers in a sword fight, the crowd overwhelmed the soldiers, pelting them with stones and belting them with clubs. Dhan was in several places at once, wielding a heavy stave and smashing skulls. As the battle ended, the Malabaris moved inside the fort to ransack it. Mohamed went in search of Lord Meedhoo.

At the secret gate Abdullah had shown him, he tripped over a body lying in the path. He bent down and saw it was someone wearing the livery of a fort servant. He lifted the body gently and walked with it to the light of a flambeau. He gazed down and saw with sorrow that he was holding the body of Abdullah, slain by one of the Malabar cut-throats.

Mohamed carried Abdullah's body away from the pile of Portuguese bodies and laid him gently on the grass. Dhan stood by him, joining him in a silent prayer.

Hassan's cry of alarm broke into his grief. "The Malabaris! They're taking Andhirin's treasure chests from his chamber. We must stop them." They ran to where Hassan was shouting for them to help put the Malabaris to rout.

When dawn broke on the morning of 1 July 1573, the 15-year-long occupation of the Maldives had come to an end. Mohamed was acclaimed in triumph as the Maldives avenger.

CHAPTER 28

"There's more to do," said Mohamed. The gentle sway of *Kaluoh Fummi* bobbing at anchor off the Male' waterfront was soothing. After spending so many months on board her, the ship was home for him and he felt uncomfortable at having to sleep ashore. In the cool of the evening, he sat under a sky brimming with stars while he discussed events with Hassan, Dhan and the two Hajji brothers.

"Mohamed, why did you refuse to become Sultan?" Hassan's question had a note of frustration to it. After the years of struggle, he seemed to think that becoming the Sultan and ruling the Maldives in place of the Portuguese was a just reward for Mohamed. The people of Male' had thought so as well for, led by Aboobakur, they had urged him to accept the Sultan's throne.

"As I told Aboobakur," said Mohamed, "a religious leader is more important to re-establish our country. I am not learned enough for that. Because there has been no leader for fifteen years, our people have lapsed. Even those, like Aboobakur, who have kept Islam strong in their hearts, have lost their way."

"What more is there to do?" Dhan, as ever, was impatient. "We have routed the Malabaris and secured the treasury, we have buried the dead, we have prayed, we have sent vessels to the islands to announce the end of Andhirin's reign. I say a man's stomach needs a reward as much as his heart needs guidance."

Mohamed laughed. "A task for you, Dhan, is to take *Kaluoh Fummi* to Minicoy and bring our wives and my son here and my sister. Hassan, you should go too and bring the wife and children of our brother Ali from Thakandhoo."

Dhan pouted, looking miserable.

"What ails you?"

I have an ache." Dhan was sitting cross-legged on the deck, his eyes twinkling in the dim light thrown from a lantern hanging from the mast.

"Should I ask where?" Mohamed suspected this was another of Dhan's riddles.

"Baarah is where. If you are all bringing wives, I ache if I cannot bring one too."

"So you shall!" Mohamed was pleased. "Who is the one in Baarah you have been fighting for?"

"No fight. She is mine, I'm sure. Queen Aisha's maid, Fulu. She waits for me."

"Since we are speaking of marriage," said Ali Hajji in his deep voice. "Have I your permission to wed your sister, Fathimafaan? I have wanted to ask you since she came to Minicoy four years ago. The time was never right."

Mohamed bowed his head. "It is an honour to have you as my brother-in-law, as well as my brother-in-arms." He paused as he looked at his four companions, the bravest friends a man could have. If ever he did become Sultan, he would govern only with their help. In the meantime there were other things to do.

"While you are away with *Kaluoh Fummi*," he said, "I will spend time ashore in Male'. I will go from house to house, meeting people, seeing what are their needs and how I can help. I will build a house here in Male' and prepare for our wives, including yours, Dhan."

"I thought we had more than that to do." Dhan got to his feet. "This doing is no more than done."

"We still have one enemy to root out. We can be sure that Lord Meedhoo will not retire to grow yams."

"He has certainly left Male'," said Hassan. "He took a boat and his followers and sailed south."

"Let's go after him. Tonight!" Dhan walked to the bow as though he was going to pull up the anchor.

"And leave Fulu to wait another year for you?" It was Hassan Hajji who spoke. He sounded weary.

"There is nothing to gain by chasing him, Dhan. We will let him find an island where he can settle, where he feels safe. We shall soon learn where he is and then we can take him."

Hassan Hajji looked relieved. He lay back on the deck, cradled his head in his arms, and swiftly fell asleep. His brother Hajji moved to a more comfortable spot and lay down, watching the stars.

"Will you come ashore with me?" Hassan quietly asked Mohamed. "Let us pay a visit to Princess Sitti's half sister, Kamanafaan, Sultan Ali's daughter by his second wife. Have you seen how pretty she is? I would marry her but I need your help to ask her grandmother."

Mohamed was tired too, but he agreed. It made him recall the day, almost sixteen years before, when was a boy and had helped Queen Aisha and her two children flee to safety. He stroked his beard slowly and sighed. So much had happened since then.

♦ ♦ ♦ ♦ ♦

The sail slapped in the wind, white eddies splashing the bow as *Kaluoh Fummi* sliced through the water. She was running smoothly with the sea, aided by the breeze that also served to clear Mohamed's mind. He felt good to be standing on her deck again after three months in Male'. When he was at the tiller, gazing at the open sea and feeling the throb of her progress under his bare feet, he felt as one with *Kaluoh Fummi*.

Dhan had warned him that she was getting old and should be replaced. He wanted to take her on this voyage south, to complete the mission he had begun with her the day Dom Gaspar was murdered on board. Afterwards, he planned to let Dhan career her and replace her timbers.

She was a noble ship and deserved a rest.

Mohamed glanced at his crew, reunited for this voyage to assess the needs of the islands in the south, and also to seek out Lord Meedhoo. He observed how his comrades looked sleeker, less rugged than when they stayed for months on board the boat. All, except Hassan Hajji, had their wives in Male'. Even he, Mohamed had noticed, had a glint of happiness in his eye whenever he was with Ali's widow. A marriage of Hassan Hajji and Ali's widow would complete the bond that united them all.

The three months he had spent in Male' showed him what he needed to do to restore Islamic values in the country. Everything, not just the religious way of life, had collapsed under the Portuguese. As colonisers, the Portuguese had made all the decisions; Maldivians had become accustomed to being told what to do and what not to do. The administration had to be re-built. He wanted to set up a permanent military force so that the islands would never be conquered again. He wanted to ensure a lasting peace so that trade and fishing would resume, and the islands would become prosperous with their return to independence.

He was doubtful about becoming the Sultan although everyone in Male' begged him to take the throne. He awaited the return, after years in exile during the Portuguese regime, of the Maldivian religious scholar, Sheikh Mohamed Jamaludeen. A man like him was needed to restore Islam so the Maldives would become a peaceful, God-fearing nation, once again.

Mohamed thought long and hard as he stood with the tiller in his hand, bracing himself against its thrust, guiding *Kaluoh Fummi* to the will of the sea. His destination was the island of Kilege Meedhoo in Nilandu atoll, south of Male'. Hassan had learned from fishermen who came to Male' that Lord Meedhoo had fled there and was building a boat. He hoped to raise popular support so that he could return to Male' and be installed as Sultan since Mohamed had declined the throne.

The sight of *Kaluoh Fummi* approaching his island must have terrified Lord Meedhoo. When Mohamed sent Hassan and the Hajji brothers ashore to find him, he had already disappeared. The islanders said that he had paddled off on a raft as soon as *Kaluoh Fummi* appeared on the horizon. The boat he had been building, according to Hassan, was nearly ready to launch. To stop anyone putting to sea in it, he and the Hajji brothers set fire to it, black smoke curling up into the cloudless, bright blue sky.

Now Mohamed had to track down Lord Meedhoo. He looked up at the sky, listened to the wind, and felt the tug of the sea through his toes on the boat's deck. He considered the currents that served the island and where they meandered afterwards. Hassan wanted to sail south, to search the deserted islands in the centre of the atoll. Mohamed thought the currents would take Meedhoo's tiny craft northwest. He set course, caught the wind, and was soon in the open channel.

"We shall find him there." After three hours, Mohamed pointed to an island that lay ahead at the southern tip of the northern part of Nilandu atoll. "That's where the current would take a raft. Don't you feel how happily *Kaluoh Fummi* sails along on its crest?"

"She is old," warned Dhan, listening to her timbers creek. "She cannot stand this pace for long."

"We fed the carpenters well, Dhan. She will not let us down."

Mohamed left Hassan on board while he and the others went ashore. There was a raft on the beach. Two sullen boys who crouched in the shade of a sea grape tree said that Lord Meedhoo had gone inland. They were waiting only for the current to turn so they could row back to their island. They disclaimed any connection with Lord Meedhoo, other than being forced to row him across the channel. Mohamed bid them go in peace.

They found Lord Meedhoo by following the path he had made as he blundered through the undergrowth. He was in a cave where he had stored dried fish and jars of water, as though he thought he might have to hide there a long time.

He must have heard Mohamed coming through the jungle because his eyes were still open and the blood was warm as it gushed from the gaping gash he had hacked through the flesh of his throat. His struggle to die and the agony of his death left his bloated face twisted and bitter.

◆ ◆ ◆ ◆ ◆

The storm came up suddenly. Mohamed smelt it in the wind when they were crossing the rough seas of the channel south of Mulaku Atoll. He expected *Kaluoh Fummi* to outrun it so they could make the safety of a lagoon until it passed. Yet however much he urged her to greater speed, the slower she became. The sails broadened with the gusting wind, but she was sluggish, meeting the high swells as though an anchor stone was trailing behind her.

Dhan stood in the bow, willing her to make some speed and move faster. Mohamed noticed the telltale seeping of water through the planks of her hull. He looked westwards at the clouds heavy with rain and could see the fierce gale winds that were bearing down.

"Can you see land?" he shouted to Dhan.

"I see only clouds and sea. And danger."

"What course, Dhan?" Mohamed was loath to admit to the others that this was an area of the Maldives he did not know well. He realised he should have respected Dhan's warnings about *Kaluoh Fume*'s deterioration through age and hard work. Her leaking planks prevented her from sailing with her usual smooth speed. They were off course in the open sea with a storm about to burst upon them.

"Can we remain afloat until we reach land?" Hassan asked.

"With God's will." Even as he spoke, the thunder roared and the sky opened, pelting them with rain so heavy, it was like daggers pricking the skin. Mohamed shouted at his comrades to start bailing. The wind tore at the mat sail, snapping it off so it flew across the water like an albatross. Another followed.

Suddenly *Kaluoh Fummi* stopped. The wave that had been bearing her along abandoned her and washed past. She remained poised on an unseen reef, unable to move forward or backward. She was wedged between towers of coral that the sea's race obscured. Fortunately, the coral had not pierced her hull but water was rushing through gaps in the boards. With the thunder and rain came the night, drowning them in darkness.

The five of them bailed all night. Sleep was impossible. Each lurch of the boat as the waves battered her made them feel the end was approaching. Even when the rain eased off and the wind dropped, there was still a danger that the boat would be swamped by the waves. Mohamed scanned the night anxiously for shreds of dawn; if they could survive until light, they might be able to save themselves. The reef indicated that land, whether a sandbank or an island, was near.

Daybreak brought relief. *Kaluoh Fummi* was perched on coral that ringed a lagoon. The white sand and green palm trees of an island were no more than a long swim away. Even as they stared in disbelief, people began to gather on the beach as dawn broke. A rowing boat set out across the lagoon towards them. Dhan, however, wanted to jump in the lagoon and swim ashore.

The island, called Kolufushi, was large and long, at the southern tip of Mulaku Atoll. The people welcomed Mohamed and his crew and then stood silently, watching them as they sank to their knees on the beach in prayer. When Mohamed asked why they were reluctant to join them on their knees, the people told him they had lost their knowledge of Islam. The Portuguese had killed their religious leader and their mosque had long been destroyed.

Glancing out to see where *Kaluoh Fummi* was stranded, Mohamed was struck by the realisation that the boat had been driven there for a purpose.

"*Kaluoh Fummi* served us well," he said to Hassan. "Now it is time for us to serve her. Let her stay here. We shall use her timbers to build these islanders a mosque where they can pray."

They remained in Kolufishi until the mosque was finished. The days spent dismantling *Kaluoh Fummi* board by board, ferrying her timber and masts to the shore, and in constructing the mosque, were the happiest Mohamed had known. He slept under a thatch shelter on the beach at night, lived on fish he and the others caught and prepared for themselves every day. The islanders were poor with little to offer beyond their sincerity. Their simple way of life reminded him of the days of his youth at Utheem.

One afternoon, when work on the mosque had finished for the day, he sat alone on the beach, watching the birds swoop down to pick crabs from the sand. He kept very still until they forgot he was there. Slowly, he reached out his hand and caught one. He raised it to his eyes and looked into its startled, frightened face. He stroked its head to calm it, recalling how his father had rebuked him when he was a boy for doing just that.

In his mind the words he had overheard his father say to his brother, Ali, came back to him. "Mohamed is touched by destiny. We must feed and care for him so that he can prepare his body and soul for a great cause."

He raised his hands above his head and released the bird. "Yes," he said aloud as he watched it soar into the sky. "Vengeance is mine." He turned to face the setting sun on the horizon. "Now it is time for me to fly too and embrace my destiny."

He turned to face the setting sun. "Now is the time."

AFTERWORD

Mohamed Thakurufaan, known in the Maldives today as Bodu (the Great) Thakurufaan, became the first Sultan of the Utheem dynasty that ruled the Maldives for over a century. After 16 years he was succeeded by his son Ibrahim Kalaafaan. A great grandson of Ali Thakurufaan also became a Sultan.

In *Excerpta Maldiviana* by H C P Bell, quoting the *Tarikh* or *Maldivian State Chronicle* it states:

The Maldivians at once elected Bodu Thakurufaan as their Sultan. In organising the State Administration, he associated himself with his brother, Hassan, under the title Ranna Baderi Kilegefanu. Hajji Ali and Hajji Hassan were appointed Dhoshumeyma and Shar Bandar, Vazirs.

Sultan Ghazi Mohamed Thakurufaan ruled wisely, being just and considerate, protecting the poor, and ever solicitous for the people's interest while earnestly feeling the pressing call for religious revival.

He was the first Maldives Sultan to form the Askarun into a military body. Under his brilliant sway the islands remained wholly peaceful and free from all injustice, like unto a festival or marriage day.

GLOSSARY

Ashi: a dais in a room, used for sitting, eating and sleeping

Batteli: a large sailing vessel

Beyru-ge: a hall for the men of the family, and for visitors

Bodu ashi: a dais used by family members and guests

Cadjan: coconut thatch

Ethere-ge: the inner room of a house

Gifili: an open air bathing place with a fence of *cadjan* around it for privacy

Katheeb: island chief

Kuda ashi: a dais reserved for visiting dignitaries

Malin: government functionary who, in addition to performing the duties of a Mudin, also conducted religious ceremonies related to royalty

Mudin: person appointed to give the call for prayers, lead prayers and look after a mosque

Odi: large sailing vessel used for inter-island voyages and foreign trading

Ramazan: Ramadan, the month of fasting, which is the ninth month of the Muslim calendar.

END

IMHOTEP
QUO
VADIS